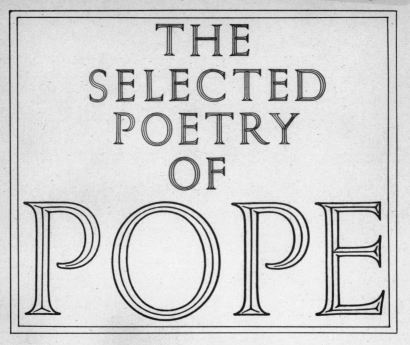

THE SELECTED POETRY OF POPE

Edited and with an Introduction by
Martin Price

A MERIDIAN BOOK

NEW AMERICAN LIBRARY

NEW YORK AND SCARBOROUGH, ONTARIO

Copyright © 1970, 1980 by Martin Price
All rights reserved

The Selected Poetry of Pope was originally published
in the Signet Classics Poetry Series, under the general editorship of
poet, lecturer, and teacher John Hollander.

Library of Congress Catalog Card Number: 80–80243

MERIDIAN TRADEMARK REG. U.S. PAT. OFF. AND FOREIGN COUNTRIES
REGISTERED TRADEMARK—MARCA REGISTRADA
HECHO EN FORGE VILLAGE, MASS., U.S.A.

SIGNET, SIGNET CLASSIC, MENTOR, PLUME, MERIDIAN and NAL BOOKS
are published *in the United States* by New American Library,
1633 Broadway, New York, New York 10019, *in Canada* by The New American
Library of Canada Limited, 81 Mack Avenue, Scarborough, Ontario M1L 1M8

First Meridian Printing, March, 1980
4 5 6 7 8 9 10 11 12
PRINTED IN THE UNITED STATES OF AMERICA

THE
SELECTED
POETRY
OF
POPE

CONTENTS

Introduction   *vii*

A General Note on the Text   *xxxv*

A Note on This Edition   *xxxv*

Chronology   *xxxvii*

Selected Bibliography   *xl*

An Essay on Criticism   *45*

Windsor Forest   *68*

The Rape of the Lock
    Canto I   *83*
    Canto II   *88*
    Canto III   *92*
    Canto IV   *98*
    Canto V   *103*

**Elegy to the Memory of an
Unfortunate Lady**   *109*

Eloïsa to Abelard   *112*

An Essay on Man
    Epistle I   *123*
    Epistle II   *133*
    Epistle III   *142*
    Epistle IV   *152*

To Richard Boyle, Earl of Burlington: Of the Use of Riches (Moral Essay IV) *164*

To a Lady: Of the Characters of Women (Moral Essay II) *172*

Satires and Epistles of Horace Imitated
Epistle to Dr. Arbuthnot: Being the Prologue to the Satires *185*
The First Satire of the Second Book of Horace (Satire II, i) *199*
The Second Satire of the Second Book of Horace (Satire II, ii) *205*
The First Epistle of the First Book of Horace (Epistle I, i) *211*
The Sixth Epistle of the First Book of Horace (Epistle I, vi) *218*

Epilogue to the Satires
Dialogue I *223*
Dialogue II *230*

The Dunciad
Book the First *240*
Book the Second *252*
Book the Third *266*
Book the Fourth *278*

INTRODUCTION

I

"To imagine a language is to imagine a form of life."
Ludwig Wittgenstein

Like all great poets, Alexander Pope is first of all a master of language. There are styles more idiosyncratic and more varied than his. Yet if he cannot be said to have created a language in the sense that Milton or Wallace Stevens did, he realized all the possibilities of the language he inherited. He made of the couplet a form more precisely controlled and therefore more subtly expressive than it had ever been before, and he used the couplet as the module with which to build a world. To begin to understand Pope, we must come to see what his language can do.

So long as the couplet remains open and does not close off a distinct unit of meaning, it plays against the longer, continuous sequence. One hears the rhyme and is aware of the regularity of meter and line structure, as one is to some degree in all verse; but there is counterpoint between the regular repetition of the form and the ongoing movement of meaning. At times the two coincide, and the rhyming word becomes all the more telling.

But to close the couplet is to define a small field wherein the order of words can become intensely important. The rhyming words divide the couplet into two distinct lines, and this division in turn encourages further division, such as we see in balance and antithesis, between the parts of each line. This elaborate internal structure requires diction of a distinctive sort; we cannot frame a striking antithesis without some fundamental similarity. We oppose good to evil, light to dark, sweet to bitter; behind each opposition lies the common class to which the two opposed members belong. Or if there is no obvious common class, the very antithesis or balance suggests one:

And now a bubble burst, and now a world.

Nor over-dress, nor leave her wholly bare.

Dost sometimes counsel take—and sometimes tea.

The more surprising the suggestion of a common class, the more play is required of the related terms. In this last instance "take" applies equally well but in different senses to "counsel" and "tea"; to yoke these two senses together in one word is a rhetorical device (called in fact *zeugma*, or "yoking") very close to a pun. Wit, as Dr. Johnson observed, may "yoke heterogeneous ideas by violence together." The surprise of wit always depends upon some degree of violence, some energy that forces two disparate meanings into one word by a kind of implosion. The evaporation of a bubble and the explosion of a star, in the first instance, are forced into the one word "burst"; and the violence that has yoked them together is the violence not simply of words but of a vision, which can see the fragility and the episodic nature of vast cosmic structures. Pope catches the impassive vision of a God whose infinity reduces vast and small, enduring and ephemeral, to much the same status.

There is wit in this compression, and it requires play upon words that awakens us to dormant meanings we easily neglect. This kind of wit is analytic: it separates out the meanings that are held together in ordinary language, for it requires meaning that can yield antitheses. The framing of contrasts demands words that name aspects of things rather than things themselves; it pushes concrete words toward greater abstractness. Each term of the antithesis is seen in its opposition to the other:

. . . some to church repair,
Not for the doctrine, but the music there.

Wrapped in a gown, for sickness, and for show.

In the closing lines of the *Essay on Criticism* we see
some of the peculiar resources of the couplet, a logic
heightened by balance and antithesis, further reinforced
by the sound pattern of the verse.

Careless of censure, nor too fond of fame;
Still pleased to praise, yet not afraid to blame;
Averse alike to flatter, or offend;
Not free from faults, nor yet too vain to mend.

The alliteration of consonants within each phrase gives the
terms a rightness confirmed by their sound—"fond of
fame," "pleased to praise." At the same time, the vowel
sounds create a contrapuntal pattern: in the second line,
we move through a series of more and more open vowels
until we reach the "a" of "blame." At that point, the
emphatic final word, the resultant of all the forces of the
preceding words in the line, is given further weight by
the rhyme (recalled by the "f" sound in "afraid" just a
moment before). As William K. Wimsatt has shown,
Pope's rhymes are remarkably strong; not only are they
typically monosyllabic, but there is almost always some
logical play between the rhyme words. It may be the play
of confirmation or of contrast; the sameness of sound may
underline an ironic difference, as here, or support an
implicit logical similarity. The critic must risk unpopu-
larity, and he may sacrifice "fame" by his need to "blame."
Again in the second couplet, there is the implicit contrast
of the aggressive "offend" and of the humble "mend."
There is a comparable effect, not of rhyme but of more
general sound pattern, in the second couplet: the lines open
with "averse," and after a succession of "f" sounds, the
"v" returns in "vain"—once more in a term that catches
the critic's moral resolution, his avoidance of both syco-
phancy and arrogance.

One might also note the kind of logical connectives Pope
uses through these four lines: "nor," "yet not," "alike . . .

or," "not . . . nor yet." The first "nor" is given some
stress by the meter, but it is comparatively weak; the same
is true of the "or" in the third line. In contrast the second
and fourth lines come down strongly, with full stress, on
the "yet not" and especially on the "nor yet," which com-
bines full stress with the vowel sound of the rhyming
words. These small and often unnoticed effects of stress
support the logic, as I have said; but in a truer sense, they
create a language that is saturated with meaning, where
each element becomes a delicate part of the structure of
meanings. The final phrase, "nor yet too vain to mend,"
catches the distinctive temptation of the critic as judge.
It is an appropriate close to an essay on the nature of
criticism—ironic, disarming, as much challenge as precept.

In narrative passages the architectural nicety may be
somewhat sacrificed for effects of motion. When the god-
dess of Dulness summons her devotees from the univer-
sities, we have an impression of sheer mindless numbers:

> Prompt at the call, around the Goddess roll
> Broad hats, and hoods, and caps, a sable shoal;
> Thick and more thick the black blockade extends,
> A hundred head of Aristotle's friends.

The alacrity of the followers becomes a vast swirling
motion of things; the academic gowns preempt the identity
of men; and "sable shoal" catches the swarming in a term
most often applied to schools of fish. As the crowd be-
comes more and more oppressively solid, the terms shift to
"blockade" and a "hundred head," as of herded cattle.
At just this point the sheer mass is identified as "Aristotle's
friends," at once suggesting the intellectual pride and the
unthinking conformity of Oxford's scholasticism. The play
of rhyming words produces an emphatic equation in the
first couplet—the insensible motion of "roll" is apt for a
"shoal." In the second couplet we find the massed array
implied by "extends" ironically likened to "Aristotle's
friends"; not individuals, as the term might at first glance
imply, but robot-like adherents. Pope's use of "friends" is
a good instance of his uncovering the meanings that lurk
beneath a bland phrase.

We may see this again in a dialogue between Pope and
the Friend who would disarm his satire. Pope asks whom
he can risk attacking:

> P.   Suppose I censure—you know what I mean—
>   To save a Bishop, may I name a Dean?
> F.   A Dean, Sir? no, his fortune is not made,
>   You hurt a man that's rising in the trade.

Here the couplet admits the free colloquial movement of
dialogue while it catches succinctly the opposition of a
moral and an expedient view. The friend unhesitantly
equates the hierarchy of the church with the ladder of the
success and its sacred offices with the free market. The
use of "rising" is given all the more force by earlier lines
in the same poem, where Pope exclaims over the difficulty
of writing satire:

> Vice with such giant strides comes on amain,
> Invention strives to be before in vain;
> Feign what I will, and paint it e'er so strong,
> Some rising genius sins up to my song.

The more familiar "lives up" is beautifully transformed to
"sins up." It is only the satirist who can give meaning to
the word "sins," and the blandness with which it replaces
"lives" suggests the outrageousness of a corrupt society
where careerism and vice are neither distinguished nor
questioned.

As these examples may show, Pope's language says at
once with astonishing compression what we can only dis-
entangle at length. It creates a tissue of expectations, some
of which are triumphantly met, others seemingly disap-
pointed only to be met in oblique and surprising ways,
some met in part and then surpassed. This tissue of expec-
tations is created by the meter, by the rhetorical pattern,
by verbal wit, and by the controlled interplay of idioms.
More than most poets before him or since, Pope draws
upon the colloquial idiom of ordinary life, naming familiar
objects and common sentiments. Often he places this within
a high epic style to produce those dissonances of the mock
heroic that depend upon shocking disparities and surprising

resemblances. Another language upon which Pope draws
is that of Roman satire, notably the urbanity of Horace's
sermones, those free, conversational, sometimes mordant
satires that Pope adapts to the London of his own day.
We get from both satire and the mock heroic a double
vision caught in a double idiom: the past opposed to the
present, the past in the present, both past and present as
a stereoscopic view of man's nature.

Perhaps the most persistent theme in Pope's poetry is
that of moral alertness. This may take the form of outrage,
of contempt, of compassion, of dry and playful amuse-
ment. In each case, the tone is carried through the speaker
in the poem, sometimes unnamed, sometimes named Pope.
This persona, or mask, is clearly in some sense the actual
Pope, but it is no less a fiction; it is Pope transformed into
a man of simple ingenuousness, mature candor, or intense
moral passion. All poets invent selves to be part of their
poems. The persona is at once simpler, more clearly de-
fined, and more dramatically appropriate to the occasion.
It is part of the structure of dialogue and debate, explora-
tion and discovery, that makes up the life of each poem.
Since Pope was a public figure better known in his time
than most poets have been, his contemporaries were always
aware of the natural man who stood behind the mask.
They might resent the pose the poet assumed or dispute
its accuracy, but they could hardly mistake the fictional
speaker for a simple self-portrait. To imagine a language
is to imagine its speaker, and to imagine its speaker is to
take, at least for the duration of the poem, a perspective
on the world.

II

The two poems that present Pope's theory of art most
fully are the early *Essay on Criticism* (1711) and the later
verse epistle *To Richard Boyle, Earl of Burlington*, origi-
nally called *Of Taste* and later *Of False Taste* (1731). The
problem of taste is much like that of reason. Swift wrote
in a sermon: "Reason itself is true and just, but the reason

of every particular man is weak and wavering, perpetually swayed and ruled by his interest, his passions, and his vices." In a similar vein, Pope writes of taste:

> 'Tis with our judgments as our watches, none
> Go just alike, yet each believes his own.
> In poets as true genius is but rare,
> True taste as seldom is the critic's share;
> Both must alike from Heaven derive their light,
> These born to judge, as well as those to write.

Here the figure of the watch catches the weak and wavering nature of individual taste: all watches derive their correctness from solar time, as private judgments derive their light from a common divine source.

> Most have the seeds of judgment in their mind:
> Nature affords at least a glimmering light.

But the innate judgment can be perverted by dogmatism, fashion, false learning, and pride. In fact, false taste, or, as we might say, the idea of Taste, can corrupt the native sensibility, as Pope makes clear in the epistle to Burlington. There we have the spectacle of vain and ostentatious men seeking to make a reputation for taste by elaborate constructions in defiance of nature. The elaboration is at once ingenious and conspicuous, begging with the unconscious servility of ill-founded pride for admiration and awe. The deviations from the natural and convenient solicit attention, for they involve great labor and expense. They are like the futilities described in Swift's *Gulliver's Travels,* where the proud experimenters in the Grand Academy of Lagado devote their own lives and others' fortunes to such exploits as extracting sunbeams from cucumbers or making pincushions of marble.

The corrective to vain eccentricity—to the frigidity of false art—is Nature. Nature, in Pope's sense, is the art of God; the divine handiwork is revealed in delicacies of organic harmony and ecological balance such as the wit of man can rarely attain in words.

> Unerring Nature, still divinely bright,
> One clear, unchanged, and universal light,

> Life, force, and beauty, must to all impart,
> At once the source, and end, and test of art.

Like Heaven itself, Nature provides the common truth and just standard. Its light is steady and clear; false eloquence, "like the prismatic glass," splits light into "gaudy colors,"

> But true expression, like the unchanging sun,
> Clears and improves whate'er it shines upon,
> It gilds all objects, but it alters none.

Here true wit or expression becomes that sharpening of detail and self-effacing lucidity that we recognize in the painting of Raphael or Poussin, the light that creates space by defining objects clearly within it, that may fall with love or grace upon them, as in Claude's landscapes, or fix them with almost startling precision, as in Canaletto's scenes of Venice or London. It differs from those more violent effects of chiaroscuro and brilliant highlights that give the baroque its splendid theatricality. Pope likens these latter effects to the play of conceit and extravagant wit in Metaphysical poetry.

Nature reveals an art that does not call attention to itself, absorbed in the product rather than in the process, imparting vitality to what it portrays rather than stressing the act of portrayal. Nature, in the largest sense, is both the creative force and the created world; but at best, one can scarcely distinguish between them, for one can scarcely imagine her works more perfectly realized. Nature in the world is like the soul informing and directing the body with which it is one. Nature cannot always, and human art can never, attain this inevitability, but true wit aspires to such an end rather than the self-conscious display of ingenuity; it is directed to its object rather than to itself, and it is fully realized in its object. As we shall see, Pope takes a similar view of man's self-love, which finds its truest expression in his selfless love of all men and therefore in his creation of the "according music" of society.

To follow Nature, then, requires a fulfillment of personality through a surrender of eccentricity. Pope ironically shows young Virgil's ambition to create an immortal work that would be wholly his own. The young poet repudiates all literary traditions and models, but, as he seeks to return directly to Nature, to his amazement, "Nature and Homer were, he found, the same." That is, the epic imagination has realized itself in Homer, and all future efforts to create its vision must return to Homer as the first and foremost translator of Nature into human terms.

Since Nature is a term used for both the visible and outward creation and the divine principle of artistic creativity that informs those works, Sir Joshua Reynolds wrote later in the century that the arts "in their highest province, are not addressed to the gross senses, but to the desires of the mind, to that spark of divinity which we have within, impatient of being circumscribed by the world which is about us." The task of the artist is to recover, as best he can, the divine principle of Nature; and for the young poet this principle has been caught, applied, and demonstrated in the great poets of the past. The novice seeks to be wholly original, only painfully and reluctantly to discover that his own feelings have been shared by others, that the images he seeks to create afresh have already been generated by the imagination in patterns that seem essential to human nature. There is, in effect, an archetypal human imagination, which is the poet's true Nature.

He learns from this discovery that those rules that critics have devised are not, at their best, a violence upon imaginative freedom. They are "Nature methodized," an empirical effort to codify what Nature's creative principle has attained in earlier poets. The rules cannot replace imagination. Pope mockingly creates a recipe for the writing of an epic poem in order to show this; and in the *Essay on Criticism* he exalts the "lucky License" and the "grace beyond the reach of art," the creative thrust that outruns all empirical rules and attains their end by a new and bold approach. Pope's intention is not to deny the power of originality but rather to warn against the effort to cultivate it for its own sake, or, what is more to the point, out of self-display. Once such a deviation from the rules has proved itself, it becomes in turn another rule—that is, a counsel of experience, not a flat prescription.

The burden of the *Essay on Criticism* is true creativity and just criticism. Both poet and critic must surrender willfulness to a deeper commitment; Nature rebukes and disciplines the personal will and private vision. History and tradition free one from the tyranny of the present, the shortsighted adherence to fashion as dogma. The most famous lines of the poem emphasize the universal Nature that controls the will. Poetry is not a mere collection of brilliant fragments or "glittering thoughts"; these produce what the late Metaphysicals too often did: "One glaring chaos and wild heap of wit."

> Poets like painters, thus, unskilled to trace
> The naked nature and the living grace,
> With gold and jewels cover every part,
> And hide with ornaments their want of art.
> True wit is Nature to advantage dressed,
> What oft was thought, but ne'er so well expressed;
> Something, whose truth convinced at sight we find,
> That gives us back the image of our mind.

Here Pope contrasts the line of the skillful drawing with the dazzling effects of color that are less essential to art, much as Aristotle decries the substitution of theatrical spectacle for the primary value of plot in tragedy. "Ornaments" are inorganic elements, disjunct, and from an artistic view frigid or dead. The true order of art achieves organic vitality and achieves it, moreover, by a respect for the stable world that abides outside the poet's willful fantasy. True wit comes out of common human awareness and finds a response in the feelings of all.

The imagery of dress recalls that favorite figure of Restoration comedy, the fop, an embodiment of false wit. He represents fatuous self-absorption, the hope that his tailor can make him more than a man. His finery is a "wild heap" of extravagant costume, glittering fragments that neither accord with the man nor with his social role. At the other extreme is nakedness, so often represented in Restoration comedy by the flagrant libertine, who defies social conventions and insists upon man's animal vigor. Both extremes ignore the essential condition of social man, part of a larger structure, requiring dress, realizing himself through forms which he neither scorns nor over-values:

> Expression is the dress of thought, and still
> Appears more decent, as more suitable.

The naked man needs social forms, and "naked Nature" needs artistic forms to acquire human meaning. The bare archetypal idea needs language to body it forth.

In each case, the forms are necessary to human life; one must only be careful that they do not overrun it or stifle it, as in foppery of dress or language. In Swift's *A Tale of a Tub* the three brothers who represent the church are left suits that will always fit them if they brush them often and keep them decent. But they find the doctrines of Christianity, which are these suits, too plain for worldly success and gradually adorn themselves with glittering ornaments so that they may rise in the world. In the process they become shallow fops who must constantly pervert the text of their father's will (the Testament) in order to shut out the "clear, unchanged, and universal light" that reveals their arrogance and betrayal. They cling to the present moment and impose the private will.

Pope's view of "Nature to advantage dressed" is a vision of art as man's effort to fulfill Nature's end, to give the universal new currency in each age, to bring to full con-sciousness what lies latent and ready to be given form. Its universality is revealed in our response: "Something whose truth . . . at sight we find." Dr. Johnson wrote of the sublime that its "first effect is sudden astonishment, and the second rational admiration." So in Pope there is the sense of return, an awakening of the depths of our aware-ness, a feeling of rightness and inevitability, "That gives us back the image of our mind." The image is confirmed by the archetype it brings to expression.

In the epistle to Burlington, Pope uses the problem of landscape gardening as a way of setting forth the prob-lems of art. The landscape improver, like any artist, works with Nature and seeks to realize its end. He can discern in the natural scene a potential design which is often frustrated by the intransigence of conditions—climate, weather, barrenness, or rank fertility. His object is not to violate the implicit "intention" of Nature but to complete that art whose vast scale may neglect or stint full realization in particular places. His object is to dress Nature to advantage, to

> . . . treat the Goddess like a modest fair
> Nor overdress, nor leave her wholly bare;
> Let not each beauty everywhere be spied,
> Where half the skill is decently to hide.

The true improver consults the "genius of the place," that tutelary spirit that summons the elements of Nature into their proper harmony:

> . . . Calls in the country, catches opening glades
> Joins willing woods, and varies shades from shades . . .
> Paints as you plant, and, as you work, designs.

This cooperation with Nature is quite different from the rigid assertion of the whim or dogma of false taste. That may impose geometric design, flatten or thin the rich order of Nature, and violate her spirit. The slow-growing yews are destroyed to make formal walks. This violation becomes a little drama of conquerors enslaving royal captives, who must "sweep those alleys they were born to shade." Throughout the poem, vitality is sacrificed to sterile and functionless formality:

> With here a fountain, never to be played;
> And there a summerhouse that knows no shade.

The culmination of this pattern of false art is Timon's Villa, where an ostentatious host imposes every discomfort upon his guests in order to vent his pride. Everything about his country house is an instance of "inverted Nature": the chapel whose baroque ceiling and "quirks of music" distract from prayer, the library where the most costly editions are displayed but the books unread, the vast marble dining hall where no one is nourished.

In a great passage, Timon's Villa is recaptured at last by Nature:

> Another age shall see the golden ear
> Embrown the slope, and nod on the parterre,
> Deep harvests bury all his pride has planned,
> And laughing Ceres reasumme the land.

After false art, living Nature returns. After the "huge heaps of littleness" come the true gold of the wheat and the true majesty of a vital goddess. The "civil pride" by which guests have been "tantalized in state" is replaced by the joyous bounty of a life-giving force, and the formal gardens now bear the freer beauty of the harvest.

A second opposition in the poem is that of the trivial decadence of ostentation to the true magnificence of Roman manliness and public spirit. Burlington had revived a more severely classical architecture, but lesser imitators were turning the architectonic elements of a dignified style into glittering ornaments. Rome was being trivialized as much as were those authors who filled Timon's shelves, all in the name of Taste. Burlington can restore the sense of function that gives all building vitality:

> You show us, Rome was glorious not profuse
> And pompous buildings once were things of use.

The poem closes with another vision, comparable to Nature's recapture of Timon's Villa: the "ideas" of Burlington's mind will be restored to their true expression by the dignified use of them in public works—harbors, bridges, churches. The private will and the ornament of pride give way to public utility, a vital sense of function, a return to Nature.

III

The order of art pervades Pope's thought. His cosmic vision rebukes the scoffer: "See Nature is but Art, unknown to thee." His vision of political order culminates in "the according music of a well-mixed state." For the organic order of which I have spoken—a complex harmony of disparate elements, each preserving its identity even as each depends on the whole—governs Pope's thoughts in every sphere. We can see it in his early poem *Windsor Forest* (1714) as well as in the *Essay on Man* (1733–34); and what is made explicit in those poems underlies all the others as well.

Windsor Forest is at first glance a descriptive poem about the hunting preserve beside the royal castle. But the poem opens into a vision of the English nation at the moment when it can once more look forward to peace after a long series of wars with France. It is a poem about the English past and its promise for the future; the poem closes with a political prophecy that approaches a messianic vision.

The landscape of *Windsor Forest* shows the order of art we have already seen:

> Here hills and vales, the woodland and the plain,
> Here earth and water seem to strive again;
> Not chaos-like together crushed and bruised,
> But, as the world, harmoniously confused:
> Where order in variety we see,
> And where, though all things differ, all agree.

The fullness and inclusiveness of this *discordia concors* sets the note for the political liberty Pope defends. The fertility that includes the riches of the Edenic past has been restored after a time of sterility—a "dreary desert, and a gloomy waste"—when the country was ravaged by conquerors and tyrants. Tyranny created disorder by its mockery of justice and aspiration. The nation was forced to serve the will of the King; the farms were enclosed to provide royal pastime. But tyranny is self-destructive, like the short-lived imposition of Timon's Villa. The tyrant dies by the savagery he introduces: "At once the chaser, and at once the prey." To war and tyranny succeed the more innocent games of spirited youth, deflected from fellow men to beasts, more sport than exploitation.

Pope beautifully catches this substitute for destructive war, recognizing fully the pain it creates in the small world of pheasant and fish. The "thoughtless town, with ease and plenty blest" is threatened no more, but we can see the vestige of doomed regality in the dying pheasant—"The

vivid green his shining plumes unfold,/His painted wings,
and breast that flames with gold"——or the snared perch
"with fins of Tyrian dye." This is "sylvan war," war trans-
formed to a game, innocent of human blood, a sublima-
tion of the cruel energies that have made history a record
of terror.

At the close of this account of rural sports, Pope pre-
sents the legend of the nymph Lodona. Pan has pursued
her with all the predatory fury of the hunter. As he over-
takes her, she is saved through miraculous metamorphosis
into a "soft, silver stream." Lodona, now the river Loddon,
provides in her "chaste current" the mirror of art, reflect-
ing the peaceful landscape through which she flows. Once
more the energies that might produce violence are con-
verted to the ends of peace and the beauty of art.

Windsor Forest becomes the scene of study and contem-
plation, where the retired man can "be to himself a friend,"
and the home of poets, who can achieve innocent con-
quests in art. The center of England's peace, it can become
the center of the world's new glory. As Father Thames
foresees, the oaks that once furnished navies for war will
now produce a fleet for commerce. Trade will achieve
more authentic riches than the spoils of conquest. It will
bring men to England from all parts of the earth: "feath-
ered people" and "painted chiefs" will come as admiring
visitors, not as slaves. This vision is one of "order in vari-
ety," of all peoples "harmoniously confused," with each
nation freed from bondage and allowed its distinctive cul-
ture:

> Till the freed Indians in their native groves
> Reap their own fruits, and woo their sable loves,
> Peru once more a race of kings behold,
> And other Mexicos be roofed with gold.

The world embodies in political freedom and peaceful
interchange the order of art we have seen in the land-
scape—"though all things differ, all agree."

What Pope presents as a political prophecy in *Windsor
Forest,* he later defends as a cosmic vision in the *Essay on
Man.* That poem, so often misunderstood, takes for granted

the traditional doctrine of divine order in the world; and it sets out to meet the doubts and complaints that arise from insatiable self-pity and querulous pride. The doubts of God's order are the result of man's overvaluation of himself. The overvaluation takes several forms: claiming man as the sole end of the universe; expecting of him perfect rational control; demanding for him unvaried happiness. In place of these Pope offers a universe in which man is one creature among many, peculiarly gifted but scarcely supreme. Man is, moreover, as much a creature of passion as of reason; he is not stable and self-sufficient but by his very nature dependent upon others. Finally, his happiness must be made by man through a recognition of this dependence. By discerning order in the universe man recognizes his nature and his limitations; he can move from narrow self-love toward love of the whole. In doing so he becomes like God, and he finds (in Milton's terms) "a paradise within . . . happier far" or (in Wordsworth's) "All gratulant, if rightly understood." He can accept his life as a good, and in a sense Eden is restored: "Earth smiles around, with boundless bounty blest."

The traditional doctrine of order which Pope invokes is the Great Chain of Being, the scale of all creation from insensate to vegetable to animal to rational, a scale in which there is constant variety as well as an ascending hierarchical structure. Moreover, the principle of plenitude declares that God's creative power will, by its nature, produce every possible kind of creature; no one is more essential to His creation than any other, and none can be spared if the chain is to be continuous. Such a vision of the universe as both hierarchy and organism may recall the structure of a feudal society, and it may suggest as well the Newtonian scheme, where gravity binds together all bodies in systems and all systems in a universe. Pope invokes both the loyalty and love that bind the feudal society and the intricacy and mutual limitation that mark the cosmic scheme.

Essential to the Great Chain of Being is the idea of station: each creature has its proper, in fact inevitable, place. To rebel is to claim a higher place, and the sin of pride becomes a violation of order like the war of the Titans against the Olympian Zeus or, even more, of the rebellious angels against God in *Paradise Lost*. Yet the order that Pope presents, for all its inevitability, is not a static one; it is a system of interrelatedness, a field of forces in tension, a dancelike structure that preserves itself in constant movement. Pope insists upon the vitality as well as the design. God is not merely the remote engineer or Pantocrator; he is an immanent presence:

> To him no high, no low, no great no small;
> He fills, he bounds, connects, and equals all.

It is in this sense that Pope can assert, "Whatever is, is right." He does not claim that the cosmic order brings full satisfaction to all or even to any. Much less does he claim that the existing social order is sacrosanct. These meanings have been given to the sentence in order to dismiss it as fatuous complacency. What it does assert is that there is apparent design in the universe, that we are (in George Eliot's phrase) "children of a large family" rather than spoiled favorites, that what seems to us pointless sacrifice may be necessary help to others. Most of all, Pope's sentence is a reassertion of faith. Beneath the apparent discord and confusing variety lies a larger and deeper concord or harmony; once more, the order of art.

The same faith is tested and reasserted as it applies to man's inner nature and to his society. Man is a creature of passion, and his reason can at most direct, not suppress or alter, the energies of passion. What makes for order in this variety is the Ruling Passion, that dominant motive that controls or unifies all others. It can, in turn, by being directed, direct the whole man to virtuous ends.

> Reason the bias turns to good from ill,
> And Nero reigns a Titus, if he will.

If man cannot direct himself, the hand of God will restore order in spite of him. If he cannot transcend self-love, his self-love can still be made to serve others' needs. In short, the individual can destroy himself but not the divine order, which will use him in the one way or the other, as willing participant or as unknowing instrument. Pope insists upon the powerlessness of evil as seen in this large perspective ("All partial evil, universal good"). Milton's Satan, too, seeks to uncreate God's cosmos, but he is powerless for all his grandeur, exerting his rebellious force only to fulfill God's ultimate design.

In the political realm as well, Pope shows a design that relates all creatures

> All forms that perish other forms supply . . .
>
> All served, all serving; nothing stands alone . . .
>
> On mutual wants built mutual happiness. . . .

Society is natural to man, as it is to all animals, and Pope suggests this in a picture of the golden age of patriarchal rule and simple faith, when man "owned a Father when he owned a God." The violation of this order, as in *Windsor Forest,* is tyranny, "The enormous faith of many made for one." The tyrant fosters an image of God not as father but as irascible and whimsical tyrant: "Gods partial, changeful, passionate, unjust . . ./Such as the souls of cowards might conceive." The cowed slave lives in a world of brute power, and he can imagine no order except the private will. Yet such a world becomes intolerable; and man is "Forced into virtue . . . by self-defense." As in Hobbes' *Leviathan,* where man is naturally a wolf to man—predatory, self-seeking, both hunter and prey—he must break this cycle of self-torture by establishing laws. Necessity forces him back to law, and the state evolves naturally; yet for Pope (in contrast to Hobbes) its evolution is also a restoration of man's true nature:

> Man, like the generous vine, supported lives;
> The strength he gains is from the embrace he gives.

Finally, Pope draws upon the whole vast metaphorical pattern of the cosmos to bring man to the only stability he can achieve. A creature of passion, he cannot fix himself by sedate reason. A creature of wants and dependency, he cannot be self-subsistent. A member of the whole order, he cannot be its stable end. Rather, he gains stability in identifying himself with the whole order and finding his peculiar happiness in that acceptance, the "soul's calm sunshine and the heartfelt joy." This kind of virtue is the "only point where human bliss stands still." Man's consciousness permits his spontaneous participation where other creatures are compelled by mechanical force or ruled by infallible instinct. Man is free to convert his self-love into social and at last to "Take every creature in, of every kind." He is part of a vital organism, always in movement, held together by infinite relatedness. His moral end comes in recognizing the claim of that organic harmony and in contributing freely and voluntarily to its order. In this way man becomes an artist of himself as well as a contributor to the larger order of art.

IV

The range of Pope's poetry can be seen in his treatment of women. In *The Rape of the Lock* Pope creates the charming and light-headed coquette, Belinda, who has been outraged by her suitor's passionate snipping of one of her locks. The poem was written at the urging of Pope's friend John Caryll; the incident it celebrates had actually taken place, and the offended Arabella Fermor had broken her engagement with Lord Petre as a result. Pope's poem was originally designed to laugh Arabella out of her anger and into marriage. It failed in that aim, but it had meanwhile become something more than a gesture of reconciliation. Pope had amplified the poem, by the addition of "epic machinery," into a great mock epic, and he later added Clarissa's speech in Canto V to heighten the epic parallel.

The mock epic, in this case, treats a trivial episode with all the weight of language that might be given heroic action. It takes a light, gay, and thoughtless world with apparent high seriousness, lavishing on beau and coquette alike the gravity of tone and poetic diction that might be appropriate to Achilles or Aeneas. Belinda is surrounded by Sylphs, diminutive spirits (drawn from the Rosicrucian mythology) that play the part of Homer's gods or of Milton's guardian angels. All of this is made plausible by a delicate shift of scale. For while these modern lovers and their friends are morally shallow and trivial, the epic form does not reduce them to grotesques, as happens in travesty and burlesque. Instead, it catches with brilliant closeness of detail the charm and rococo beauty of their world. We do not take it seriously, but we feel something far more complex than moral superiority.

Pope's language celebrates the value that forms acquire within a society. Belinda at her dressing table is mockingly presented as an epic hero arming himself for battle and a goddess worshiping her own image in the mirror; yet we see her using art to realize nature to the full, calling "forth all the wonders of her face" with cosmetics. The art is as genuine as the beauty. All that it lacks is what the poem, at this point, indulgently holds at a distance—a sense of proportion and value. Belinda's dressing table reveals her lack of discrimination. It contains alike, "puffs, powders, patches, bibles, billet-doux." Yet stability of character and moral consistency are cheerfully sacrificed for a fragile, youthful charm. As Pope writes elsewhere,

> Ladies, like variegated tulips, show;
> 'Tis by their changes half their charms we owe.

And Pope proceeds to do in his mock-heroics what a simple high style would avoid, to "number the streaks of the tulip."

Belinda's charm has its element of pride and assurance, its unconscious wish to lead men on and to reward them only with smiles; but the smiles have genuine beauty: "Belinda smiled, and all the world was gay." We see her surrounded by anxious Sylphs, intent to protect her lest "she stain her honor, or a new brocade." (Here zeugma is used to catch the true heroic and the light mock-heroic values in one line.) The principal image associated with Belinda is the "frail China jar," the small and beautiful vase, fragile, easily flawed. It is not a noble statue or a splendid temple, but it is a work of art no less genuine for its diminutive scale.

Into this world, which is the measure of Belinda's mind, other forces intrude. One couplet mordantly catches the cruel obliviousness of its self-absorption:

> The hungry judges soon the sentence sign,
> And wretches hang that jurymen may dine.

In the great contest on the card table, the old heroic figures emerge as diminutive playing cards. The card table becomes a "velvet plain," and on it we see the formidable armies led by such heroic figures as the "hoary Majesty of Spades" and the "Club's black tyrant." But Belinda's victory at cards only induces the reckless pride, the *hubris*, that will cause her to lose another game. As the Baron raises the scissors, now the "glittering forfex," irreversible doom confronts her:

> The meeting points the sacred hair dissever
> From the fair head, for ever, and for ever!

In what follows, the moral values of the poem are made clear. It is a poem that celebrates not heroic obduracy but serene good humor. Belinda's outrage becomes a case of "vapors," of self-indulgent grief, brought from the Cave of Spleen. The cave is the Hell of this social world, a place of rancor, hypocrisy, and prim frustration, where the passions that are repressed explode in grotesque libidinal fantasy: "Men prove with child, as powerful fancy works, /And maids, turned bottles, call aloud for corks." Belinda, in her outrage, turns from coquette to prude, longing for the improbable life of a pious rustic retreat and revealing herself all unconsciously: "Oh hadst Thou, cruel! been content to seize/Hairs less in sight, or any hairs but these!" Belinda quits the game she has played with supreme charm, the only game for which she has really lived. Now a spoil-sport, she denounces the game in unconvincing moral protestations; but even her ill temper has more charm than she knows. Yet it is good humor, finally, that is the virtue of this world—a grace of spirit and temper than can outlast physical charm. The lock remains more lovely than its possessor, and it is finally snatched from the chaos of bick-

ering to preserve, as a constellation, the permanent beauty
that Pope celebrates.

In contrast with the charm and loveliness of Belinda are
the two heroines to whom Pope devoted early "romantic"
poems. *Elegy to the Memory of an Unfortunate Lady*
(1717) celebrates a woman of intransigent passion, whose
soul has aspired "above the vulgar flight of low desire."
Scorned by her guardian uncle, denied Christian burial, she
transcends the rigidity of those "whose breast ne'er learned
to glow/For others' good or melt at others' woe." If men
do not honor her, Nature does. If no monumental "Loves"
of marble adorn her grave, "Angels with their silver wings"
pay tribute to the sanctity of her love; her ashes are now a
saint's "reliques." The poem is a generous and unguarded
tribute to the value of intensity, to the self-transcendence
of passion, to a "brave disorder" that outshines unfeeling
respectability.

In *Eloïsa to Abelard* (1717) Pope attempts a more
complex problem. Eloïsa has retired into a convent after
her illicit affair with her teacher, Abelard. He, castrated
by her angry family, has retired into a monastic life; but
one of his letters reaches Eloïsa and reawakens her pas-
sion. The poem, as Pope tells us, is "a picture of the
struggles of grace and nature, virtue and passion." We see
Eloïsa struggling to overcome her renewed passion, call-
ing upon images of grace to preserve her in her vocation.
The Gothic gloom of her setting evokes the dark uncon-
scious passions we have seen comically presented in the
Cave of Spleen. And those unconscious forces fight with
tenacity, infecting her visions of grace with a strain of
erotic fantasy. As spiritual and carnal ecstasy intermix in
her mind, the struggle becomes a tremendous torture. Its
very force is a tribute to the energies of passion, a tribute
that takes full account of their cost.

The comic and tragic modes we see in these three early
poems are fused in the later work *To a Lady* (1735). This
poem is concerned with the problem of character as op-
posed to role. It opens with a wry account of one lady
posing for portraits in various guises, "All how unlike
each other, all how true!" If all the roles are equally apt,

can this lady or any lady be said to have a character at all? The poet as portrait painter cannot hope to sketch in firm lines; he can only use strokes of color (like the streaks of a tulip) to create a shimmering impression of his insubstantial subject.

The poem is largely made up of a series of portraits which stress the inconsistencies of female temperament and range in tone from mild amusement to near-tragic awe. For the inconsistencies reveal strain and torture in many cases, such as the volatile Flavia, who dies "of nothing but a rage to live." The violent thrust of aspiration constantly overshoots the possibilities of the actual, and Flavia's disappointment with all that might give pleasure is her one constancy. Chloe, on the other hand, is icily egocentric. All her virtues are those of omission; she neither slanders nor betrays, not, however, through loyalty but through sheer indifference. The most impressive portrait is that of Atossa, "Scarce once herself, by turns all womankind!" The scale of Atossa's life is magnified throughout, but the vastness of her torrential energy is directed to self-destruction. Every victory in her long warfare contributes to inevitable defeat: "Sick of herself through very selfishness!"

These ladies reveal a design they never perceive, as the tyrant or rebel in the *Essay on Man* serves an end in which he refuses to believe or as Timon unknowingly provides benefit to others through his ostentatious waste. In contrast the true artist creates a deliberate order; the Lady whom Pope addresses achieves the good humor Belinda neglects and the tact and self-knowledge Flavia and Atossa never glimpse. Her inner stability fuses feminine charm and masculine "character." She is flexible and varied, but she has not lost a true self in the roles she assumes.

V

It is satire that we think of as Pope's most characteristic work. The turning to Horace as a model to be imitated and freely adapted to contemporary England marks a new phase in Pope's poetic career. His earlier work had often been satirical and always witty. Now he undertakes to write with a new freedom, informality, and colloquial directness. The poetic imagination becomes more self-effacing, throwing away effects more readily, ironically creating a persona through which it speaks and against which it sometimes turns. Pope is sometimes engaged in self-defense: in the assertion that satire is forced upon him by his age, in his scorn for the slander of his enemies and the oblique self-portrait that he creates in response. But, like most great satirists, he also presents himself as the satirist satirized.

For satire demands an excess. It compels attention by overstatement or powerful reductive images; it overleaps the literal in order to force us into an awareness that comes hard and is easily lost. In doing so it claims to be the language of an innocent man stung into rage and even into madness, tortured by a swarm of insect tormentors (*Epistle to Dr. Arbuthnot*), urged to deny truth and good sense by a time-serving careerist (*Epilogue to the Satires*), affronted by the public adulation of material success (*Epistle* I, vi). To catch this tone of outrage and to dramatize its outrageous assertions, Pope risks the appearance of both naïveté and arrogance. Yet the mockery moves toward celebration. Worldliness can go only so far without corruption; beyond it lies intransigence and a higher claim. We see this most sharply in those famous lines:

> F. You're strangely proud.
> P.   So proud, I am no Slave:
> So impudent, I own myself no Knave:
> So odd, my Country's Ruin makes me grave.
> Yes, I am proud; I must be proud to see
> Men not afraid of God, afraid of me.

The satirist must always make clear that the fury of his attack is a measure of the power of his devotion. It is callousness that compromises, indifference that condones. If the satirist remains intransigent in spite of all the appeals to his charity, it is because he cares too much for what he sees being destroyed to remain tactfully silent or to find a comforting rationalization. The technique of satire is in large part that of delimiting sympathy and identification, of so characterizing the opponent that he becomes too trivial, too contemptible, or too revolting to deserve our sympathy. The opponent may be plausible and, up to a point, persuasive; but he must be revealed finally as insensible or obtuse, unfeeling or self-deluded. The satirist creates a persona who is too naïve to conform, too rational to be deceived, too angry to be deterred. Against him is set an adversary who may give friendly counsels of caution or who may attack the speaker's motives—charging him with spite, envy, or fanaticism.

Out of this dramatic opposition comes the satiric dialectic. In the *Epistle to Dr. Arbuthnot*, Pope's friend, the court doctor, voices caution; but the true adversaries are to be found in the brilliant portraits of Atticus, Bufo, and Sporus. Atticus is too weak to attack directly, too vain to put up with genuine emulation. A gifted man, he becomes the enemy of excellence. Bufo is the patron who likes safe reputations that can further his own name; he is afraid to take risks, for he has no power to discern real merit. Sporus is the most complex and corrupt: a perverse and mincing courtier, all charm and treachery in contrast to the openness and independence of the honest satirist. Pope creates a persona in studied contrast to each of these three portraits.

The self that speaks through the persona of these satires becomes the best dramatization we have of what Pope's age sought to cultivate: flexibility, self-awareness, ironic discrimination, a warm generosity of spirit. There is a skeptical distrust of formulas and systems, of the externals whose care preempts the free life of the soul, of all the unlimited claims of power that exact joyless and unthinking adherence. Pope values the freedom to choose and therefore to refuse; he can withdraw from mindless activity to the solitude of his grotto, where he asks "sober questions" of his heart. The self that Pope presents is often presented in Christian terms but as often in a Socratic guise; it is not his ability to find absolute answers so much as to ask the ultimate questions that matters.

In *The Dunciad* Pope achieved his masterpiece. It is a

mock-heroic poem of a different kind from *The Rape of the Lock*. There is once more play upon scale, in the contrast of modern dunces and ancient heroes. But while the dunces are trivial enough, they compose together a massive force of blind energy, mythically represented by the goddess Dulness, the daughter of Chaos and Night. Dulness is a force of epic proportions, a monster worthy of the sword of any hero, strangely invincible because her power is that of inertia. She represents sluggishness of mind, relaxation of will, a surrender to ease and undemanding pleasure. She rules wherever men substitute fantasy for truth, self-flattery for effort, passivity for alertness. In that sense she fosters both darkness and disorder, and her only energy is a rolling vortex which moves viscously but powerfully to "blot out order and extinguish light."

The action of *The Dunciad* is a parody of the westward movement of the Trojans under Aeneas' guidance to found a new empire in Latium. Dulness' hero is the laureate Bays (based on the shameless figure of Colley Cibber), and her followers are men of the commercial city of London who move westward (in the Lord Mayor's procession) to found their empire in the court itself by imposing their standards. For the poem deals with the eclipse of culture. Art becomes trifling or self-seeking hackwork, and the tawdriest publisher governs public taste. In the first three books we move in widening circles from a shallow, cynical plagiarist-laureate to the debased world of literary trade and at last (through the vision of the city laureate, Elkanah Settle) to a long vision of the progress of Dulness as it has crept slowly from east to west, leveling and darkening one culture after another throughout human history. In the fourth book, which Pope added more than a dozen years later, we trace the force of Dulness in the mind itself and its perversion of those forms through which the mind has created order and art.

As the arts degenerate they become something more spectacular and less substantial, able to dazzle but no longer able to move heart or mind. They become more and more external, an appeal to sensation but to nothing deeper. Education becomes fixed at the level of verbal ingenuity; words become ends in themselves and in the process the very frustration of thought. Study turns more and more to the trivial, the minute, the disjunct detail; history becomes antiquarianism, learning becomes pedantry.

There emerges by the close of *The Dunciad* a picture of a world immersed in furious activity that is the very denial of life. The Grand Tour of the young wastrel is a tour of every form of decadence. Venice once a great maritime power is now the brothel of Europe. At Paris, the Seine, "obsequious as she runs,/Pours at great Bourbon's feet her silken sons." The young traveler returns with "nothing but a solo in his head," accompanied by a dissolute fugitive nun. Those who remain at home become collectors and amateur scientists, worshipers of the curious and rare regardless of its intrinsic worth:

> The dull may waken to a hummingbird;
> The most recluse, discreetly opened, find
> Congenial matter in the cockle kind;
> The mind, in metaphysics at a loss,
> May wander in a wilderness of moss.

In such a world the image of God dwindles; he is at best engineer of a mechanical universe, or, like Dulness herself,

> Wrapped up in self, a God without a thought
> Regardless of our merit or default.

The insensible materialism of the dunces encourages a tyranny that rules by corruption. The condition toward which the world moves is the lethargy of satiation, the torpor of passivity, the comfort of sleep. At the close, only the poet himself is awake to see the lights going out, the eclipse of each value by a debased substitute. The pain of beholding the death of culture is heightened by the obliviousness of those who contribute to its death. Evil need not assume the guise of terror or of violence; it becomes the more frightening, less overt process of insensible self-betrayal. Such a process requires no villains, and its appropriate presiding deity is a large, blowsy, self-absorbed goddess all of whose blind energy serves to uncreate, to reduce the painfully earned order of culture to a primal chaos of private will and gross appetite.

Dulness achieves her full meaning as the false art that replaces the true. All that we have seen in Pope's artistic theory and his social or cosmic vision celebrates a rich order holding together diversity without crushing it into uniformity, an order that allows the individual his identity and yet forms of all individuals a tissue of relatedness that creates an organism. In contrast Dulness allows each individual to fly off into eccentricity and to become all the more impoverished as he loses relationship with others and all sense of the whole. The world itself, devoted more and more to spectacle and stupefying sensation, becomes a "glittering chaos and wild heap of wit." The order it achieves is the involuntary vortex-like movement of material bodies; the dunces are impelled about Dulness not by love but by "strong impulsive gravity of head," like dead planets about a dying sun. Pope never relinquishes the awareness that the goddess who seems to control men is nothing more than a barbaric force within them given power by their surrender to it.

In *The Dunciad* we can see the way in which Pope's satire includes a tragic dimension even while it refuses to admit whatever glamor tragedy might confer. The mystery of evil is tremendous if we regard its scope, but a rather contemptible business as we close in upon the individual dunces. We can see the weight of the theme—and the epic framework reminds us constantly of that—but we can see the irremediable lightness of mind that makes the tragic action possible. The awe we feel is a measure of the grandeur that has been achieved by art and destroyed by blind selfhood. We are reminded here, as everywhere, of those paradoxes Pope sets forth in his description of man:

> Created half to rise, and half to fall;
> Great lord of all things, yet a prey to all;
> Sole judge of Truth, in endless Error hurled:
> The glory, jest, and riddle of the world!

—MARTIN PRICE

A NOTE ON THIS EDITION

The text of this edition is eclectic, largely based upon the Warburton octavo edition of 1751, but with some earlier readings restored. The punctuation is modernized wherever this seems helpful, and capitalization is almost entirely reduced to modern usage. I have preserved capital letters in cases of clearly allegorical nouns and in some terms of direct address that might be read as titles. In a few instances, I have preserved capitalization of such a term as "Nature" in order to make clear that it carries a fuller meaning than its modern counterpart.

Elliptical spellings have been expanded, in the belief that the visual pattern they present is distracting and that an adequate reading cannot help but enforce the elisions that the earlier spelling indicated. Archaic spellings have been modernized where this causes no change in pronunciation.

I have glossed as fully as seemed possible in this format, trying to give at least the import of the many proper names, and citing Pope's notes or those of Pope and Warburton (as P–W) where they were inescapably apt. Occasionally Pope is cited from a letter or other source without specific indication. The task, as I have pursued it, has been to provide a serviceable text for the general reader and student. I am deeply indebted to the Twickenham Edition, which all readers are urged to consult.

The selections are such as seemed to me essential. I regret several omissions, notably the epistles to Cobham and Bathurst and the imitation of Horace's epistle to Augustus.

CHRONOLOGY

1688   21 May. Alexander Pope born in London of Roman Catholic parents, Alexander Pope, a linen merchant, and Editha Turner Pope.

c. 1700 Pope's family moved to Binfield, in Windsor Forest.

1705   Pope first entered the literary society of London, notably that of Will's coffeehouse, the resort of Dryden until his death in 1700.

1709   May. Pope's *Pastorals*, begun in 1704, published in Tonson's *Poetical Miscellanies*.

1711   May. *An Essay in Criticism* published, praised by Addison in *Spectator* No. 253, attacked by the established critic, John Dennis.

1712   May. The *Messiah* (conflating Isaiah and Virgil) published in *Spectator* No. 378. The early two-canto version of *The Rape of the Lock* published in Lintot's *Miscellaneous Poems*. Pope became friendly with Addison, Steele, and other Whig wits who met at Button's coffeehouse.

1713   March. *Windsor Forest*. April. A prologue to Addison's tragedy, *Cato*. Contributions to Steele's *Guardian*. October. Proposals for a translation of the *Iliad*.

1714   March. The enlarged version of *The Rape of the Lock*. Pope was attending meetings of the Scriblerus Club with such Tory wits as Jonathan Swift, Dr. John Arbuthnot, John Gay, Thomas Parnell, and the two chief ministers of the government, Robert Harley, Earl of Oxford,

	and Henry St. John, Viscount Bolingbroke. The group was dispersed and the ministry fell with the death of Queen Anne on August 1.
1715	June. *Iliad*, Books I–IV (a translation which was to occupy him for the next five years and win him economic independence of patrons).
1716	March. *Iliad*, volume II. Pope's family moved to Chiswick on the Thames outside London.
1717	June. *Iliad*, volume III and the first collected volume of Pope's *Works*, containing *Eloïsa to Abelard* and *Elegy to the Memory of an Unfortunate Lady*. October. Death of Pope's father.
1718	June. *Iliad*, volume IV.
1719	Pope and his mother moved to the villa at Twickenham on the Thames, where he was to become much involved in building and gardening.
1720	May. *Iliad*, volumes V and VI.
1725	March. Pope's edition of Shakespeare (begun in 1721) published in six volumes. April. The translation of the *Odyssey*, assisted by William Broome and Elijah Fenton, began to appear: volumes I–III. Bolingbroke, returned from exile, settled near Pope at Dawley Farm, Uxbridge.
1726	March. Lewis Theobald's *Shakespeare Restored*, with attacks upon errors and omissions of Pope's edition. June. *Odyssey*, volumes IV–V. Pope visited by Swift, whose *Gulliver's Travels* appeared in October.
1727	June. The first two volumes of the *Miscellanies* by Pope and Swift.
1728	March. The "last" volume of the *Miscellanies*. May. The first version of *The Dunciad* in three books, with Lewis Theobald as hero.
1729	April. *The Dunciad Variorum*, amplified with burlesque critical apparatus, including the "prolegomena" of Martinus Scriblerus.
1731	December. *Epistle to the Earl of Burlington* (*Moral Essay* IV).
1733	January. *Epistle to Bathurst* (*Moral Essay* III).

February. The first of the Imitations of Horace, *Satire* II, i. February–May. The first three epistles of the *Essay on Man* published anonymously and widely praised.

1734   January. *Epistle to Cobham* (*Moral Essay* I) and the fourth epistle of the *Essay on Man*. June. Pope's mother died at the age of ninety-one.

1735   January. *Epistle to Dr. Arbuthnot*. February. *To a Lady* (*Moral Essay* II). May. Edmund Curll published an unauthorized edition of Pope's letters.

1737   May. Pope's own edition of his letters.

1738   May–July. *Epilogue to the Satires*. Pope by now was close to the leaders of the opposition to Sir Robert Walpole.

1740   Pope's meeting with William Warburton, later his literary executor and editor of the posthumous edition of his *Works* in 1751.

1742   March. *The New Dunciad*, the fourth book, published and attacked by Colley Cibber.

1743   October. *The Dunciad* in four books, with Cibber replacing Theobald as hero.

1744   Pope and Warburton worked on a collected edition of Pope's works. May 30. Death of Pope.

SELECTED BIBLIOGRAPHY

Editions of the Works

The Twickenham Edition of the Poems of Alexander Pope. 10 vols. John Butt (general editor). New Haven: Yale University Press, London: Methuen & Co., 1939–1968.
  I *Pastoral Poetry and An Essay in Criticism.* E. Audra and Aubrey Williams (eds.).
  II *The Rape of the Lock and Other Poems.* Geoffrey Tillotson (ed.).
  III, i *An Essay on Man.* Maynard Mack (ed.).
  III, ii *Epistles to Several Persons (Moral Essays).* F. W. Bateson (ed.).
  IV *Imitations of Horace.* John Butt (ed.).
  V *The Dunciad.* James Sutherland (ed.).
  VI *Minor Poems.* Norman Ault and John Butt (eds.).
  VII–VIII *The Iliad.* Maynard Mack and others (eds.).
  IX–X *The Odyssey.* Maynard Mack and others (eds.).
The Correspondence of Alexander Pope. 5 vols. George Sherburn (ed.). Oxford: Clarendon Press, 1956.
The Prose Works of Alexander Pope. Norman Ault (ed.). Vol. I only. Oxford: Shakespeare Head Press, 1936.
Memoirs of the Extraordinary Life, Works, and Discoveries of Martinus Scriblerus. Charles Kerby-Miller (ed.). New Haven: Yale University Press, 1950.
The Art of Sinking in Poetry. Edna Leake Stevens (ed.). New York: King's Crown Press, 1952.

Biographical and Related Materials

Sherburn, George. *The Early Career of Alexander Pope.* Oxford: Clarendon Press, 1956.
Elwin, Whitwell and Courthope, W. J. (eds.). *The Works of Alexander Pope.* 10 vols. London: J. Murray, 1871–89. Vol. V contains the *Life* by W. J. Courthope.

Spence, Joseph (ed.). *Anecdotes, Observations and Characters of Books and Men.* 2 vols. Oxford: Clarendon Press, 1966.

Wimsatt, William K. *The Portraits of Alexander Pope.* New Haven: Yale University Press, 1965.

Griffith, R. H. *Alexander Pope: A Bibliography.* 2 vols. Austin: University of Texas Studies, 1922, 1927.

Abbott, Edwin. *A Concordance to the Works of Alexander Pope.* New York: Kraus Reprint, 1965.

Barnard, John (ed.). *Pope: The Critical Heritage.* London and Boston: Routledge, 1973.

Guerinot, Joseph V. *Pamphlet Attacks on Alexander Pope, 1711–1744:* A Descriptive Bibliography. London: Methuen, 1969.

Winn, James A. *A Window in the Bosom: The Letters of Alexander Pope.* Hamden, Conn.: Archon Books, 1977.

Critical and Related Studies

Aden, John M. *Something Like Horace: Studies in the Art and Allusion of Pope's Horatian Satires.* Nashville: Vanderbilt University Press, 1969.

———. *Pope's Once and Future Kings: Satire and Politics in the Early Career.* Knoxville: University of Tennessee Press, 1978.

Adler, Jacob H. *The Reach of Art: A Study of the Prosody of Pope.* Gainesville: University of Florida Press, 1964.

Blanchard, Rufus A. *Discussions of Alexander Pope.* Boston: D. C. Heath & Co., 1960.

Brower, Reuben Arthur. *Alexander Pope: The Poetry of Allusion.* Oxford: Clarendon Press, 1959.

Brownell, Morris R. *Alexander Pope and the Arts of Georgian England.* Oxford: Clarendon Press, 1978.

Clifford, James L. and Landa, Louis A. *Pope and His Contemporaries: Essays presented to George Sherburn.* Oxford: Clarendon Press, 1949.

Dixon, Peter. *The World of Pope's Satires: An Introduction to the Epistles and Imitations of Horace.* London: Methuen, 1968.

Edwards, Thomas R., Jr. *This Dark Estate: A Reading of Pope.* Berkeley and Los Angeles: University of California Press, 1963.

Elkin, P. K. *The Augustan Defence of Satire.* Oxford: Clarendon Press, 1973.

Erskine-Hill, H. R. *The Social Milieu of Alexander Pope.* New Haven: Yale University Press, 1975.

Griffin, Dustin H. *Alexander Pope: The Poet in the Poems.* Princeton: Princeton University Press, 1978.

Jack, Ian. *Augustan Satire.* Oxford: Clarendon Press, 1952.

Keener, Frederick M. *An Essay on Pope.* New York: Columbia University Press, 1974.

Kernan, Alvin. *The Plot of Satire.* New Haven: Yale University Press, 1965.

Knight, Douglas. *Pope and the Heroic Tradition: A Critical Study of His Iliad.* New Haven: Yale University Press, 1951.

Knight, G. Wilson. *Laureate of Peace: On the Genius of Alexander Pope.* New York: Oxford University Press, 1955.

Leavis, F. R. *The Common Pursuit.* London: Chatto and Windus, 1958.

Leranbaum, Miriam. *Alexander Pope's "Opus Magnum", 1729–1744.* New York: Oxford University Press, 1977.

Mack, Maynard. *Essential Articles for the Study of Pope.* Hamden, Conn.: Archon Books, 1964; 2nd ed., 1968.
———. *The Garden and the City: Retirement and Politics in the Later Poetry of Pope, 1731–1743.* Toronto: University of Toronto Press, 1969.

Maresca, Thomas E. *Pope's Horatian Poems.* Columbus: Ohio State University Press, 1966.

Mason, H. A. *To Homer through Pope: An Introduction to Homer's Iliad and Pope's Translation.* New York: Barnes and Noble, 1972.

Parkin, Rebecca Price. *The Poetic Workmanship of Alexander Pope.* Minneapolis: University of Minnesota Press, 1955.

Rogers, Robert W. *The Major Satires of Alexander Pope.* Urbana: University of Illinois Press, 1955.

Root, Robert K. *The Poetical Career of Alexander Pope.* Princeton, N.J.: Princeton University Press, 1938.

Rousseau, George S. and Nicolson, Marjorie. *"This Long Disease, My Life": Alexander Pope and the Sciences.* Princeton: Princeton University Press, 1968.

Russo, John Paul. *Alexander Pope: Tradition and Identity.* Cambridge, Mass: Harvard University Press, 1972.

Sitter, John E. *The Poetry of Pope's Dunciad.* Minneapolis: University of Minnesota Press, 1971.

Sitwell, Edith. *Alexander Pope.* London: Faber and Faber, 1930 (chiefly of interest for formal analysis).

Spacks, Patricia A. *An Argument of Images: The Poetry of Alexander Pope.* Cambridge, Mass.: Harvard University Press, 1971.

Tillotson, Geoffrey. *Augustan Studies.* London: Athlone Press, 1961.

———. *On the Poetry of Pope.* Oxford: Clarendon Press, 1938, 1950.

———. *Pope and Human Nature.* Oxford: Clarendon Press, 1958.

Trickett, Rachel. *The Honest Muse: A Study in Augustan Verse.* Oxford: Clarendon Press, 1967.

Warren, Austin. *Alexander Pope as Critic and Humanist.* Princeton: Princeton University Press, 1929.

Wasserman, Earl R. *Epistle to Bathhurst: A Critical Reading, with an Edition of the Manuscripts.* Baltimore: Johns Hopkins Press, 1960.

———. *The Subtler Language.* Baltimore: Johns Hopkins Press, 1959.

Weinbrot, Howard D. *The Formal Strain: Studies in Augustan Imitation and Satire.* Chicago, University of Chicago Press, 1969.

———. *Augustus Caesar in "Augustan" England: The Decline of a Classical Norm.* Princeton: Princeton University Press, 1977.

White, Douglas E. *Pope and the Context of Controversy: The Manipulation of Ideas in An Essay on Man.* Chicago: University of Chicago Press, 1970.

Williams, Aubrey L. *Pope's Dunciad: A Study of its Meaning.* London: Methuen and Co.; Baton Rouge, La.: Louisiana State University Press, 1955.

Wimsatt, William K. *The Verbal Icon: Studies in the Meaning of Poetry.* Lexington: University of Kentucky Press, 1954.

Biographical and Related Materials

Barnard, John (ed.). *Pope: The Critical Heritage.* London and Boston: Routledge, 1973.

Guerinot, Joseph V. *Pamphlet Attacks on Alexander Pope, 1711–1744: A Descriptive Bibliography.* London: Methuen, 1969.

Winn, James A. *A Window in the Bosom: The Letters of Alexander Pope.* Hamden, Conn.: Archon Books, 1977.

Critical and Related Studies

Aden, John M. *Something Like Horace: Studies in the Art and Allusion of Pope's Horatian Satires*. Nashville: Vanderbilt University Press, 1969.

————. *Pope's Once and Future Kings: Satire and Politics in the Early Career*. Knoxville: University of Tennessee Press, 1978.

Brownell, Morris R. *Alexander Pope and the Arts of Georgian England*. Oxford: Clarendon Press, 1978.

Dixon, Peter. *The World of Pope's Satires: An Introduction to the Epistles and Imitations of Horace*. London: Methuen,' 1968.

Elkin, P. K., *The Augustan Defence of Satire*. Oxford: Clarendon Press, 1973.

Erskine-Hill, H. R. *The Social Milieu of Alexander Pope*. New Haven: Yale University Press, 1975.

Griffin, Dustin H. *Alexander Pope: The Poet in the Poems*. Princeton: Princeton University Press, 1978.

Keener Frederick M. *An Essay on Pope*. New York: Columbia University Press, 1974.

Leranbaum, Miriam. *Alexander Pope's "Opus Magnum", 1729–1744*. New York: Oxford University Press. 1977.

Mason, H. A. *To Homer through Pope: An Introduction to Homer's Iliad and Pope's Translation*. New York: Barnes and Noble, 1972.

Russo, John Paul. *Alexander Pope: Tradition and Identity*. Cambridge, Mass: Harvard University Press, 1972.

Sitter, John E. *The Poetry of Pope's Dunciad*. Minneapolis: University of Minnesota Press, 1971.

Spacks, Patricia A. *An Argument of Images: The Poetry of Alexander Pope*. Cambridge, Mass: Harvard University Press, 1971.

Trickett, Rachel. *The Honest Muse: A Study in Augustan Verse*. Oxford: Clarendon Press, 1967.

Weinbrot, Howard D. *The Formal Strain: Studies in Augustan Imitation and Satire*. Chicago, University of Chicago Press, 1969.

————. *Augustus Caesar in "Augustan" England: The Decline of a Classical Norm*. Princeton: Princeton University Press, 1977.

White, Douglas E. *Pope and the Context of Controversy: The Manipulation of Ideas in An Essay of Man*. Chicago: University of Chicago Press, 1970.

AN ESSAY ON CRITICISM

(1711)

'Tis hard to say, if greater want of skill
Appear in writing or in judging ill;
But, of the two, less dangerous is the offense
To tire our patience, than mislead our sense.
Some few in that, but numbers err in this,   *5*
Ten censure wrong for one who writes amiss;
A fool might once himself alone expose,
Now one in verse makes many more in prose.
   'Tis with our judgments as our watches; none
Go just alike, yet each believes his own.   *10*
In poets as true genius is but rare,
True taste as seldom is the critic's share;
Both must alike from Heaven derive their light,
These born to judge, as well as those to write.
Let such teach others who themselves excel,   *15*
And censure freely who have written well.
Authors are partial to their wit,° 'tis true,
But are not critics to their judgment too?
   Yet if we look more closely, we shall find
Most have the seeds of judgment in their mind;   *20*
Nature affords at least a glimmering light;
The lines, though touched but faintly, are drawn right.
But as the slightest sketch, if justly traced,
Is by ill coloring but the more disgraced,

17 **wit** For the senses of this word, see Introduction, pp. xix–xxxix

25 So by false learning is good sense° defaced;
  Some are bewildered in the maze of schools,°
  And some made coxcombs° Nature meant but fools.
  In search of wit these lose their common sense,
  And then turn critics in their own defense.
30 Each burns alike, who can, or cannot write,
  Or with a rival's or an eunuch's spite.
  All fools have still an itching to deride,
  And fain would be upon the laughing side;
  If Mævius° scribble in Apollo's° spite,
35 There are who judge still worse than he can write.
    Some have at first for wits, then poets past,
  Turned critics next, and proved plain fools at last;
  Some neither can for wits nor critics pass,
  As heavy mules are neither horse nor ass.
40 Those half-learned witlings, numerous in our isle,
  As half-formed insects on the banks of Nile;
  Unfinished things, one knows not what to call,
  Their generation's so equivocal:°
  To tell° 'em, would a hundred tongues require,
45 Or one vain wit's, that might a hundred tire.
    But you who seek to give and merit fame,
  And justly bear a critic's noble name,
  Be sure yourself and your own reach to know,
  How far your genius, taste, and learning go;
50 Launch not beyond your depth, but be discreet,
  And mark that point where sense and dulness meet.
    Nature to all things fixed the limits fit,
  And wisely curbed proud man's pretending wit:
  As on the land while here the ocean gains,
55 In other parts it leaves wide sandy plains;
  Thus in the soul while memory prevails,

25 **good sense** This looks back to the "glimmering light" and "seeds of judgment," which may be fulfilled through learning (as the drawn sketch is by coloring) or may be destroyed through its misuse. 26 **schools** schools of thought or criticism, with a glance at the schoolmen or scholastics, whose learning often seemed arid. 27 **coxcombs** vain pretenders. 34 **Maevius** a bad poet of Virgil's age. 34 **Apollo** as god and inspirer of true poetry. 43 **equivocal** Insects and vermin were supposed to be bred spontaneously from the mud of the Nile. 44 **tell** count.

The solid power of understanding fails;
Where beams of warm imagination play,
The memory's soft figures melt away.
One science° only will one genius fit,   60
So vast is art, so narrow human wit;
Not only bounded to peculiar arts,
But oft in those confined to single parts.
Like kings we lose the conquests gained before,
By vain ambition still to make them more;   65
Each might his several province well command,
Would all but stoop to what they understand.
      First follow Nature,° and your judgment frame
By her just standard, which is still° the same:
Unerring NATURE, still divinely bright,   70
One clear, unchanged, and universal light,
Life, force, and beauty, must to all impart,
At once the source, and end, and test of art.
Art from that fund each just supply provides,
Works without show, and without pomp presides: 75
In some fair body thus the informing soul
With spirits feeds, with vigor fills the whole,
Each motion guides, and every nerve sustains;
Itself unseen, but in the effects, remains.
Some to whom Heaven in wit has been profuse,   80
Want as much more, to turn it to its use;
For wit and judgment often are at strife,
Though meant each other's aid, like man and wife.
'Tis more to guide than spur the Muse's steed;°
Restrain his fury, than provoke his speed;   85
The wingèd courser, like a generous° horse,
Shows most true mettle when you check his course.
      Those RULES of old discovered, not devised,
Are Nature still, but Nature methodized;
Nature, like liberty, is but restrained   90
By the same laws which first herself ordained.
      Hear how learnèd Greece her useful rules indites,
When to repress, and when indulge our flights:

60 **science** art or type of knowledge.   68 **Nature** See Introduction,
pp. xiii ff.   69 **still** always.   84 **Muse's steed** Pegasus.   86 **generous**
high-bred.

High on Parnassus' top her sons she showed,
95 And pointed out those arduous paths they trod,
Held from afar, aloft, the immortal prize,
And urged the rest by equal steps to rise;
Just precepts thus from great examples given,
She drew from them what they derived from Heaven.
100 The generous critic fanned the poet's fire,
And taught the world with reason to admire.
Then criticism the Muses' handmaid proved,
To dress her charms, and make her more beloved;
But following wits from that intention strayed,
105 Who could not win the mistress, wooed the maid;
Against the poets their own arms they turned,
Sure to hate most the men from whom they learned.
So modern 'pothecaries, taught the art
By doctor's bills° to play the doctor's part,
110 Bold in the practice of mistaken° rules,
Prescribe, apply, and call their masters fools.
Some on the leaves° of ancient authors prey,
Nor time nor moths e'er spoiled so much as they:
Some drily plain, without invention's° aid,
115 Write dull receipts° how poems may be made:
These leave the sense, their learning to display,
And those explain the meaning quite away.
    You then whose judgment the right course would
        steer,
Know well each ancient's proper character;
120 His fable,° subject, scope° in every page;
Religion, country, genius of his age:
Without all these at once before your eyes,
Cavil you may, but never criticize.
Be Homer's works your study and delight,
125 Read them by day, and meditate by night;
Thence form your judgment, thence your maxims bring,
And trace the Muses upward to their spring;
Still with itself compared, his text peruse;

109 **bills** prescriptions.   110 **mistaken** misunderstood.   112 **leaves**
The scholiasts and textual editors are seen as insects and vermin.
114 **invention's** imagination's.   115 **receipts** formulas.   120 **fable**
plot. 120 **scope** aim, chosen form.

And let your comment be the Mantuan Muse.°
   When first young Maro° in his boundless mind   *130*
A work to outlast immortal Rome designed,
Perhaps he seemed° above the critic's law,
And but from Nature's fountains scorned to draw:
But when to examine every part he came,
Nature and Homer were, he found, the same: *135*
Convinced, amazed, he checks the bold design,
And rules as strict his labored work confine,
As if the Stagirite° o'erlooked each line.
Learn hence for ancient rules a just esteem;
To copy nature is to copy them.   *140*
   Some beauties yet no precepts can declare,
For there's a happiness° as well as care.
Music resembles poetry, in each
Are nameless graces which no methods teach,
And which a master hand alone can reach.   *145*
If, where the rules not far enough extend,
(Since rules were made but to promote their end)
Some lucky licence answer to the full
The intent proposed, that licence is a rule.
Thus Pegasus, a nearer way to take,   *150*
May boldly deviate from the common track;
From vulgar bounds with brave° disorder part,
And snatch a grace beyond the reach of art,
Which, without passing through the judgment, gains
The heart, and all its end at once attains.   *155*
In prospects, thus, some objects please our eyes,
Which out of nature's common order rise,
The shapeless rock, or hanging precipice.
Great wits sometimes may gloriously offend,
And rise to faults true critics dare not mend.   *160*
But though the ancients thus their rules invade,
(As kings dispense with laws themselves have made)
Moderns, beware! or if you must offend

---

129 **Mantuan Muse** Virgil's poetry, the best commentary on Homer's. 130 **Maro** Virgil. 132 **seemed** i.e., to himself. 138 **Stagirite** Aristotle, whose *Poetics* analyzed the forms of tragedy and epic. 142 **happiness** felicity, good fortune (as opposed to "care"); cf. "lucky license" (line 148). 152 **brave** (1) daring (2) brilliant, vivid.

Against the precept, ne'er transgress its end;
165 Let it be seldom, and compelled by need,
And have, at least, their precedent to plead.
The critic else proceeds without remorse,
Seizes your fame, and puts his laws in force.
  I know there are, to whose presumptuous thoughts
170 Those freer beauties, even in them, seem faults:
Some figures monstrous and misshaped appear,
Considered singly, or beheld too near,
Which, but proportioned to their light or place,
Due distance reconciles to form and grace.
175 A prudent chief not always must display
His powers in equal ranks, and fair array,
But with the occasion and the place comply,
Conceal his force, nay seem sometimes to fly.
Those oft are stratagems which error seem,
180 Nor is it Homer nods, but we that dream.
   Still green with bays° each ancient altar° stands,
Above the reach of sacrilegious hands,
Secure from flames, from envy's fiercer rage,
Destructive war, and all-involving age.
185 See, from each clime the learned their incense bring!
Hear, in all tongues consenting° paeans ring!
In praise so just, let every voice be joined,
And fill the general chorus of mankind!
Hail Bards triumphant! born in happier days;
190 Immortal heirs of universal praise!
Whose honors with increase of ages grow,
As streams roll down, enlarging as they flow!
Nations unborn your mighty names shall sound,
And worlds applaud that must not yet be found!
195 Oh may some spark of your celestial fire,
The last, the meanest of your sons inspire,
(That on weak wings, from far, pursues your flights;
Glows while he reads, but trembles as he writes)
To teach vain wits a science little known,
200 To admire superior sense, and doubt their own!

181 **bays** the laurel that crowns the poet. 181 **altar** the works of
the ancients. 186 **consenting** in harmony, unanimous.

OF all the causes which conspire to blind
Man's erring judgment, and misguide the mind,
What the weak head with strongest bias rules,
Is *pride,* the never-failing vice of fools.
Whatever Nature has in worth denied,   *205*
She gives in large recruits° of needful° pride;
For as in bodies, thus in souls, we find
What wants° in blood and spirits, swelled with wind;
Pride, where wit fails, steps in to our defense,
And fills up all the mighty void of sense.   *210*
If once right reason drives that cloud away,
Truth breaks upon us with resistless day;
Trust not yourself; but your defects to know,
Make use of every friend—and every foe.

A *little learning* is a dangerous thing;   *215*
Drink deep, or taste not the Pierian spring:°
There shallow draughts intoxicate the brain,
And drinking largely° sobers us again.
Fired at first sight with what the Muse imparts,
In fearless youth we tempt the heights of arts,   *220*
While from the bounded level of our mind,
Short views we take, nor see the lengths behind,
But more advanced, behold with strange surprise
New, distant scenes of endless science° rise!
So pleased at first, the towering Alps we try,   *225*
Mount o'er the vales, and seem to tread the sky;
The eternal snows appear already past,
And the first clouds and mountains seem the last:
But those attained, we tremble to survey
The growing labors of the lengthened way,   *230*
The increasing prospect tires our wandering eyes,
Hills peep o'er hills, and Alps on Alps arise!
A perfect judge will read each work of wit
With the same spirit that its author writ:
Survey the WHOLE, nor seek slight faults to find,   *235*
Where nature moves, and rapture warms the mind;

206 **recruits** additional supplies. 206 **needful** (1) needed (2) de-
manding, arrogant. 208 **wants** is lacking. 216 **Pierian spring** a
spring sacred to the Muses (the Pierides). 218 **largely** deeply, fully.
224 **science** knowledge.

Nor lose, for that malignant dull delight,
The generous pleasure to be charmed with wit.
But in such lays as neither ebb, nor flow,
240 Correctly cold, and regularly° low,
That shunning faults, one quiet tenor keep;
We cannot blame indeed—but we may sleep.
In wit, as nature, what affects our hearts
Is not the exactness° of peculiar° parts;
245 'Tis not a lip, or eye, we beauty call,
But the joint force and full result of all.
Thus when we view some well-proportioned dome,°
(The world's just wonder, and even thine O Rome!)
No single parts unequally surprise;
250 All comes united to the admiring° eyes;
No monstrous height, or breadth, or length appear;
The whole at once is bold, and regular.
    Whoever thinks a faultless piece to see,
Thinks what ne'er was, nor is, nor e'er shall be.
255 In every work regard the writer's end,
Since none can compass more than they intend;
And if the means be just, the conduct° true,
Applause, in spite of trivial faults, is due.
As men of breeding, sometimes men of wit,°
260 To avoid great errors, must the less commit,
Neglect the rules each verbal critic° lays,
For not to know some trifles, is a praise.
Most critics, fond of some subservient art,
Still make the whole depend upon a part,
265 They talk of principles, but notions° prize,
And all to one loved folly sacrifice.
    Once on a time, La Mancha's knight,° they say,

240 **correctly . . . regularly** obedient to the rules but without imagination. 244 **exactness** correctness. 244 **peculiar** particular. 247 **dome** building, whether domed or not, although the dome provides a fine instance of unifying structure, as in Michelangelo's dome for St. Peter's. 250 **admiring** wondering, awestruck, as well as approving. 257 **conduct** execution. 259 **breeding . . . wit** The analogy is of manners and poetic composition. 261 **verbal critic** are concerned with details of language, with form rather than function. 265 **notions** prejudices, unexamined ideas. 267 **La Mancha's knight** Don Quixote (in a sequel to Cervantes' novel).

A certain bard encountering on the way,
Discoursed in terms as just, with looks as sage,
As e'er could Dennis° of the Grecian stage; 270
Concluding all were desperate sots and fools,
Who durst depart from Aristotle's rules.
Our author, happy in a judge so nice,
Produced his play, and begged the knight's advice,
Made him observe the subject and the plot, 275
The manners, passions, unities,° what not?
All which, exact to rule, were brought about,
Were but a combat in the lists left out.
"What! leave the Combat out?" exclaims the knight;
Yes, or we must renounce the Stagirite. 280
"Not so by Heaven" (he answers in a rage)
"Knights, squires, and steeds, must enter on the stage."
So vast a throng the stage can ne'er contain.
"Then build a new, or act it in a plain."
        Thus critics, of less judgment than caprice, 285
Curious,° not knowing, not exact, but nice,°
Form short ideas; and offend in arts
(As most in manners) by a love to parts.°
        Some to *conceit*° alone their taste confine,
And glittering thoughts struck out at every line; 290
Pleased with a work where nothing's just or fit;
One glaring chaos and wild heap of wit:
Poets like painters, thus, unskilled to trace
The naked nature and the living grace,
With gold and jewels cover every part, 295
And hide with ornaments their want of art.
True wit° is nature to advantage dressed,
What oft was thought, but ne'er so well expressed,

270 **Dennis** John Dennis, a gifted but self-important critic of Pope's
day.   276 **manners . . . unities** critical terms derived from Aristotle,
sometimes legalistically applied, as in the doctrine of the three
unities (of time, place, and subject) limiting a play to one revolution
of the sun, one locale, and a uniform tone.   286 **curious** laborious,
fussy.   286 **nice** squeamishly fastidious.   288 **parts** isolated gifts, as
in "a man of parts."   289 **conceit** farfetched comparisons or meta-
phors, such as had been favored by the Metaphysical poets.   297
True wit See Introduction, p. xvi f.

Something, whose truth convinced at sight we find,
300   That gives us back the image of our mind:
As shades° more sweetly recommend the light,
So modest plainness sets off sprightly wit:
For works may have more wit than does 'em good,
As bodies perish through excess of blood.°
305   Others for *language* all their care express,
And value books, as women men, for dress:
Their praise is still—the style is excellent:
The sense, they humbly take upon content.°
Words are like leaves; and where they most abound,
310   Much fruit of sense beneath is rarely found.
False eloquence, like the prismatic glass,
Its gaudy colors spreads on every place;
The face of nature we no more survey,
All glares alike, without distinction gay:
315   But true expression, like the unchanging sun,
Clears and improves whate'er it shines upon,
It gilds all objects, but it alters none.
Expression is the dress of thought, and still
Appears more decent° as more suitable;
320   A vile° conceit in pompous words expressed,
Is like a clown° in regal purple dressed;
For different styles with different subjects sort,
As several garbs with country, town, and court.
Some by old words° to fame have made pretence;
325   Ancients in phrase, mere moderns in their sense!
Such labored nothings, in so strange a style,
Amaze the unlearned, and make the learnèd smile.
Unlucky, as Fungoso in the play,°
These sparks° with awkward vanity display
330   What the fine gentleman wore yesterday;
And but so mimic ancient wits at best,

---

301 **As shades** Cf. *Windsor Forest,* lines 17–18, and *Epistle to Bur-
lington,* lines 53–6.   304 **excess of blood** as it was believed, in apo-
plexy.   308 **upon content** on trust.   319 **decent** appropriate, attrac-
tive.   320 **vile** inept or low in tone.   321 **clown** rustic.   324 **old
words** archaic diction, such as Spenser affects at times, but used
more crudely by lesser poets of Pope's day.   328 **play** Ben John-
son's *Every Man Out of His Humor.*   329 **sparks** wits, fops.

As apes° our grandsires in their doublets drest.
In words, as fashions, the same rule will hold;
Alike fantastic, if too new, or old;
Be not the first by whom the new are tried,   335
Nor yet the last to lay the old aside.
   But most by *numbers*° judge a poet's song,
And smooth or rough, with them, is right or wrong;
In the bright Muse though thousand charms conspire,
Her voice is all these tuneful fools admire,   340
Who haunt Parnassus but to please their ear,
Not mend their minds; as some to church repair,
Not for the doctrine but the music there.
These equal syllables alone require,
Though oft the ear the open vowels tire,°   345
While expletives their feeble aid do join,
And ten low words oft creep in one dull line,
While they ring round the same unvaried chimes,
With sure returns of still expected rhymes.
Where'er you find "the cooling western breeze,"   350
In the next line, it "whispers through the trees;"
If crystal streams "with pleasing murmurs creep,"
The reader's threatened (not in vain) with "sleep."
Then, at the last and only couplet fraught
With some unmeaning thing they call a thought,   355
A needless Alexandrine° ends the song,
That, like a wounded snake, drags its slow length along.
Leave such to tune their own dull rhymes, and know
What's roundly smooth, or languishingly slow;
And praise the easy vigor of a line   360
Where Denham's strength, and Waller's sweetness° join.
True ease in writing comes from art, not chance,

332 **apes** Monkeys were often dressed in elaborate dress for entertainment.   337 **numbers** versification, sound patterns.   345 The line illustrates the pattern of "equal syllables" (line 344).   356 **Alexandrine** a line of twelve syllables and six stresses, illustrated in line 357.   **361 Denham's strength . . . Waller's sweetness** These two poets of the 17th century were praised for complementary virtues, which the Augustans sought to fuse. Sir John Denham (1615–69) wrote concisely, sometimes harshly; Sir Edmund Waller (1606–87) was celebrated for the harmony and musicality of his verse.

As those move easiest who have learned to dance.
'Tis not enough no harshness gives offense,
365   The sound must seem an echo to the sense.
Soft is the strain° when Zephyr° gently blows,
And the smooth stream in smoother numbers flows;
But when loud surges lash the sounding shore,
The hoarse, rough verse should like the torrent roar.
370   When Ajax° strives, some rock's vast weight to throw,
The line too labors, and the words move slow;
Not so, when swift Camilla° scours the plain,
Flies o'er the unbending corn, and skims along the main.
Hear how Timotheus'° varied lays surprise,
375   And bid alternate passions fall and rise!
While, at each change, the son of Libyan Jove°
Now burns with glory, and then melts with love;
Now his fierce eyes with sparkling fury glow;
Now sighs steal out, and tears begin to flow:
380   Persians and Greeks like turns of nature° found,
And the world's victor stood subdued by sound!
The power of music all our hearts allow,
And what Timotheus was, is DRYDEN now.
    Avoid extremes; and shun the fault of such
385   Who still are pleased too little or too much.
At every trifle scorn to take offense;
That always shows great pride, or little sense;
Those heads, as stomachs, are not sure the best,
Which nauseate all, and nothing can digest.
390   Yet let not each gay turn° thy rapture move,
For fools admire,° but men of sense approve;°
As things seem large which we through mists descry,
Dulness is ever apt to magnify.
    Some foreign writers, some our own despise;

---

366 **Soft is the strain** Here and throughout the next eight lines, Pope illustrates line 365. 366 **Zephyr** the west wind. 370 **Ajax** the rough hero in Homer's *Iliad*. 372 **Camilla** the female warrior in Virgil's *Aeneid*. 374 **Timotheus** the bard is shown in Dryden's ode, *Alexander's Feast, or the Power of Music*. 376 **son . . . Jove** Alexander the Great. 380 **turns of nature** emotions. 390 **turn** play on words or sound. 391 **admire** are filled with awe. 391 **approve** (1) test (2) judge favorably.

The ancients only, or the moderns prize: *395*
(Thus wit, like faith, by each man is applied
To one small sect, and all are damned beside.)
Meanly they seek the blessing to confine,
And force that sun but on a part to shine,
Which not alone the southern wit sublimes,°   *400*
But ripens spirits in cold northern climes;
Which from the first has shone on ages past,
Enlights the present, and shall warm the last:
(Though each may feel increases and decays,
And see now clearer and now darker days.)   *405*
Regard not then if wit be old or new,
But blame the false, and value still the true.
    Some ne'er advance a judgment of their own,
But catch the spreading notion of the town;
They reason and conclude by precedent,   *410*
And own stale nonsense which they ne'er invent.
Some judge of authors' names, not works, and then
Nor praise nor blame the writings, but the men.
Of all this servile herd the worst is he
That in proud dulness joins with quality,   *415*
A constant critic at the great man's board,
To fetch and carry nonsense for my lord.
What woeful stuff this madrigal would be,
In some starved hackney sonneteer, or me?
But let a lord once own the happy lines,   *420*
How the wit brightens! how the style refines!
Before his sacred name flies every fault,
And each exalted stanza teems with thought!
    The vulgar thus through imitation err;
As oft the learned by being singular;   *425*
So much they scorn the crowd, that if the throng
By chance go right, they purposely go wrong;
So schismatics the plain believers quit,
And are but damned for having too much wit.
    Some praise at morning what they blame at night;   *430*
But always think the last opinion right.
A Muse by these is like a mistress used,

400 **sublimes** raises, purifies.

This hour she's idolized, the next abused,
While their weak heads, like towns unfortified,
435 Twixt sense and nonsense daily change their side.
Ask them the cause; they're wiser still, they say;
And still tomorrow's wiser than today.
We think our fathers fools, so wise we grow;
Our wiser sons, no doubt, will think us so.
440 Once school-divines° this zealous isle o'erspread;
Who knew most sentences° was deepest read;
Faith, Gospel, all, seemed made to be disputed,
And none had sense enough to be confuted.
Scotists and Thomists,° now, in peace remain,
445 Amidst their kindred cobwebs in Duck Lane.°
If faith itself has different dresses worn,
What wonder modes in wit should take their turn?
Oft, leaving what is natural and fit,
The current folly proves the ready wit,
450 And authors think their reputation safe,
Which lives as long as fools are pleased to laugh.
    Some valuing those of their own side or mind,
Still make themselves the measure of mankind;
Fondly° we think we honor merit then,
455 When we but praise ourselves in other men.
Parties in wit attend on those of state,°
And public faction doubles private hate.
Pride, malice, folly, against Dryden rose,
In various shapes of parsons, critics, beaus;
460 But sense survived, when merry jests were past;
For rising merit will buoy up at last.
Might he return, and bless once more our eyes,
New Blackmores and new Milbourns° must arise;

---

440 **school-divines** schoolmen, scholastic theologians.   441 **sentences**
maxims and precepts; religious *sententiae* used in debate.   444 **Scot-
ists and Thomists** followers of Duns Scotus and St. Thomas Aquinas,
opposed on theological issues.   445 **Duck Lane** a London street
where old and secondhand books were sold.   454 **Fondly** foolishly,
complacently.   456 **state** This refers both to the state's hiring of
hack writers to further political interests and to the political element
that entered into literary judgments.   463 **Blackmores . . . Milbourns**
Sir Richard Blackmore and Luke Milbourn were among the lesser
writers who attacked Dryden.

Nay should great Homer lift his awful° head,
Zoilus° again would start up from the dead.   *465*
Envy will merit, as its shade, pursue;
But like a shadow, proves the substance true;
For envied wit, like Sol eclipsed, makes known
The opposing body's grossness, not its own.
When first that sun too powerful beams displays,   *470*
It draws up vapors which obscure its rays;
But even those clouds at last adorn its way,
Reflect new glories, and augment the day.
   Be thou the first true merit to befriend;
His praise is lost, who stays till all commend.   *475*
Short is the date, alas, of modern rhymes;
And 'tis but just to let them live betimes.
No longer now that golden age appears,
When patriarch wits survived a thousand years;
Now length of fame (our second life) is lost,   *480*
And bare threescore is all even that can boast:
Our sons their fathers' failing language see,
And such as Chaucer is,° shall Dryden be.
So when the faithful pencil has designed
Some bright idea° of the master's mind,   *485*
Where a new world leaps out at his command,
And ready nature waits upon his hand;
When the ripe colors soften and unite,
And sweetly melt into just shade and light,
When mellowing years their full perfection give,   *490*
And each bold figure just begins to live;
The treacherous colors the fair art betray,
And all the bright creation fades away!
   Unhappy wit, like most mistaken things,
Atones not for that envy which it brings.   *495*
In youth alone its empty praise we boast,
But soon the short-lived vanity is lost:

464 **awful** awe-inspiring.   465 **Zoilus** grammarian and pedantic com-
mentator on Homer.   483 **as Chaucer is** Pope foresees continuing
change in the English language, such as had made interpreting
Chaucer difficult and reading his words aloud most uncertain.
485 **bright idea** with suggestions of the Platonic ideas by which the
world is formed.

Like some fair flower the early spring supplies,
That gaily blooms, but even in blooming dies.
500 What is this wit which must our cares employ?
The owner's wife, that other men enjoy;
Then most our trouble still when most admired,
And still the more we give, the more required;
Whose fame with pains we guard, but lose with ease,
505 Sure some to vex, but never all to please;
'Tis what the vicious fear, the virtuous shun;
By fools 'tis hated, and by knaves undone!
    If wit so much from ignorance undergo,
Ah let not learning too commence its foe!
510 Of old, those met rewards who could excel,
And such were praised who but endeavored well:
Though triumphs were to generals only due,
Crowns were reserved to grace the soldiers too.
Now, they who reach Parnassus' lofty crown,
515 Employ their pains to spurn some others down;
And while self-love each jealous writer rules,
Contending wits become the sport of fools:
But still the worst with most regret commend,
For each ill author is as bad a friend.
520 To what base ends, and by what abject ways,
Are mortals urged through sacred° lust of praise!
Ah ne'er so dire a thirst of glory boast,
Nor in the critic let the man be lost!
Good nature and good sense must ever join;
525 To err is human, to forgive, divine.
    But if in noble minds some dregs remain,
Not yet purged off, of spleen and sour disdain,
Discharge that rage on more provoking crimes,
Nor fear a dearth in these flagitious° times.
530 No pardon vile obscenity should find,
Though wit and art conspire to move your mind;
But dulness with obscenity must prove
As shameful sure as impotence in love.
In the fat age° of pleasure, wealth, and ease,

521 **sacred** in its other meaning of "accursed."   529 **flagitious** wicked.
534 **fat age** the Restoration reign of Charles II.

Sprung the rank weed, and thrived with large increase;   *535*
When love was all an easy monarch's care;
Seldom at council, never in a war:
Jilts° ruled the state, and statesmen farces writ;
Nay wits had pensions, and young lords had wit:
The fair sat panting at a courtier's play,   *540*
And not a mask° went unimproved away:
The modest fan was lifted up no more,
And virgins smiled at what they blushed before.
The following licence of a foreign reign
Did all the dregs of bold Socinus° drain;   *545*
Then unbelieving priests reformed the nation,
And taught more pleasant methods of salvation;
Where Heaven's free subjects might their rights dispute,
Lest God himself should seem too absolute.
Pulpits their sacred satire learned to spare,   *550*
And vice admired to find a flatterer there!
Encouraged thus, wit's Titans° braved the skies,
And the press groaned with licensed blasphemies.
These monsters, critics! with your darts engage,
Here point your thunder,° and exhaust your rage!   *555*
Yet shun their fault, who, scandalously nice,
Will needs mistake° an author into vice;
All seems infected that the infected spy,
As all looks yellow to the jaundiced eye.

LEARN then what MORALS critics ought to show,   *560*
For 'tis but half a judge's task, to know.
'Tis not enough, taste, judgment, learning, join;
In all you speak, let truth and candor° shine:
That not alone what to your sense is due
All may allow; but seek your friendship too.   *565*

---

538 **jilts** harlots.   541 **mask** Women wore masks at the theatre in the
Restoration period.   545 **Socinus** (1539–1604) the religious teacher
who denied the divinity of Christ. In William's reign greater reli-
gious toleration was permitted, and this early version of Unitarian-
ism was among the doctrines freed from censorship.   552 **Titans**
the gods, pent up in the earth, who fought Zeus in the heavens;
here deistic writers.   555 **thunder** recalling Zeus' thunderbolts.   557
mistake misread.   563 **candor** generosity, openness of mind.

Be silent always when you doubt your sense;
And speak, though sure, with seeming diffidence:
Some positive persisting fops we know,
Who, if once wrong, will needs be always so;
570 But you, with pleasure own your errors past,
And make each day a critic on the last.
    'Tis not enough your counsel still be true;
Blunt truths more mischief than nice° falsehoods do;
Men must be taught as if you taught them not,
575 And things unknown proposed as things forgot.
Without good breeding, truth is disapproved;
That only makes superior sense beloved.
    Be niggards of advice on no pretense;
For the worst avarice is that of sense:
580 With mean complacence° ne'er betray your trust,
Nor be so civil as to prove unjust;
Fear not the anger of the wise to raise;
Those best can bear reproof, who merit praise.
    'Twere well might critics still this freedom take;
585 But Appius° reddens at each word you speak,
And stares, tremendous!° with a threatening eye,
Like some fierce tyrant in old tapestry.
Fear most to tax an honorable° fool,
Whose right it is, uncensured to be dull;
590 Such without wit are poets when they please,
As without learning they can take degrees.°
Leave dangerous truths to unsuccessful satires,
And flattery to fulsome dedicators,
Whom, when they praise, the world believes no more,
595 Than when they promise to give scribbling o'er.
'Tis best sometimes your censure to restrain,
And charitably let the dull be vain:
Your silence there is better than your spite,
For who can rail so long as they can write?

573 **nice** delicate.   580 **mean complacence** timidly uncritical approval.   585 **Appius** John Dennis, author of the unsuccessful tragedy *Appius and Virginia,* was sensitive to criticism.   586 **tremendous** Dennis was fond of this word and used it often.   588 **honorable** noble.   591 **degrees** unearned degrees could be awarded to privy councilors and other noblemen.

Still humming on, their drowsy course they keep,   600
And lashed so long, like tops, are lashed asleep.°
False steps but help them to renew the race,
As after stumbling, jades° will mend their pace.
What crowds of these, impenitently bold,
In sounds and jingling syllables grown old,   605
Still run on poets in a raging vein,
Even to the dregs and squeezings of the brain;
Strain out the last, dull droppings of their sense,
And rhyme with all the rage of impotence!
    Such shameless bards we have; and yet 'tis true,   610
There are as mad, abandoned critics too.
The bookful blockhead, ignorantly read,
With loads of learnèd lumber in his head,
With his own tongue still edifies his ears,
And always listening to himself appears.   615
All books he reads, and all he reads assails,
From Dryden's Fables down to Durfey's Tales.°
With him, most authors steal their works, or buy;
Garth° did not write his own Dispensary.
Name a new play, and he's the poet's friend,   620
Nay showed his faults—but when would poets mend?
No place so sacred from such fops is barred,
Nor is Paul's church° more safe than Paul's churchyard:
Nay, fly to altars; there they'll talk you dead;
For fools rush in where angels fear to tread.   625
Distrustful sense with modest caution speaks;
It still looks home, and short excursion makes;
But rattling nonsense in full volleys breaks,
And never shocked,° and never turned aside,
Bursts out, resistless, with a thundering tide!   630
    But where's the man who counsel can bestow,

601 **asleep** A top is said to "sleep" when its motion is so rapid as to
be imperceptible.   603 **jades** worn-out horses.   617 **Dryden's . . .
Tales** Dryden's *Fables* includes excellent verse translations of
Chaucer, Boccaccio, and Ovid. Thomas Durfey, best known as a
writer and collector of songs, was also a literary hack.   619 **Garth**
Sir Samuel Garth, author of *The Dispensary*.   623 **Paul's church** St.
Paul's Cathedral and its churchyard were often places of meeting in
the 17th century.   629 **shocked** checked.

Still pleased to teach, and yet not proud to know?
Unbiased, or by favor or by spite;
Not dully prepossessed, nor blindly right;
635 Though learned, well-bred; and though well-bred,
    sincere;
Modestly bold, and humanly° severe?
Who to a friend his faults can freely show,
And gladly praise the merit of a foe?
Blest with a taste exact, yet unconfined;
640 A knowledge both of books and human kind;
Generous converse; a soul exempt from pride;
And love to praise, with reason on his side?
    Such once were critics, such the happy few,
Athens and Rome in better ages knew.
645 The mighty Stagirite first left the shore,
Spread all his sails, and durst the deeps explore;
He steered securely, and discovered far,
Led by the light of the Maeonian star.°
Poets, a race long unconfined and free,
650 Still fond and proud of savage liberty,
Received his laws, and stood convinced 'twas fit
Who conquered nature,° should preside o'er wit.
    Horace still charms with graceful negligence,
And without method° talks us into sense,
655 Will like a friend familiarly convey
The truest notions in the easiest way.
He, who supreme in judgment, as in wit,
Might boldly censure, as he boldly writ,
Yet judged with coolness though he sung with fire;°
660 His precepts teach but what his works inspire.
Our critics take a contrary extreme,
They judge with fury, but they write with fle'me:°
Nor suffers Horace more in wrong translations
By wits, than critics in as wrong quotations.

---

636 **humanly** humanely.   648 **Maeonian star** Homer.   652 **nature** re-
ferring to Aristotle's scientific works.   654 **without method** Horace's
chief critical work, the *Ars Poetica,* is written as an informal verse
letter to friends, unlike the more methodical *Poetics* of Aristotle.
659 **sung with fire** referring to Horace's odes.   662 **fle'me** phlegm,
coldness.

AN ESSAY ON CRITICISM

See Dionysius° Homer's thoughts refine,   *665*
And call new beauties forth from every line!
Fancy and art in gay Petronius please,
The scholar's learning, with the courtier's ease.
In grave Quintilian's copious work we find
The justest rules, and clearest method joined; *670*
Thus useful arms in magazines° we place,
All ranged in order, and disposed with grace,
But less to please the eye, than arm the hand,
Still fit for use, and ready at command.
Thee, bold Longinus!° all the Nine inspire,   *675*
And bless their critic with a poet's fire.
An ardent judge, who zealous in his trust,
With warmth gives sentence, yet is always just;
Whose own example strengthens all his laws,
And is himself that great sublime he draws.   *680*
Thus long succeeding critics justly reigned,
Licence repressed, and useful laws ordained.
Learning and Rome alike in empire grew,
And arts still followed where her eagles° flew;
From the same foes, at last, both felt their doom, *685*
And the same age saw learning fall, and Rome.
With tyranny, then superstition joined,
As that the body, this enslaved the mind;
Much was believed, but little understood,
And to be dull was construed to be good;   *690*
A second deluge learning thus o'errun,
And the monks finished what the Goths begun.
At length Erasmus,° that great injured name,
(The glory of the priesthood, and the shame!)
Stemmed the wild torrent of a barbarous age, *695*
And drove those holy Vandals off the stage.

---

665 **Dionysius** i.e., of Halicarnassus, Greek rhetorician, first century
A.D. 671 **magazines** armories. 675 **Longinus** Greek author of *On
the Sublime*, the most enthusiastic and least rule-bound of ancient
critics, first century A.D. 684 **eagles** the insignia of her armies.
693 **Erasmus** (1466–1536), humanist and moderate churchman (cf.
Satire II, i, 66–7). Pope felt that Erasmus had been "oppressed and
persecuted" by narrower fellow-Catholics and was at last "vindi-
cated after a whole age of obloquy" (cf. "shame," line 694).

    But see! each Muse, in Leo's golden days,°
    Starts from her trance, and trims her withered bays!
    Rome's ancient genius, o'er its ruins spread,
700 Shakes off the dust, and rears his reverend head!
    Then sculpture and her sister arts revive;
    Stones leaped to form, and rocks began to live;
    With sweeter notes° each rising temple rung;
    A Raphael° painted, and a Vida° sung!
705 Immortal Vida! on whose honored brow
    The poet's bays and critic's ivy° grow:
    Cremona° now shall ever boast thy name,
    As next in place to Mantua, next in fame!
    But soon by impious arms° from Latium chased,
710 Their ancient bounds the banished muses passed;
    Thence arts o'er all the northern world advance;
    But critic learning flourished most in France.
    The rules, a nation born to serve,° obeys,
    And Boileau° still in right of Horace sways.
715 But we, brave Britons, foreign laws despised,
    And kept unconquered, and uncivilized,
    Fierce for the liberties of wit, and bold,
    We still defied the Romans, as of old.°
    Yet some there were, among the sounder few
720 Of those who less presumed, and better knew,

697 **Leo's . . . days** Leo X, the son of Lorenzo de' Medici, the Magnificent, was pope from 1513 to 1521. A patron of learning and the arts, he established the first Greek printing press in Rome and made Raphael (line 704) custodian of classical antiquities. 703 **sweeter notes** recalling the myth of Amphion, who built the walls of Thebes by drawing stones into place with the music of his lyre; referring as well to Leo's love and sponsorship of music. 704 **Raphael** (1483–1520) named chief architect of St. Peter's in 1514, painted many of his greatest frescoes and prepared the great tapestry cartoons (now in London) under Leo X. 704 **Vida** (1490?–1566) a celebrated neo-Latin poet who was treated with favor by Leo X. 706 As the bays, or laurel, were originally associated with the conqueror or emperor, so was ivy with the poet; but as the bays became identified with the poet, so was the ivy with the man of learning, here the critic (Vida was the author of an "art of poetry" in verse). 707 **Cremona** the birthplace of Vida, as Mantua (708) was of Virgil. 709 **impious arms** the Sack of Rome in 1527 by the troops of the Emperor Charles V. 713 **nation . . . serve** Cf. *Dunciad* IV, 297–8. 714 **Boileau** (1636–1711) published a verse *Art of Poetry* and satires in imitation of Horace. 718 As the Britons resisted Roman rule, so these writers resisted classical form and precept.

Who durst assert the juster ancient cause,
And here restored wit's fundamental laws.
Such was the muse,° whose rules and practice tell,
"Nature's chief masterpiece is writing well."
Such was Roscommon°—not more learned than good,   *725*
With manners generous as his noble blood;
To him the wit of Greece and Rome was known,
And every author's merit,° but his own.
Such late was Walsh,°—the Muse's judge and friend,
Who justly knew to blame or to commend;   *730*
To failings mild, but zealous for desert;
The clearest head, and the sincerest heart.
This humble praise, lamented shade! receive,
This praise at least a grateful Muse may give!
The Muse, whose early voice you taught to sing,   *735*
Prescribed her heights, and pruned her tender wing,
(Her guide now lost) no more attempts to rise,
But in low numbers short excursions tries:
Content, if hence the unlearned their wants may view,
The learned reflect on what before they knew: *740*
Careless of censure, nor too fond of fame,
Still pleased to praise, yet not afraid to blame,
Averse alike to flatter, or offend,
Not free from faults, nor yet too vain to mend.

723 **muse** John Sheffield, Duke of Buckingham and Normandy (1648–1721), whose *Essay upon Poetry* is quoted in the next line. He had been a patron of Dryden and was a friend of the young Pope.   725 **Roscommon** translated Horace's *Art of Poetry* and wrote *An Essay on Translated Verse.*   728 **merit** Roscommon was one of the first to praise Milton's *Paradise Lost.*   729 **Walsh** William Walsh (1662–1708), poet and critic, whose advice was valued by both Dryden and Pope.

WINDSOR FOREST

(1713)

Thy forests, Windsor! and thy green retreats,
At once the Monarch's and the Muse's seats,°
Invite my lays. Be present, sylvan maids!
Unlock your springs, and open all your shades.
5   Granville° commands; your aid, O Muses, bring!
What Muse for Granville can refuse to sing?
  The groves of Eden,° vanished now so long,
Live in description, and look green in song:
These, were my breast inspired with equal flame,
10 Like them in beauty, should be like in fame.
Here hills and vales, the woodland and the plain,
Here earth and water seem to strive again;
Not chaos-like together crushed and bruised,
But, as the world, harmoniously confused:°
15 Where order in variety we see,
And where, though all things differ, all agree.
Here waving groves a chequered scene display,
And part admit and part exclude the day;
As some coy nymph her lover's warm address
20 Nor quite indulges, nor can quite repress.
There, interspersed in lawns and opening glades,

---

2 **At once . . . seats** the royal forest preserve of Queen Anne seen as
the center of both England's natural beauty and its culture, later of
its history and its empire.   5 **Granville** a poet and friend of Pope,
made Secretary of War in 1710 and created a peer in 1712.   7 **Eden**
an allusion to Milton, *Paradise Lost*, IV.   14 **harmoniously con-
fused** an echo of Ovid's *discors concordia* (*Metamorphoses*, I, 433).

Thin trees arise that shun each other's shades.
Here in full light the russet plains extend:
There wrapped in clouds the bluish hills ascend.
Even the wild heath displays her purple dyes, 25
And midst the desert° fruitful fields arise,
That crowned with tufted trees and springing corn,
Like verdant isles the sable waste adorn.
Let India boast her plants, nor envy we
The weeping amber or the balmy tree,° 30
While by our oaks° the precious loads are borne,
And realms commanded which those trees adorn.
Not proud Olympus° yields a nobler sight,
Though gods assembled grace his towering height,
Than what more humble mountains offer here, 35
Where, in their blessings,° all those gods appear.
See Pan° with flocks, with fruits Pomona° crowned,
Here blushing Flora paints the enamelled ground,°
Here Ceres' gifts° in waving prospect stand,
And nodding tempt the joyful reaper's hand; 40
Rich Industry° sits smiling on the plains,
And peace and plenty tell, a Stuart reigns.
    Not thus the land appeared in ages past,
A dreary desert and a gloomy waste,
To savage beasts and savage laws a prey, 45
And kings more furious and severe than they:
Who claimed the skies, dispeopled air and floods,°
The lonely lords of empty wilds and woods:

26 **desert** barrenness; cf. "waste" (line 28). 30 **weeping . . . tree** Cf.
Milton, *Paradise Lost*, IV, 248: "Groves whose rich Trees wept
odorous Gums and Balm." 31 **oaks** in the form of the British ships
of the spice trade or (line 32) the Royal Navy. 33 **Olympus** the
high Greek mountain where the gods dwelled. 36 **blessings** in the
form of their gifts. 37 **Pan** as shepherd. 37 **Pomona** as goddess of
fruit. 38 **blushing Flora . . . ground** The goddess of flowers, herself
suffused with their color, paints the earth as if it were a painter's
surface, prepared with a background coating. 39 **Ceres' gifts** wheat.
41 **Industry** Pope domesticates Virgil's account of the Golden Age,
Eclogue IV, as a picture of English prosperity in a time of peace,
This is a tribute to the Peace of Utrecht (1713), which ended the
War of the Spanish Succession, begun under William of Orange in
1701. 47 **claimed . . . floods** a reference to the wide hunting pre-
serves claimed by earlier kings.

Cities laid waste, they stormed the dens and caves,
50 (For wiser brutes were backward to be slaves.)
What could be free when lawless beasts obeyed,
And even the elements a Tyrant swayed?°
In vain kind seasons swelled the teeming grain,
Soft showers distilled, and suns grew warm in vain;
55 The swain with tears his frustrate labor yields,
And famished dies amidst his ripened fields.
What wonder then, a beast or subject slain
Were equal crimes in a despotic reign;
Both doomed alike, for sportive tyrants bled,
60 But while the subject starved, the beast was fed.
Proud Nimrod° first the bloody chase began,
A mighty hunter, and his prey was man.
Our haughty Norman° boasts that barbarous name,
And makes his trembling slaves the royal game.
65 The fields are ravished from the industrious swains,
From men their cities, and from Gods their fanes:
The levelled towns with weeds lie covered o'er;
The hollow winds through naked temples roar;
Round broken columns clasping ivy twined;
70 O'er heaps of ruin stalked the stately hind;
The fox obscene to gaping tombs retires,
And savage howlings fill the sacred choirs.
Awed by his Nobles, by his Commons curst,
The oppressor ruled tyrannic where he durst,
75 Stretched o'er the poor and church his iron rod,
And served alike his vassals and his God.
Whom even the Saxon spared and bloody Dane,
The wanton victims of his sport° remain.

49–52 **Cities . . . swayed** The metaphor of hunting expands to all
predatory use of power, and possibly (in line 52) to the doctrine of
a God in the image of the tyrant (cf. *Essay on Man*, III, 241–68).
Tyranny is associated throughout with social disorder, in contrast
to the "peace and plenty" of a just reign.   61 **Nimrod** described in
Genesis 10:8–9 as "a mighty one in the earth" and a "mighty hunter
before the lord"; by Milton, *Paradise Lost*, XII, 24–47, as the first
tyrant and hunter of men.   63 **Norman** William the Conqueror, who
created the New Forest by destroying the existing towns, farms, and
churches (cf. "fanes," line 66; "temples," 68; "choirs," 72).   78 **sport**
(1) hunting (2) scornful whim.

But see, the man who spacious regions gave
A waste for beasts, himself denied a grave!°   *80*
Stretched on the lawn his second hope° survey,
At once the chaser, and at once the prey:
Lo Rufus, tugging at the deadly dart,
Bleeds in the forest like a wounded hart.
Succeeding monarchs heard the subjects' cries,   *85*
Nor saw displeased the peaceful cottage rise.
Then gathering flocks on unknown mountains fed,
O'er sandy wilds were yellow harvests spread,
The forests wondered at the unusual grain,
And secret transport touched the conscious° swain.   *90*
Fair Liberty, Britannia's goddess, rears
Her cheerful head, and leads the golden years.
> Ye vigorous swains! while youth ferments your
>   blood,
And purer spirits swell the sprightly flood,°
Now range the hills, the gameful woods beset,   *95*
Wind the shrill horn, or spread the waving net.
When milder autumn summer's heat succeeds,
And in the new-shorn field the partridge feeds,
Before his lord the ready spaniel bounds,
Panting with hope, he tries the furrowed grounds;   *100*
But when the tainted gales° the game betray,
Couched close he lies, and meditates the prey:
Secure they° trust the unfaithful field beset,
Till hovering o'er 'em sweeps the swelling net.
Thus (if small things we may with great compare)   *105*
When Albion sends her eager sons to war,
Some thoughtless town, with ease and plenty blest,
Near, and more near, the closing lines° invest;
Sudden they seize the amazed, defenseless prize,
And high in air Britannia's standard flies.   *110*

---

80 **grave** William's burial place at Caen was claimed by another and
had to be bought anew by his son.   81 **second hope** William's sec-
ond son, Richard, who died in the New Forest, like his brother,
William Rufus (line 83).   90 **conscious** responsive.   94 **spirits . . .
sprightly flood** a reference to the animal spirits, believed to be a
subtle vapor-like substance that moved in the blood and animated
the body.   101 **tainted gales** breezes that carry the scent of game.
103 **they** the partridges.   108 **lines** of siege.

See! from the brake° the whirring pheasant springs,
And mounts exulting on triumphant wings;
Short is his joy! he feels the fiery wound,
Flutters in blood, and panting beats the ground.
115 Ah! what avail his glossy, varying dyes,°
His purple crest, and scarlet-circled eyes,
The vivid green his shining plumes unfold,
His painted wings, and breast that flames with gold?
Nor yet, when moist Arcturus° clouds the sky,
120 The woods and fields their pleasing toils deny.
To plains with well-breathed beagles we repair,
And trace the mazes of the circling hare:
(Beasts, urged by us, their fellow-beasts pursue,
And learn of man each other to undo.)
125 With slaughtering guns the unwearied fowler roves,
When frosts have whitened all the naked groves;
Where doves in flocks the leafless trees o'ershade,
And lonely woodcocks haunt the watery glade.
He lifts the tube, and levels with his eye;
130 Straight a short thunder breaks the frozen sky.
Oft, as in airy rings they skim the heath,
The clamorous lapwings feel the leaden death:
Oft, as the mounting larks their notes prepare,
They fall, and leave their little lives in air.
135 In genial spring, beneath the quivering shade,
Where cooling vapors breathe along the mead,
The patient fisher takes his silent stand,
Intent, his angle trembling in his hand;
With looks unmoved, he hopes the scaly breed,
140 And eyes the dancing cork and bending reed.
Our plenteous streams a various race supply,
The bright-eyed perch with fins of Tyrian dye,°
The silver eel, in shining volumes° rolled,
The yellow carp, in scales bedropped with gold,
145 Swift trouts, diversified with crimson stains,

---

111 **brake** thicket.   115 **glossy . . . dyes** the pheasant's plumage seen
as regal splendor.   119 **moist Arcturus** associated with storms as it
rose in September.   142 **Tyrian dye** crimson or purple.   143 **volumes** coils.

And pikes, the tyrants° of the watery plains.
  Now Cancer° glows with Phoebus' fiery car;
The youth rush eager to the sylvan war,
Swarm o'er the lawns, the forest walks surround,
Rouse the fleet hart, and cheer the opening° hound.   *150*
The impatient courser pants in every vein,
And, pawing, seems to beat the distant plain:
Hills, vales, and floods appear already crossed,
And ere he starts, a thousand steps are lost.
See the bold youth strain up the threatening steep,   *155*
Rush through the thickets, down the valleys sweep,
Hang o'er their coursers' heads with eager speed,
And earth rolls back beneath the flying steed.
Let old Arcadia° boast her ample plain,
The immortal huntress,° and her virgin train;   *160*
Nor envy, Windsor! since thy shades have seen
As bright a goddess, and as chaste a Queen,°
Whose care, like hers, protects the sylvan reign,
The earth's fair light, and empress of the main.
  Here too, 'tis sung, of old Diana strayed,   *165*
And Cynthus'° top forsook for Windsor shade;
Here was she seen o'er airy wastes to rove,
Seek the clear spring, or haunt the pathless grove;
Here armed with silver bows, in early dawn,
Her buskined virgins° traced° the dewy lawn.   *170*
  Above the rest a rural nymph was famed,
Thy offspring, Thames! the fair Lodona° named;
(Lodona's fate, in long oblivion cast,
The Muse shall sing, and what she sings shall last.)
Scarce could the goddess from her nymph be known,   *175*

---

146 **tyrants** so called for their voraciousness. 147 **Cancer** the zodiacal sign for the season that begins with the summer solstice, when the sun is at its height ("Phoebus' fiery car"). 150 **opening** giving tongue, baying. 159 **Arcadia** the area of Greece celebrated in pastoral poetry. 160 **huntress** Diana, celebrated for chastity and as goddess of the moon (cf. line 162). 162 **Queen** Anne, who often hunted. 166 **Cynthus** the mountain on the island of Delos where Diana was born. 170 **buskined virgins** the nymphs who joined Diana in the hunt, wearing high-laced sandals. 170 **traced** traversed. 172 **Lodona** the mythical form of the river Loddon, here imagined as Diana's nymph.

But by the crescent° and the golden zone.°
She scorned the praise of beauty and the care;
A belt her waist, a fillet binds her hair;
A painted quiver on her shoulder sounds,
180 And with her dart the flying deer she wounds.
It chanced, as eager of the chase, the maid
Beyond the forest's verdant limits strayed,
Pan° saw and loved, and, burning with desire,
Pursued her flight; her flight increased his fire.
185 Not half so swift the trembling doves can fly,
When the fierce eagle cleaves the liquid° sky;
Not half so swiftly the fierce eagle moves,
When through the clouds he drives the trembling doves;
As from the god she flew with furious pace,
190 Or as the god, more furious, urged the chase.
Now fainting, sinking, pale, the nymph appears;
Now close behind, his sounding steps she hears;
And now his shadow reached her as she run
(His shadow lengthened by the setting sun),
195 And now his shorter breath, with sultry air,
Pants on her neck, and fans her parting hair.
In vain on father Thames she calls for aid,
Nor could Diana help her injured maid.
Faint, breathless, thus she prayed, nor prayed in vain;
200 "Ah, Cynthia!° ah—though banished from thy train,
Let me, O let me, to the shades repair,
My native shades—there weep and murmur there"
She said, and melting as in tears she lay,
In a soft, silver stream dissolved away.
205 The silver stream her virgin coldness keeps,
For ever murmurs, and for ever weeps;
Still bears the name the hapless virgin bore,
And bathes the forest where she ranged before.
In her chaste current oft the goddess laves,
210 And with celestial tears augments the waves.
Oft in her glass° the musing shepherd spies

---

176 crescent the moon emblem of Diana.   **176 zone** belt.   **183 Pan**
as the God of shepherds, often imagined as a goatlike satyr.   **186**
liquid clear.   **200 Cynthia** Diana, so named for Mt. Cynthus.   **211**
glass mirror.

The headlong mountains and the downward skies,
The watery landscape of the pendent woods,
And absent° trees that tremble in the floods;
In the clear azure gleam the flocks are seen,   215
And floating forests paint the waves with green,
Through the fair scene roll slow the lingering streams,
Then foaming pour along, and rush into the Thames.
    Thou, too, great father° of the British floods!°
With joyful pride surveyst our lofty woods;   220
Where towering oaks their growing honors° rear,
And future navies on thy shores appear.
Not Neptune's° self from all his streams receives
A wealthier tribute than to thine he gives.
No seas so rich, so gay no banks appear,   225
No lake so gentle, and no spring so clear.
Nor Po° so swells the fabling poet's lays,
While led along the skies his current strays,
As thine,° which visits Windsor's famed abodes,
To grace the mansion of our earthly gods: 230
Nor all his stars above a lustre show
Like the bright beauties on thy banks below;
Where Jove, subdued by mortal° passion still,
Might change Olympus for a nobler hill.
    Happy the man whom this bright court approves,   235
His sovereign favors, and his country loves;
Happy next him, who to these shades retires,
Whom Nature charms, and whom the Muse inspires,
Whom humbler joys of home-felt quiet please,
Successive study, exercise, and ease.   240
He gathers health from herbs the forest yields,
And of their fragrant physic spoils the fields:
With chymic° art exalts the mineral powers,
And draws° the aromatic souls of flowers.

---

214 **absent** unseen except in reflection. 219 **father** Thames. 219 **floods** rivers. 221 **honors** foliage. 223 **Neptune** as the sea receiving the tribute of the rivers; in return a source of trade. 227 **Po** the Italian river seen as the constellation Eridanus, flowing through the heavens (cf. line 231). 229 **thine** the Thames as it flows by the royal castle. 233 **mortal** for a mortal woman. 243 **chymic** chemical or alchemical (converting baser elements to gold). 244 **draws** extracts in essences.

245 Now marks the course of rolling orbs on high;
O'er figured° worlds now travels with his eye.
Of ancient writ° unlocks the learnèd store,
Consults the dead, and lives past ages o'er.
Or wandering thoughtful in the silent wood,
250 Attends the duties of the wise and good,
To observe a mean,° be to himself a friend,
To follow Nature, and regard his end;°
Or looks on heaven with more than mortal eyes,
Bids his free soul expatiate° in the skies,
255 Amid her kindred stars familiar roam,
Survey the region, and confess her home!
Such was the life great Scipio° once admired;
Thus Atticus,° and Trumbull° thus retired.
  Ye sacred Nine! that all my soul possess,
260 Whose raptures fire me, and whose visions bless,
Bear me, oh bear me to sequestered scenes,
The bowery mazes, and surrounding greens:
To Thames's banks, which fragrant breezes fill,
Or where ye Muses sport on Cooper's Hill.°
265 (On Cooper's Hill eternal wreaths shall grow,
While lasts the mountain, or while Thames shall flow.)
I seem through consecrated walks to rove,
I hear soft music die along the grove:
Led by the sound, I roam from shade to shade
270 By godlike poets venerable made:
Here his first lays majestic Denham° sung;
There the last numbers flowed from Cowley's° tongue.
O early lost! what tears the river shed,

246 **figured** charted, as on a globe of the heavens. 247 **writ** writ-
ings. 251 **mean** the golden mean, or temperate life. 252 **end** proper
function as well as fate. 254 **expatiate** wander at will. 257 **Scipio**
the Roman general who retired to his country estate. 258 **Atticus**
the friend of Cicero who repudiated public life out of devotion to
study. 258 **Trumbull** Sir William, the retired statesman and friend
of the young Pope. 264 **Cooper's Hill** the scene of Sir John Den-
ham's poem (1642), a model for this one. 271 **Denham** Sir John,
the Royalist poet, "majestic" because of his epic vein (1615–69).
272 **Cowley** the poet Abraham Cowley, who died near Windsor
Forest at the age of forty-nine.

When the sad pomp° along his banks was led!
His drooping swans on every note expire,   275
And on his willows hung each Muse's lyre.°
   Since fate relentless stopped their heavenly voice,
No more the forests ring or groves rejoice;
Who now shall charm the shades, where Cowley strung
His living harp, and lofty Denham sung?   280
But hark! the groves rejoice, the forest rings!
Are these revived? or is it Granville sings?
'Tis yours, my Lord, to bless our soft retreats,
And call the Muses to their ancient seats;
To paint anew the flowery sylvan scenes,   285
To crown the forests with immortal greens,
Make Windsor hills in lofty numbers° rise,
And lift her turrets nearer to the skies;
To sing those honors you deserve to wear,
And add new lustre to her silver star.°   290
   Here noble Surrey° felt the sacred rage,
Surrey, the Granville of a former age:
Matchless his pen, victorious was his lance,
Bold in the lists, and graceful in the dance:
In the same shades the cupids tuned his lyre,   295
To the same notes, of love, and soft desire:
Fair Geraldine,° bright object of his vow,
Then filled the groves, as heavenly Mira now.
   Oh wouldst thou sing what heroes Windsor bore,
What kings first breathed upon her winding shore,   300
Or raise old warriors, whose adored remains
In weeping vaults her hallowed earth contains!
With Edward's acts° adorn the shining page,
Stretch his long triumphs down through every age,

---

274 **pomp** Cowley's body was borne down the Thames to London,
where it was buried in Westminster Abbey. 276 **each Muse's lyre**
a reference to the many forms of poetry in which Cowley excelled.
287 **lofty numbers** exalted or heroic verse. 290 **silver star** the em-
blem of the Order of the Garter, founded at Windsor by Edward
III. It was these "honors" (line 289) that Granville deserved. 291
Surrey "one of the refiners of the English poetry, who flourished
in the time of Henry the VIIIth" (Pope). 297 **Geraldine** the object
of Surrey's love poems, as "Mira" was of Granville's (line 298).
303 **Edward's acts** the victories of Edward III, whose forces cap-
tured kings of Scotland and of France (line 305).

305   Draw monarchs chained, and Cressy's glorious field,°
      The lilies blazing on the regal shield:
      Then, from her roofs when Verrio's colors° fall,
      And leave inanimate the naked wall,
      Still in thy song should vanquished France appear,
310   And bleed for ever under Britain's spear.
         Let softer strains ill-fated Henry° mourn,
      And palms eternal° flourish round his urn.
      Here o'er the Martyr King the marble weeps,
      And, fast beside him, once-feared Edward° sleeps:
315   Whom not the extended Albion° could contain,
      From old Belerium° to the northern main,
      The grave unites; where e'en the great find rest,
      And blended lie the oppressor and the opprest!
         Make sacred Charles's° tomb for ever known
320   (Obscure the place, and uninscribed the stone),
      Oh fact accurst! what tears has Albion shed,
      Heavens, what new wounds! and how her old have bled!
      She saw her sons with purple deaths° expire,
      Her sacred domes involved in rolling fire,°
325   A dreadful series of intestine wars,
      Inglorious triumphs and dishonest° scars.
      At length great Anna said—"Let Discord cease!"
      She said! the world obeyed, and all was Peace!

         In that blest moment from his oozy bed
330   Old father Thames advanced his reverend head.
      His tresses dropped with dews, and o'er the stream

305 **Cressy's . . . field** Crécy was a great victory of Edward's son,
the Black Prince, which confirmed Edward's claim to France and
his quartering of her fleur-de-lys on his shield.   307 **Verrio's colors**
the ceiling paintings at Windsor which represented Charles II with
France at his feet.   311 **Henry** Henry VI (1421–71), probably mur-
dered and regarded as a royal martyr.   312 **palms eternal** as em-
blems of martyrdom.   314 **Edward** Edward IV (1442–83), rival
claimant to the throne, buried near Henry VI at Windsor.   315 **ex-
tended Albion** all of Britain, since Henry VI fled from Edward IV
to the north.   316 **Belerium** Land's End, Cornwall.   319 **Charles**
Charles I, another royal martyr, buried in some tomb as Henry VIII
without any service.   323 **purple deaths** the Great Plague (1665).
324 **rolling fire** the Great Fire of London (1666).   326 **dishonest**
shameful, especially if the plague and fire are seen as divine retribu-
tion for the execution of Charles I.

His shining horns° diffused a golden gleam:
Graved on his urn appeared the moon, that guides
His swelling waters, and alternate tides;
The figured° streams in waves of silver rolled,   335
And on their banks Augusta° rose in gold.
Around his throne the sea-born° brothers stood,
Who swell with tributary urns his flood.
First the famed authors of his ancient name,°
The winding Isis and the fruitful Thame: 340
The Kennet swift, for silver eels renowned;
The Loddon slow, with verdant alders crowned;
Cole, whose dark streams his flowery islands lave;
And chalky Wey, that rolls a milky wave:
The blue, transparent Vandalis appears;   345
The gulfy Lee his sedgy tresses rears;
And sullen Mole, that hides his diving flood;°
And silent Darent, stained with Danish blood.°

    High in the midst, upon his urn reclined
(His sea-green mantle waving with the wind),   350
The God appeared: he turned his azure eyes
Where Windsor domes and pompous turrets rise;
Then bowed and spoke; the winds forget to roar,
And the hushed waves glide softly to the shore.

    "Hail, sacred Peace! hail, long-expected days,   355
That Thames's glory to the stars shall raise!
Though Tiber's streams immortal Rome behold,
Though foaming Hermus° swells with tides of gold,
From heaven itself though sevenfold Nilus° flows,
And harvests on a hundred realms bestows;   360
These now no more shall be the Muse's themes,
Lost in my fame, as in the sea their streams.

---

332 **shining horns** The horns of a bull were the usual mythical attri-
butes of river-gods, perhaps suggesting natural energy. The "urn"
(line 333), from which the river flows, is commonly shown with the
river-god.   335 **figured** represented on the urn.   336 **Augusta** Lon-
don.   337 **sea-born** born, like all rivers, of Oceanus.   339 **authors**
. . . name The Latin name Tamesis is taken as a fusion of Thame
and Isis.   347 **diving flood** underground stream.   348 **Danish blood**
at Otford in 1016.   358 **Hermus** a river of Asia Minor whose sands
were covered with gold.   359 **Nilus** The source of the Nile was still
undiscovered in Pope's day.

Let Volga's bank with iron squadrons° shine,
And groves of lances glitter on the Rhine,°
365 Let barbarous Ganges° arm a servile train;
Be mine the blessings of a peaceful reign.
No more my sons shall dye with British blood
Red Iber's sands,° or Ister's foaming flood;°
Safe on my shore each unmolested swain
370 Shall tend the flocks, or reap the bearded grain;
The shady empire shall retain no trace
Of war or blood, but in the sylvan chase;
The trumpet sleep, while cheerful horns are blown,
And arms employed on birds and beasts alone.
375 Behold! the ascending villas on my side,
Project long shadows o'er the crystal tide.
Behold! Augusta's glittering spires increase,
And temples° rise, the beauteous works of Peace.
I see, I see, where two fair cities° bend
380 Their ample bow, a new Whitehall° ascend!
There mighty nations shall inquire their doom,
The world's great oracle in times to come;
There kings shall sue, and suppliant states be seen
Once more to bend before a British Queen.
385   "Thy trees, fair Windsor! now shall leave their woods,
And half thy forests rush into thy floods,
Bear Britain's thunder,° and her cross° display,
To the bright regions of the rising day;°
Tempt icy seas, where scarce the waters roll,
390 Where clearer flames glow round the frozen Pole;

---

363 **iron squadrons** presumably of Charles XII of Sweden, finally
defeated by Peter the Great in 1709. 364 **Rhine** a reference to
Marlborough's campaigns in the recent war. 365 **Ganges** reference
to wars of the Mogul Emperor Aurangzeb against the rebellious
Marathar (1689–1705). 368 **Iber's sands** the Ebro river in Spain,
where the English fought victoriously in 1710. 368 **Ister's . . . flood**
the Danube, where Marlborough achieved the victory of Blenheim
in 1704. 378 **temples** the fifty new churches commissioned by
Queen Anne. 379 **two fair cities** London and Westminster meet at
a circular sweep of the Thames. 380 **Whitehall** the royal palace
mostly destroyed by fire in 1698, for which many new plans were
considered, notably Sir Christopher Wren's. 387 **thunder** naval can-
nons. 387 **cross** of Saint George on the Union Jack. 388 **rising
day** Orient.

Or under southern skies exalt their sails,
Led by new stars,° and borne by spicy gales!
For me the balm° shall bleed, and amber flow,
The coral redden, and the ruby glow,
The pearly shell its lucid globe infold,　　　　　　*395*
And Phoebus° warm the ripening ore to gold.
The time shall come, when free as seas or wind
Unbounded Thames° shall flow for all mankind,
Whole nations enter with each swelling tide,
And seas but join the regions they divide;　　　　　*400*
Earth's distant ends our glory shall behold,
And the new world launch forth to seek the old.
Then ships of uncouth form shall stem the tide,
And feathered people° crowd my wealthy side,
And naked youths and painted chiefs admire　　　*405*
Our speech, our color, and our strange attire!
O stretch thy reign, fair Peace! from shore to shore,
Till conquest cease, and slavery be no more;
Till the freed Indians in their native groves
Reap their own fruits, and woo their sable loves,　*410*
Peru once more a race of kings behold,
And other Mexicos be roofed with gold.
Exiled by thee from earth to deepest hell,
In brazen bonds, shall barbarous Discord° dwell;
Gigantic Pride, pale Terror, gloomy Care,　　　　*415*
And mad Ambition shall attend her there:
There purple Vengeance bathed in gore retires,
Her weapons blunted, and extinct her fires:
There hateful Envy her own snakes shall feel,
And Persecution mourn her broken wheel:°　　　*420*
There Faction roar, Rebellion bite her chain,

---

392 **new stars** the southern constellations.　393 **balm** from openings
cut in the bark to secure precious gums.　396 **Phoebus** The sun was
believed to ripen precious minerals in the earth.　398 **Unbounded
Thames** "A wish that London may be made a free port" (Pope).
Cf. Isaiah 60:3, "And the Gentiles shall come to thy light, and kings
to the brightness of thy rising," or 60:11, "Therefore thy gates shall
be open continually; they shall not be shut day nor night."　404
feathered people like the four Iroquois chiefs who were received by
Queen Anne in 1710.　414 **Discord** banished from Heaven by Ju-
piter, but here by Anne (l. 327).　420 **Wheel** the torturing rack.

And gasping Furies thirst for blood in vain."
    Here cease thy flight, nor with unhallowed lays
Touch the fair fame of Albion's golden days:
The thoughts of gods let Granville's verse recite,
And bring the scenes of opening fate to light.
My humble Muse, in unambitious strains,
Paints the green forests and the flowery plains,
Where Peace descending bids her olives spring,
And scatters blessings from her dovelike wing.
Even I more sweetly pass my careless days,
Pleased in the silent shade with empty praise;
Enough for me, that to the listening swains
First in these fields I sung the sylvan strains.

THE RAPE OF THE LOCK

AN HEROI-COMICAL POEM

TO MRS. ARABELLA FERMOR°

(1712–1714)

CANTO I

WHAT dire offense from amorous causes springs,
What mighty contests rise from trivial things,
I sing—This verse to CARYLL, Muse! is due;
This, even Belinda may vouchsafe to view:
Slight is the subject, but not so the praise,   5
If she inspire, and he approve my lays.
   Say what strange motive, Goddess! could compel
A well-bred Lord to assault a gentle Belle?
O say what stranger cause, yet unexplored,
Could make a gentle Belle reject a Lord?   10
In tasks so bold, can little men engage,

To Mrs. Arabella Fermor John Caryll, Pope's friend, was concerned about the estrangement between two families caused when Robert, Lord Petre, cut off a lock of Arabella (known as "Belle") Fermor's hair. As Pope explained it, Caryll, a "common acquaintance and well-wisher to both, desired me to write a poem and make a jest of it, and laugh them together again." Pope published an earlier version in two cantos and, a year later, amplified it with full mock-heroic devices.

And in soft bosoms dwells such mighty rage?
   Sol through white curtains shot a timorous ray,
And oped those eyes that must eclipse the day:
15 Now lapdogs give themselves the rousing shake,
And sleepless lovers, just at twelve, awake:
Thrice rung the bell, the slipper knocked the ground,
And the pressed watch° returned a silver sound.
Belinda still her downy pillow prest,
20 Her guardian Sylph° prolonged the balmy rest.
'Twas he had summoned to her silent bed
The morning dream that hovered o'er her head.
A youth more glittering than a birth-night Beau,°
(That even in slumber caused her cheek to glow)
25 Seemed to her ear his winning lips to lay,
And thus in whispers said, or seemed to say:
   Fairest of mortals, thou distinguished care
Of thousand bright inhabitants of air!
If e'er one vision touched thy infant thought,
30 Of all the nurse and all the priest° have taught,
Of airy elves by moonlight shadows seen,
The silver token, and the circled green,°
Or virgins visited by angel powers,
With golden crowns and wreaths of heavenly flowers,
35 Hear and believe! thy own importance know,
Nor bound thy narrow views to things below.
Some secret truths, from learnèd pride concealed,
To maids alone and children are revealed:
What though no credit doubting wits may give?
40 The fair and innocent shall still believe.
Know, then, unnumbered spirits round thee fly,
The light militia of the lower sky;

18 **pressed watch** It responds with chimes for the hour and the near-
est quarter hour.   20 **Sylph** one of the aerial creatures serving as
a counterpart to a guardian angel, although his whisper (lines 25–6)
may recall Satan's first temptation of Eve in *Paradise Lost*, Book
IV, and his appeal to her pride in the later, successful temptation
of Book IX.   23 **birth-night beau** courtier splendidly dressed for the
royal birthday.   30 **nurse . . . priest** considered as teachers of super-
stition.   32 Referring to the phosphoric light ("fairy sparks") and
the withered circles in the grass ("fairy rings") that were taken as
signs of fairies' presence.

These, though unseen, are ever on the wing,
Hang o'er the box, and hover round the Ring.°
Think what an equipage thou hast in air,   45
And view with scorn two pages and a chair.
As now your own, our beings were of old,
And once enclosed in woman's beauteous mold;
Thence, by a soft transition, we repair
From earthly vehicles° to these of air.   50
Think not, when woman's transient breath is fled,
That all her vanities at once are dead:
Succeeding vanities she still regards,
And though she plays no more, o'erlooks the cards.
Her joy in gilded chariots, when alive,   55
And love of ombre,° after death survive.
For when the fair in all their pride expire,
To their first elements° their souls retire:
The sprites of fiery termagants in flame
Mount up, and take a Salamander's name.°   60
Soft yielding minds to water glide away,
And sip, with nymphs, their elemental tea.°
The graver prude sinks downward to a Gnome,
In search of mischief still on earth to roam.
The light coquettes in Sylphs aloft repair,   65
And sport and flutter in the fields of air.
   Know farther yet; whoever fair and chaste
Rejects mankind, is by some Sylph embraced:
For spirits, freed from mortal laws, with ease
Assume what sexes and what shapes they please.°   70
What guards the purity of melting maids,
In courtly balls and midnight masquerades,
Safe from the treacherous friend, the daring spark,
The glance by day, the whisper in the dark;

44 The theater **box** and the circular drive (Ring) in Hyde Park were common scenes of flirtation.   50 **vehicles** both (1) the equipage (45) and (2) the form, ethereal or terrestrial, in which the soul is embodied.   56 **ombre** See note to Canto III, line 27.   58 **first elements** the preponderant elements of the four (air, earth, fire, water) of which all material things are composed.   60 **Salamander's name** for the animal which, traditionally, could live unharmed in the midst of fire.   62 **tea** a perfect rhyme in Pope's time for "away."   70 As can the angels in *Paradise Lost*.

75   When kind occasion prompts their warm desires,
     When music softens, and when dancing fires?
     'Tis but their Sylph, the wise celestials know,
     Though *honor* is the word with men below.
          Some nymphs there are, too conscious of their face,
80   For life predestined to the Gnomes' embrace.
     These swell their prospects and exalt their pride,
     When offers are disdained, and love denied.
     Then gay ideas crowd the vacant brain,
     While peers and dukes, and all their sweeping train,
85   And garters, stars, and coronets° appear,
     And in soft sounds, *Your Grace*° salutes their ear.
     'Tis these that early taint the female soul,
     Instruct the eyes of young coquettes to roll,
     Teach infant cheeks a bidden blush to know,
90   And little hearts to flutter at a beau.
          Oft when the world imagine women stray,
     The Sylphs through mystic mazes guide their way
     Through all the giddy circle they pursue,
     And old impertinence° expel by new.
95   What tender maid but must a victim fall
     To one man's treat, but for another's ball?
     When Florio speaks what virgin could withstand,
     If gentle Damon did not squeeze her hand?
     With varying vanities, from every part,
100 They shift the moving toyshop of their heart;
     Where wigs with wigs, with sword-knots sword-knots
          strive,
     Beaux banish beaux, and coaches coaches drive.°
     This erring mortals levity may call,
     Oh blind to truth! the Sylphs contrive it all.
105   Of these am I, who thy protection claim,
     A watchful sprite, and Ariel is my name.
     Late, as I ranged the crystal wilds of air,

85 **Garters . . . coronets** emblems of high court honors.   86 **Your
Grace** the salutation to a peeress.   94 **impertinence** (1) triviality or
frivolity (2) excessive freedoms.   101–2 Cf. *Iliad* IV, 508–9: "Now
shield with shield, with helmet helmet closed,/To armor armor,
lance to lance opposed." ("sword-knots," ornaments tied to the hilts
of swords.)

In the clear mirror of thy ruling star
I saw, alas! some dread event impend,
Ere to the main this morning sun descend.   110
But heaven reveals not what, or how, or where:
Warned by the Sylph, oh pious maid, beware!
This to disclose is all thy guardian can:
Beware of all, but most beware of man!
    He said; when Shock, who thought she slept too long, 115
Leaped up, and waked his mistress with his tongue.
'Twas then, Belinda, if report say true,
Thy eyes first opened on a billet-doux;
Wounds, charms and ardors were no sooner read,
But all the vision vanished from thy head.   120
    And now, unveiled, the toilet° stands displayed,
Each silver vase in mystic order laid.
First, robed in white, the nymph intent adores,
With head uncovered, the cosmetic powers.
A heavenly image in the glass appears,   125
To that she bends, to that her eyes she rears;
The inferior priestess,° at her altar's side,
Trembling, begins the sacred rites of pride.
Unnumbered treasures ope at once, and here
The various offerings of the world appear;   130
From each she nicely culls with curious° toil,
And decks the goddess with the glittering spoil.
This casket India's glowing gems unlocks,
And all Arabia° breathes from yonder box.
The tortoise here and elephant unite,   135
Transformed to combs, the speckled and the white.°
Here files° of pins extend their shining rows,
Puffs, powders, patches,° bibles, billet-doux.

---

121 **toilet** The dressing table is ironically presented as an altar,
where "cosmetic powers" (line 124) replace cosmic powers.   127 **The
inferior priestess** the maid Betty (see line 148).   Belinda is superior
priestess as well as the source of the "heavenly image" (line 125)
that is adored.   131 **curious** elaborately careful.   134 **Arabia** the
source of perfumes.   136 **speckled . . . white** tortoiseshell and ivory.
137 **files** as of soldiers in ranks.   138 **patches** tiny pieces of black
silk or court plaster worn on the face to heighten the whiteness of
the skin.

Now awful° beauty puts on all its arms;
140 The fair each moment rises in her charms,
Repairs her smiles, awakens every grace,
And calls forth all the wonders of her face;
Sees by degrees a purer blush° arise,
And keener lightnings° quicken in her eyes.
145 The busy Sylphs surround their darling care;
These set the head, and those divide the hair,
Some fold the sleeve, whilst others plait the gown;
And Betty's praised for labors not her own.

CANTO II

Not with more glories, in the ethereal plain,°
The sun first rises o'er the purpled main,°
Than issuing forth, the rival of his beams
Launched on the bosom of the silver Thames.°
5 Fair nymphs, and well-dressed youths around her shone,
But every eye was fixed on her alone.
On her white breast a sparkling cross she wore,
Which Jews might kiss, and infidels adore.°
Her lively looks a sprightly mind disclose,
10 Quick as her eyes, and as unfixed as those:
Favors to none, to all she smiles extends,
Oft she rejects, but never once offends.
Bright as the sun, her eyes the gazers strike,
And, like the sun, they shine on all alike.
15 Yet graceful ease, and sweetness void of pride,
Might hide her faults, if belles had faults to hide:

139 **awful** majestic or awe-inspiring, like the epic hero arming himself. 143 **purer blush** a more even redness, the result of rouge.
144 **keener lightnings** achieved by drops of belladonna. 1 **ethereal plain** the heavens. 2 **purpled main** the sea reddened by dawn to the color of "royal purple." 4 Belinda is about to sail from London to Hampton Court. 8 The kissing or adoration of the cross would mark conversion to a new faith.

If to her share some female errors fall,
Look on her face, and you'll forget 'em all.
   This nymph, to the destruction of mankind,
Nourished two locks, which graceful hung behind   *20*
In equal curls, and well conspired to deck
With shining ringlets the smooth ivory neck.
Love in these labyrinths his slaves detains,
And mighty hearts are held in slender chains.
With hairy springes° we the birds betray,   *25*
Slight lines of hair surprise the finny prey,
Fair tresses man's imperial race ensnare,
And beauty draws us with a single hair.
   The adventurous Baron the bright locks admired,
He saw, he wished, and to the prize aspired: *30*
Resolved to win, he meditates the way,
By force to ravish, or by fraud betray;
For when success a lover's toil attends,
Few ask, if fraud or force attained his ends.
   For this, ere Phoebus rose,° he had implored   *35*
Propitious heaven, and every power adored,
But chiefly Love—to Love an altar built,
Of twelve vast French romances,° neatly gilt.
There lay three garters, half a pair of gloves;
And all the trophies of his former loves.   *40*
With tender billets-doux he lights the pyre,
And breathes three amorous sighs to raise the fire;
Then prostrate falls, and begs with ardent eyes
Soon to obtain, and long possess, the prize:
The powers gave ear, and granted half his prayer;   *45*
The rest, the winds dispersed in empty air.°
   But now secure the painted vessel glides,
The sunbeams trembling on the floating tides,
While melting music steals upon the sky,
And softened sounds along the waters die.   *50*

---

25 **hairy springes** traps, often nooses, delicately woven. 35 **ere Phoebus rose** before sunrise. 38 **French romances** notoriously long and highly formalized love stories, here handsomely bound as well ("neatly gilt"). 45–6 Cf. *Aeneid*, II, 794–5: "Apollo heard, and granting half his prayer,/Shuffled in winds the rest, and tossed in empty air" (Dryden).

Smooth flow the waves, the zephyrs gently play,
Belinda smiled, and all the world was gay.
All but the Sylph—with careful thoughts opprest,
The impending woe sat heavy on his breast.
55 He summons strait his denizens° of air;
The lucid squadrons round the sails repair:
Soft o'er the shrouds° aërial whispers breathe,
That seemed but zephyrs to the train beneath.
Some to the sun their insect wings unfold,
60 Waft on the breeze, or sink in clouds of gold;
Transparent forms, too fine for mortal sight,
Their fluid bodies half dissolved in light.
Loose to the wind their airy garments flew,
Thin glittering textures of the filmy dew;
65 Dipped in the richest tincture of the skies,
Where light disports in ever-mingling dyes,
While every beam new transient colors flings,
Colors that change whene'er they wave their wings.
Amid the circle, on the gilded mast,
70 Superior° by the head, was Ariel placed;
His purple pinions opening to the sun,
He raised his azure wand, and thus begun.
      Ye Sylphs and Sylphids, to your chief give ear,
Fays, Fairies, Genii, Elves, and Daemons, hear!°
75 Ye know the spheres and various tasks assigned
By laws eternal to the aërial kind.
Some in the fields of purest aether play,
And bask and whiten in the blaze of day.
Some guide the course of wandering orbs° on high,
80 Or roll the planets through the boundless sky.
Some less refined, beneath the moon's pale light
Pursue the stars that shoot athwart the night,
Or suck the mists in grosser air below,
Or dip their pinions in the painted bow,°

55 denizens inhabitants; more strictly, naturalized aliens. **57 shrouds** ropes (appropriate to a grander vessel than this rivercraft). **70 Superior** taller, as is the typical epic hero. **73–4** Cf. *Paradise Lost* V, 600–2: "Hear all ye Angels, Progeny of Light,/Thrones, Dominations, Princedoms, Virtues, Powers,/Hear my Decree. . . ." **79 wandering orbs** comets? **84 bow** rainbow.

Or brew fierce tempests on the wintry main, 85
Or o'er the glebe° distil the kindly rain.
Others on earth o'er human race preside,
Watch all their ways, and all their actions guide:
Of these the chief the care of nations own,
And guard with arms divine the British throne. 90
    Our humbler province is to tend the fair,
Not a less pleasing, though less glorious care.
To save the powder from too rude a gale,°
Nor let the imprisoned essences° exhale,
To draw fresh colors from the vernal flowers, 95
To steal from rainbows e'er they drop in showers
A brighter wash;° to curl their waving hairs,
Assist their blushes, and inspire their airs;
Nay oft, in dreams, invention we bestow,
To change a flounce, or add a furbelow.° 100
    This day, black omens threat the brightest fair
That e'er deserved a watchful spirit's care;
Some dire disaster, or by force, or slight,
But what, or where, the fates have wrapped in night.
Whether the nymph shall break Diana's law,° 105
Or some frail China jar receive a flaw,
Or stain her honor, or her new brocade,
Forget her prayers, or miss a masquerade,
Or lose her heart, or necklace, at a ball;
Or whether Heaven has doomed that Shock must fall. 110
Haste then, ye spirits! to your charge repair:
The fluttering fan be Zephyretta's care;
The drops to thee, Brillante, we consign;
And, Momentilla, let the watch be thine;
Do thou, Crispissa,° tend her favorite lock; 115
Ariel himself shall be the guard of Shock.
    To fifty chosen Sylphs, of special note,
We trust the important charge, the petticoat:

---

86 **glebe** farmland. 93 **too rude a gale** too rough a breeze. 94 **essences** perfumes. 97 **wash** tinting rinse. 100 **furbelow** ruffle. 105 **Diana's law** virginity. 115 **Crispissa** derives from "crisp," in its old sense of "curl."

Oft have we known that sevenfold fence to fail,
120   Though stiff with hoops, and armed with ribs of whale.°
Form a strong line° about the silver bound,
And guard the wide circumference around.°
    Whatever spirit, careless of his charge,
His post neglects, or leaves the fair at large,
125   Shall feel sharp vengeance soon o'ertake his sins,
Be stopped in vials, or transfixed with pins;
Or plunged in lakes of bitter washes lie,
Or wedged whole ages in a bodkin's° eye:
Gums and pomatums shall his flight restrain,
130   While clogged he beats his silken wings in vain;
Or alum styptics with contracting power
Shrink his thin essence like a rivelled flower.
Or as Ixion° fixed, the wretch shall feel
The giddy motion of the whirling mill,
135   In fumes of burning chocolate shall glow,
And tremble at the sea that froths below!
    He spoke; the spirits from the sails descend;
Some, orb in orb, around the nymph extend,
Some thrid the mazy ringlets of her hair,
140   Some hang upon the pendants of her ear;
With beating hearts the dire event they wait,
Anxious, and trembling for the birth of fate.

CANTO III

CLOSE by those meads, for ever crowned with flowers,
Where Thames with pride surveys his rising towers,
There stands a structure° of majestic frame,
Which from the neighboring Hampton takes its name.

120 **whale** whalebone. 121 **line** that is, of defense. 119–22 The
petticoat is described in terms that recall the hero's shield in epic.
128 **bodkin's** needle's. 133 **Ixion** was tortured. 3 **structure** Hamp-
ton Court, a royal residence.

Here Britain's statesmen oft the fall foredoom   5
Of foreign tyrants, and of nymphs at home;
Here thou, great Anna!° whom three realms obey,
Dost sometimes counsel take—and sometimes tea.
   Hither the heroes and the nymphs resort,
To taste awhile the pleasures of a court;   10
In various talk the instructive hours they past,
Who gave the ball, or paid the visit last;
One speaks the glory of the British queen,
And one describes a charming Indian screen;
A third interprets motions, looks, and eyes;   15
At every word a reputation dies.
Snuff, or the fan, supply each pause of chat,
With singing, laughing, ogling, *and all that.*
   Meanwhile, declining from the noon of day,
The sun obliquely shoots his burning ray;   20
The hungry judges soon the sentence sign,
And wretches hang that jurymen may dine;
The merchant from the Exchange returns in peace,
And the long labors of the toilet cease—
Belinda now, whom thirst of fame invites,   25
Burns to encounter two adventurous knights,
At ombre° singly to decide their doom;
And swells her breast with conquests yet to come.
Straight the three bands prepare in arms to join,
Each band the number of the sacred nine.°   30
Soon as she spread her hand, the aërial guard
Descend, and sit on each important card:
First Ariel perched upon a Matadore,°
Then each, according to the rank they bore;
For Sylphs, yet mindful of their ancient race,   35
Are, as when women, wondrous fond of place.°
   Behold, four Kings in majesty revered,°

---

7 great Anna Queen Anne, ruler of Great Britain and Ireland and
claimant to France. **27 ombre** a card game related to whist or
modern bridge, played with forty cards, the 10's, 9's, and 8's re-
moved from the deck. The taking of each trick is here presented as
epic combat. **29–30** There were three players, each holding nine
cards. **30 sacred nine** the Muses. **33 Matadore** the highest trump
card. **36 place** rank. **37 ff.** The epic review of forces is parodied.

With hoary whiskers and a forky beard;
And four fair Queens whose hands sustain a flower,
40   The expressive emblem of their softer power;
Four Knaves in garbs succinct,° a trusty band,
Caps on their heads, and halberts° in their hand;
And particolored troops, a shining train,
Draw forth to combat on the velvet plain.°
45   The skilful nymph reviews her force with care;
Let spades be trumps! she said, and trumps they were.°
        Now move to war her sable Matadores,°
In show like leaders of the swarthy Moors.
Spadillio first, unconquerable lord!
50   Led off two captive trumps, and swept the board.
As many more Manillio forced to yield,
And marched a victor from the verdant field.
Him Basto followed, but his fate more hard
Gained but one trump and one plebeian card.
55   With his broad sabre next, a chief in years,
The hoary Majesty of Spades appears,
Puts forth one manly leg, to sight revealed;
The rest, his many-colored robe concealed.
The rebel Knave, who dares his prince engage,
60   Proves the just victim of his royal rage.
Even mighty Pam,° that kings and queens o'erthrew,
And mowed down armies in the fights of Lu,
Sad chance of war! now, destitute of aid,
Falls undistinguished by the victor spade!
65   Thus far both armies to Belinda yield;
Now to the Baron fate inclines the field.
His warlike Amazon° her host invades,

41 **succinct** tucked up.   42 **halberts** battle-axes and pikes on long
handles.   44 **velvet plain** typical epic term for a field, here the
velvet-covered card table. Cf. "verdant field" (line 52) and "level
green" (line 80).   46 Cf. Genesis 1:3: "And God said, 'Let there
be light,' and there was light."   47 **Matadores** The highest trumps
seen as epic heroes taking the field. They are the ace of spades
(Spadillio), the two of spades (Manillio), the ace of clubs (Basto).
61 **Pam** knave of clubs, strongest card in the game of loo.   67 **Ama-
zon** the queen of spades seen as a female warrior. This is the first
of the four tricks the Baron takes in turn.

The imperial consort of the crown of spades.
The club's black tyrant first her victim died,
Spite of his haughty mien, and barbarous pride: 70
What boots the regal circle on his head,
His giant limbs in state unwieldy spread?
That long behind he trails his pompous robe,
And of all monarchs only grasps the globe?°
    The Baron now his diamonds pours apace;   75
The embroidered King who shows but half his face,
And his refulgent Queen, with powers combined,
Of broken troops an easy conquest find.
Clubs, diamonds, hearts, in wild disorder seen,
With throngs promiscuous strew the level green.   80
Thus when dispersed a routed army runs,
Of Asia's troops, and Afric's sable sons,
With like confusion different nations fly,
Of various habit and of various dye,
The pierced battalions disunited fall,   85
In heaps on heaps; one fate o'erwhelms them all.°
    The Knave of Diamonds tries his wily arts,
And wins (oh shameful chance!) the Queen of Hearts.
At this, the blood the virgin's cheek forsook,
A livid paleness spreads o'er all her look;   90
She sees, and trembles at the approaching ill,
Just in the jaws of ruin, and Codille.°
And now (as oft in some distempered state)
On one nice trick° depends the general fate.
An Ace of Hearts steps forth: the King unseen   95
Lurked in her hand, and mourned his captive Queen.
He springs to vengeance with an eager pace,
And falls like thunder on the prostrate Ace.°
The nymph exulting fills with shouts the sky,
The walls, the woods, and long canals reply.   100

71–4 Typical epic lament for the decline of glory. Cf. *Windsor Forest*, lines 115 ff.   81–6 A parody of the epic simile.   92 **Codille** the "elbow," defeat if the Baron gains a fifth trick.   94 **trick** used in a double sense, referring to both the game and the politics of "some distempered state" (line 93).   98 **prostrate Ace** outranked by the king in the red suits.

Oh thoughtless mortals! ever blind to fate,
Too soon dejected, and too soon elate!
Sudden these honors shall be snatched away,
And cursed for ever this victorious day.°
105   For lo! the board with cups and spoons is crowned,
The berries° crackle, and the mill turns round.
On shining altars of Japan° they raise
The silver lamp; the fiery spirits° blaze.
From silver spouts the grateful liquors glide,
110 While China's earth° receives the smoking tide.
At once they gratify their scent and taste,
And frequent cups prolong the rich repast.
Straight hover round the fair her airy band;
Some, as she sipped, the fuming liquor fanned,
115 Some o'er her lap their careful plumes displayed,
Trembling, and conscious of the rich brocade.
Coffee, (which makes the politician wise,
And see through all things with his half-shut eyes)
Sent up in vapors to the Baron's brain
120 New stratagems, the radiant lock to gain.
Ah cease, rash youth! desist ere 'tis too late,
Fear the just gods, and think of Scylla's fate!°
Changed to a bird, and sent to flit in air,
She dearly pays for Nisus' injured hair!
125   But when to mischief mortals bend their will,
How soon they find fit instruments of ill!
Just then, Clarissa drew with tempting grace
A two-edged weapon from her shining case;
So ladies in romance assist their knight,
130 Present the spear, and arm him for the fight.
He takes the gift with reverence, and extends
The little engine on his fingers' ends;

101–4 the epic warning in the moment of pride.   106 **berries** coffee
beans. The coffee service parodies the epic feast. 107 **Japan**
japanned or lacquered tables. 108 **spirits** in the spirit lamps that
heat the coffee.   110 **China's earth** the cups of earthenware or china.
122 **Scylla's fate** Scylla plucked a purple hair (upon which his power
depended) from the head of her father, Nisus, in order to give it to
her lover. She was repudiated by her lover, and both were changed
to birds. Cf. Ovid, *Metamorphoses*, VIII.

This just behind Belinda's neck he spread,
As o'er the fragrant steams she bends her head.
Swift to the lock a thousand sprites repair,   *135*
A thousand wings, by turns, blow back the hair,
And thrice they twitched the diamond in her ear;
Thrice she looked back, and thrice the foe drew near.
Just in that instant, anxious Ariel sought
The close recesses of the virgin's thought;   *140*
As, on the nosegay° in her breast reclined,
He watched the ideas rising in her mind,
Sudden he viewed, in spite of all her art,
An earthly lover lurking at her heart.
Amazed, confused, he found his power expired,   *145*
Resigned to fate, and with a sigh retired.
      The peer now spreads the glittering forfex° wide,
To enclose the lock; now joins it, to divide.
Even then, before the fatal engine closed,
A wretched Sylph too fondly interposed;   *150*
Fate urged the shears, and cut the Sylph in twain
(But airy substance soon unites° again),
The meeting points the sacred hair dissever
From the fair head, for ever and for ever!
      Then flashed the living lightning from her eyes,   *155*
And screams of horror rend the affrighted skies.
Not louder shrieks to pitying heaven are cast,
When husbands or when lapdogs breathe their last,
Or when rich China vessels, fallen from high,
In glittering dust and painted fragments lie!   *160*
      Let wreaths of triumph now my temples twine,
(The victor cried) the glorious prize is mine!
While fish in streams, or birds delight in air,
Or in a coach and six the British fair,
As long as Atalantis° shall be read,   *165*
Or the small pillow grace a lady's bed,
While visits shall be paid on solemn days,

---

141 **nosegay** corsage of flowers.   147 **forfex** high diction for the
pair of scissors.   152 **soon unites** Cf. Milton, *Paradise Lost*, VI,
330–1.   165 **Atalantis** a popular book of the day, full of court
scandal.

When numerous wax-lights in bright order blaze,
While nymphs take treats, or assignations give,
170 So long my honor, name, and praise shall live!"
    What time would spare, from steel° receives its date,
And monuments, like men, submit to fate!
Steel could the labor of the gods destroy,
And strike to dust the imperial towers of Troy;°
175 Steel could the works of mortal pride confound,
And hew triumphal arches to the ground.
What wonder then, fair nymph! thy hairs should feel
The conquering force of unresisted steel?

CANTO IV

BUT anxious cares the pensive nymph oppressed,
And secret passions labored in her breast.
Not youthful kings in battle seized alive,
Not scornful virgins who their charms survive,
5 Not ardent lovers robbed of all their bliss,
Not ancient ladies when refused a kiss,
Not tyrants fierce that unrepenting die,
Not Cynthia when her manteau's° pinned awry,
E'er felt such rage, resentment, and despair,
10 As thou, sad virgin! for thy ravished hair.
    For, that sad moment, when the Sylphs withdrew,
And Ariel weeping from Belinda flew,
Umbriel,° a dusky melancholy sprite
As ever sullied the fair face of light,
15 Down to the central earth, his proper scene,

---

171 **steel** the fatal power of arms and warfare. 174 **Troy** supposed
to have been built by the gods Apollo and Poseidon. 8 **manteau**
mantua, loose upper gown or hood. 13 **Umbriel** a gnome and for-
mer prude, named from "umbra," or shadow.

Repaired to search the gloomy Cave of Spleen.°
  Swift on his sooty pinions flits the Gnome,
And in a vapor reached the dismal dome.°
No cheerful breeze this sullen region knows,
The dreaded East° is all the wind that blows.   20
Here, in a grotto, sheltered close from air,
And screened in shades from day's detested glare,
She sighs for ever on her pensive bed,
Pain at her side, and Megrim° at her head.
  Two handmaids wait the throne: alike in place,   25
But differing far in figure and in face.
Here stood Ill Nature like an ancient maid,
Her wrinkled form in black and white arrayed;
With store of prayers, for mornings, nights, and noons,
Her hand is filled; her bosom with lampoons.   30
  There Affectation, with a sickly mien
Shows in her cheek the roses of eighteen,
Practiced to lisp, and hang the head aside,
Faints into airs, and languishes with pride;
On the rich quilt sinks with becoming woe,   35
Wrapped in a gown, for sickness, and for show.
The fair ones feel such maladies as these,
When each new nightdress gives a new disease.
  A constant vapor o'er the palace flies;
Strange phantoms° rising as the mists arise;   40
Dreadful, as hermit's dreams in haunted shades,
Or bright as visions of expiring° maids.
Now glaring fiends, and snakes on rolling spires,
Pale spectres, gaping tombs, and purple fires:
Now lakes of liquid gold, Elysian scenes,°   45
And crystal domes, and angels in machines.
  Unnumbered throngs on every side are seen

16 **Cave of Spleen** epic visit to the underworld; suggestive also of
Spenser's caves of Mammon, Despair, and Night. Spleen was the
name for the fashionable psychosomatic ailment of the day, whose
symptoms were melancholy, self-pity, and hypochondria, sometimes
called a "fit of vapors." 18 **dome** dwelling. 20 **East** the east wind
was taken as a cause of spleen. 24 **Megrim** migraine headache.
40 **phantoms** fantasies. 42 **expiring** literally, dying; in the punning
sense, reaching sexual climax. 45 **Elysian scenes** not only fantasies
of heaven but scenes such as the contemporary stage featured in
lavish operas and pantomimes.

Of bodies changed° to various forms by Spleen.
Here living teapots stand, one arm held out,
50 One bent; the handle this, and that the spout:
A pipkin° there like Homer's tripod walks;
Here sighs a jar, and there a goose-pie° talks;
Men prove with child, as powerful fancy works,
And maids turned bottles, call aloud for corks.
55   Safe passed the Gnome through this fantastic band,
A branch of healing spleenwort° in his hand.
Then thus addressed the power: "Hail, wayward Queen!
Who rule the sex to fifty from fifteen,
Parent of vapors and of female wit,
60 Who give the hysteric, or poetic fit,
On various tempers act by various ways,
Make some take physic,° others scribble plays;
Who cause the proud their visits to delay,
And send the godly in a pet to pray.
65 A nymph there is, that all thy power disdains,
And thousands more in equal mirth maintains.
But oh! if e'er thy Gnome could spoil a grace,°
Or raise a pimple on a beauteous face,
Like citron-waters° matrons' cheeks inflame,
70 Or change complexions at a losing game;
If e'er with airy horns° I planted heads,
Or rumpled petticoats, or tumbled beds,
Or caused suspicion when no soul was rude,
Or discomposed the headdress of a prude,
75 Or e'er to costive° lapdog gave disease,
Which not the tears of brightest eyes could ease:
Hear me, and touch Belinda with chagrin;
That single act gives half the world the spleen."
    The goddess with a discontented air

---

48 **bodies changed** fantasies more psychotic than neurotic, clearly
sexual in some cases, as the prudish world of gnomes would lead
one to expect.   51 **pipkin** small earthenware boiler on a tripod. For
Vulcan's walking tripods, see *Iliad*, XVIII, 439 ff.   52 **goose-pie**
"Alludes to a real fact, a Lady of Distinction imagined herself in
this condition" (Pope).   56 **spleenwort** a protection against the
powers of spleen.   62 **physic** medicine.   67 **grace** both (1) charm
and (2) prayer (as in line 64).   69 **citron-waters** brandy flavored
with citron.   71 **horns** as signs of the cuckold.   75 **costive** con-
stipated.

Seems to reject him, though she grants his prayer.   80
A wondrous bag with both her hands she binds,
Like that where once Ulysses° held the winds;
There she collects the force of female lungs,
Sighs, sobs, and passions, and the war of tongues.
A vial next she fills with fainting fears,   85
Soft sorrows, melting griefs, and flowing tears.
The Gnome rejoicing bears her gifts away,
Spreads his black wings, and slowly mounts to day.
  Sunk in Thalestris'° arms the nymph he found,
Her eyes dejected and her hair unbound.   90
Full o'er their heads the swelling bag he rent,
And all the furies issued at the vent.
Belinda burns with more than mortal ire,
And fierce Thalestris fans the rising fire.
"O wretched maid!" she spread her hands, and cried,   95
(While Hampton's echoes, "Wretched maid!" replied)
"Was it for this you took such constant care
The bodkin,° comb, and essence to prepare;
For this your locks in paper durance° bound,
For this with torturing irons wreathed around?   100
For this with fillets° strained your tender head,
And bravely bore the double loads of lead?
Gods! shall the ravisher display your hair,
While the fops envy, and the ladies stare!
Honor forbid! at whose unrivalled shrine   105
Ease, pleasure, virtue, all, our sex resign.
Methinks already I your tears survey,
Already hear the horrid things they say,
Already see you a degraded toast,°
And all your honor in a whisper lost!   110
How shall I, then, your helpless fame defend?
'Twill then be infamy to seem your friend!
And shall this prize,° the inestimable prize,
Exposed through crystal to the gazing eyes,

82 **Ulysses** when he was given the winds by Aeolus, *Odyssey*, X,
19 ff.   89 **Thalestris** named for the Queen of the Amazons.   98
bodkin hairpin.   99 **paper durance** high diction for curling papers.
101 **fillets** headbands, worn by priestesses in the *Aeneid*, here ma-
chinery of hairdressing.   109 **toast** one whose health is often drunk.
113 **this prize** the lock encased in a ring.

115 And heightened by the diamond's circling rays,
     On that rapacious hand for ever blaze?
     Sooner shall grass in Hyde Park Circus° grow,
     And wits take lodgings in the sound of Bow;°
     Sooner let earth, air, sea, to chaos fall,
120 Men, monkeys, lapdogs, parrots, perish all!"
         She said; then raging to Sir Plume repairs,
     And bids her beau demand the precious hairs:
     (Sir Plume, of amber snuffbox justly vain,
     And the nice conduct of a clouded° cane)
125 With earnest eyes, and round unthinking face,
     He first the snuffbox opened, then the case,
     And thus broke out—"My Lord, why, what the devil?
     Z—ds! damn the lock! 'fore Gad, you must be civil!
     Plague on't! 'tis past a jest—nay prithee, pox!
130 Give her the hair"—he spoke, and rapped his box.
         "It grieves me much" (replied the peer again)
     "Who speaks so well should ever speak in vain.
     But by this lock, this sacred lock I swear,
     (Which never more shall join its parted hair,
135 Which never more its honors shall renew,
     Clipped from the lovely head where late it grew)
     That while my nostrils draw the vital air,
     This hand, which won it, shall for ever wear."
     He spoke, and speaking, in proud triumph spread
140 The long-contended honors° of her head.
         But Umbriel, hateful Gnome! forbears not so;
     He breaks the vial whence the sorrows flow.
     Then see! the nymph in beauteous grief appears,
     Her eyes half languishing, half drowned in tears;
145 On her heaved bosom hung her drooping head,
     Which, with a sigh, she raised; and thus she said.
         "For ever cursed be this detested day,
     Which snatched my best, my favorite curl away!
     Happy! ah ten times happy had I been,
150 If Hampton Court these eyes had never seen!

117 **Hyde Park Circus** the fashionable Ring (I, 44).   118 **Bow** near
St. Mary-le-Bow, in the unfashionable merchants' quarter, as op-
posed to Westminster.   124 **clouded** fashionably mottled or veined.
140 **honors** beauties.

Yet am not I the first mistaken maid,
By love of courts to numerous ills betrayed.
Oh had I rather unadmired remained
In some lone isle, or distant northern land;
Where the gilt chariot never marks the way,   155
Where none learn ombre; none e'er taste bohea!°
There kept my charms concealed from mortal eye,
Like roses that in deserts bloom and die.
What moved my mind with youthful lords to roam?
O had I stayed, and said my prayers at home!   160
'Twas this, the morning omens seemed to tell;
Thrice from my trembling hand the patch box fell;
The tottering china shook without a wind,
Nay, Poll sat mute, and Shock was most unkind!
A Sylph too warned me of the threats of fate,   165
In mystic visions, now believed too late!
See the poor remnants of these slighted hairs!
My hands shall rend what even thy rapine spares:
These, in two sable ringlets taught to break,
Once gave new beauties to the snowy neck;   170
The sister lock now sits uncouth, alone,
And in its fellow's fate foresees its own;
Uncurled it hangs, the fatal shears demands;
And tempts once more thy sacrilegious hands.
Oh hadst thou, cruel! been content to seize   175
Hairs less in sight, or any hairs but these!"

CANTO V

SHE said: the pitying audience melt in tears,
But fate and Jove had stopped the Baron's ears.
In vain Thalestris with reproach assails,
For who can move when fair Belinda fails?
Not half so fixed the Trojan could remain,   5

156 **bohea** a kind of tea.

While Anna° begged and Dido raged in vain.
Then grave Clarissa° graceful waved her fan;
Silence ensued, and thus the nymph began.
   "Say why are beauties praised and honored most,
10 The wise man's passion, and the vain° man's toast?
Why decked with all that land and sea afford,
Why angels called, and angel-like adored?
Why round our coaches crowd the white-gloved beaux,
Why bows the side-box from its inmost rows?
15 How vain are all these glories, all our pains,
Unless good sense preserve what beauty gains:
That men may say, when we the front-box grace,
'Behold the first in virtue, as in face!'
Oh! if to dance all night, and dress all day,
20 Charmed the smallpox,° or chased old age away,
Who would not scorn what housewife's cares produce,
Or who would learn one earthly thing of use?
To patch, nay ogle, might become a saint,
Nor could it sure be such a sin to paint.
25 But since, alas! frail beauty must decay,
Curled or uncurled, since locks will turn to gray;
Since painted or not painted, all shall fade,
And she who scorns a man, must die a maid;
What then remains, but well our power to use,
30 And keep good humor still whate'er we lose?
And trust me, dear! good humor can prevail,
When airs, and flights, and screams, and scolding fail.
Beauties in vain their pretty eyes may roll;
Charms strike the sight, but merit wins the soul."
35   So spoke the dame, but no applause ensued;
Belinda frowned, Thalestris called her prude.
"To arms, to arms!" the fierce virago cries,
And swift as lightning to the combat flies.
All side in parties, and begin the attack;
40 Fans clap, silks rustle, and tough whalebones crack;

6 **Anna** Dido's sister, who failed to persuade Aeneas to remain with Dido; *Aeneid,* IV. 7 **Clarissa** "A new character introduced in the subsequent editions, to open more clearly the moral of the poem, in a parody of the speech of Sarpedon to Glaucus in Homer [*Iliad,* XII]" (Pope). 10 **vain** both foolish and boastful. 20 **smallpox** This disfiguring disease was still very common.

Heroes' and heroines' shouts confusedly rise,
And bass and treble voices strike the skies.
No common weapons in their hands are found,
Like gods they fight, nor dread a mortal wound.
    So when bold Homer makes the gods engage,   *45*
And heavenly breasts with human passions rage;
'Gainst Pallas, Mars; Latona, Hermes arms;
And all Olympus rings with loud alarms.
Jove's thunder roars, heaven trembles all around;
Blue Neptune storms, the bellowing deeps resound;   *50*
Earth shakes her nodding towers, the ground gives way;
And the pale ghosts start at the flash of day!
    Triumphant Umbriel on a sconce's height
Clapped his glad wings, and sat to view the fight:
Propped on their bodkin spears, the sprites survey   *55*
The growing combat, or assist the fray.
    While through the press enraged Thalestris flies,
And scatters death around from both her eyes,
A beau and witling perished in the throng,
One died in metaphor, and one in song.   *60*
"O cruel nymph! a living death I bear,"
Cried Dapperwit, and sunk beside his chair.
A mournful glance Sir Fopling upwards cast,
"Those eyes are made so killing"—was his last.
Thus on Maeander's flowery margin lies   *65*
The expiring swan,° and as he sings he dies.
    When bold Sir Plume had drawn Clarissa down,
Chloe stepped in, and killed him with a frown;
She smiled to see the doughty hero slain,
But at her smile, the beau revived again.   *70*
    Now Jove suspends his golden scales° in air,
Weighs the men's wits against the lady's hair;
The doubtful beam long nods from side to side;
At length the wits mount up, the hairs subside.
    See, fierce Belinda on the Baron flies,   *75*
With more than usual lightning in her eyes;

66 **swan** The swan, dying on the banks of the river Maeander, is
supposed to sing most sweetly as he dies.   71 **golden scales** a typical
epic omen, here at the expense of the light-witted men.

Nor feared the Chief the unequal fight to try,
Who sought no more than on his foe to die.°
But this bold lord, with manly strength endued,
80   She with one finger and a thumb subdued:
Just where the breath of life his nostrils drew,
A charge of snuff the wily virgin threw;
The Gnomes direct, to every atom just,
The pungent grains of titillating dust.
85   Sudden, with starting tears each eye o'erflows,
And the high dome re-echoes to his nose.
        "Now meet thy fate," incensed Belinda cried,
And drew a deadly bodkin from her side.
(The same,° his ancient personage to deck,
90   Her great great grandsire wore about his neck
In three seal rings; which after, melted down,
Formed a vast buckle for his widow's gown:
Her infant grandame's whistle next it grew,
The bells she jingled, and the whistle blew;
95   Then in a bodkin graced her mother's hairs,
Which long she wore, and now Belinda wears.)
        "Boast not my fall" (he cried) "insulting foe!
Thou by some other shalt be laid as low.
Nor think, to die dejects my lofty mind;
100   All that I dread is leaving you behind!
Rather than so, ah let me still survive,
And burn in Cupid's flames—but burn alive."
        "Restore the lock!" she cries; and all around
"Restore the lock!" the vaulted roofs rebound.
105   Not fierce Othello in so loud a strain
Roared for the handkerchief that caused his pain.
But see how oft ambitious aims are crossed,
And chiefs contend till all the prize is lost!
The lock, obtained with guilt, and kept with pain,
110   In every place is sought, but sought in vain:
With such a prize no mortal must be blest,
So heaven decrees! with heaven who can contest?

78 to die in the double sense of "expiring" (IV, 42), as elsewhere in
this section.   **89 The same** a parody of epic accounts of the descent
of armor or of Agamemnon's scepter.

Some thought it mounted to the lunar sphere,°
Since all things lost on earth are treasured there.
There heroes' wits are kept in ponderous vases,   *115*
And beaus' in snuffboxes and tweezer cases.
There broken vows, and deathbed alms are found,
And lovers' hearts with ends of riband bound;
The courtier's promises, and sick man's prayers,
The smiles of harlots, and the tears of heirs,   *120*
Cages for gnats, and chains to yoke a flea,
Dried butterflies, and tomes of casuistry.
But trust the Muse—she saw it upward rise,
Though marked by none but quick, poetic eyes:
(So Rome's great founder° to the heavens withdrew,   *125*
To Proculus alone confessed in view.)
A sudden star, it shot through liquid° air,
And drew behind a radiant trail of hair.
Not Berenice's locks° first rose so bright,
The heavens bespangling with dishevelled light.   *130*
The Sylphs behold it kindling as it flies,
And pleased pursue its progress through the skies.
This the beau monde° shall from the Mall° survey,
And hail with music its propitious ray.
This, the blest lover shall for Venus take,   *135*
And send up vows from Rosamonda's lake.°
This Partridge° soon shall view in cloudless skies,
When next he looks through Galileo's eyes;°
And hence the egregious wizard shall foredoom
The fate of Louis, and the fall of Rome.   *140*
Then cease, bright nymph! to mourn thy ravished hair
Which adds new glory to the shining sphere!
Not all the tresses that fair head can boast

---

113 **lunar sphere** reminiscent of Milton's Limbo of Vanity in *Paradise Lost*. Cf. Ariosto, *Orlando Furioso*, XXXIV, stanzas 68 ff. for a common source.   125 **Rome's . . . founder** Romulus, whose translation to heaven was witnessed by the senator Proculus.   127 **liquid** clear.   129 **Berenice's locks** The Queen's hair, offered by her to ensure her husband's safety in battle, was translated into a constellation.   133 **beau monde** fashionable world.   133 **Mall** the promenade in St. James's Park.   136 **Rosamonda's lake** a pond in St. James's Park, associated with unhappy love.   137 **Partridge** an astrologer who predicted momentous public events.   138 **Galileo's eyes** telescope.

Shall draw such envy as the lock you lost.
145 For, after all the murders of your eye,
     When, after millions slain, yourself shall die;
     When those fair suns shall set, as set they must,
     And all those tresses shall be laid in dust;
     This lock, the Muse shall consecrate to fame,
150 And midst the stars inscribe Belinda's name!

ELEGY TO THE MEMORY OF AN UNFORTUNATE LADY

(1717)

WHAT beckoning ghost, along the moonlight shade
Invites my steps, and points to yonder glade?
'Tis she!—but why that bleeding bosom gored,
Why dimly gleams the visionary sword?
Oh ever beauteous, ever friendly! tell,   *5*
Is it, in heaven, a crime to love too well?
To bear too tender, or too firm a heart,
To act a lover's or a Roman's part?°
Is there no bright reversion° in the sky,
For those who greatly think, or bravely die?   *10*
  Why bade ye else, ye Powers! her soul aspire
Above the vulgar flight of low desire?
Ambition first sprung from your blest abodes;
The glorious fault of angels and of gods:°
Thence to their images on earth it flows,   *15*
And in the breasts of kings and heroes glows.
Most souls, 'tis true, but peep out once an age,
Dull sullen prisoners in the body's cage:
Dim lights of life, that burn a length of years
Useless, unseen, as lamps in sepulchres;   *20*

8 **act . . . a Roman's part** commit suicide.   9 **reversion** return to the
former state; used legally of the return of an estate to the owner
after the expiration of a temporary grant.   14 **angels . . . gods** re-
ferring to the rebellious angels of Milton's *Paradise Lost* or to the
wars of the Titans in classical mythology.

Like eastern kings a lazy state they keep,
And close confined to their own palace, sleep.
   From these perhaps (ere nature bade her die)
Fate snatched her early to the pitying sky.
25 As into air the purer spirits flow,
And separate from their kindred dregs below;°
So flew the soul to its congenial place,
Nor left one virtue to redeem her race.
   But thou, false guardian of a charge too good,
30 Thou, mean deserter of thy brother's blood!
See on these ruby lips the trembling breath,
These cheeks, now fading at the blast of death;
Cold is that breast which warmed the world before,
And those love-darting eyes must roll no more.
35 Thus, if eternal justice rules the ball,
Thus shall your wives, and thus your children fall:
On all the line a sudden vengeance waits,
And frequent hearses shall besiege your gates.
There passengers shall stand, and pointing say,
40 (While the long funerals blacken all the way)
Lo these were they, whose souls the Furies steeled,
And cursed with hearts unknowing how to yield.
Thus unlamented pass the proud away,
The gaze of fools, and pageant of a day!
45 So perish all, whose breast ne'er learned to glow
For others' good, or melt at others' woe.
   What can atone (oh ever-injured shade!)
Thy fate unpitied, and thy rites unpaid?
No friend's complaint, no kind domestic tear
50 Pleased thy pale ghost, or graced thy mournful bier.
By foreign hands thy dying eyes were closed,
By foreign hands thy decent limbs composed,
By foreign hands thy humble grave adorned,
By strangers honored, and by strangers mourned!
55 What though no friends in sable weeds appear,
Grieve for an hour, perhaps, then mourn a year,
And bear about the mockery of woe
To midnight dances, and the public show?

25–6 The image is of chemical distillation.

What though no weeping Loves° thy ashes grace,
Nor polished marble emulate° thy face?   *60*
What though no sacred earth° allow thee room,
Nor hallowed dirge be muttered o'er thy tomb?
Yet shall thy grave with rising flowers be drest,
And the green turf lie lightly on thy breast:
There shall the morn her earliest tears bestow,   *65*
There the first roses of the year shall blow;
While angels with their silver wings o'ershade
The ground, now sacred by thy reliques° made.
    So peaceful rests, without a stone, a name,
What once had beauty, titles, wealth, and fame.   *70*
How loved, how honored once, avails thee not,
To whom related, or by whom begot;
A heap of dust alone remains of thee,
'Tis all thou art, and all the proud shall be!
    Poets themselves must fall, like those they sung,   *75*
Deaf the praised ear, and mute the tuneful tongue.
Even he, whose soul now melts in mournful lays,
Shall shortly want the generous tear he pays;
Then from his closing eyes thy form shall part,
And the last pang shall tear thee from his heart,   *80*
Life's idle business at one gasp be o'er,
The Muse forgot, and thou beloved no more!

59 **Loves** funeral monuments in the form of mourning cupids.   60
emulate rival, reproduce.   61 **sacred earth** Presumably because of
her suicide, the lady is not allowed Christian burial.   68 **reliques**
remains, often used of saint's remains; here they sanctify the ground,
just as nature pays the tribute man has denied (lines 63–6).

ELOISA TO ABELARD

(1717)

ARGUMENT

Abelard and Eloïsa flourished in the twelfth century; they were two
of the most distinguished persons of their age in learning and
beauty, but for nothing more famous than for their unfortunate
passion. After a long course of calamities, they retired each to a
several convent, and consecrated the remainder of their days to
religion. It was many years after this separation, that a letter of
Abelard's to a friend, which contained the history of his misfor-
tune, fell into the hands of Eloïsa. This awakening all her tender-
ness, occasioned those celebrated letters (out of which the following
is partly extracted) which give so lively a picture of the struggles of
grace and nature, virtue and passion.

IN these deep solitudes and awful cells,
Where heavenly-pensive contemplation dwells,
And ever-musing melancholy reigns;
What means this tumult in a Vestal's° veins?
5   Why rove my thoughts beyond this last retreat?
Why feels my heart its long-forgotten heat?
Yet, yet I love!—From Abelard it° came,
And Eloïsa yet must kiss the name.
     Dear fatal name! rest ever unrevealed,
10   Nor pass these lips in holy silence sealed.
Hide it, my heart, within that close disguise,
Where mixed with God's, his loved idea° lies:
O write it not, my hand—the name appears
Already written—wash it out, my tears!

4 **Vestal's** nun's.   7 **it** the letter (see Argument).   12 **idea** image.

In vain lost Eloïsa weeps and prays,   15
Her heart still dictates, and her hand obeys.
    Relentless walls! whose darksome round contains
Repentant sighs, and voluntary pains:
Ye rugged rocks! which holy knees have worn;
Ye grots and caverns shagged with horrid thorn!°   20
Shrincs! where their vigils pale-eyed virgins keep,
And pitying saints, whose statues learn to weep!
Though cold like you, unmoved and silent grown,
I have not yet forgot myself to stone.°
All is not Heaven's while Abelard has part,   25
Still rebel nature holds out half my heart;
Nor prayers nor fasts its stubborn pulse restrain,
Nor tears for ages taught to flow in vain.
    Soon as thy letters trembling I unclose,
That well-known name awakens all my woes.   30
Oh name for ever sad! for ever dear!
Still breathed in sighs, still ushered with a tear.
I tremble too, where'er my own I find,
Some dire misfortune follows close behind.
Line after line my gushing eyes o'erflow,   35
Led through a sad variety of woe:
Now warm in love, now withering in thy bloom,
Lost in a convent's° solitary gloom!
There stern religion quenched the unwilling flame,
There died the best of passions, love and fame.   40
    Yet write, oh write me all, that I may join
Griefs to thy griefs, and echo sighs to thine.
Nor foes nor fortune take this power away.
And is my Abelard less kind than they?
Tears still are mine, and those I need not spare,   45
Love but demands what else were shed in prayer;
No happier task these faded eyes pursue;
To read and weep is all they now can do.
    Then share thy pain, allow that sad relief;
Ah, more than share it, give me all thy grief.   50
Heaven first taught letters for some wretch's aid,

20 Cf. Milton, *Comus*, 429: "By grots, and caverns shag'd with hor-
rid shades."   24 Cf. Milton, *Il Penseroso*, 42: "Forget thy self to
marble."   **38 convent** monastery.

Some banished lover, or some captive maid;
They live, they speak, they breathe what love inspires,
Warm from the soul, and faithful to its fires,
55 The virgin's wish without her fears impart,
Excuse° the blush, and pour out all the heart,
Speed the soft intercourse from soul to soul,
And waft a sigh from Indus° to the Pole.
    Thou knowst how guiltless first I met thy flame,
60 When Love approached me under Friendship's name;
My fancy formed thee of angelic kind,
Some emanation° of the all-beauteous Mind.
Those smiling eyes, attempering every ray,
Shone sweetly lambent° with celestial day.
65 Guiltless I gazed; heaven listened while you sung;
And truths divine came mended° from that tongue.
From lips like those what precept failed to move?
Too soon they taught me 'twas no sin to love:
Back through the paths of pleasing sense I ran,
70 Nor wished an angel whom I loved a man.
Dim and remote the joys of saints I see,
Nor envy them that heaven I lose for thee.
    How oft, when pressed to marriage, have I said,
Curse on all laws but those which love has made?
75 Love, free as air, at sight of human ties,
Spreads his light wings, and in a moment flies.
Let wealth, let honor, wait the wedded dame,
August her deed, and sacred be her fame;
Before true passion all those views remove;°
80 Fame, wealth, and honor! what are you to Love?
The jealous god, when we profane his fires,
Those restless passions in revenge inspires,
And bids them make mistaken mortals groan,
Who seek in love for aught but love alone.
85 Should at my feet the world's great master fall,
Himself, his throne, his world, I'd scorn 'em all:
Not Caesar's empress would I deign to prove;

56 **excuse** make unnecessary. 58 **Indus** the large river flowing from Tibet to the Indian Sea. 62 **emanation** as in Neoplatonic thought, a radiation or flowing forth from Godhead. 64 **lambent** radiant. 66 **mended** improved. 79 **remove** depart.

No, make me mistress to the man I love;
If there be yet another name more free,
More fond than mistress, make me that to thee!   90
Oh! happy state! when souls each other draw,
When love is liberty, and nature, law:
All then is full, possessing, and possessed,
No craving void left aching in the breast:
Even thought meets thought ere from the lips it part,   95
And each warm wish springs mutual from the heart.
This sure is bliss (if bliss on earth there be)
And once the lot of Abelard and me.

   Alas, how changed! what sudden horrors rise!
A naked lover bound and bleeding lies!   100
Where, where was Eloïse? her voice, her hand,
Her poniard, had opposed the dire command.
Barbarian, stay! that bloody stroke° restrain;
The crime was common, common be the pain.
I can no more; by shame, by rage suppressed,   105
Let tears and burning blushes speak the rest.

   Canst thou forget that sad, that solemn day,
When victims at yon altar's foot we lay?
Canst thou forget what tears that moment fell,
When, warm in youth, I bade the world farewell?   110
As with cold lips I kissed the sacred veil,
The shrines all trembled, and the lamps grew pale:
Heaven scarce believed the conquest it surveyed,
And saints with wonder heard the vows I made.
Yet then, to those dread altars as I drew,   115
Not on the cross my eyes were fixed, but you:
Not grace, or zeal, love only was my call,
And if I lose thy love, I lose my all.
Come! with thy looks, thy words, relieve my woe;
Those still at least are left thee to bestow.   120
Still on that breast enamored let me lie,
Still drink delicious poison from thy eye,
Pant on thy lip, and to thy heart be pressed;
Give all thou canst—and let me dream the rest.
Ah no! instruct me other joys to prize,   125

103 **bloody stroke** referring to the emasculation of Abelard upon
the orders of Eloïsa's uncle.

With other beauties charm my partial eyes,
Full in my view set all the bright abode,
And make my soul quit Abelard for God.
    Ah, think at least thy flock° deserves thy care,
130 Plants of thy hand, and children of thy prayer.
From the false world in early youth they fled,
By thee to mountains, wilds, and deserts led.
You raised these hallowed walls; the desert smiled,
And paradise was opened in the wild.
135 No weeping orphan saw his father's stores
Our shrines irradiate, or emblaze the floors;
No silver saints, by dying misers given,
Here bribed the rage of ill-requited heaven:
But such plain roofs as piety could raise,
140 And only vocal with the Maker's praise.
In these lone walls (their days eternal bound)
These moss-grown domes with spiry turrets crowned,
Where awful arches make a noonday night,
And the dim windows shed a solemn light;
145 Thy eyes diffused a reconciling ray,
And gleams of glory brightened all the day.
But now no face divine contentment wears,
'Tis all blank sadness or continual tears.
See how the force of others' prayers I try,
150 (O pious fraud of amorous charity!)
But why should I on others' prayers depend?
Come thou, my father, brother, husband, friend!
Ah let thy handmaid, sister, daughter move,
And all those tender names in one, thy love!
155 The darksome pines that o'er yon rocks reclined
Wave high, and murmur to the hollow wind,
The wandering streams that shine between the hills,
The grots that echo to the tinkling rills,
The dying gales that pant upon the trees,
160 The lakes that quiver to the curling breeze;
No more these scenes my meditation aid
Or lull to rest the visionary maid.
But o'er the twilight groves and dusky caves,

129 **flock** Eloïsa's convent, the Paraclete, was founded by Abelard
and given to her nuns.

Long-sounding aisles, and intermingled graves,
Black Melancholy sits, and round her throws   165
A deathlike silence, and a dread repose:
Her gloomy presence saddens all the scene,
Shades every flower, and darkens every green,
Deepens the murmur of the falling floods,
And breathes a browner horror on the woods.   170
    Yet here for ever, ever must I stay;
Sad proof how well a lover can obey!
Death, only death, can break the lasting chain;
And here, even then, shall my cold dust remain,
Here all its frailties, all its flames resign,   175
And wait till 'tis no sin to mix with thine.
    Ah wretch! believed the spouse of God in vain,
Confessed within the slave of love and man.
Assist me, heaven! but whence arose that prayer?
Sprung it from piety, or from despair?   180
Even here, where frozen chastity retires,
Love finds an altar for forbidden fires.
I ought to grieve, but cannot what I ought;
I mourn the lover, not lament the fault;
I view my crime, but kindle at the view,   185
Repent old pleasures, and solicit new;
Now turned to heaven, I weep my past offense,
Now think of thee, and curse my innocence.
Of all affliction taught a lover yet,
'Tis sure the hardest science to forget!   190
How shall I lose the sin, yet keep the sense,
And love the offender, yet detest the offense?
How the dear object from the crime remove,
Or how distinguish penitence from love?
Unequal task! a passion to resign,   195
For hearts so touched, so pierced, so lost as mine.
Ere such a soul regains its peaceful state,
How often must it love, how often hate!
How often hope, despair, resent, regret,
Conceal, disdain,—do all things but forget.   200
But let heaven seize it, all at once 'tis fired:
Not touched, but rapt; not wakened, but inspired!
Oh come! oh teach me nature to subdue,

Renounce my love, my life, myself—and you.
205 Fill my fond heart with God alone, for he
Alone can rival, can succeed to thee.
How happy is the blameless Vestal's lot!
The world forgetting, by the world forgot:
Eternal sunshine of the spotless mind!
210 Each prayer accepted, and each wish resigned;
Labor and rest, that equal periods keep;
"Obedient slumbers that can wake and weep;"°
Desires composed, affections ever even;
Tears that delight, and sighs that waft to heaven.
215 Grace shines around her with serenest beams,
And whispering angels prompt her golden dreams.
For her the unfading rose of Eden blooms,
And wings of Seraphs shed divine perfumes,
For her the spouse prepares the bridal ring,
220 For her white virgins hymeneals° sing,
To sounds of heavenly harps she dies away,
And melts in visions of eternal day.
Far other dreams my erring soul employ,
Far other raptures, of unholy joy:
225 When at the close of each sad, sorrowing day,
Fancy restores what vengeance snatched away,
Then conscience sleeps, and leaving nature free,
All my loose soul unbounded springs to thee.
Oh cursed, dear horrors of all-conscious night!
230 How glowing guilt exalts the keen delight!
Provoking demons all restraint remove,
And stir within me every source of love.
I hear thee, view thee, gaze o'er all thy charms,
And round thy phantom glue my clasping arms.
235 I wake:—no more I hear, no more I view,
The phantom flies me, as unkind as you.
I call aloud; it hears not what I say:
I stretch my empty arms; it glides away.
To dream once more I close my willing eyes;
240 Ye soft illusions, dear deceits, arise!

212 Taken from Richard Crashaw, *Description of a Religious House,*
line 16.   220 **hymeneals** wedding songs for the *spouse of God* (cf.
line 177).

Alas, no more! methinks we wandering go
Through dreary wastes, and weep each other's woe,
Where round some moldering tower pale ivy creeps,
And low-browed rocks hang nodding o'er the deeps.
Sudden you mount, you beckon from the skies;   *245*
Clouds interpose, waves roar, and winds arise.
I shriek, start up, the same sad prospect find,
And wake to all the griefs I left behind.
    For thee the fates, severely kind, ordain
A cool suspense from pleasure and from pain;   *250*
Thy life a long dead calm of fixed repose;
No pulse that riots, and no blood that glows.
Still as the sea, ere winds were taught to blow,
Or moving spirit bade the waters flow;
Soft as the slumbers of a saint forgiven,   *255*
And mild as opening gleams of promised heaven.
    Come, Abelard! for what hast thou to dread?
The torch of Venus burns not for the dead.
Nature stands checked; religion disapproves;
Even thou art cold—yet Eloïsa loves.   *260*
Ah hopeless, lasting flames! like those that burn
To light the dead, and warm the unfruitful urn.
    What scenes appear where'er I turn my view?
The dear ideas, where I fly, pursue,
Rise in the grove, before the altar rise,   *265*
Stain all my soul, and wanton in my eyes.
I waste the matin lamp in sighs for thee,
Thy image steals between my God and me,
Thy voice I seem in every hymn to hear,
With every bead I drop too soft a tear.   *270*
When from the censer clouds of fragrance roll,
And swelling organs lift the rising soul,
One thought of thee puts all the pomp to flight,
Priests, tapers, temples, swim before my sight:
In seas of flame my plunging soul is drowned,   *275*
While altars blaze, and angels tremble round.
    While prostrate here in humble grief I lie,
Kind, virtuous drops just gathering in my eye,
While praying, trembling, in the dust I roll,
And dawning grace is opening on my soul: *280*

Come, if thou darst, all charming as thou art!
Oppose thyself to heaven; dispute my heart;
Come, with one glance of those deluding eyes,
Blot out each bright idea of the skies;
285 Take back that grace, those sorrows, and those tears;
Take back my fruitless penitence and prayers;
Snatch me, just mounting, from the blest abode;
Assist the fiends, and tear me from my God!
      No, fly me, fly me, far as Pole from Pole;
290 Rise Alps between us! and whole oceans roll!
Ah, come not, write not, think not once of me,
Nor share one pang of all I felt for thee.
Thy oaths I quit, thy memory resign;
Forget, renounce me, hate whate'er was mine.
295 Fair eyes, and tempting looks (which yet I view!)
Long loved, adored ideas, all adieu!
Oh Grace serene! oh virtue heavenly fair!
Divine oblivion of low-thoughted care!
Fresh blooming Hope, gay daughter of the sky!
300 And Faith, our early immortality!
Enter, each mild, each amicable guest;
Receive, and wrap me in eternal rest!
      See in her cell sad Eloïsa spread,
Propped on some tomb, a neighbor of the dead.
305 In each low wind methinks a Spirit calls,
And more than echoes talk along the walls.
Here, as I watched the dying lamps around,
From yonder shrine I heard a hollow sound.
"Come, sister, come!" (it said, or seemed to say)
310 "Thy place is here, sad sister, come away!
Once like thyself, I trembled, wept, and prayed,
Love's victim then, though now a sainted maid:
But all is calm in this eternal sleep;
Here grief forgets to groan, and love to weep,
315 Even superstition loses every fear:
For God, not man, absolves our frailties here."
      I come, I come! prepare your roseate bowers,
Celestial palms, and ever-blooming flowers.
Thither, where sinners may have rest, I go,
320 Where flames refined in breasts seraphic glow:

Thou, Abelard! the last sad office pay,
And smooth my passage to the realms of day;
See my lips tremble, and my eyeballs roll,
Suck my last breath, and catch my flying soul!
Ah no—in sacred vestments mayst thóu stand,   *325*
The hallowed taper trembling in thy hand,
Present the cross before my lifted eye,
Teach me at once, and learn of me to die.
Ah then, thy once-loved Eloïsa see!
It will be then no crime to gaze on me.   *330*
See from my cheek the transient roses fly!
See the last sparkle languish in my eye!
Till every motion, pulse, and breath be o'er,
And even my Abelard be loved no more.
O Death all-eloquent! you only prove   *335*
What dust we dote on, when 'tis man we love.
    Then too, when fate shall thy fair frame destroy,
(That cause of all my guilt, and all my joy)
In trance ecstatic may thy pangs be drowned,
Bright clouds descend, and angels watch thee round, *340*
From opening skies may streaming glories shine,
And saints embrace thee with a love like mine.
    May one kind grave unite each hapless name,°
And graft my love immortal on thy fame!
Then, ages hence, when all my woes are o'er,   *345*
When this rebellious heart shall beat no more;
If ever chance two wandering lovers brings
To Paraclete's white walls and silver springs,
O'er the pale marble shall they join their heads,
And drink the falling tears each other sheds;   *350*
Then sadly say, with mutual pity moved,
"Oh may we never love as these have loved!"
From the full choir when loud hosannas rise,
And swell the pomp of dreadful sacrifice,
Amid that scene if some relenting eye   *355*
Glance on the stone where our cold relics° lie,
Devotion's self shall steal a thought from heaven,

343 "Abelard and Eloïsa were interred in the same grave, or in monuments adjoining in the monastery of the Paraclete: he died in the year 1142, she in 1163" (Pope).   356 **relics** remains.

One human tear shall drop, and be forgiven.
And sure, if fate some future bard shall join
360 In sad similitude of griefs to mine,
Condemned whole years in absence to deplore,
And image charms he must behold no more;
Such if there be, who loves so long, so well;
Let him our sad, our tender story tell;
365 The well-sung woes will soothe my pensive ghost;
He best can paint 'em who shall feel 'em most.

AN ESSAY ON MAN

IN FOUR EPISTLES

TO HENRY ST. JOHN, LORD BOLINGBROKE°

(1733–1734)

EPISTLE I

AWAKE, my ST. JOHN! leave all meaner things
To low ambition, and the pride of kings.
Let us (since life can little more supply
Than just to look about us and to die)
Expatiate free o'er all this scene of Man;   *5*
A mighty maze! but not without a plan;
A wild, where weeds and flowers promiscuous shoot,
Or garden, tempting with forbidden fruit.°
Together let us beat this ample field,°
Try what the open, what the covert yield;   *10*
The latent tracts, the giddy heights, explore
Of all who blindly creep, or sightless soar;
Eye nature's walks, shoot folly as it flies,
And catch the manners living as they rise;

Bolingbroke See *Imitations of Horace*, Epistle I, i. 7–8 **A wild . . .
fruit** with suggestions of Milton's Eden, which required cultivation
by Adam and Eve, fused goodness with latent evil and disorder,
and was the scene of their fall. 9 **beat . . . field** as might hunters
of birds.

15   Laugh where we must, be candid where we can;
    But vindicate the ways of God to man.°
        I.   Say first, of God above, or Man below,
    What can we reason, but from what we know?
    Of Man, what see we but his station here,
20   From which to reason, or to which refer?
    Through worlds unnumbered though the God be known,
    'Tis ours to trace him only in our own.
    He, who through vast immensity can pierce,
    See worlds on worlds compose one universe,
25   Observe how system into system runs,
    What other planets circle other suns,
    What varied being peoples every star,
    May tell why Heaven has made us as we are.
    But of this frame the bearings, and the ties,
30   The strong connections, nice° dependencies,
    Gradations just, has thy pervading soul
    Looked through? or can a part contain the whole?
        Is the great chain,° that draws all to agree,
    And drawn supports, upheld by God, or thee?
35   II.   Presumptuous Man! the reason wouldst thou
           find,
    Why formed so weak, so little, and so blind!
    First, if thou canst, the harder reason guess,
    Why formed no weaker, blinder, and no less!
    Ask of thy mother earth,° why oaks are made
40   Taller or stronger than the weeds they shade?
    Or ask of yonder argent fields above,
    Why Jove's satellites° are less than Jove?
        Of systems possible, if 'tis confest

15–16 **laugh . . . God to man** echoing in a lighter vein (the tentative tone of an "essay") Milton's "justify the ways of God to man" (*Paradise Lost*, I, 26).   30 **nice** subtle, precise (here as throughout lines 29–31 the delicate equilibrium of the "plan" is stressed).   33 **great chain** the Great Chain of Being, the metaphor which sees all kinds of creatures as links in a continuous chain descending from God through the levels of being: from angelic to human, from intelligent to merely sentient, from animate to inanimate. Man's place is the most precarious, for he is the lowest of rational creatures and the highest of passionate, most complex and unstable in his structure, free to fall and easily deluded by pride.   39 **thy mother earth** a reminder of man's less than angelic nature.   42 **Jove's satellites** i.e., of the planet Jupiter; but also the lesser Olympian gods.

That wisdom infinite must form the best,
Where all must full or not coherent° be,   *45*
And all that rises, rise in due degree;
Then, in the scale of reasoning life, 'tis plain
There must be, somewhere, such a rank as Man;
And all the question (wrangle e'er so long)
Is only this, if God has placed him wrong?°   *50*
 Respecting Man, whatever wrong we call,
May, must be right, as relative to all.°
In human works, though labored on with pain,
A thousand movements scarce one purpose gain;
In God's, one single can its end produce;   *55*
Yet serves to second too some other use.
So Man, who here seems principal alone,
Perhaps acts second to some sphere unknown,
Touches some wheel, or verges to some goal;°
'Tis but a part we see, and not a whole.   *60*
 When the proud steed shall know why Man restrains
His fiery course, or drives him o'er the plains;
When the dull ox, why now he breaks the clod,
Is now a victim, and now Egypt's god:°
Then shall Man's pride and dulness comprehend   *65*
His actions', passions', being's use and end;
Why doing, suffering, checked, impelled; and why
This hour a slave, the next a deity.
 Then say not Man's imperfect, Heaven in fault;
Say rather, Man's as perfect as he ought: *70*

45 **full or not coherent** According to the principle of plenitude, the
Great Chain must include every possible kind of creature if it is to
represent God's goodness and omnipotence; any gaps would be de-
nials of these qualities, and any failure to preserve an exact hier-
archy of kinds ("due degree," line 46) in the chain would represent
a disordering or unmaking of God's creation (see I, lines 243–6,
249–50). 49–50 **all the question . . . wrong** alluding to the frequent
complaints (1) that man was insufficiently prepared to maintain his
place, (2) that he was denied powers granted other creatures, or (3)
that he should be able to move freely throughout the chain, assum-
ing whatever place he chose. 52 **as relative to all** when considered
not as an end in himself ("principal," line 57) but as part of a large
plan, in which his existence serves the needs of other creatures as
well ("to second too some other use," as in line 56). 59 **Touches
. . . goal** recalling the imagery of a delicate machine, so delicate as
to suggest an organism, as in lines 29–31. 64 **Egypt's god** Apis, the
sacred bull worshiped at Memphis.

His knowledge measured to his state and place,
His time a moment, and a point his space.°
If to be perfect in a certain sphere,
What matter, soon or late, or here or there?
75 The blest today is as completely so,
As who began a thousand years ago.

    III.   Heaven from all creatures hides the book of
     Fate,
All but the page prescribed, their present state;
From brutes what men, from men what spirits know:
80 Or who could suffer Being here below?
The lamb thy riot° dooms to bleed today,
Had he thy Reason, would he skip and play?
Pleased to the last, he crops the flowery food,
And licks the hand just raised to shed his blood.°
85 Oh blindness to the future! kindly given,
That each may fill the circle marked by Heaven;
Who sees with equal° eye, as God of all,
A hero perish, or a sparrow fall,°
Atoms or systems into ruin hurled,
90 And now a bubble burst, and now a world.
    Hope humbly then; with trembling pinions soar;
Wait the great teacher Death, and God adore!
What future bliss, he gives not thee to know,
But gives that hope to be thy blessing now.
95 Hope springs eternal in the human breast:
Man never Is, but always To be blest:
The soul, uneasy and confined from home,°
Rests and expatiates in a life to come.
    Lo, the poor Indian, whose untutored mind
100 Sees God in clouds, or hears him in the wind;
His soul proud Science never taught to stray

72 **His time . . . space** This contraction of man's mortal life both
stresses the limit of his knowledge and contrasts with the eternity of
beatitude of lines 75–6 (where timelessness makes a difference of a
"thousand years" meaningless). 81 **riot** self-indulgence. 84 **And licks
. . . blood** stressing (1) blessed ignorance of "the book of Fate"
(line 77) and (2) the inevitable cruelty of man's dispensations when
he assumes a role like God's, as in lines 117–18. 87 **equal** impar-
tial. 88 **a sparrow fall** Cf. Matthew 10:29: "Are not two sparrows
sold for a farthing? and one of them shall not fall to the ground
without your Father." 97 **home** Heaven.

Far as the solar walk, or milky way;
Yet simple Nature to his hope has given,
Behind the cloud-topped hill, an humbler heaven;
Some safer world in depth of woods embraced,   *105*
Some happier island in the watery waste,
Where slaves° once more their native land behold,
No fiends torment, no Christians thirst for gold!
To Be, contents his natural desire,
He asks no angel's wing, no seraph's fire;°   *110*
But thinks, admitted to that equal° sky,
His faithful dog shall bear him company.
    IV.   Go, wiser thou! and in thy scale of sense
Weigh thy Opinion against Providence;
Call imperfection what thou fanciest such,   *115*
Say, here he° gives too little, there too much;
Destroy all creatures for thy sport or gust,°
Yet cry, If Man's unhappy, God's unjust;
If Man alone ingross° not Heaven's high care,
Alone made perfect here, immortal there: *120*
Snatch from his hand the balance and the rod,°
Re-judge his justice, be the GOD of GOD!
In Pride, in reasoning Pride, our error lies;
All quit their sphere, and rush into the skies.
Pride still is aiming at the blest abodes,   *125*
Men would be Angels, Angels would be Gods.
Aspiring to be Gods, if Angels fell,°
Aspiring to be Angels, Men rebel:
And who but wishes to invert the laws
Of ORDER, sins against the Eternal Cause.   *130*
    V.   Ask for what end the heavenly bodies shine,
Earth for whose use? Pride answers, " 'Tis for mine:

---

107 **slaves** presumably, as an example, the Indians who work the gold mines of Spanish America. 110 **seraph's fire** a traditional attribute based on the supposed derivation of "seraph" from the Hebrew root meaning "to burn"; here associated with the consuming ambition of more sophisticated men. 111 **equal** available to all (see line 87). 116 **he** God. 117 **gust** taste (food or pleasure). 119 **ingross** monopolize. 121 **balance . . . rod** symbols of justice and power. 127 **Aspiring . . . fell** recalling the rebellion of Satan and the war in Heaven of *Paradise Lost* and (in line 128) Satan's temptation of Eve.

For me kind Nature wakes her genial° power,
Suckles each herb, and spreads out every flower;
135 Annual for me, the grape, the rose renew
The juice nectareous, and the balmy dew;°
For me, the mine a thousand treasures brings;
For me, health gushes from a thousand springs;
Seas roll to waft me, suns to light me rise;
140 My footstool earth, my canopy the skies."°
    But errs not Nature from this gracious end,
From burning suns when livid deaths° descend,
When earthquakes swallow, or when tempests sweep
Towns to one grave, whole nations to the deep?
145 "No" ('tis replied)° "the first Almighty Cause
Acts not by partial, but by general laws;
The exceptions few; some change since all began,
And what created perfect?"—Why then Man?°
If the great end be human Happiness,
150 Then Nature deviates; and can Man do less?
As much that end a constant course requires
Of showers and sunshine, as of Man's desires;
As much eternal springs and cloudless skies,
As men for ever temperate, calm, and wise.
155 If plagues or earthquakes break not Heaven's design,
Why then a Borgia,° or a Catiline?°
Who knows but he, whose hand the lightning forms,
Who heaves old Ocean, and who wings the storms,
Pours fierce ambition in a Caesar's mind,
160 Or turns young Ammon° loose to scourge mankind?

---

133 **genial** generative.   136 **balmy dew** fragrance.   140 **My footstool . . . skies** Cf. Isaiah 66:1: "Thus saith the Lord, the heaven is my throne, and the earth my footstool." Here it is man who speaks as the "God of God" (line 122).   142 **livid deaths** plagues, believed to be caused by the sun's heat.   145 **'tis replied** by Pride, qualifying the anthropocentric view with a recognition of some limitations in God's design, but never questioning whether the end of that design may be misunderstood.   148 **Why then Man?** Why should Pride expect Man to be created full of imperfections?   156 **Borgia** one of the Italian Renaissance family that ruled with murder and deceit; Cesare Borgia was the model of Machiavelli's "Prince."   156 **Catiline** the conspirator against the Roman Republic, attacked by Cicero for treachery and licentiousness.   160 **young Ammon** Alexander the Great, who claimed descent from Jupiter Ammon.

From Pride, from Pride, our very reasoning springs;
Account for moral as for natural things:
Why charge° we Heaven in those, in these acquit?
In both, to reason right is to submit.
   Better for us, perhaps, it might appear,   *165*
Were there all harmony, all virtue here;
That never air or ocean felt the wind;
That never passion discomposed the mind:
But ALL subsists by elemental strife;°
And passions are the elements of life.   *170*
The general ORDER, since the whole began,
Is kept in Nature, and is kept in Man.
   VI.   What would this Man? Now upward will he
      soar,
And little less than Angel, would be more;
Now looking downwards,° just as grieved appears   *175*
To want the strength of bulls, the fur of bears.
Made for his use all creatures if he call,
Say what their use, had he the powers of all?
Nature to these, without profusion° kind,
The proper organs, proper powers assigned;   *180*
Each seeming want compénsated of course,°
Here with degrees of swiftness, there of force;
All in exact proportion to the state;
Nothing to add, and nothing to abate.
Each beast, each insect, happy in its own: *185*
Is Heaven unkind to Man, and Man alone?
Shall he alone, whom rational we call,
Be pleased with nothing, if not blessed with all?
   The bliss of Man (could Pride that blessing find)
Is not to act or think beyond mankind;   *190*
No powers of body or of soul to share,
But what his nature and his state can bear.

---

163 **charge** with error, in making Man less than perfect.   169 **But
all . . . strife** The Whole is created by the harmony of apparently
discordant elements, as man's mind is seen as a harmony of four
humors, each corresponding in turn to one of the elements, each
capable of becoming a violent force without the restraining power
of the others.   175 **downwards** in the scale of creatures in the Great
Chain of Being.   179 **profusion** excess.   181 **of course** in due course.

Why has not Man a microscopic eye?
For this plain reason, Man is not a Fly.
195 Say what the use, were finer optics° given,
To inspect a mite, not comprehend the heaven?
Or touch, if tremblingly alive all o'er,
To smart and agonize at every pore?
Or quick effluvia° darting through the brain,
200 Die of a rose in aromatic pain?
If nature thundered in his opening° ears,
And stunned him with the music of the spheres,°
How would he wish that Heaven had left him still
The whispering zephyr, and the purling rill?
205 Who finds not Providence all good and wise,
Alike in what it gives, and what denies?
　　VII.　Far as creation's ample range extends,
The scale of sensual,° mental powers ascends:
Mark how it mounts, to Man's imperial race,
210 From the green myriads in the peopled grass:
What modes of sight betwixt each wide extreme,
The mole's dim curtain, and the lynx's beam:°
Of smell, the headlong° lioness between,
And hound sagacious° on the tainted° green:
215 Of hearing, from the life that fills the flood,°
To that which warbles through the vernal wood:
The spider's touch, how exquisitely fine!
Feels at each thread, and lives along the line:
In the nice bee, what sense so subtly true
220 From poisonous herbs extracts the healing dew:°
How Instinct varies in the groveling swine,

---

195 **finer optics** like the fly, which was believed to have microscopic powers (contrasted in the next line with telescopic). 199 **quick effluvia** streams of invisible particles carrying odors. 201 **opening** more perceptive. 202 **music of the spheres** the music, audible to angels but not to men, supposedly produced by the motion of the heavenly spheres that held stars, planets, etc. 208 **sensual** sensuous. 212 **lynx's beam** traditionally the keenest of all eyebeams. 213 **headlong** lioness who hunted by the sound rather than the scent of the prey. 214 **sagacious** quick of scent. 214 **tainted** with an animal's scent. 215 **life . . . flood** fish, like the lioness an extreme of insensitivity. 220 **healing dew** honey, once believed to be a dew and still used medicinally.

Compared, half-reasoning elephant,° with thine:
Twixt that, and Reason, what a nice barrier;
For ever separate, yet for ever near!
Remembrance and Reflection how allied;   225
What thin partitions Sense from Thought divide:°
And middle natures,° how they long to join,
Yet never pass the insuperable line!
Without this just gradation, could they be
Subjected these to those, or all to thee?   230
The powers of all subdued by thee alone,
Is not thy Reason all these powers in one?
    VIII.   See, through this air, this ocean, and this earth,
All matter quick,° and bursting into birth.
Above, how high progressive life may go!   235
Around, how wide! how deep extend below!
Vast chain of being, which from God began,
Natures ethereal, human, angel, man,
Beast, bird, fish, insect! what no eye can see,
No glass can reach! from Infinite to thee,°   240
From thee to Nothing!—On superior powers
Were we to press, inferior might on ours:
Or in the full creation leave a void,
Where, one step broken, the great scale's destroyed:
From Nature's chain whatever link you strike,   245
Tenth or ten thousandth, breaks the chain alike.
    And if each system in gradation roll,°
Alike essential to the amazing Whole,
The least confusion but in one, not all
That system only, but the Whole must fall.   250
Let Earth unbalanced from her orbit fly,
Planets and suns run lawless through the sky,
Let ruling Angels° from their spheres be hurled,
Being on being wrecked, and world on world,

222 **elephant** famous for its memory and credited with other mental powers.   225–6 **Remembrance . . . divide** making two parallel distinctions (1) between simple memory and the ability to draw conclusions or make plans; (2) between sensation and rationality.   227 **middle natures** animals that fall between classes, transitional species, that almost but not quite join the powers distinguished in lines 225–6.   234 **quick** pregnant, living.   240 **thee** Man.   247 **roll** revolve and rotate.   253 **ruling Angels** believed to rule or govern the movement of each sphere.

255 Heaven's whole foundations to their center nod,
And Nature tremble to the throne of God:
All this dread ORDER break—for whom? for thee?
Vile worm!—Oh madness, pride, impiety!
     IX.   What if the foot, ordained the dust to tread,
260 Or hand to toil, aspired to be the head?
What if the head, the eye, or ear repined
To serve mere engines° to the ruling mind?
Just as absurd for any part of claim
To be another, in this general frame:
265 Just as absurd, to mourn the tasks or pains
The great directing MIND of ALL ordains.
     All are but parts of one stupendous whole,
Whose body Nature is, and God the soul;
That, changed through all, and yet in all the same,
270 Great in the earth, as in the ethereal frame,
Warms in the sun, refreshes in the breeze,
Glows in the stars, and blossoms in the trees,
Lives through all life, extends through all extent,
Spreads undivided, operates unspent,
275 Breathes in our soul, informs our mortal part,
As full, as perfect, in a hair as heart;
As full, as perfect, in vile Man that mourns,
As the rapt Seraph that adores and burns;
To him no high, no low, no great, no small;
280 He fills, he bounds, connects, and equals all.°
     X.   Cease then, nor ORDER imperfection name:
Our proper bliss depends on what we blame.
Know thy own point:° this kind, this due degree
Of blindness, weakness, Heaven bestows on thee.
285 Submit—in this, or any other sphere,
Secure to be as blest as thou canst bear:
Safe in the hand of one disposing Power,
Or in the natal, or° the mortal hour.
All Nature is but Art, unknown to thee:°

262 **engines** instruments. For a scriptural parallel to this passage see
I Corinthians 12:12–27. 280 **equals all** makes all equal. 283 **point**
as in line 72. 288 **Or . . . or** whether . . . or. 289 **All Nature . . .
thee** alluding to the traditional view that nature is the handiwork or
art of God.

All Chance, Direction, which thou canst not see;   *290*
All Discord, Harmony, not understood;
All partial Evil,° universal Good:
And, spite of Pride, in erring Reason's spite,
One truth is clear, "WHATEVER IS, IS RIGHT."

EPISTLE II

I.   KNOW then thyself, presume not God to scan;°
The proper study of mankind is Man.
Placed on this isthmus of a middle state,
A being darkly wise, and rudely° great:
With too much knowledge for the Sceptic side,°   *5*
With too much weakness for the Stoic's pride,°
He hangs between; in doubt to act, or rest,
In doubt to deem himself a God, or Beast;°
In doubt his Mind or Body to prefer,
Born but to die, and reasoning but to err;   *10*
Alike in ignorance, his reason such,
Whether he thinks too little, or too much:
Chaos of Thought and Passion, all confused;
Still by himself abused, or disabused;
Created half to rise, and half to fall;   *15*
Great lord of all things, yet a prey to all;
Sole judge of Truth, in endless Error hurled:
The glory, jest, and riddle of the world!
     Go, wondrous creature! mount where Science guides,
Go, measure earth, weigh air, and state the tides;   *20*
Instruct the planets in what orbs to run,

292 **partial Evil** evil to individuals.   1 **scan** criticize, judge.   4 **rudely**
roughly, turbulently.   5 **Sceptic side** the distrust of all possibility of
certain knowledge.   6 **Stoic's pride** the mastery of all passions.   7–8
in doubt . . . or Beast choosing between the impassivity and serenity
("rest") of a God or the restless activity of satisfying animal appe-
tite; so again in line 9, Mind and Body as opposed principles.

Correct old Time, and regulate the Sun;
Go, soar with Plato to the empyreal sphere,°
To the first good, first perfect, and first fair;
25 Or tread the mazy round° his followers trod,
And quitting sense call imitating God;
As Eastern priests in giddy circles run,
And turn their heads to imitate the sun.
Go, teach Eternal Wisdom how to rule—
30 Then drop into thyself, and be a fool!
    Superior beings, when of late they saw
A mortal Man unfold all Nature's law,
Admired such wisdom in an earthly shape,
And showed a NEWTON as we show an Ape.°
35   Could he, whose rules the rapid comet bind,
Describe or fix one movement of his mind?
Who saw its fires here rise, and there descend,
Explain his own beginning, or his end?
Alas what wonder! Man's superior part
40 Unchecked may rise, and climb from art to art:
But when his own great work is but begun,
What Reason weaves, by Passion is undone.°
    Trace Science° then, with modesty thy guide;
First strip off all her equipage of pride,
45 Deduct what is but vanity, or dress,
Or learning's luxury,° or idleness;
Or tricks to show the stretch of human brain,
Mere curious pleasure, or ingenious pain:
Expunge the whole, or lop the excrescent parts
50 Of all, our Vices have created Arts:

23 **empyreal sphere** the outermost, where might dwell Plato's arche-
typal ("first," line 24) Ideas of the Good, True, and Beautiful (as in
line 24) from which all earthly instances are imitated. 25 **mazy
round** Neoplatonists often fused metaphysics and mysticism, seek-
ing to transcend the flesh in rapturous trances and to become god-
like; likened here to the self-induced obliviousness of Eastern mys-
tics who dizzy themselves (lines 27–8). 34 **And showed . . . ape**
with real esteem for his powers but with powers of their own that
far surpass his; at once a tribute to Newton and a warning against
pride. 42 **What Reason . . . undone** as in Penelope's undoing by
night what she weaved by day; here the distinctive problem of man's
knowledge of Man where his passions and interests are involved.
43 **Science** knowledge in general. 46 **luxury** self-display.

Then see how little the remaining sum,
Which served the past, and must the times to come!
   II.   Two principles in human nature reign;
Self-love, to urge, and Reason, to restrain;
Nor this a good, nor that a bad we call,   *55*
Each works its end, to move or govern all:
And to their proper operation still,
Ascribe all good; to their improper, ill.
   Self-love,° the spring of motion, acts° the soul;
Reason's comparing balance rules the whole.   *60*
Man, but for that, no action could attend,°
And, but for this, were active to no end;
Fixed like a plant on his peculiar spot,
To draw nutrition, propagate, and rot;
Or, meteor-like, flame lawless through the void,   *65*
Destroying others, by himself destroyed.
   Most strength the moving principle requires;
Active its task, it prompts, impels, inspires.
Sedate and quiet the comparing lies,
Formed but to check, deliberate, and advise.   *70*
Self-love still stronger, as its objects nigh;
Reason's at distance, and in prospect lie:
That sees immediate good by present sense;
Reason, the future and the consequence.
Thicker than arguments, temptations throng,   *75*
At best more watchful this, but that more strong.
The action of the stronger to suspend
Reason still use, to Reason still attend:
Attention, habit and experience gains,
Each strengthens Reason, and Self-love restrains.° *80*
   Let subtle schoolmen° teach these friends to fight,

59 **Self-love** in the sense of gratification of appetite, not merely self-regard; see note to II, 7–8. 59 **acts** activates. 61 **attend** give himself to. 75–80 **thicker than . . . restrains** The linkages are arguments –watchfulness–reason and temptations–strength–self-love. In order to suspend the strength of self-love one must invoke reason; attention to her dictates builds habits which strengthen reason and enable her to restrain the initially stronger power of self-love. 81 **subtle schoolmen** scholastic philosophers, or any rigid theologians and moralists.

More studious to divide than to unite,
And Grace and Virtue,° Sense° and Reason split,
With all the rash dexterity of wit:
85 Wits, just like fools, at war about a name,
Have full as oft no meaning, or the same.
Self-love and Reason to one end aspire,
Pain their aversion, pleasure their desire;
But greedy that its object would devour,
90 This taste the honey, and not wound the flower:
Pleasure, or wrong or rightly understood,
Our greatest evil, or our greatest good.
    III.   Modes of Self-love the Passions we may call;
'Tis real good, or seeming, moves them all;
95 But since not every good we can divide,
And Reason bids us for our own provide;
Passions, though selfish, if their means be fair,
List° under Reason, and deserve her care;
Those, that imparted,° court a nobler aim,
100 Exalt their kind, and take some Virtue's name.
    In lazy apathy° let Stoics boast
Their virtue fixed; 'tis fixed as in a frost,
Contracted all, retiring to the breast;
But strength of mind is Exercise, not Rest:
105 The rising tempest puts in act the soul,
Parts it may ravage, but preserves the whole.°
On life's vast ocean diversely we sail,
Reason the card,° but Passion is the gale;
Nor God alone in the still calm we find,
110 He mounts the storm, and walks upon the wind.°

83 **Grace and Virtue** a much-discussed issue during the rise of radi-
cal Protestantism, which dissociated the state of grace from mere
worldly morality or good works; the moderate position saw virtue
as a probable sign of grace and thus held them together. 83 **Sense**
probably used as "sensuality" or passion rather than "sensation" or
empiricism. 98 **List** enlist. 99 **that imparted** under the guide of
reason. 101 **apathy** impassivity, a conquest of passion or feeling.
106 **Parts . . . whole** suggesting the analogy of a ship, torn by winds
but lost without them. 108 **card** mariner's chart. 110 **He mounts
. . . wind** Cf. among other scriptural passages, Psalms 104:3: "who
maketh the clouds his chariot: who walketh upon the wings of the
wind."

Passions, like elements,° though born to fight,
Yet, mixed and softened, in his work unite:
These 'tis enough to temper and employ;
But what composes Man, can Man destroy?°
Suffice that Reason keep to Nature's road,   *115*
Subject, compound them, follow her and God.
Love, Hope, and Joy, fair pleasure's smiling train,
Hate, Fear, and Grief, the family of pain;
These mixed with art, and to due bounds confined,
Make and maintain the balance of the mind: *120*
The lights and shades, whose well-accorded strife
Gives all the strength and color of our life.
     Pleasures are ever in our hands or eyes,
And when in act they cease, in prospect rise;
Present to grasp, and future still to find,   *125*
The whole employ of body and of mind.
All spread their charms, but charm not all alike;
On different senses different objects strike;
Hence different Passions more or less inflame,
As strong or weak, the organs of the frame;   *130*
And hence one MASTER PASSION in the breast,
Like Aaron's serpent,° swallows up the rest.
     As Man, perhaps, the moment of his breath,
Receives the lurking principle of death;
The young disease, that must subdue at length,   *135*
Grows with his growth, and strengthens with his strength:
So, cast and mingled with his very frame,
The mind's disease, its RULING PASSION came;
Each vital humor° which should feed the whole,
Soon flows to this, in body and in soul.   *140*
Whatever warms the heart, or fills the head,
As the mind opens, and its functions spread,

111 **elements** as in "elemental strife," I, 169, and note.   114 **can Man destroy,** i.e., can man hope to suppress his passions entirely? 132 **Aaron's serpent** When Aaron cast down his rod before the Pharaoh, it became a serpent; when the Egyptian magicians did the same, Aaron's serpent devoured theirs (Exodus 7:10–12).   139 **vital humor** The "vital spirits" (found in the heart) and "animal spirits" (found in the head) were believed to nourish the power of body and soul.

Imagination plies her dangerous art,
And pours it all upon the peccant part.°
145   Nature its mother, Habit is its nurse;
Wit, Spirit, Faculties, but make it worse;
Reason itself but gives it edge and power;
As Heaven's blest beam turns vinegar more sour;
We, wretched subjects though to lawful sway,
150 In this weak queen,° some favorite still obey.
Ah! if she lend not arms, as well as rules,
What can she more than tell us we are fools?
Teach us to mourn our nature, not to mend,
A sharp accuser, but a helpless friend!
155 Or from a judge turn pleader, to persuade
The choice we make, or justify it made;
Proud of an easy conquest all along,
She but removes weak passions for the strong:
So, when small humors gather to a gout,°
160 The doctor fancies he has driven them out.
     Yes, Nature's road must ever be preferred;
Reason is here no guide, but still a guard:
'Tis hers to rectify, not overthrow,
And treat this passion more as friend than foe:
165 A mightier Power the strong direction sends,
And several men impels to several° ends.
Like varying winds, by other passions tossed,
This drives them constant to a certain coast.°
Let power or knowledge, gold or glory, please,
170 Or (oft more strong than all) the love of ease;
Through life 'tis followed, even at life's expense;
The Merchant's toil, the sage's indolence,
The monk's humility, the hero's pride,
All, all alike, find Reason on their side.
175   The Eternal Art educing good from ill,
Grafts on this Passion our best principle:

143–44 **Imagination . . . peccant part** Imagination disruptively directs the nourishing vital humors to the already excessive ("peccant") growth of the one ruling passion. 150 **weak queen** Reason. 159 **gout** supposedly caused by a gathering into an extremity of redundant humors. 166 **several** different. 168 **constant . . . coast** The ruling passions differentiate men but give each man his distinctive constancy of nature.

'Tis thus the mercury° of Man is fixed,
Strong grows the virtue with his nature mixed;
The dross cements what else were too refined,°
And in one interest body acts with mind.   *180*
    As fruits ungrateful° to the planter's care
On savage stocks inserted learn to bear;
The surest virtues thus from passions shoot,
Wild Nature's vigor working at the root.
What crops of wit and honesty appear   *185*
From spleen, from obstinacy, hate, or fear!
See anger, zeal and fortitude supply;
Even avarice, prudence; sloth, philosophy;
Lust, through some certain strainers well refined,
Is gentle love, and charms all womankind: *190*
Envy, to which the ignoble mind's a slave,
Is emulation in the learned or brave:
Nor virtue, male or female, can we name,
But what will grow on pride, or grow on shame.
    Thus Nature gives us (let it check our pride)°   *195*
The virtue nearest to our vice allied;
Reason the bias turns to good from ill,
And Nero reigns a Titus,° if he will.
The fiery soul abhorred in Catiline,
In Decius charms, in Curtius° is divine.   *200*
The same ambition can destroy or save,
And makes a patriot as it makes a knave.
    IV.   This light and darkness in our chaos joined,
What shall divide?° The God within the mind.
    Extremes in Nature equal ends produce,°   *205*
In Man they join to some mysterious use;
Though each by turns the other's bound invade,

---

177 **mercury** volatility, changeableness.   179 **the dross . . . refined**
i.e., both appetite and aspiration are satisfied at once.   181 **ungrate-
ful** unresponsive.   195 **pride** the "Stoic's pride" in conquering his
passions, which are in fact necessary; or our pride in noble virtues,
which depend in turn upon our "baser" passions; see II, 231–4.
198 **Titus** a virtuous Roman emperor of first century A.D.   200 **De-
cius . . . Curtius** legendary Roman heroes who gave their lives for
their country.   204 **divide** As God divides the light from the dark-
ness in Genesis 1:4, so man must create order out of the chaos of
his nature by an act of "will" (see line 198).   205 **Extremes . . .
produce** Opposites have comparable ends or, perhaps, cooperate to
the same end.

As, in some well-wrought picture, light and shade,
And oft so mix, the difference is too nice
210 Where ends the virtue, or begins the vice.
  Fools! who from hence into the notion fall,
That vice or virtue there is none at all.
If white and black blend, soften, and unite
A thousand ways, is there no black or white?
215 Ask your own heart; and nothing is so plain;
'Tis to mistake them, costs the time and pain.
  V. Vice is a monster of so frightful mien,
As, to be hated, needs but to be seen;
Yet seen too oft, familiar with her face,
220 We first endure, then pity, then embrace.°
But where the extreme of Vice, was ne'er agreed:
Ask where's the North? at York, 'tis on the Tweed;°
In Scotland, at the Orcades;° and there,
At Greenland, Zembla, or the Lord knows where:
225 No creature owns it in the first degree,
But thinks his neighbor further gone than he.
Even those who dwell beneath its very zone,
Or never feel the rage, or° never own;°
What happier natures shrink at with affright,
230 The hard inhabitant° contends is right.
  VI. Virtuous and vicious every Man must be,
Few in the extreme, but all in the degree;
The rogue and fool by fits is fair and wise,
And even the best, by fits, what they despise.
235 'Tis but by parts we follow good or ill,
For, vice or virtue, Self directs it still;
Each individual seeks a several goal;
But HEAVEN's great view is One, and that the Whole.
That counterworks each folly and caprice;
240 That disappoints the effect of every vice:
That happy° frailties to all ranks applied,

219–20 **familiar . . . embrace** Cf. *Paradise Lost,* II, 761–3, where
Sin recalls that "familiar grown,/I pleas'd, and with attractive
graces won/The most averse. . . ." 222 **Tweed** the river dividing
England from Scotland. 223 **Orcades** the Orkney Islands, north of
Scotland. 228 **Or . . . or** either . . . or. 228 **own** admit it. 230
hard inhabitant the dweller in an extreme climate. 241 **happy**
fortunate, useful.

Shame to the virgin, to the matron pride,
Fear to the statesman, rashness to the chief,
To kings presumption, and to crowds belief:
That virtue's ends from vanity can raise,   *245*
Which seeks no interest, no reward but praise;
And build on wants, and on defects of mind,
The joy, the peace, the glory of Mankind.
   Heaven forming each on other to depend,
A master, or a servant, or a friend,   *250*
Bids each on other for assistance call,
Till one man's weakness grows the strength of all.
Wants, frailties, passions, closer still ally
The common interest, or endear the tie:
To these we owe true friendship, love sincere,   *255*
Each home-felt joy that life inherits here:
Yet from the same we learn, in its decline,
Those joys, those loves, those interests to resign:
Taught half by Reason, half by mere decay,
To welcome death, and calmly pass away.   *260*
   Whate'er the passion, knowledge, fame, or pelf,
Not one will change his neighbor with himself.
The learned is happy nature to explore,
The fool is happy that he knows no more;
The rich is happy in the plenty given,   *265*
The poor contents him with the care of Heaven.
See the blind beggar dance, the cripple sing,
The sot a hero, lunatic a king;
The starving chemist° in his golden views
Supremely blest, the poet in his Muse.   *270*
   See some strange comfort every state attend,
And Pride bestowed on all, a common friend;
See some fit Passion every age supply,
Hope travels through, nor quits us when we die.
   Behold the child, by Nature's kindly law,   *275*
Pleased with a rattle, tickled with a straw:
Some livelier plaything gives his youth delight,
A little louder, but as empty quite:
Scarfs,° garters, gold, amuse his riper stage;

269 **chemist** alchemist, hoping to create gold.   279 **scarfs** badges of
the Doctors of Divinity or trophies of lovers.

280 And beads° and prayer books are the toys of age:
     Pleased with this bauble still, as that before;
     Till tired he sleeps, and Life's poor play is o'er!
         Meanwhile Opinion gilds with varying rays
     Those painted clouds that beautify our days;
285 Each want of happiness by Hope supplied,
     And each vacuity of sense by Pride:
     These build as fast as knowledge can destroy;
     In Folly's cup still laughs the bubble,° joy;
     One prospect lost, another still we gain;
290 And not a vanity is given in vain;
     Even mean Self-love becomes, by force divine,
     The scale to measure others' wants by thine.
     See! and confess, one comfort still must rise,
     'Tis this, though Man's a fool, yet GOD IS WISE.

EPISTLE III

     HERE then we rest: "The Universal Cause
     Acts to one end,° but acts by various laws."
     In all the madness of superfluous health,
     The trim of pride, the impudence of wealth,
5   Let this great truth be present night and day;
     But most be present, if we preach or pray.
         I.   Look round our world; behold the chain of love°
     Combining all below and all above.
     See plastic° Nature working to this end,
10   The single atoms each to other tend,
     Attract, attracted to, the next in place

280 **beads** rosaries.   288 **bubble** with secondary meaning of "decep-
tion."   2 **one end** the "general good" as in line 14.   7 **chain of love**
The Chain of Being is here seen as a unity held together by mutual
attention, relatedness, or love, of which divine love for all creatures
is the exemplar.   9 **plastic** forming, creative.

Formed and impelled its neighbor to embrace.°
See matter next, with various life endued,
Press to one center still, the general Good.
See dying vegetables life sustain,   *15*
See life dissolving vegetate again:
All forms that perish other forms supply,
(By turns we catch the vital breath, and die)
Like bubbles on the sea of matter born,
They rise, they break, and to that sea return.   *20*
Nothing is foreign: parts relate to whole;
One all-extending all-preserving Soul
Connects each being, greatest with the least;
Made beast in aid of Man, and Man of beast;
All served, all serving: nothing stands alone;   *25*
The chain holds on, and where it ends, unknown.
   Has God, thou fool! worked solely for thy good,
Thy joy, thy pastime, thy attire, thy food?
Who for thy table feeds the wanton° fawn,
For him as kindly spread the flowery lawn.   *80*
Is it for thee the lark ascends and sings?
Joy tunes his voice, joy elevates his wings.
Is it for thee the linnet pours his throat?
Loves of his own and raptures swell the note.
The bounding steed you pompously bestride,   *85*
Shares with his lord the pleasure and the pride.
Is thine alone the seed that strews the plain?
The birds of heaven shall vindicate° their grain.
Thine the full harvest of the golden year?
Part pays, and justly, the deserving steer: *40*
The hog, that ploughs not nor obeys thy call,
Lives on the labors of this lord of all.
   Know, Nature's children all divide her care;
The fur that warms a monarch, warmed a bear.
While Man exclaims, "See all things for my use!"   *45*
"See man for mine!" replies a pampered goose:
And just as short of reason he must fall,

---

12 **embrace** like "attracted" and "impelled," interpreting the mechanical motion as gestures of "love." 29 **wanton** untamed. 38 **vindicate** lay claim to.

Who thinks all made for one, not one for all.
    Grant that the powerful still the weak control;
50 Be Man the wit° and tyrant of the whole:
Nature that tyrant checks; he only knows,
And helps, another creature's wants and woes.
Say, will the falcon, stooping from above,
Smit with her varying plumage, spare the dove?
55 Admires the jay the insect's gilded wings?
Or hears the hawk when Philomela° sings?
Man cares for all: to birds he gives his woods,
To beasts his pastures, and to fish his floods;
For some his interest prompts him to provide,
60 For more his pleasure, yet for more his pride:
All feed on one vain patron, and enjoy
The extensive blessing of his luxury.
That very life his learnèd° hunger craves,
He saves from famine, from the savage° saves;
65 Nay, feasts the animal he dooms his feast,
And, till he ends the being, makes it blest;
Which sees no more the stroke, or feels the pain,
Than favored° Man by touch ethereal slain.
The creature had his feast of life before;
70 Thou too must perish, when thy feast is o'er!
    To each unthinking being, Heaven a friend,
Gives not the useless knowledge of its end:
To Man imparts it; but with such a view
As, while he dreads it, makes him hope it too:
75 The hour concealed, and so remote the fear,
Death still draws nearer, never seeming near.
Great standing miracle! that Heaven assigned
Its only thinking thing this turn of mind.
    II.   Whether with Reason, or with Instinct blest,
80 Know, all enjoy that power which suits them best;
To bliss alike by that direction tend,
And find the means proportioned to their end.
Say, where full Instinct is the unerring guide,

---

50 **wit** only intellectual being. 56 **Philomela** the nightingale. 63 **learnèd** artificial, not arising from nature. 64 **savage** wild animal. 68 **favored** those struck by lightning were held as sacred among some people.

What Pope or Council° can they need beside?
Reason, however able, cool at best,   *85*
Cares not for service, or but serves when pressed,°
Stays till we call, and then not often near;
But honest Instinct comes a volunteer;
Sure never to o'ershoot, but just to hit,
While still too wide or short is human wit;   *90*
Sure by quick Nature happiness to gain,
Which heavier Reason labors at in vain.
This too serves always, Reason never long;
One must go right, the other may go wrong.
See then the acting and comparing powers   *95*
One in their nature, which are two in ours,
And Reason raise o'er Instinct as you can,
In this 'tis God directs, in that 'tis Man.
    Who taught the nations of the field and wood
To shun their poison, and to choose their food?   *100*
Prescient, the tides or tempests to withstand,
Build on the wave, or arch beneath the sand?°
Who made the spider parallels design,
Sure as Demoivre,° without rule or line?
Who bid the stork, Columbus-like, explore   *105*
Heavens not his own, and worlds unknown before?
Who calls the council, states the certain day,
Who forms the phalanx, and who points the way?
    III.   God in the nature of each being founds
Its proper bliss, and sets its proper bounds: *110*
But as he framed a Whole, the Whole to bless,
On mutual wants built mutual happiness:
So from the first eternal Order ran,
And creature linked to creature, man to man.
Whate'er of life all-quickening aether° keeps,   *115*
Or breathes through air, or shoots beneath the deeps,
Or pours profuse on earth, one nature feeds

---

84 **Pope or Council** the latter claiming infallibility. 86 **pressed**
forced into service rather than a "volunteer" (line 88). 102 **Build
. . . sand** nesting on the waves, as the halcyon was believed to do,
or in the sand, as the kingfisher does. 104 **Demoivre** an eminent
French mathematician. 115 **all-quickening aether** thought of as the
divine breath that gives life to all things.

The vital flame, and swells the genial° seeds.
Not Man alone, but all that roam the wood,
120　Or wing the sky, or roll along the flood,
Each loves itself, but not itself alone,
Each sex desires alike, till two are one.
Nor ends the pleasure with the fierce embrace;
They love themselves, a third time, in their race.
125　Thus beast and bird their common charge attend,
The mothers nurse it, and the sires defend;
The young dismissed to wander earth or air,
There stops the Instinct, and there ends the care;
The link dissolves, each seeks a fresh embrace,
130　Another love succeeds, another race.
A longer care Man's helpless kind demands;
That longer care contracts more lasting bands:
Reflection, Reason, still the ties improve,
At once extend the interest, and the love;
135　With choice we fix, with sympathy we burn;
Each Virtue in each Passion takes its turn;
And still new needs, new helps, new habits rise,
That graft benevolence on charities.°
Still as one brood, and as another rose,
140　These natural love maintained, habitual those:
The last, scarce ripened into perfect Man,
Saw helpless him from whom their life began:
Memory and forecast just returns engage,
That pointed back to youth, this on to age:
145　While pleasure, gratitude, and hope, combined,
Still spread the interest, and preserved the kind.
　　IV.　Nor think, in NATURE'S STATE they blindly trod;
The state of Nature° was the reign of God:
Self-love and Social at her birth began,
150　Union the bond of all things, and of Man.
Pride then was not; nor Arts, that Pride to aid;
Man walked with beast, joint tenant of the shade;

118 **genial** procreative.　138 **benevolence on charities** virtuous habits
of fellow-feeling on instinctive or natural affections.　148 **The state
of Nature** rejecting Thomas Hobbes' view of the original state of
nature as a state of war in which each man was a "wolf to man"
and human life was "nasty, brutish, and short"; social love is not,
for Pope, artificial, but natural (line 149).

The same his table, and the same his bed;
No murder clothed him, and no murder fed.
In the same temple, the resounding wood,   *155*
All vocal beings hymned their equal° God:
The shrine with gore unstained, with gold undressed,
Unbribed, unbloody,° stood the blameless priest:
Heaven's attribute was Universal Care,
And Man's prerogative to rule, but spare.   *160*
Ah! how unlike the man of times to come!
Of half that live the butcher and the tomb;°
Who, foe to Nature, hears the general groan,
Murders their species and betrays his own.
But just disease to luxury succeeds,   *165*
And every death its own avenger breeds;
The Fury-passions from that blood began,
And turned on Man a fiercer savage, Man.
   See him from Nature rising slow to Art!
To copy Instinct then was Reason's part;   *170*
Thus then to Man the voice of Nature spake—
"Go, from the creatures thy instructions take:
Learn from the birds what food the thickets yield;
Learn from the beasts the physic° of the field;
Thy arts of building from the bee° receive;   *175*
Learn of the mole to plough, the worm° to weave;
Learn of the little nautilus° to sail,
Spread the thin oar, and catch the driving gale.
Here too all forms of social union find,
And hence let Reason, late, instruct Mankind: *180*
Here subterranean works and cities see;
There towns aerial on the waving tree.
Learn each small people's genius, policies,
The Ant's republic, and the realm of Bees;°
How those in common all their wealth bestow,   *185*

156 **equal** common, impartial.   158 **unbloody** not yet sacrificing animals or fellowmen.   162 **butcher . . . tomb** slayer and devourer.   174 **physic** medicinal herbs.   175 **bee** the architect of honeycombed hives.   176 **worm** silkworm.   177 **nautilus** believed to swim on the back of their shells, which resemble the hulks of ships, to extend a membrane between as a sail, and to use their other feet as oars.   184 **The Ant's . . . Bees** seen as democratic or socalistic and monarchical respectively, in the next four lines.

And anarchy without confusion know;
And these for ever, though a monarch reign,
Their separate cells and properties maintain.
Mark what unvaried laws preserve each state,
190 Laws wise as Nature, and as fixed as Fate.
In vain thy Reason finer webs shall draw,
Entangle Justice in her net of Law,
And right, too rigid, harden into wrong;
Still for the strong too weak, the weak too strong.
195 Yet go! and thus o'er all the creatures sway,
Thus let the wiser make the rest obey,
And, for those Arts mere Instinct could afford,
Be crowned as monarchs, or as Gods adored."
    V. Great Nature spoke; observant men obeyed;
200 Cities were built, societies were made:
Here rose one little state; another near
Grew by like means, and joined, through love or fear.
Did here the trees with ruddier burdens bend,
And there the streams in purer rills descend?
205 What War could ravish, Commerce could bestow,
And he returned a friend, who came a foe.
Converse and Love mankind might strongly draw,
When Love was Liberty, and Nature Law.
Thus states were formed; the name of King unknown,
210 Till common interest placed the sway in one.
'Twas Virtue only (or in arts or arms,
Diffusing blessings, or averting harms)
The same which in a sire the sons obeyed,
A prince the father of a people made.
215   VI. Till then, by Nature crowned, each patriarch
        sate,
King, priest, and parent of his growing state;
On him, their second Providence, they hung,
Their law his eye, their oracle his tongue.
He from the wondering° furrow called the food,
220 Taught to command the fire, control the flood,
Draw forth the monsters of the abyss profound,
Or fetch the aërial eagle to the ground.

219 **wondering** sharing in the amazement of the people.

Till drooping, sickening, dying they began
Whom they revered as God to mourn as Man:
Then, looking up from sire to sire, explored°   *225*
One great first father, and that first adored.
Or plain tradition that this All begun,°
Conveyed unbroken faith from sire to son,
The worker from the work distinct was known,
And simple Reason never sought but one: *230*
Ere wit oblique° had broke that steady light,
Man, like his Maker, saw that all was right,°
To Virtue, in the paths of Pleasure, trod,
And owned a Father when he owned a God.
Love all the faith, and all the allegiance then;   *235*
For Nature knew no right divine° in Men,
No ill could fear in God; and understood
A sovereign being but a sovereign good.
True faith, true policy,° united ran,
This was but love of God, and this of Man.   *240*
   Who first taught souls enslaved, and realms undone,
The enormous° faith of many made for one;°
That proud exception to all Nature's laws,
To invert the world, and counterwork its Cause?°
Force first made Conquest, and that conquest, Law;   *245*
Till Superstition taught the tyrant awe,
Then shared the tyranny, then lent it aid,
And gods of conquerors, slaves of subjects made:
She,° midst the lightning's blaze, and thunder's sound,
When rocked the mountains, and when groaned the   *250*
      ground,

225 **explored** discovered by inference.   227 **this All begun** the
world was created rather than subsisted eternally, a theistic rather
than a pantheistic view (see lines 229–30).   231 **wit oblique** pris-
matically breaking the "steady light"; see *Essay on Criticism*, II, 2,
232 **saw . . . right** Cf. Genesis 1:21: "And God saw every thing that
he had made, and, behold, it was very good."   236 **right divine**
power conferred upon specific men by God, as was claimed by the
divine right of kings.   239 **policy** government.   242 **enormous** mon-
strous.   242 **many made for one** "In this Aristotle placeth the dif-
ference between a King and a tyrant, that the first supposeth him-
self made for the people, the other that the people are made for
him" (Warburton, citing *Politics*, V. 10).   244 **To invert . . . Cause**
i.e., repudiating God: design as presented in III, 22–5, 111–12.   249
She superstition.

She taught the weak to bend, the proud to pray,
To Power unseen, and mightier far than they:
She, from the rending earth and bursting skies,
Saw Gods descend, and fiends infernal rise:
255 Here fixed the dreadful, there the blest abodes;
Fear made her Devils, and weak Hope her Gods;
Gods partial, changeful, passionate, unjust,
Whose attributes were rage, revenge, or lust;
Such as the souls of cowards might conceive,
260 And, formed like tyrants, tyrants would believe.°
Zeal° then, not charity, became the guide,
And hell was built on spite, and heaven on pride.
Then sacred seemed the ethereal vault no more;
Altars grew marble then, and reeked with gore:
265 Then first the flamen tasted living food;
Next his grim idol smeared with human blood;°
With Heaven's own thunders shook the world below,
And played the God an engine on his foe.°
So drives Self-love, through just and through unjust,
270 To one man's power, ambition, lucre, lust:
The same Self-love, in all, becomes the cause
Of what restrains him, Government and Laws.
For, what one likes if others like as well,
What serves one will,° when many wills rebel?
275 How shall he keep, what, sleeping or awake,
A weaker may surprise, a stronger take?
His safety must his liberty restrain:
All join to guard what each desires to gain.
Forced into virtue thus by self-defense,
280 Even kings learned justice and benevolence:
Self-love forsook the path it first pursued,

253–60 **She . . . believe** a religion "grounded not on love but fear."
The "superstitious man looks on the great Father of all as a tyrant.
. . . Accordingly he serves his Maker but as slaves do their tyrants,
with a gloomy savage zeal against his fellow creatures . . . at the
same time he trembles with the dread of being ill-used himself"
(Pope, cited by Mack, Twickenham edition, III, i, 117–18). 261
zeal fanaticism. 266 **smeared . . . blood** Cf. *Paradise Lost*, I,
392–3: "First Moloch, horrid King, besmear'd with blood/Of
human sacrifice. . . ." 268 **And played . . . foe** i.e., turn God into
a piece of artillery, an instrument of man's will and vengeance.
274 **What . . . will** Of what force is one will?

And found the private in the public good.
   'Twas then, the studious head or generous mind,
Follower of God or friend of humankind,
Poet or patriot, rose but to restore   285
The faith and moral,° Nature gave before;
Relumed her ancient light, not kindled new;
If not God's image, yet his shadow drew:
Taught power's due use to people and to kings,
Taught nor to slack, nor strain its tender strings,°   290
The less, or greater, set so justly true,
That touching one must strike° the other too;
Till jarring° interests of themselves create
The according music of a well-mixed state.°
Such is the world's great harmony, that springs   295
From order, union, full consent of things!
Where small and great, where weak and mighty, made
To serve, not suffer, strengthen, not invade,
More powerful each as needful to the rest,
And, in proportion as it blesses, blest,   300
Draw to one point, and to one center bring
Beast, Man, or Angel, Servant, Lord, or King,
   For forms of government let fools contest;
Whate'er is best administered is best:°
For modes of faith, let graceless° zealots fight;   305
His can't be wrong whose life is in the right:
In faith and hope the world will disagree,
But all mankind's concern is charity:°
All must be false that thwart this one great end,
And all of God, that bless mankind or mend.   *310*

286 **moral** moral principles, as in III, 235–40.   290 **its tender strings**
of musical instruments, where harmony was a common figure for
political structure, as in lines 294–5.   292 **strike** cause to reverber-
ate.   293 **jarring** conflicting, discordant.   294 **well-mixed state** The
mixed state was conceived as a balance of the power of the One
(King), the Few (Lords), and the Many (Commons); such a balance
was believed to give the state the stability to endure and withstand
fluctuations among controlling factions.   303–4 **For forms . . . is**
best Pope later explained that these lines did not mean "that no one
form of government is, in itself, better than another . . . but that no
form of government, however excellent or preferable in itself, can
be sufficient to make a people happy, unless it be administered
with integrity."   305 **graceless** (1) crude (2) without divine grace.
308 **charity** Cf. I Corinthians 13:13.

Man, like the generous vine,° supported lives;
The strength he gains is from the embrace he gives.
On their own axis as the planets run,°
Yet make at once their circle round the sun:
315 So two consistent motions act the soul;
And one regards itself, and one the Whole.
    Thus God and Nature linked the general frame,
And bade Self-love and Social be the same.

EPISTLE IV

OH HAPPINESS! our being's end and aim!
Good, pleasure, ease, content! whate'er thy name:
That something still which prompts the eternal sigh,
For which we bear to live or dare to die,
5   Which still so near us, yet beyond us lies,
O'erlooked, seen double,° by the fool, and wise.
Plant of celestial seed! if dropped below,
Say, in what mortal soil thou deignst to grow?
Fair opening to some court's propitious shine,
10   Or deep with diamonds in the flaming mine?°
Twined with the wreaths Parnassian laurels yield,
Or reaped in iron harvests of the field?°
Where grows?—where grows it not? If vain our toil,
We ought to blame the culture, not the soil:
15   Fixed to no spot is Happiness sincere,°
'Tis nowhere to be found, or everywhere;
'Tis never to be bought, but always free,
And fled from monarchs, ST. JOHN! dwells with thee.

311 **generous vine** as in traditional fables of the love of vine and
elm, "generous" in the giving of oneself to another.   313 **run** rotate.
6 **O'erlooked, seen double** neglected where it is to be found, magni-
fied in other places.   10 **deep . . . mine** referring to the belief that
minerals were organisms ripened by the sun, hence blazing from
within beneath the ground.   12 **field** battlefield.   15 **sincere** pure,
genuine.

   I. Ask of the learned the way, the learned are blind,
This bids to serve, and that to shun° mankind;   *20*
Some place the bliss in action, some in ease,
Those call it pleasure, and contentment these;
Some sunk to beasts, find pleasure end in pain;
Some swelled to gods, confess even virtue vain;
Or indolent, to each extreme they fall,   *25*
To trust in every thing, or doubt of all.
   Who thus define it, say they more or less
Than this, that Happiness is Happiness?
   II. Take Nature's path, and mad Opinion's leave,
All states can reach it, and all heads conceive;   *30*
Obvious her goods, in no extreme they dwell,
There needs but thinking right, and meaning well;
And mourn our various portions as we please,
Equal is common sense, and common ease.°
   Remember, Man, "the Universal Cause   *35*
Acts not by partial, but by general laws;"°
And makes what Happiness we justly call
Subsist not in the good of one, but all.
There's not a blessing individuals find,
But some way leans and hearkens to the kind.   *40*
No bandit fierce, no tyrant mad with pride,
No caverned hermit, rests self-satisfied.
Who most to shun or hate Mankind pretend,
Seek an admirer, or would fix a friend.
Abstract° what others feel, what others think,   *45*
All pleasures sicken, and all glories sink;
Each has his share; and who would more obtain,
Shall find, the pleasure pays not half the pain.
   ORDER is Heaven's first law; and this confest,
Some are, and must be, greater than the rest,   *50*
More rich, more wise; but who infers from hence
That such are happier, shocks all common sense.
Heaven to Mankind impartial we confess,
If all are equal in their Happiness:
But mutual wants this Happiness increase,   *55*

20 **to serve ... to shun** as Stoics or Epicureans might. 34 **common ease** peace of mind. 35–6 **the Universal Cause ... general laws** Cf. II, 249–56; III, 1–2, 111–14. 45 **Abstract** remove.

All Nature's difference keeps all Nature's peace.
Condition,° circumstance is not the thing;
Bliss is the same in subject or in king,
In who obtain defense, or who defend,
60 In him who is, or him who finds a friend:
Heaven breathes through every member of the whole
One common blessing, as one common soul.
But Fortune's gifts if each alike possessed,
And each were equal, must not all contest?
65 If then to all men Happiness was meant,
God in externals could not place content.
    Fortune her gifts may variously dispose,
And these be happy called, unhappy those;
But Heaven's just balance equal will appear,
70 While those are placed in hope, and these in fear:
Not present good or ill, the joy or curse,
But future views of better, or of worse.
    Oh sons of earth! attempt ye still to rise,
By mountains piled on mountains, to the skies?
75 Heaven still with laughter the vain toil surveys,
And buries madmen in the heaps they raise.°
    III.   Know, all the good that individuals find,
Or God and Nature meant to mere Mankind,
Reason's whole pleasure, all the joys of Sense,
80 Lie in three words, Health, Peace, and Competence.°
But Health consists with Temperance alone;
And Peace, oh Virtue! Peace is all thy own.
The good or bad the gifts of Fortune gain,
But these less taste° them, as they worse obtain.°
85 Say, in pursuit of profit or delight,
Who risk the most, that take wrong means, or right?
Of Vice or Virtue, whether blest or curst,
Which meets contempt, or which compassion first?
Count all the advantage prosperous Vice attains,

57 **Condition** rank, class. 73–6 **Oh sons . . . raise** an allusion to the Titans' war against the Olympian deities where they heaped Mt. Ossa upon Mt. Pelion in order to reach heaven; also to the building of the Tower of Babel, upon which "Great laughter was in Heav'n" (*Paradise Lost*, XII, 59). 80 **Competence** sufficiency of goods to support life. 84 **taste** enjoy. 84 **worse obtain** obtain by baser means.

'Tis but what Virtue flies from and disdains: 90
And grant the bad what happiness they would,
One they must want,° which is, to pass for good.
   Oh blind to truth, and God's whole scheme below,
Who fancy bliss to Vice, to Virtue woe!
Who sees and follows that great scheme the best,   95
Best knows the blessing, and will most be blest.
But fools the Good alone unhappy call,
For ills or accidents that chance to all.
See FALKLAND° dies, the virtuous and the just!
See godlike TURENNE° prostrate on the dust!   100
See SIDNEY° bleeds amid the martial strife!
Was this their Virtue, or contempt of life?
Say, was it Virtue, more though Heaven ne'er gave,
Lamented DIGBY!° sunk thee to the grave?
Tell me, if Virtue made the son expire,   105
Why, full of days and honor, lives the sire?
Why drew Marseilles' good bishop° purer breath,
When Nature sickened, and each gale was death?
Or why so long (in life if long can be)
Lent Heaven a parent° to the poor and me?   110
   IV.   What makes all physical or moral ill?
There deviates Nature, and here wanders Will.
God sends not ill; if rightly understood,
Or partial ill is universal good,
Or change admits, or Nature lets it fall,°   115
Short and but rare, till Man improved it all.°
We just as wisely might of Heaven complain
That righteous Abel was destroyed by Cain,
As that the virtuous son is ill at ease

---

92 **want** miss. 99 **Falkland** Lucius Cary, Second Viscount Falkland, a man universally admired for his gifts and goodness, killed fighting for Charles I in 1643. 100 **Turenne** the French marshal and hero slain in battle in 1675. 101 **Sidney** Sir Philip Sidney, courtier, poet, patron, killed at Zutphen in 1586. 104 **Digby** the Hon. Robert Digby who died at forty and was celebrated in an epitaph by Pope; his father was seventy-four at the time Pope wrote. 107 **Marseilles' good bishop** François de Belsunce, who performed notable service in the plague of 1720–21, and who lived on until 1755. 110 **a parent** Pope's mother died in 1734 at the age of ninety-one. 115 **Or change ... fall** See I, 145–50. 116 **till Man ... all** until man increased the scale of evil through his "will."

120 When his lewd father gave the dire disease.
Think we, like some weak prince, the Eternal Cause,
Prone for his favorites to reverse his laws?
Shall burning Etna, if a sage° requires,
Forget to thunder, and recall her fires?
125 On air or sea new motions be imprest,
Oh blameless Bethel!° to relieve thy breast?
When the loose mountain trembles from on high,
Shall gravitation cease, if you go by?
Or some old temple, nodding to its fall,
130 For Chartres' head° reserve the hanging wall?
    V. But still this world (so fitted for the knave)
Contents us not. A better shall we have?
A kingdom of the Just then let it be:
But first consider how those Just agree.
135 The good must merit God's peculiar care;
But who, but God, can tell us who they are?
One thinks on Calvin Heaven's own spirit fell,
Another deems him instrument of hell;
If Calvin feel Heaven's blessing, or its rod,
140 This cries there is, and that, there is no God.
What shocks one part will edify the rest,
Nor with one system can they all be blest.
The very best will variously incline,
And what rewards your virtue, punish mine.
145 WHATEVER IS, IS RIGHT—This world, 'tis true,
Was made for Caesar—but for Titus too:
And which more blest? who chained his country,° say,
Or he° whose Virtue sighed to lose a day?
    "But sometimes Virtue starves, while Vice is fed."
150 What then? Is the reward of Virtue bread?
That, Vice may merit; 'tis the price of toil;
The knave deserves it, when he tills the soil,
The knave deserves it, when he tempts the main,
Where Folly fights for kings, or dives for gain.

123 **sage** the philosopher Empedocles, who perished in the crater of
Mt. Etna. 126 **Bethel** a friend of Pope who suffered from asthma.
130 **Chartres' head** a notorious scoundrel of the day; 147 **who . . .
country** Caesar. 148 **he** Titus as quoted by the historian Suetonius;
see II, 198.

The good man may be weak, be indolent,   *155*
Nor is his claim to plenty, but content.
But grant him riches, your demand is o'er?
"No—shall the good want health, the good want power?"
Add health and power, and every earthly thing;
"Why bounded power? why private? why no king?"   *160*
Nay, why external for internal given?
Why is not Man a God, and Earth a Heaven?
Who ask and reason thus, will scarce conceive
God gives enough, while he has more to give:
Immense the power, immense were the demand;   *165*
Say, at what part of nature will they stand?
    VI.   What nothing earthly gives, or can destroy,
The soul's calm sunshine, and the heartfelt joy,
Is Virtue's prize: a better would you fix?
Then give Humility a coach and six,   *170*
Justice a conqueror's sword, or Truth a gown,°
Or Public Spirit its great cure,° a Crown.
Weak, foolish man! will Heaven reward us there
With the same trash mad mortals wish for here?
The boy and man an individual makes,   *175*
Yet sighst thou now for apples and for cakes?
Go, like the Indian,° in another life
Expect thy dog, thy bottle, and thy wife:
As well as dream such trifles are assigned,
As toys and empires, for a godlike mind.   *180*
Rewards, that either would to Virtue bring
No joy, or be destructive of the thing:
How oft by these at sixty are undone
The virtues of a saint at twenty-one!
    To whom can riches give repute, or trust,   *185*
Content, or pleasure, but the Good and Just?
Judges and senates have been bought for gold,
Esteem and love were never to be sold.
Oh fool! to think God hates the worthy mind,
The lover and the love of humankind,   *190*
Whose life is healthful, and whose conscience clear;

171 **gown** academic or clerical. 172 **cure** care, change, remedy.
177 **like the Indian** See 1, 99–112.

Because he wants a thousand pounds a year.
   Honor and shame from no condition rise;
Act well your part, there all the honor lies.
195 Fortune in men has some small difference made,
One flaunts in rags, one flutters in brocade,
The cobbler aproned, and the parson gowned,
The friar hooded, and the monarch crowned.
"What differ more" (you cry) "than crown and cowl?"
200 I'll tell you, friend! a wise man and a fool.
You'll find, if once the monarch acts the monk,
Or, cobbler-like, the parson will be drunk,
Worth makes the man, and want of it, the fellow;°
The rest is all but leather or prunella.°
205   Stuck o'er with titles and hung round with strings,°
That thou mayst be by kings, or whores of kings.
Boast the pure blood of an illustrious race,
In quiet flow from Lucrece° to Lucrece;
But by your fathers' worth if yours you rate,
210 Count me those only who were good and great.°
Go! if your ancient, but ignoble blood
Has crept through scoundrels ever since the flood,
Go! and pretend your family is young;
Nor own, your fathers have been fools so long.
215 What can ennoble sots, or slaves, or cowards?
Alas! not all the blood of all the Howards.°
   Look next on Greatness; say where Greatness lies?
"Where, but among the heroes and the wise?"
Heroes are much the same, the point's agreed,
220 From Macedonia's madman° to the Swede;°
The whole strange purpose of their lives, to find
Or make, an enemy of all mankind!
Not one looks backward, onward still he goes,
Yet ne'er looks forward farther than his nose.

203 **fellow** rogue. 204 **leather or prunella** the cobbler's apron or
the parson's worsted gown. 205 **strings** ribbons, decorations. 208
Lucrece a chaste matron like the Roman victim of Tarquin's rape
who slew herself for shame. 210 **good and great** virtuous as well
as in public power. 216 **Howards** a family of highest rank and
great age. 220 **Macedonia's madman** Alexander the Great. 220
the Swede Charles XII of Sweden, whose short life included bril-
liant conquests and ultimate defeat at the hands of Peter the Great.

No less alike the politic and wise,   225
All sly slow things, with circumspective eyes:
Men in their loose unguarded hours they take,
Not that themselves are wise, but others weak.
But grant that those can conquer, these can cheat,
'Tis phrase absurd to call a villain great: 230
Who wickedly is wise, or madly brave,
Is but the more a fool, the more a knave.
Who noble ends by noble means obtains,
Or failing, smiles in exile or in chains,
Like good Aurelius° let him reign, or bleed   235
Like Socrates,° that man is great indeed.
     What's Fame? a fancied life in others' breath,
A thing beyond us, even before our death.
Just what you hear, you have, and what's unknown
The same (my Lord) if Tully's° or your own.   240
All that we feel of it begins and ends
In the small circle of our foes or friends;
To all beside as much an empty shade,
An Eugene° living, as a Caesar dead,
Alike or when, or where, they shone, or shine,   245
Or on the Rubicon, or on the Rhine.
A wit's a feather, and a chief a rod;°
An honest man's the noblest work of God.
Fame but from death a villain's name can save,
As justice tears his body from the grave,°   250
When what to oblivion better were resigned,
Is hung on high, to poison half mankind.
All fame is foreign, but of true desert;°
Plays round the head, but comes not to the heart:
One self-approving hour whole years outweighs   255
Of stupid starers, and of loud huzzas;

235 **Aurelius** Marcus Aurelius Antoninus, Roman emperor, whose
Meditations is a great work of Stoic philosophy. 236 **Socrates**
forced to drink hemlock, not a ruler but a victim of the state.
240 **Tully's** Cicero's. 244 **Eugene** Prince Eugene of Savoy, a mili-
tary hero of the day, who campaigned on the Rhine against the
French. 247 **A wit's . . . rod** A mere wit is no more than his quill,
a mere chief no more than his baton or truncheon. 250 **As Justice
. . . grave** e.g., the bodies of the judges of Charles I were exhumed
in 1661 and displayed on gallows. 253 **desert** merit.

And more true joy Marcellus° exiled feels,
Than Caesar with a senate at his heels.
    In Parts° superior what advantage lies?
260 Tell (for You° can) what is it to be wise?
'Tis but to know how little can be known;
To see all others' faults, and feel our own:
Condemned in business or in arts to drudge
Without a second,° or without a judge:
265 Truths would you teach, or save a sinking land?
All fear, none aid, you, and few understand.
Painful pre-eminence! yourself to view
Above life's weakness, and its comforts too.
    Bring then these blessings to a strict account,
270 Make fair deductions, see to what they mount.
How much of other each is sure to cost;
How each for other oft is wholly lost;
How inconsistent greater goods with these;
How sometimes life is risked, and always ease:
275 Think, and if still the things thy envy call,
Say, wouldst thou be the man to whom they fall?
To sigh for ribbands° if thou art so silly,
Mark how they grace Lord Umbra,° or Sir Billy:°
Is yellow dirt the passion of thy life?
280 Look but on Gripus,° or on Gripus' wife:
If Parts allure thee, think how Bacon° shined,
The wisest, brightest, meanest of mankind:
Or ravished with the whistling of a name,
See Cromwell,° damned to everlasting fame!
285 If all, united, thy ambition call,
From ancient story learn to scorn them all.
There, in the rich, the honored, famed, and great,
See the false scale of Happiness complete!
In hearts of kings, or arms of queens who lay,

257 **Marcellus** banished by Caesar for his loyalty to Pompey. 259 **Parts** abilities. 260 **You** Bolingbroke. 264 **second** supporter, near-equal. 277 **ribbands** decorations. 278 **Lord Umbra** "Lord Shad-ow," a nonentity. 278 **Sir Billy** any foolish nobleman. 280 **Gripus** a miser. 281 **Bacon** Sir Francis Bacon, revered as writer and phi-losopher, scorned for his dismissal from office on charges of bribery. 284 **Cromwell** Oliver Cromwell as rebel and perhaps tyrant.

How happy! those to ruin, these betray.°   290
Mark by what wretched steps their glory grows,
From dirt and seaweed as proud Venice rose;
In each how guilt and greatness equal ran,
And all that raised the Hero, sunk the Man.
Now Europe's laurels on their brows behold,   295
But stained with blood, or ill exchanged for gold:
Then see them broke with toils, or sunk in ease,
Or infamous for plundered provinces.
Oh wealth ill-fated! which no act of fame
E'er taught to shine, or sanctified from shame!   300
What greater bliss attends their close of life?
Some greedy minion,° or imperious wife,
The trophied arches, storied halls invade,
And haunt their slumbers in the pompous shade.
Alas! not dazzled with their noontide ray,   305
Compute the morn and evening to the day;
The whole amount of that enormous fame,
A tale, that blends their glory with their shame!
   VII.   Know then this truth (enough for Man to
       know)
"Virtue alone is Happiness below."   310
The only point where human bliss stands still,
And tastes the good without the fall to ill,
Where only° Merit constant pay receives,
Is blest in what it takes, and what it gives;
The joy unequalled, if its end it gain,   315
And if it lose, attended with no pain:
Without satiety, though e'er so blessed,
And but more relished as the more distressed:
The broadest mirth unfeeling Folly wears,
Less pleasing far than Virtue's very tears: 320
Good, from each object, from each place acquired,
For ever exercised, yet never tired;
Never elated, while one man's oppressed;
Never dejected, while another's blessed;
And where no wants, no wishes can remain,   325
Since but to wish more Virtue, is to gain.

290 **these betray** the monarchs are betrayed by the ambitious career-
ists.   302 **minion** favorite.   313 **where only** where alone.

See the sole bliss Heaven could on all bestow!
Which who but feels can taste, but thinks can know:
Yet poor with fortune, and with learning blind,
330 The bad must miss; the good, untaught, will find;
Slave to no sect, who takes no private road,
But looks through Nature up to Nature's God;
Pursues that Chain which links the immense design,
Joins heaven and earth, and mortal and divine;
335 Sees, that no being any bliss can know,
But touches some above, and some below;
Learns, from this union of the rising Whole,
The first, last purpose of the human soul;
And knows, where Faith, Law, Morals, all began,
340 All end, in LOVE OF GOD, and LOVE OF MAN.
For him alone, Hope leads from goal to goal,
And opens still, and opens on his soul,
Till lengthened on to Faith, and unconfined,
It pours the bliss that fills up all the mind.
345 He sees, why Nature plants in Man alone
Hope of known bliss, and Faith in bliss unknown:
(Nature, whose dictates to no other kind
Are given in vain, but what they seek they find)
Wise is her present; she connects in this
350 His greatest Virtue with his greatest Bliss,
At once his own bright prospect to be blest,
And strongest motive to assist the rest.
Self-love thus pushed to social, to divine,
Gives thee to make thy neighbor's blessing thine.
355 Is this too little for the boundless heart?
Extend it, let thy enemies have part:
Grasp the whole worlds of Reason, Life, and Sense,
In one close system of Benevolence:
Happier as kinder, in whate'er degree,
360 And height of Bliss but height of Charity.
God loves from whole to parts: but human soul
Must rise from individual to the whole.
Self-love but serves the virtuous mind to wake,
As the small pebble stirs the peaceful lake;
365 The center moved, a circle straight° succeeds,

365 **straight** straightway.

Another still, and still another spreads,
Friend, parent, neighbor, first it will embrace,
His country next; and next all human race;
Wide and more wide, the o'erflowings of the mind
Take every creature in, of every kind;   370
Earth smiles around, with boundless bounty blest,
And Heaven beholds its image in his breast.
    Come then, my Friend! my Genius!° come along,
Oh master of the poet, and the song!
And while the Muse now stoops, or now ascends,   375
To Man's low passions, or their glorious ends,
Teach me, like thee, in various nature wise,
To fall with dignity, with temper rise;
Formed by thy converse, happily to steer
From grave to gay, from lively to severe;   380
Correct with spirit, eloquent with ease,
Intent to reason, or polite to please.
Oh! while along the stream of time thy name
Expanded flies, and gathers all its fame,
Say, shall my little bark attendant sail,   385
Pursue the triumph, and partake the gale?
When statesmen, heroes, kings, in dust repose,
Whose sons shall blush their fathers were thy foes,
Shall then this verse to future age pretend°
Thou wert my guide, philosopher, and friend?   390
That urged by thee, I turned the tuneful art
From sounds to things, from fancy to the heart;
For Wit's false mirror held up Nature's light;
Showed erring Pride, WHATEVER IS, IS RIGHT;
That REASON, PASSION, answer one great aim;   395
That true SELF-LOVE and SOCIAL are the same;
That VIRTUE only makes our Bliss below;
And all our Knowledge is, OURSELVES TO KNOW.

---

373 Genius Bolingbroke as guardian spirit.   **389 pretend** assert.

TO RICHARD BOYLE, EARL OF BURLINGTON:°

OF THE USE OF RICHES

(1731)

'Tis strange, the miser should his cares employ
To gain those riches he can ne'er enjoy:
Is it less strange, the prodigal should waste
His wealth, to purchase what he ne'er can taste?
5 Not for himself he sees, or hears, or eats;
Artists must choose his pictures, music, meats:
He buys for Topham,° drawings and designs,
For Pembroke,° statues, dirty gods, and coins;
Rare monkish manuscripts for Hearne° alone,
10 And books for Mead, and butterflies for Sloane.°
Think we all these are for himself! no more
Than his fine wife, alas! or finer whore.

To . . . **Burlington** Richard Boyle, Third Earl of Burlington (1695–1753), studied architecture in Italy and upon his return designed buildings himself, commissioned works by others, and published the designs of Inigo Jones and Andrea Palladio. In opposition to the baroque of Wren and later Vanbrugh, he promoted a more severe Roman classicism and spent great sums on public buildings of such design. 7 **Topham** "A gentleman famous for a judicious collection of drawings" (Pope). 8 **Pembroke** The Earl of Pembroke had large collections at Wilton House. 9 **Hearne** an eminent medievalist and editor of early English chronicles. 10 **Mead . . . Sloane** "Two eminent physicians; the one had an excellent library, the other the finest collection in Europe of natural curiosities; both men of great learning and humanity" (Pope).

For what has Virro painted, built, and planted?
Only to show, how many tastes he wanted.°
What brought Sir Visto's ill got wealth to waste?   *15*
Some demon whispered, "Visto! have a taste."
Heaven visits with a taste the wealthy fool,
And needs no rod° but Ripley° with a rule.°
See! sportive fate, to punish awkward pride,
Bids Bubo° build, and sends him such a guide: *20*
A standing sermon, at each year's expense,
That never coxcomb° reached magnificence!°
   You° show us, Rome was glorious, not profuse,
And pompous buildings once were things of use.
Yet shall (my Lord) your just, your noble rules   *25*
Fill half the land with imitating fools;
Who random drawings from your sheets shall take,
And of one beauty many blunders make;
Load some vain church with old theatric state,°
Turn arcs of triumph° to a garden gate;   *30*
Reverse your ornaments, and hang them all
On some patched dog-hole eked with ends of wall;
Then clap four slices of pilaster° on't,
That, laced with bits of rustic,° makes a front.°
Shall call the winds through long arcades to roar,   *35*

---

14 wanted lacked.   **18 rod** punishment.   **18 Ripley** Thomas Ripley,
a mediocre but politically favored architect; as Pope put it, "a car-
penter, employed by a first Minister who raised him into an archi-
tect, without any genius in the art."   **18 rule** (1) carpenter's rule, as
a form of "rod" (2) misapplied principle, as in lines 25–6.   **20 Bubo**
Latin for owl, also a reference to Bubb Dodington who spent
£140,000 for a country house designed by Vanbrugh.   **22 coxcomb**
fop, vain fool.   **22 magnificence** not merely splendor, but according
to Aristotle (*Nicomachean Ethics*, IV, 2), expenditure on public ob-
jects rather than oneself; tasteful generosity.   **23 You** Burlington,
then publishing the *Antiquities of Rome* by the great Italian archi-
tect, Palladio, and other architectural drawings, whose "sheets"
(line 27) might be pillaged for decorative details by those without
a sense of "use" (line 24).   **29 theatric state** (1) the inappropriate
details of a Roman theatre (2) baroque theatricality based on clas-
sical details.   **30 arcs of triumph** Roman triumphal arches reduced
in scale as pompous ornament.   **33 pilaster** columns attached to the
wall.   **34 rustic** rustication, the sharp definition of massive building
stones for an effect of rough strength.   **34 front** "frontispiece," the
formal entrance to a building.

Proud to catch cold at a Venetian door;°
Conscious they act a true Palladian part,
And, if they starve,° they starve by rules of art.
    Oft have you hinted to your brother peer,
40 A certain truth, which many buy too dear:
Something there is more needful than expense,
And something previous even to taste—'tis sense:
Good sense, which only is the gift of Heaven,
And though no science, fairly worth the seven:
45 A light, which in yourself you must perceive;
Jones° and Le Nôtre° have it not to give.
    To build, to plant, whatever you intend,
To rear the column, or the arch to bend,
To swell the terrace, or to sink the grot;°
50 In all, let Nature never be forgot.
But treat the goddess like a modest fair,
Nor overdress, nor leave her wholly bare;
Let not each beauty everywhere be spied,
Where half the skill is decently° to hide.
55 He gains all points, who pleasingly confounds,
Surprises, varies, and conceals the bounds.°
    Consult the genius of the place° in all;
That tells the waters or to rise, or fall;
Or helps the ambitious hill the heavens to scale,
60 Or scoops in circling theatres° the vale;
Calls in the country, catches opening glades,
Joins willing woods, and varies shades from shades;
Now breaks, or now directs, the intending lines;

---

36 **Venetian door** Palladio invented the Venetian window or door, an arched center opening with two smaller rectangular windows on either side.   38 **starve** because of (1) cost or (2) the great distances food had to be brought.   46 **Jones** Inigo Jones, the distinguished English architect of the late Renaissance.   46 **Le Nôtre** the great French designer of formal gardens, including those at Versailles.   49 **grot** grotto, artificial cave.   54 **decently** (1) modestly (2) appropriately.   56 **bounds** Pope was one of the earliest and most influential supporters of the so-called English garden, which sought to avoid formal symmetry and sharp geometrical pattern for the sake of greater naturalness.   57 **genius of the place** (1) the character of the natural landscape (2) the tutelary deity who traditionally inhabited each place and preserved it from violation.   60 **circling theatres** the graceful curves of classical amphitheatres.

Paints° as you plant, and, as you work, designs.
    Still follow sense, of every art the soul,   *65*
Parts answering parts shall slide into a whole,
Spontaneous beauties all around advance,
Start even from difficulty, strike from chance;
Nature shall join you; time shall make it grow
A work to wonder at—perhaps a Stowe.°   *70*
    Without it, proud Versailles!° thy glory falls;
And Nero's terraces° desert their walls:
The vast parterres° a thousand hands shall make,
Lo! Cobham° comes, and floats° them with a lake:
Or cut wide views through mountains to the plains,°   *75*
You'll wish your hill or sheltered seat° again.
Even in an ornament its place remark,
Nor in an Hermitage set Dr. Clarke.°
    Behold Villario's ten years' toil complete;
His quincunx° darkens, his espaliers° meet;   *80*
The wood supports the plain, the parts unite,
And strength of shade contends with strength of light;
A waving glow the bloomy beds display,
Blushing in bright diversities of day,
With silver-quivering rills meandered o'er—   *85*
Enjoy them, you! Villario can no more;
Tired of the scene parterres and fountains yield,
He finds at last he better likes a field.

64 **paints** (1) colors (2) shapes into picturesque composition, like that of landscape paintings.   70 **Stowe** the house and gardens of Lord Cobham, of which Pope wrote, "If anything under Paradise could set me beyond all earthly cogitations, Stowe might do it." 71 **Versailles** formal as opposed to natural gardens.   72 **Nero's terraces** the elaborate works of the Golden House of the Roman Emperor.   73 **parterres** formal terraces.   74 **Cobham** as at Stowe.   74 **floats** floods.   75 "This was done . . . by a wealthy citizen . . . by which means (merely to overlook a dead plain) he let in the north-wind upon his house and parterre, which were before adorned and defended by beautiful woods" (Pope).   76 **seat** country house.   78 **Hermitage . . . Dr. Clarke** Samuel Clarke was a liberal theologian and philosopher, rationalistic and somewhat unorthodox; hence the impropriety of a "hermitage." But that is also the name of an ornamental building in Richmond Park, where Queen Caroline placed a bust of her favorite, Dr. Clarke, as well as of Locke, Newton, and others.   80 **quincunx** a planting of five trees, one in the center of the square formed by the others.   80 **espaliers** trees fastened to a garden wall.

      Through his young woods how pleased Sabinus strayed,
90 Or sat delighted in the thickening shade,
    With annual joy the reddening shoots to greet,
    Or see the stretching branches long to meet!
    His son's fine taste an opener vista loves,
    Foe to the dryads° of his father's groves;
95 One boundless green, or flourished carpet° views,
    With all the mournful family of yews;°
    The thriving plants ignoble broomsticks made,
    Now sweep those alleys they were born to shade.
      At Timon's Villa let us pass a day,
100 Where all cry out, "What sums are thrown away!"
    So proud, so grand; of that stupendous air,
    Soft and agreeable come never there.
    Greatness, with Timon, dwells in such a draught
    As brings all Brobdingnag° before your thought.
105 To compass this, his building is a town,
    His pond an ocean, his parterre a down:
    Who but must laugh, the master when he sees,
    A puny insect, shivering at a breeze!
    Lo, what huge heaps of littleness around!
110 The whole, a labored quarry above ground.
    Two cupids squirt before: a lake behind
    Improves the keenness of the northern wind.°
    His gardens next your admiration call,
    On every side you look, behold the wall!
115 No pleasing intricacies intervene,
    No artful wildness to perplex the scene;
    Grove nods at grove, each alley has a brother,
    And half the platform just reflects the other.
    The suffering eye inverted Nature sees,
120 Trees cut to statues, statues thick as trees;°

---

94 **dryads** tree nymphs.　95 **flourished carpet** a terrace elaborated in
scrolled beds as opposed to the opposite vice, the nakedness of the
"boundless green."　96 **family of yews** the typical planting of ceme-
teries, here forming "pyramids of dark green continually repeated,
not unlike a funeral procession" (Pope).　104 **Brobdingnag** the land
of giants in the second voyage of Swift's *Gulliver's Travels.*　112
northern wind See note to line 75.　120 Referring to the topiary art
of trimming trees or hedges into sculpturesque shapes and to the
common overuse of statuary in gardens.

With here a fountain, never to be played;
And there a summerhouse, that knows no shade;
Here Amphitrite° sails through myrtle bowers;
There gladiators fight, or die in flowers;
Unwatered see the drooping sea-horse mourn, 125
And swallows roost in Nilus' dusty urn.°
   My Lord advances with majestic mien,
Smit with the mighty pleasure, to be seen:
But soft—by regular approach—not yet—
First through the length of yon hot terrace sweat; 130
And when up ten steep slopes you've dragged your
     thighs,
Just at his study door he'll bless your eyes.
   His study! with what authors is it stored?
In books, not authors, curious is my Lord;
To all their dated backs° he turns you round: 135
These Aldus° printed, those Du Sueil° has bound.
Lo, some are vellum, and the rest as good
For all his Lordship knows, but they are wood.
For Locke or Milton 'tis in vain to look,
These shelves admit not any modern book. 140
   And now the chapel's silver bell you hear,
That summons you to all the pride of prayer:
Light quirks of music, broken and uneven,
Make the soul dance upon a jig to Heaven.
On painted ceilings you devoutly stare, 145
Where sprawl the saints of Verrio or Laguerre,°
On gilded clouds in fair expansion lie,
And bring all Paradise before your eye.
To rest, the cushion and soft dean invite,°

123 **Amphitrite,** a sea nymph, wife of Poseidon and mother of Triton. 126 **Nilus' . . . urn** For the river-god's urn, see Windsor *Forest,* line 332 and note. 135 **dated backs** early editions with dates stamped in gold on the binding: "many delight chiefly in the elegance of the print or the binding; some have carried it so far as to cause the upper shelves to be filled with painted books of wood" (Pope). 136 **Aldus** the great Venetian printer of the Renaissance. 136 **Du Sueil** Parisian binder of early 18th century. 146 **Verrio or Laguerre** fashionable court painters, here shown in a baroque vein. 149 Pope cites an actual Dean of Peterborough Cathedral who referred in a sermon to "a place which he did not think fit to name in that courtly audience."

150 Who never mentions Hell to ears polite.
        But hark! the chiming clocks to dinner call;
    A hundred footsteps scrape the marble hall:
    The rich buffet well-colored serpents grace,
    And gaping tritons° spew to wash your face.
155 Is this a dinner? this a genial room?
    No, 'tis a temple, and a hecatomb.°
    A solemn sacrifice, performed in state,
    You drink by measure, and to minutes eat.
    So quick retires each flying course, you'd swear
160 Sancho's dread Doctor and his wand° were there.
    Between each act the trembling salvers ring,
    From soup to sweet wine, and God bless the King.°
    In plenty starving, tantalized in state,
    And complaisantly helped to all I hate,
165 Treated, caressed, and tired, I take my leave,
    Sick of his civil pride from morn to eve;
    I curse such lavish cost, and little skill,
    And swear no day was ever passed so ill.
        Yet hence the poor are clothed, the hungry fed;
170 Health to himself, and to his infants bread
    The laborer bears: what his hard heart denies,
    His charitable vanity supplies.°
        Another age shall see the golden ear°
    Embrown the slope, and nod on the parterre,
175 Deep harvests bury all his pride has planned,
    And laughing Ceres° reassume° the land.
        Who then shall grace, or who improve the soil?

153–4 **serpents . . . tritons** "Taxes the incongruity of ornaments . . .
where an open mouth ejects the water into a fountain, or where the
shocking images of serpents, etc., are introduced in grottos or buf-
fets" (Pope).   154 **tritons** sea deities, with a human form in upper
part of the body and that of a fish in the lower.   156 **hecatomb**
slaughter of a hundred oxen.   160 **Sancho's . . . wand** Cervantes,
Don Quixote, Pt. II, Ch. 47, where Sancho's doctor forbids him all
the food he ravenously contemplates and causes each dish to be
whisked away as he touches it with a wand.   162 that is, from the
begining to the end of the meal, ending with a toast in port.   169–72
Cf. *Essay on Man*, II, 230–7, and *To a Lady*, lines 149–50.   173 **ear**
of wheat.   176 **laughing Ceres** the goddess of agriculture, (1) cheer-
fully bounteous (2) scornful of Timon's unnatural art.   176 **reas-
sume** regain possession, as a monarch reassumes a kingdom.

Who plants like Bathurst,° or who builds like Boyle.°
'Tis use alone that sanctifies expense,·
And splendor borrows all her rays from sense.   *180*
   His father's acres who enjoys in peace,
Or makes his neighbors glad, if he increase:
Whose cheerful tenants bless their yearly toil,
Yet to their Lord owe more than to the soil;
Whose ample lawns are not ashamed to feed   *185*
The milky heifer and deserving steed;
Whose rising forests, not for pride or show,
But future buildings, future navies, grow:
Let his plantations stretch from down to down,
First shade a country, and then raise a town.   *190*
   You too proceed! make falling arts your care,
Erect new wonders, and the old repair;
Jones and Palladio to themselves restore,
And be whate'er Vitruvius° was before:
Till kings call forth the ideas of your mind,   *195*
Proud to accomplish what such hands designed,
Bid harbors open, public ways extend,
Bid temples,° worthier of the God, ascend;
Bid the broad arch° the dangerous flood contain,
The mole projected break the roaring main;   *200*
Back to his bounds their subject sea command,
And roll obedient rivers through the land:
These honors, peace to happy Britain brings,
These are imperial works, and worthy kings.

178 **Bathurst** a friend of Pope's and an enthusiastic landscape gardener. 178 **Boyle** Burlington. 194 **Vitruvius** the Roman author of the most influential ancient work on architecture. 198 **temples** Some of the new churches had been built on marshy ground and sank dangerously. 199 **broad arch** A proposal to build Westminster Bridge had been rejected, but it was later undertaken with Burlington as a commissioner.

TO A LADY:

OF THE CHARACTERS OF WOMEN

(1735)

NOTHING so true as what you once let fall,
"Most women have no characters at all."
Matter too soft a lasting mark to bear,
And best distinguished by black, brown, or fair.
5   How many pictures of one nymph we view,°
All how unlike each other, all how true!
Arcardia's countess,° here, in ermined pride,
Is, there, Pastora° by a fountain side:
Here Fannia, leering on her own good man,
10   And there, a naked Leda° with a swan.
Let then the fair one beautifully cry,
In Magdalen's loose hair and lifted eye,°
Or dressed in smiles of sweet Cecilia° shine,
With simpering angels, palms, and harps divine;

5–13 "Attitudes in which several ladies affected to be drawn, and
sometimes one lady in them all." (Pope).   7 **Arcadia's countess** sug-
gested by the title of Sir Philip Sidney's romance, *The Countess of
Pembroke's Arcadia* (1590) so called in compliment to his sister;
here a possible reference to Pope's contemporary Mary Howe.
8 **Pastora** a pastoral heroine in contrast with ermined pride (line 7).
10 **naked Leda** a popular Renaissance subject, as in the influential
(but now lost) painting by Leonardo da Vinci.   12 **loose hair . . .
eye** typical attributes of the Magdalen in works of Titian, El Greco,
and others; in Titian's work the loose hair partly conceals a bare
bosom.   13 **Cecilia** St. Cecilia, as the next line suggests, was the
patron saint of music, often shown in her ascent to heaven.

Whether the charmer sinner it, or saint it,   *15*
If folly grow romantic,° I must paint it.
   Come then, the colors and the ground° prepare!
Dip in the rainbow, trick her off° in air,
Choose a firm cloud, before it fall, and in it
Catch, ere she change, the Cynthia° of this minute.   *20*
   Rufa,° whose eye quick-glancing o'er the park,
Attracts each light gay meteor of a spark,°
Agrees as ill with Rufa studying Locke,°
As Sappho's diamonds with her dirty smock,
Or Sappho° at her toilet's greasy task,   *25*
With Sappho fragrant at an evening mask:°
So morning insects that in muck° begun,
Shine, buzz, and flyblow in the setting sun.
   How soft is Silia! fearful to offend,
The frail one's advocate, the weak one's friend: *30*
To her, Calista proved her conduct nice,°
And good Simplicius° asks of her advice.
Sudden, she storms! she raves! You tip the wink,°
But spare your censure; Silia does not drink.
All eyes may see from what the change arose,   *35*
All eyes may see—a pimple on her nose.
   Papillia,° wedded to her amorous spark,
Sighs for the shades—"How charming is a park!"°
A park is purchased, but the fair he sees
All bathed in tears—"Oh, odious, odious Trees!"   *40*
   Ladies, like variegated° tulips, show;
'Tis to their changes half their charms we owe;
Fine by defect, and delicately weak,

---

16 **romantic** extravagant. 17 **ground** the painted background to
which colors will be applied. 18 **trick her off** sketch her. 20 **Cyn-
thia** Diana, here cited as the fickle goddess of the changing moon.
21 **Rufa** redhead. 22 **spark** beau. 23 **Locke** the philosopher
John Locke, made a fashionable study by *The Spectator* of Addison
and Steele. 25 **Sappho** perhaps an allusion to the brilliant but noto-
riously slovenly Lady Mary Wortley Montagu. 26 **mask** masked
ball. 27 **muck** referring to the belief that insects were generated by
corruption. 31 **nice** foolishly fastidious, overly punctilious. 32
Simplicius the name of, among others, the commentator on the Stoic
Epictetus. 33 **tip the wink** make a surmise. 37 **Papillia** Latin for
butterfly. 38 **park** rural estate. 41 **variegated** Streaked tulips were
much cultivated and prized in Pope's day.

Their happy spots the nice° admirer take,
45　'Twas thus Calypso° once each heart alarmed,
Awed without virtue, without beauty charmed;
Her tongue bewitched as oddly as her eyes,
Less wit than mimic, more a wit than wise;
Strange graces still, and stranger flights she had,
50　Was just not ugly, and was just not mad;
Yet ne'er so sure our passion to create,
As when she touched the brink of all we hate.
　　Narcissa's° nature, tolerably mild,
To make a wash,° would hardly stew a child;
55　Has even been proved to grant a lover's prayer,
And paid a tradesman once to make him stare;
Gave alms at Easter, in a Christian trim,°
And made a widow happy, for a whim.
Why then declare good-nature is her scorn,
60　When 'tis by that alone she can be borne?
Why pique all mortals, yet affect a name?
A fool to pleasure, yet a slave to fame:
Now deep in Taylor° and the Book of Martyrs,°
Now drinking citron° with his Grace° and Chartres:°
65　Now conscience chills her, and now passion burns;
And atheism and religion take their turns;
A very heathen in the carnal part,
Yet still a sad,° good Christian at her heart.
　　See Sin in state, majestically drunk;
70　Proud as a peeress, prouder as a punk;°
Chaste to her husband, frank° to all beside,
A teeming mistress, but a barren bride.
What then? let blood and body bear the fault,
Her head's untouched, that noble seat of thought:
75　Such this day's doctrine—in another fit

44 **nice** discriminating.　45 **Calypso** named for the nymph who de-
tained Odysseus for many years.　53 **Narcissa** whose name suggests
vanity.　54 **wash** i.e., for hair or skin.　57 **trim** dress.　63 **Taylor**
Jeremy Taylor's *Holy Living and Holy Dying* was an extremely
popular devotional work.　63 **Book of Martyrs** John Foxe's work
of 1563.　64 **citron** brandy flavored with lemon peel.　64 **his Grace**
a duke, perhaps her lover.　64 **Chartres** a notorious gambler and
libertine.　68 **sad** sober.　70 **punk** prostitute.　71 **frank** free.

She sins with poets through pure love of wit.
What has not fired her bosom or her brain?
Caesar and Tallboy,° Charles° and Charlemagne.
As Helluo,° late dictator of the feast,
The nose of hautgout,° and the Tip of Taste,   80
Critiqued your wine, and analyzed your meat,
Yet on plain pudding deigned at home to eat;
So Philomedé, lecturing all mankind
On the soft passion, and the taste refined,
The address, the delicacy—stoops at once,   85
And makes her hearty meal upon a dunce.

    Flavia's a wit, has too much sense to pray;
To toast our wants and wishes, is her way;
Nor asks of God, but of her stars, to give
The mighty blessing, "while we live, to live."   90
Then all for death, that opiate of the soul!
Lucretia's dagger, Rosamonda's bowl.°
Say, what can cause such impotence of mind?
A spark too fickle, or a spouse too kind.
Wise wretch! with pleasures too refined to please;   95
With too much spirit to be e'er at ease;
With too much quickness ever to be taught;
With too much thinking to have common thought:
You purchase pain with all that joy can give,
And die of nothing but a rage to live.   100

    Turn then from wits; and look on Simo's mate,
No ass so meek, no ass so obstinate.
Or her, that owns her faults, but never mends,
Because she's honest, and the best of friends.
Or her, whose life the Church and scandal share,   105
For ever in a passion, or a prayer.
Or her, who laughs at Hell, but (like her Grace)
Cries, "Ah! how charming, if there's no such place!"
Or who in sweet vicissitude appears
Of mirth and opium, ratafie° and tears,   110

78 **Tallboy** a booby lover in a popular comedy.   78 **Charles** a com-
mon name for a footman.   79 **Helluo** Latin for glutton.   80 **hautgout**
anything with a strong scent, such as overkept game.   92 **Lucretia's
. . . bowl** forms of suicide of wronged women.   110 **ratafie** cherry
brandy.

The daily anodyne, and nightly draught,
To kill those foes to fair ones, time and thought.
Woman and fool are two hard things to hit;
For true no-meaning puzzles more than wit.
115   But what are these to great Atossa's° mind?
Scarce once herself, by turns all womankind!
Who, with herself, or others, from her birth
Finds all her life one warfare upon earth:
Shines, in exposing knaves, and painting fools,
120 Yet is, whate'er she hates and ridicules.
No thought advances, but her eddy brain
Whisks it about, and down it goes again.
Full sixty years the world has been her trade,
The wisest fool much time has ever made.
125 From loveless youth to unrespected age,
No passion gratified except her rage.
So much the fury still outran the wit,
The pleasure missed her, and the scandal hit.
Who breaks with her, provokes revenge from hell,
130 But he's a bolder man who dares be well.
Her every turn with violence pursued,
Nor more a storm her hate than gratitude:
To that each passion turns, or soon or late;
Love, if it makes her yield, must make her hate:
135 Superiors? death! and equals? what a curse!
But an inferior not dependent? worse.
Offend her, and she knows not to forgive;
Oblige her, and she'll hate you while you live:
But die, and she'll adore you—Then the bust°
140 And temple° rise—then fall again to dust.
Last night, her Lord was all that's good and great;
A knave this morning, and his will a cheat.
Strange! by the means defeated of the ends,
By spirit robbed of power, by warmth of friends,
145 By wealth of followers! without one distress,
Sick of herself through very selfishness!
Atossa, cursed with every granted prayer,
Childless with all her children, wants an heir.

115 **Atossa** named for the great Persian princess.   139 **bust** funerary
monument.   140 **temple** sepulchre.

To heirs unknown descends the unguarded store,
Or wanders, Heaven-directed, to the poor.   *150*
   Pictures like these, dear Madam, to design,
Asks no firm hand, and no unerring line;
Some wandering touches, some reflected light,
Some flying stroke alone can hit 'em right:
For how should equal° colors do the knack?   *155*
Chameleons who can paint in white and black?
   "Yet Chloe sure was formed without a spot"—
Nature in her then erred not, but forgot.
"With every pleasing, every prudent part,
Say, what can Chloe want?"—She wants a heart.   *160*
She speaks, behaves, and acts just as she ought;
But never, never, reached one generous thought.
Virtue she finds too painful an endeavor,
Content to dwell in decencies° for ever.
So very reasonable, so unmoved,   *165*
As never yet to love, or to be loved.
She, while her lover pants upon her breast,
Can mark the figures on an Indian chest;
And when she sees her friend in deep despair,
Observes how much a chintz exceeds mohair.   *170*
Forbid it Heaven, a favor or a debt
She e'er should cancel—but she may forget.
Safe is your secret still in Chloe's ear;
But none of Chloe's shall you ever hear.
Of all her dears she never slandered one,   *175*
But cares not if a thousand are undone.
Would Chloe know if you're alive or dead?
She bids her footman put it in her head.
Chloe is prudent—Would you too be wise?
Then never break your heart when Chloe dies.   *180*
   One certain portrait may (I grant) be seen,
Which Heaven has varnished out, and made a *Queen*:°
The same for ever! and described by all

---

155 **equal** unvaried. 164 **decencies** proprieties. 182 **Queen** with
reference to Queen Caroline, who exercised influence over George II
in behalf of Sir Robert Walpole and favored Lord Hervey, whom
Pope presents as Sporus in the *Epistle to Dr. Arbuthnot*. This por-
trait is in part a satire on court flattery.

With truth and goodness, as with crown and ball.°
185 Poets heap virtues, painters gems at will,
And show their zeal, and hide their want of skill.°
'Tis well—but, artists! who can paint or write,
To draw the naked is your true delight.
That robe of quality so struts and swells,
190 None see what parts of nature it conceals:
The exactest traits of body or of mind,
We owe to models of an humble kind.
If Queensbury° to strip there's no compelling,
'Tis from a handmaid we must take a Helen.
195 From peer or bishop 'tis no easy thing
To draw the man who loves his God, or king:
Alas! I copy (or my draught° would fail)
From honest Máhomet,° or plain Parson Hale.°
   But grant, in public men sometimes are shown,
200 A woman's seen in private life alone:
Our bolder talents in full light displayed;
Your virtues open fairest in the shade.
Bred to disguise, in public 'tis you hide;
There, none distinguish twixt your shame or pride,
205 Weakness or delicacy; all so nice,
That each may seem a virtue, or a vice.
   In men, we various ruling passions° find;
In women, two almost divide the kind;
Those, only fixed, they first or last obey,
210 The love of pleasure, and the love of sway.
   That, Nature gives; and where the lesson taught
Is but to please, can pleasure seem a fault?
Experience, this; by man's oppression curst,
They seek the second not to lose the first.
215   Men, some to business, some to pleasure take;
But every woman is at heart a rake:

184 **ball** orb (and scepter), symbols of rule. 185–6 Cf. *Essay on Criticism*, lines 293–6. 193 **Queensbury** Catherine Hyde, Duchess of Queensbury, one of the most beautiful women of her day. 197 **draught** sketch. 198 **Máhomet** "Servant to the late King, said to be the son of a Turkish Bassa, whom he took at the siege of Buda, and constantly kept about his person" (Pope). 198 **Parson Hale Dr.** Stephen Hales, notable physiologist and admirable parish priest, a friend of Pope's. 207 **ruling passions** See *Essay on Man*, II, 123 ff.

Men, some to quiet, some to public strife;
But every lady would be queen for life.
   Yet mark the fate of a whole sex of queens!
Power all their end, but beauty all the means: 220
In youth they conquer, with so wild a rage,
As leaves them scarce a subject in their age:
For foreign glory, foreign joy, they roam;
No thought of peace or happiness at home.
But wisdom's triumph is well-timed retreat,   225
As hard a science to the fair as great!
Beauties, like tyrants, old and friendless grown,
Yet hate repose, and dread to be alone,
Worn out in public, weary every eye,
Nor leave one sigh behind them when they die.   230
   Pleasures the sex, as children birds, pursue,
Still out of reach, yet never out of view;
Sure, if they catch, to spoil the toy at most,
To covet flying, and regret when lost:
At last, to follies youth could scarce defend,   235
It grows their age's prudence to pretend;
Ashamed to own they gave delight before,
Reduced to feign it, when they give no more:
As hags° hold sabbaths, less for joy than spite,
So these their merry, miserable night;°   240
Still round and round the ghosts of beauty glide,
And haunt the places where their honor died.
   See how the world its veterans rewards!
A youth of frolics, an old age of cards;
Fair to no purpose, artful to no end,   245
Young without lovers, old without a friend;
A fop their passion, but their prize a sot;
Alive, ridiculous, and dead, forgot!
   Ah! Friend!° to dazzle let the vain design;
To raise the thought, and touch the heart be thine!   250
That charm shall grow, while what fatigues the Ring°
Flaunts and goes down, an unregarded thing:
So when the sun's broad beam has tired the sight,

239 **hags** witches.   240 **night** visiting night.   249 **Friend** Martha
Blount, neighbor and close friend of Pope's.   251 **Ring** a fashion-
able drive in Hyde Park.

All mild ascends the moon's more sober light,
255 Serene in virgin modesty° she shines,
And unobserved the glaring orb declines.
    Oh! blest with temper, whose unclouded ray
Can make tomorrow cheerful as today;
She, who can love a sister's charms, or hear
260 Sighs for a daughter with unwounded ear;
She, who ne'er answers till a husband cools,
Or, if she rules him, never shows she rules;
Charms by accepting, by submitting sways,
Yet has her humor most, when she obeys;
265 Let fops or fortune fly which way they will;
Disdains° all loss of tickets,° or Codille;°
Spleen, vapors,° or smallpox, above them all,
And mistress of herself, though China° fall.
    And yet, believe me, good as well as ill,
270 Woman's at best a contradiction still.
Heaven, when it strives to polish all it can
Its last best work, but forms a softer man;
Picks from each sex, to make the favorite blest,
Your love of pleasure, our desire of rest:
275 Blends, in exception to all general rules,
Your taste of follies, with our scorn of fools:
Reserve with frankness, art with truth allied,
Courage with softness, modesty with pride;
Fixed principles, with fancy ever new;
280 Shakes all together, and produces—You.
    Be this a woman's fame: with this unblest,
Toasts live a scorn, and queens may die a jest.
This Phoebus° promised (I forget the year)
When those blue eyes first opened on the sphere;
285 Ascendant Phoebus watched that hour with care,
Averted half your parents' simple prayer;
And gave you beauty, but denied the pelf

---

255 **virgin modesty** with recollection of Diana as the virgin goddess
of the moon. 266 **Disdains** disregards as trifling. 266 **tickets** in
lotteries. 266 **Codille** a list game of ombre (cf. *Rape of the Lock*,
III, 92). 267 **vapors** hypochondria, melancholy. 268 **China** for its
double sense, cf. *Rape of the Lock*, III, 110, and III, 159. 283
Phoebus as god of prophecy.

That buys your sex a tyrant o'er itself.
The generous god, who wit and gold° refines,
And ripens spirits as he ripens mines,   *290*
Kept dross for duchesses, the world shall know it,
To you gave sense, good humor,° and a poet.

289 **wit and gold** Phoebus as god of poetry, which fosters true wit, and as god of the sun, by which gold generates in the earth.   292 **good humor** Cf. *Rape of the Lock*, V, 29–34.

Satires and Epistles of Horace Imitated

EPISTLE TO DR. ARBUTHNOT:

BEING THE PROLOGUE
TO THE SATIRES

(1735)

P.   SHUT, shut the door, good John!° fatigued, I said,
Tie up the knocker, say I'm sick, I'm dead.
The dog-star° rages! nay 'tis past a doubt,
All Bedlam, or Parnassus,° is let out:
Fire in each eye, and papers in each hand,   5
They rave, recite, and madden round the land.
    What walls can guard me, or what shades can hide?
They pierce my thickets, through my grot° they glide;
By land, by water,° they renew the charge;
They stop the chariot, and they board the barge.   10
No place is sacred, not the Church is free;
Even Sunday shines no sabbath-day to me:
Then from the Mint° walks forth the man of rhyme,
Happy! to catch me just at dinner time.

1 **good John** Pope's servant, John Searl.   3 **dog-star** Sirius, which
reappears in the season of late summer heat; traditionally a time of
satiric rage, occasioned for Juvenal by the reading of pompous epic
poems in August (see "Parnassus" in line 4).   4 **Bedlam, or Parnassus**
inhabitants of the madhouse or of Parnassus, the mountain of the
Muses.   8 **grot** Pope's grotto at Twickenham was an underground
retreat, an artificial cave.   9 **by water** Pope's house was on the
Thames; one could be rowed from London by watermen.   13 **Mint**
a sanctuary for debtors, who, however, were free of arrest elsewhere
on Sunday.

15   Is there a Parson, much bemused in° beer,
        A maudlin poetess, a rhyming peer,
        A clerk, foredoomed his father's soul to cross,
        Who pens a stanza, when he should *engross.*°
        Is there, who, locked from ink and paper, scrawls
20   With desperate charcoal round his darkened walls?°
        All fly to TWITNAM, and in humble strain
        Apply to me, to keep them mad or vain.
        Arthur,° whose giddy son neglects the Laws,
        Imputes to me and my damned works the cause:
25   Poor Cornus° sees his frantic wife elope,
        And curses wit, and poetry, and Pope.
           Friend to my Life! (which did not you prolong,
        The world had wanted many an idle song)
        What drop or nostrum° can this plague remove?
30   Or which must end me, a fool's wrath or love?
        A dire dilemma! either way I'm sped,
        If foes, they write, if friends, they read me dead.
        Seized and tied down to judge, how wretched I!
        Who can't be silent, and who will not lie;
35   To laugh, were want of goodness and of grace,
        And to be grave, exceeds all power of face.
        I sit with sad civility, I read
        With honest anguish, and an aching head;
        And drop at last, but in unwilling ears,
40   This saving counsel, "Keep your piece nine years."°
           "Nine years!" cries he, who high in Drury Lane,°
        Lulled by soft zephyrs through the broken pane,
        Rhymes ere he wakes, and prints before Term° ends,
        Obliged by hunger, and request of friends:°
45   "The piece, you think, is incorrect? why, take it,

---

15 bemused in rhyming with the name of Laurence Eusden, a parson
and poet laureate much given to drink.   **18 engross** copy a legal
document.   **20 darkened walls** i.e., in restful confinement, perhaps
Bedlam.   **23 Arthur** in fact Arthur Moore, a Member of Parlia-
ment; but the name is generic, like *Cornus* (line 25).   **25 Cornus**
"horned"; a cuckold.   **29 drop or nostrum** cures.   **40 keep . . . years**
the advice of Horace, *Ars Poetica*, 386–9.   **41 Drury Lane** resort of
prostitutes and, here, writers in garrets.   **43 Term** court term, which
was also the publishing season.   **44 obliged . . . friends** i.e., cover-
ing the first reason with the second, a frequent apology in prefaces.

I'm all submission; what you'd have it, make it."
   Three things another's modest wishes bound,
My friendship, and a prologue,° and ten pound.
   Pitholeon° sends to me: "You know his Grace,
I want a patron; ask him for a place."°   *50*
Pitholeon libelled me—"but here's a letter
Informs you, sir, 'twas when he knew no better.
Dare you refuse him? Curll° invites to dine,
He'll write a Journal, or he'll turn Divine."°
   Bless me! a packet.—" 'Tis a stranger sues,   *55*
A virgin tragedy, an orphan Muse."
If I dislike it, "Furies, death and rage!"
If I approve, "Commend it to the stage."
There (thank my stars) my whole commission ends,
The players and I are, luckily, no friends.   *60*
Fired that the house° reject him, " 'Sdeath I'll print it,
And shame the fools——Your Interest, sir, with Lintot."°
Lintot, dull rogue! will think your price too much:
"Not, sir, if you revise it, and retouch."
All my demurs but double his attacks;   *65*
At last he whispers, "Do; and we go snacks."°
Glad of a quarrel, straight I clap the door,
"Sir, let me see your works and you no more."
   'Tis sung, when Midas' ears° began to spring,
(Midas, a sacred person and a King)   *70*
His very Minister who spied them first,
(Some say his Queen) was forced to speak, or burst.
And is not mine, my friend, a sorer case,
When every coxcomb perks them in my face?
   "Good friend, forbear! you deal in dangerous things.   *75*
I'd never name Queens, Ministers, or Kings;
Keep close to ears, and those let asses prick;

---

48 **prologue** often sought from famous writers to promote a new play. 49 **Pitholeon** a foolish and pretentious poet mentioned by Horace. 50 **place** position, sinecure. 53 **Curll** Edmund Curll, notorious publisher of hacks, might commission another libel. 54 **Journal ... Divine** become a party writer in politics or religion. 61 **house** theatre. 62 **Lintot** Pope's publisher. 66 **snacks** shares. 69 **Midas' ears** the ass's ears given him by Apollo for preferring Pan's music. Midas' queen whispered it into a hole in the earth and covered the place, but the reeds which grew there repeated the message in the wind.

'Tis nothing—" Nothing? if they bite and kick?
Out with it, DUNCIAD! let the secret pass,
80 That secret to each fool, that he's an ass:
The truth once told (and wherefore should we lie?)
The Queen of Midas slept, and so may I.
    You think this cruel? take it for a rule,
No creature smarts so little as a fool.
85 Let peals of laughter, Codrus!° round thee break,
Thou unconcerned canst hear the mighty crack:°
Pit, box, and gallery in convulsions hurled,
Thou standst unshook amidst a bursting world.
Who shames a scribbler? break one cobweb through,
90 He spins the slight, self-pleasing thread anew:
Destroy his fib or sophistry, in vain,
The creature's at his dirty work° again,
Throned in the center of his thin designs,
Proud of a vast extent of flimsy lines!
95 Whom have I hurt? has poet yet, or peer,
Lost the arched eyebrow, or Parnassian sneer?°
And has not Colley still his Lord, and whore?
His butchers Henley,° his Freemasons Moore?°
Does not one table Bavius° still admit?
100 Still to one bishop Philips° seem a wit?
Still Sappho—"Hold! for God's sake—you'll offend,
No names—be calm—learn prudence of a friend:
I too could write, and I am twice as tall;
But foes like these—" One flatterer's worse than all.
105 Of all mad creatures, if the learned are right,
It is the slaver kills, and not the bite.
A fool quite angry is quite innocent:
Alas! 'tis ten times worse when they *repent.*

85 **Codrus** a poet ridiculed by Virgil and Juvenal. 86 **mighty crack**
This phrase of Addison's amused Pope by its inadequacy to the
conception of a cosmic catastrophe; here it seems reduced to stage
thunder. 92 **dirty work** the point (as with the spider in Swift's
The Battle of the Books) is that he spins a structure out of his
excrement. 96 **Parnassian sneer** referring to Colley Cibber, the
shameless poet laureate, as in *Dunciad*, I. 98 **his butchers Henley**
See *Dunciad*, III, 199, 209. 98 **Moore** See *Dunciad*, II, 50. Moore
used to head Freemasons' processions. 99 **Bavius** the bad poet of
Virgil and Horace's day. 100 **Philips** Ambrose Philips was secretary
to the Bishop of Armagh.

One dedicates in high heroic prose,
And ridicules beyond a hundred foes: *110*
One from all Grubstreet° will my fame defend,
And, more abusive, calls himself my friend.
This prints my *Letters,*° that expects a bribe,
And others roar aloud, "Subscribe, subscribe."°
 There are, who to my person pay their court: *115*
I cough like Horace, and, though lean, am short,
Ammon's great son° one shoulder had too high,
Such Ovid's nose, and "Sir! you have an eye"—
Go on, obliging creatures, make me see
All that disgraced my betters, met in me.   *120*
Say for my comfort, languishing in bed,
"Just so immortal Maro° held his head":
And when I die, be sure you let me know
Great Homer died three thousand years ago.
 Why did I write? what sin to me unknown   *125*
Dipped me in ink, my parents' or my own?
As yet a child, nor yet a fool to fame,
I lisped in numbers,° for the numbers came.
I left no calling for this idle trade,
No duty broke, no father disobeyed.   *130*
The Muse but served to ease some friend, not wife,
To help me through this long disease, my life,
To second, ARBUTHNOT! thy art and care,
And teach the being you preserved, to bear.
 But why then publish? Granville° the polite,   *135*
And knowing Walsh, would tell me I could write;
Well-natured Garth inflamed with early praise;
And Congreve loved, and Swift endured my lays;
The courtly Talbot, Somers, Sheffield read,
Even mitred Rochester° would nod the head,   *140*
And St. John's self° (great Dryden's friends before)

111 **Grubstreet** the center of hack writers.   113 **Letters** pirated or
forged.   114 **subscribe** Books were published with advance sub-
scriptions.   117 **Ammon's . . . son** Alexander the Great.   122 **Maro**
Virgil.   128 **numbers** verses.   135 **Granville** the first of a series of
peers, writers, and critics of reputation in contrast to the hacks;
see *Windsor Forest,* line 6.   140 **mitred Rochester** Francis Atter-
bury, Bishop of Rochester.   141 **St. John's self** Henry St. John,
Viscount Bolingbroke.

With open arms received one poet more.
Happy my studies, when by these approved!
Happier their author, when by these beloved!
145 From these the world will judge of men and books,
Not from the Burnets, Oldmixons, and Cookes.°
    Soft were my numbers; who could take offense
While pure description held the place of sense?
Like gentle Fanny's° was my flowery theme,
150 A painted mistress, or a purling stream.
Yet then did Gildon° draw his venal quill;
I wished the man a dinner, and sat still.
Yet then did Dennis° rave in furious fret;
I never answered—I was not in debt.
155 If want provoked, or madness made them print,
I waged no war with Bedlam or the Mint.
    Did some more sober critic come abroad;
If wrong, I smiled; if right, I kissed the rod.
Pains, reading, study, are their just pretense,
160 And all they want is spirit, taste, and sense.
Commas and points° they set exactly right,
And 'twere a sin to rob them of their mite.
Yet ne'er one sprig of laurel° graced these ribalds,°
From slashing Bentley down to pidling Tibalds:°
165 Each wight, who reads not, and but scans and spells,
Each word-catcher, that lives on syllables,
Even such small critics some regard may claim,
Preserved in Milton's or in Shakespeare's name.
Pretty! in amber° to observe the forms
170 Of hairs, or straws, or dirt, or grubs, or worms!

146 **Burnets . . . Cookes** "authors of secret and scandalous history"
(Pope).   149 **gentle Fanny's** Lord Hervey or some other conven-
tional poet.   151 **Gildon** a critic who had attacked Pope personally.
153 **Dennis** See note to *Essay on Criticism*, lines 585–6.   161 **points**
periods.   163 **laurel** the crown of the true poet.   163 **ribalds** buf-
foons.   164 **slashing Bentley . . . pidling Tibalds** Richard Bentley
and Lewis Theobald were, among other things, textual scholars.
Bentley's great learning was not infused with literary sense, and his
arrogant handling of Milton's *Paradise Lost* calls forth the "slash-
ing" (although Bentley's personality might as well; see *Dunciad*,
IV, 201). Theobald made a few great emendations of Shakespeare's
text and many that have been happily forgotten.   169 **in amber** as
flies and other creatures have been decoratively preserved.

The things, we know, are neither rich nor rare,
But wonder how the devil they got there.
   Were others angry? I excused them too;
Well might they rage; I gave them but their due.
A man's true merit 'tis not hard to find;   *175*
But each man's secret standard in his mind,
That casting-weight° pride adds to emptiness,
This, who can gratify? for who can guess?
The bard° whom pilfered pastorals renown,
Who turns a Persian tale for half a crown,°   *180*
Just writes to make his barrenness appear,
And strains, from hard-bound brains, eight lines a year;
He, who still wanting, though he lives on theft,
Steals much, spends little, yet has nothing left:
And he, who now to sense, now nonsense leaning,   *185*
Means not, but blunders round about a meaning:
And he, whose fustian's so sublimely bad,
It is not poetry, but prose run mad:
All these, my modest satire bade translate,
And owned that nine such poets made a Tate.°   *190*
How did they fume, and stamp, and roar, and chafe!
And swear, not *Addison*° himself was safe.
   Peace to all such! but were there one whose fires
True genius kindles, and fair fame inspires;
Blest with each talent and each art to please,   *195*
And born to write, converse, and live with ease:
Should such a man, too fond to rule alone,
Bear, like the Turk,° no brother near the throne,
View him with scornful, yet with jealous eyes,
And hate for arts that caused himself to rise;   *200*
Damn with faint praise, assent with civil leer,
And without sneering, teach the rest to sneer;
Willing to wound, and yet afraid to strike,

---

177 **casting-weight** ballast.   179 **bard** Ambrose Philips, author of
derivative pastorals and a book of *Persian Tales*.   180 **half a crown**
a prostitute's customary fee.   190 **Tate** Nahum Tate, former poet
laureate, "a cold writer of no invention" (Pope).   192 **Addison** who
is clearly meant in the following portrait of Atticus, named for the
friend of Cicero and, later, of Augustus; himself an author.   198
like the Turk To forestall rivalry and assassination, the Turkish
rulers often eliminated their close kinsmen.

Just hint a fault, and hesitate dislike;
205 Alike reserved to blame, or to commend,
A timorous foe, and a suspicious friend;
Dreading even fools, by flatterers besieged,
And so obliging, that he ne'er obliged;
Like Cato,° give his little Senate laws,
210 And sit attentive to his own applause;
While wits and templars° every sentence raise,
And wonder with a foolish face of praise—
Who but must laugh, if such a man there be?
Who would not weep, if Atticus were he?
215   What though my name stood rubric° on the walls,
Or plastered posts, with claps,° in capitals?
Or smoking forth, a hundred hawkers' load,
On wings of wind came flying all abroad?
I sought no homage from the race that write;
220 I kept, like Asian monarchs,° from their sight:
Poems I heeded (now berhymed so long)
No more than thou, great GEORGE! a birthday song.°
I ne'er with wits or witlings passed my days,
To spread about the itch of verse and praise;
225 Nor like a puppy, daggled° through the town,
To fetch and carry singsong up and down;
Nor at rehearsals sweat, and mouthed, and cried,
With handkerchief and orange° at my side;
But sick of fops, and poetry, and prate,
230 To *Bufo* left the whole Castalian state.°
    Proud as Apollo on his forkèd hill,
Sat full-blown Bufo,° puffed by every quill;
Fed with soft dedication all day long,

---

209 **like Cato** the Roman leader of the Senate, the hero of Addison's famous play. 211 **templars** law students, often more interested in writing than law. 215 **stood rubric** was posted in booksellers' advertisements. 216 **with claps** (1) on posters (2) with advertisements for quack cures for gonorrhea. 220 **like . . . monarchs** Cf. *Elegy to . . . Unfortunate Lady,* lines 21–2. 222 **birthday song** the official ode of the poet laureate. 225 **daggled** moved in a slovenly way or through mud. 228 **orange** commonly sold at theatres. 230 **Castalian state** poetry, named for the spring on Mt. Parnassus (the *forkèd hill* of line 231), sacred to Apollo and the Muses. 232 **Bufo** a patron, from the Latin for "toad," a creature that swells up with air.

Horace and he° went hand in hand in song.
His library (where busts of poets dead   235
And a true Pindar stood without a head)
Received of wits an undistinguished race,
Who first his judgment asked, and then a place:
Much they extolled his pictures, much his seat,°
And flattered every day, and some days eat: 240
Till grown more frugal in his riper days,
He paid some bards with port, and some with praise;
To some a dry rehearsal was assigned,
And others (harder still) he paid in kind.°
Dryden alone (what wonder?) came not nigh,   245
Dryden alone escaped this judging eye:
But still the Great have kindness in reserve,
He helped to bury° whom he helped to starve.
     May some choice patron bless each gray goose quill!
May every Bavius have his Bufo still!   250
So, when a statesman wants a day's defense,
Or envy holds a whole week's war with sense,
Or simple pride for flattery makes demands,
May dunce by dunce be whistled off my hands!
Blest be the Great! for those they take away,   255
And those they left me; for they left me GAY,°
Left me to see neglected genius bloom,
Neglected die, and tell it on his tomb:°
Of all thy blameless life the sole return
My Verse, and QUEENSBURY° weeping o'er thy urn!   260
     Oh let me live my own, and die so too!
(To live and die is all I have to do:)
Maintain a poet's dignity and ease,
And see what friends, and read what books I please:
Above a patron, though I condescend   26:
Sometimes to call a Minister my friend.
I was not born for courts or great affairs;

234 **Horace and he** as a modern Maecenas, Horace's patron.   239
seat estate.   244 **in kind** with his own verses.   248 **helped to bury**
Dryden, although poor much of his life, was given a lavish funeral.
255–6 Cf. Job: "The Lord gave and the Lord hath taken away;
blessed be the name of the Lord."   258 **on his tomb** Pope wrote
Gay's epitaph.   260 **Queensbury** with his Duchess patron and friend
of Gay.

    I pay my debts, believe, and say my prayers;
    Can sleep without a poem in my head,
270 Nor know, if Dennis be alive or dead.
       Why am I asked what next shall see the light?
    Heavens! was I born for nothing but to write?
    Has life no joys for me? or (to be grave)
    Have I no friend to serve, no soul to save?
275 "I found him close with Swift"—"Indeed? no doubt,"
    (Cries prating Balbus) "something will come out."
    'Tis all in vain, deny it as I will.
    "No, such a Genius never can lie still";
    And then for mine obligingly mistakes
280 The first Lampoon Sir *Will.* or *Bubo*° makes.
    Poor guiltless I! and can I choose but smile,
    When every coxcomb knows me by my *style?*
       Cursed be the verse, how well soe'er it flow,
    That tends to make one worthy man my foe,
285 Give Virtue scandal, Innocence a fear,
    Or from the soft-eyed virgin steal a tear!
    But he who hurts a harmless neighbor's peace,
    Insults fallen worth, or beauty in distress,
    Who loves a lie, lame slander helps about,
290 Who writes a libel, or who copies out:
    That fop, whose pride affects a patron's name,
    Yet absent, wounds an author's honest fame:
    Who can your merit selfishly approve,
    And show the sense of it without the love;°
295 Who has the vanity to call you friend,
    Yet wants the honor, injured, to defend;
    Who tells whate'er you think, whate'er you say,
    And, if he lie not, must at least betray:
    Who to the *Dean,* and *silver bell* can swear,
300 And sees at *Canons* what was never there;°

---

280 **Sir Will. or Bubo** Yonge or Bubb Dodington, but any feeble
writers will do. 293–4 **Who can . . . the love** who can win merit
for himself by seeming to approve of ours but actually placing an
invidious interpretation on your words. 299–300 **Who . . . never
there** who makes false identifications of characters and places in
Pope's *Epistle to Burlington.* The gossip that linked Timon's villa
and the Duke of Chandos's estate, Cannons, was used unjustly to
convict Pope of ingratitude.

Who reads, but with a lust to misapply,
Make Satire a Lampoon, and Fiction, Lie.
A lash like mine no honest man shall dread,
But all such babbling blockheads in his stead.
    Let *Sporus*° tremble—"What? that thing of silk,   *305*
Sporus, that mere white curd of ass's milk?
Satire or sense, alas! can Sporus feel?
Who breaks a butterfly upon a wheel?"°
Yet let me flap this bug with gilded wings,
This painted child of dirt that stinks and stings;   *310*
Whose buzz the witty and the fair annoys,
Yet wit ne'er tastes, and beauty ne'er enjoys:
So well-bred spaniels civilly delight
In mumbling of the game they dare not bite.
Eternal smiles his emptiness betray,   *315*
As shallow streams run dimpling all the way.
Whether in florid impotence he speaks,
And, as the prompter breathes, the puppet squeaks;
Or at the ear of Eve,° familiar Toad,
Half froth, half venom, spits himself abroad,   *320*
In puns, or politics, or tales, or lies,
Or spite, or smut, or rhymes, or blasphemies.
His wit all seesaw, between *that* and *this,*
Now high, now low, now master up, now miss,
And he himself one vile antithesis.   *325*
Amphibious thing! that acting either part,
The trifling head, or the corrupted heart,
Fop at the toilet, flatterer at the board,
Now trips a Lady, and now struts a Lord.
Eve's tempter thus the Rabbins° have exprest,   *330*
A Cherub's face, a reptile all the rest;
Beauty that shocks you, parts that none will trust,
Wit that can creep, and pride that licks the dust.

---

305 **Sporus** Nero's homosexual favorite; appropriately used for Lord
Hervey, prominent in the court of George II and Queen Caroline,
of which he left memoirs; a long-time enemy of Pope. 308 **wheel**
the instrument of torture on which men were disjointed. 319 **at the
ear of Eve** Cf. *Paradise Lost,* IV, 800, where Satan is found "squat
like a Toad, close at the ear of Eve." 330 **Rabbins** rabbis, inter-
preters of the Old Testament.

Not Fortune's worshipper, nor fashion's fool,
335 Not lucre's madman, nor ambition's tool,
Not proud, nor servile; be one poet's praise,
That, if he pleased, he pleased by manly ways:
That flattery, even to kings, he held a shame,
And thought a lie in verse or prose the same.
340 That not in fancy's maze he wandered long,
But stooped° to truth and moralized his song:
That not for fame, but virtue's better end,
He stood° the furious foe, the timid friend,
The damning critic, half-approving wit,
345 The coxcomb hit, or fearing to be hit;
Laughed at the loss of friends he never had,
The dull, the proud, the wicked, and the mad;
The distant threats of vengeance on his head,
The blow unfelt, the tear he never shed;
350 The tale revived, the lie so oft o'erthrown,
The imputed trash, and dulness not his own;
The morals blackened when the writings 'scape,
The libeled person, and the pictured shape;
Abuse, on all he loved, or loved him, spread,
355 A friend in exile, or a father, dead;
The whisper,° that to greatness still too near,
Perhaps, yet vibrates on his SOVEREIGN'S ear—
Welcome for thee, fair Virtue! all the past:
For thee, fair Virtue! welcome even the *last!*
360   "But why insult the poor, affront the great?"
A knave's a knave, to me, in every state:
Alike my scorn, if he succeed or fail,
Sporus at court, or Japhet° in a jail,
A hireling scribbler, or a hireling peer,
365 Knight of the post° corrupt, or of the shire;°
If on a pillory, or near a throne,
He gain his Prince's ear, or lose his own.°
    Yet soft by nature, more a dupe than wit,

---

341 **stooped** as a falcon is said to "stoop" to its prey.   343 **stood** withstood, endured.   356 **whisper** by Hervey.   363 **Japhet** Japhet Crook, a forger.   365 **Knight . . . post** a false witness.   365 **of the shire** of the county, a legitimate knight.   367 **lose his own** as did Japhet Crook, as well as stand in the pillory.

Sappho° can tell you how this man was bit:°
This dreaded satirist Dennis will confess   370
Foe to his pride, but friend to his distress,°
So humble, he has knocked at Tibbald's door,
Has drunk with Cibber, nay, has rhymed for Moore.°
Full ten years slandered, did he once reply?
Three thousand suns went down on Welsted's lie.   375
To please a mistress one aspersed his life;
He lashed him not, but let her be his wife:
Let Budgell charge low Grubstreet° on his quill,
And write whate'er he pleased, except his will;°
Let the two Curlls° of town and court, abuse   380
His father, mother, body, soul, and Muse.
Yet why? that Father held it for a rule,
It was a sin to call our neighbor fool:
That harmless Mother thought no wife a whore:
Hear this, and spare his family, *James Moore!*   385
Unspotted names, and memorable long!
If there be force in virtue, or in song.

    Of gentle blood (part shed in honor's cause,
While yet in *Britain* honor had applause)
Each parent sprung—"What fortune, pray?"—Their   390
    own,
And better got, than Bestia's° from the throne.
Born to no pride, inheriting no Strife,
Nor marrying discord in a noble wife,
Stranger to civil and religious rage,
The good man walked innoxious through his age.   395
No courts he saw, no suits would ever try,
Nor dared an oath, nor hazarded a lie.
Unlearned, he knew no schoolman's subtle art,°
No language, but the language of the heart.

369 **Sappho** Lady Mary Wortley Montagu, to whom Pope had once
been close, after their estrangement joined Lord Hervey in attack-
ing him.   369 **bit** cheated, deceived.   371 **his distress** Pope had been
of help in Dennis' last years.   373 **for Moore** unintentionally, for
Moore plagiarized from Pope.   378 **low Grubstreet** contributions to
the *Grub Street Journal.*   379 **except his will** Budgell seems to have
forged a will in which he displaced a nephew as heir.   380 **two
Curlls** the publisher (line 53) and Lord Hervey.   391 **Bestia** a Ro-
man consul bribed with a dishonorable peace.   398 **schoolman's
. . . art** casuistry.

400 By nature honest, by experience wise,
     Healthy by temperance and by exercise;
     His life, though long, to sickness passed unknown,
     His death was instant, and without a groan.
     O grant me, thus to live, and thus to die!
405 Who sprung from kings shall know less joy than I.
       O Friend!° may each domestic bliss be thine!
     Be no unpleasing melancholy mine:
     Me, let the tender office long engage,
     To rock the cradle of reposing Age,
410 With lenient arts extend a Mother's breath,°
     Make Languor smile, and smooth the bed of Death,
     Explore the thought, explain the asking eye,
     And keep a while one parent from the sky!
     On cares like these if length of days attend,
415 May Heaven, to bless those days, preserve my friend,
     Preserve him social, cheerful, and serene,
     And just as rich as when he served a Queen.°
     A.   Whether that blessing be denied or given,
     Thus far was right, the rest belongs to Heaven.

---

406 **Friend** Arbuthnot.   410 **Mother's breath** Although Pope's
mother died before the *Epistle* was published, this passage had been
written during her illness.   417 **Queen** Anne, to whom Arbuthnot
was physician.

THE FIRST SATIRE OF THE SECOND BOOK OF HORACE

TO MR. FORTESCUE°

(1733)

P.   THERE are (I scarce can think it, but am told),
There are, to whom my satire seems too bold:
Scarce to wise Peter° complaisant enough,
And something said of Chartres° much too rough.
The lines are weak, another's pleased to say,   *5*
Lord Fanny° spins a thousand such a day.
Timorous by nature, of the rich in awe,
I come to counsel learned in the law:
You'll give me, like a friend, both sage and free,°
Advice; and (as you use) without a fee.   *10*
  F.   I'd write no more.
  P.   Not write? but then I *think,*
And for my soul I cannot sleep a wink.
I nod in company, I wake at night,
Fools rush into my head, and so I write.
  F.   You could not do a worse thing for your life.   *15*

To Mr. Fortescue William Fortescue was a friend and legal adviser
of Pope as well as a friend and supporter of Sir Robert Walpole.
He was later to become Baron of the Exchequer and Master of the
Rolls. He appears in Pope's dialogue as the celebrated Roman law-
yer Trebatius does in Horace's poem.   3 **wise Peter** Peter Walter,
land steward to the Duke of Newcastle, Member of Parliament,
wealthy moneylender to the aristocracy; cf. *Epilogue to the Satires*
I, 121; II, 57.   4 **Chartres** Cf. *Epistle* I, vi, 120 and note.   6 **Lord
Fanny** Lord Hervey; see note to *Epistle to Dr. Arbuthnot,* line 305.
9 **free** generous, open.

Why, if the nights seem tedious, take a wife;
Or rather truly, if your point be rest,
Lettuce and cowslip wine;° *Probatum est.*°
But talk with Celsus,° Celsus will advise
20 Hartshorn,° or something that shall close your eyes.
Or, if you needs must write, write CAESAR'S° praise,
You'll gain at least a *knighthood,* or the *bays.*°
    P.   What? like Sir Richard,° rumbling, rough, and
       fierce,
With ARMS, and GEORGE, and BRUNSWICK° crowd the
    verse,
25 Rend with tremendous sound your ears asunder,
With gun, drum, trumpet, blunderbuss, and thunder?
Or nobly wild, with Budgell's° fire and force,
Paint angels trembling round his falling horse?
    F.   Then all your Muse's softer art display,
30 Let CAROLINA° smooth the tuneful lay,
Lull with AMELIA'S° liquid name the Nine,
And sweetly flow through all the royal line.
    P.   Alas! few verses touch their nicer° ear;
They scarce can bear their *laureate* twice a year;°
35 And justly CAESAR scorns the poet's lays,
It is to *history* he trusts for Praise.
    F.   Better be Cibber, I'll maintain it still,
Than ridicule all taste, blaspheme Quadrille,°
Abuse the City's best good men° in meter,
40 And laugh at Peers that put their trust in Peter.
Even those you touch not, hate you.
    P.   What should ail them?
    F.   A hundred smart in Timon and in Balaam.°

18 **lettuce . . . wine** inducers of sleep.   18 **Probatum est** It is approved.   19 **Celsus** the chief Roman writer on medicine.   20 **Hartshorn** ammonia.   21 **Caesar** King George II.   22 **bays** poet-laureateship.   23 **Sir Richard** Blackmore, poet and physician; author of several wretched epics.   24 **Brunswick** a German duchy of the Hanoverian George II.   27 **Budgell** author of a ludicrous celebration of George II.   30 **Carolina** Queen Caroline.   31 **Amelia** the third of the royal children.   33 **nicer** more delicate.   34 **twice a year** at the New Year and the Royal Birthday, occasions for odes. George II, who disliked poetry, was reported to have complained of Pope, "Why will not my subjects write in prose?"   38 **Quadrille** a fashionable card game.   39 **City . . . men** merchants.   42 **Timon . . . Balaam** fictitious characters in earlier satires.

The fewer still you name,° you wound the more;
Bond° is but one, but Harpax° is a score.
   P.   Each mortal has his pleasure: none deny   45
Scarsdale his bottle, Darty his ham-pie;
Ridotta° sips and dances, till she see
The doubling lustres° dance as fast as she;
F—— loves the Senate, Hockley Hole° his brother,
Like in all else, as one egg to another.   50
I love to pour out all my self, as plain
As downright SHIPPEN° or as old MONTAIGNE:°
In them, as certain to be loved as seen,
The soul stood forth, nor kept a thought within;
In me what spots (for spots I have) appear,   55
Will prove at least the medium must be clear.
In this impartial glass, my Muse intends
Fair to expose myself, my foes, my friends;
Publish the present age; but where my text
Is vice too high, reserve it for the next: 60
My foes shall wish my life a longer date,
And every friend the less lament my fate.
My head and heart thus flowing through my quill,
Verse-man or prose-man, term me which you will,
Papist or Protestant, or both between,   65
Like good Erasmus in an honest Mean,
In moderation placing all my glory,
While Tories call me Whig, and Whigs a Tory.
Satire's my weapon, but I'm too discreet
To run amuck, and tilt at all I meet;   70
I only wear it in a land of hectors,°
Thieves, supercargoes,° sharpers, and directors.°
Save but our army! and let Jove encrust
Swords, pikes, and guns, with everlasting rust!

43 **Name** identify accurately. 44 **Bond** See note, *Epilogue to the Satires* I, 121. 44 **Harpax** from Greek for "robber." 47 **Ridotta** a type of society woman. 48 **lustres** crystal chandeliers. 49 **Hockley Hole** scene of bear-baiting. 52 **Shippen** leading Jacobite in Commons, an incorruptible man. 52 **Montaigne** whose *Essays* are candidly self-revealing and self-exploring. 71 **hectors** bullies. 72 **supercargoes** officers concerned not with the sailing of the vessel but only with its trade. 72 **directors** Those of the South Sea Company had been particularly notorious for fraud.

75 Peace is my dear delight—not Fleury's° more:
But touch me, and no Minister so sore.
Whoe'er offends, at some unlucky time
Slides into verse, and hitches in a rhyme,
Sacred to Ridicule his whole life long,
80 And the sad burden of some merry song.
  Slander or Poison dread from Delia's rage,
Hard words or hanging, if your judge be Page.
From furious Sappho scarce a milder fate,
P—xed° by her love, or libelled by her hate.
85 Its proper power to hurt, each creature feels;
Bulls aim their horns, and asses lift their heels;
'Tis a bear's talent not to kick, but hug;
And no man wonders he's not stung by Pug.°
So drink with Walters, or with Chartres eat,
90 They'll never poison you, they'll only cheat.
  Then, learnèd sir! (to cut the matter short)
Whate'er my fate, or well or ill at Court,
Whether old age, with faint but cheerful ray,
Attends to gild the evening of my day,
95 Or death's black wing already be displayed,
To wrap me in the universal shade;
Whether the darkened room to muse invite,
Or whitened wall provoke the skewer to write:°
In durance, exile, Bedlam, or the Mint,°
100 Like Lee or Budgell,° I will rhyme and print.
  F. Alas, young man! your days can ne'er be long,
In flower of age you perish for a song!
Plums° and directors, Shylock° and his wife,
Will club their testers,° now, to take your life!
105   P. What? armed for virtue when I point the pen,
Brand the bold front° of shameless guilty men;
Dash the proud gamester in his gilded car;

75 **Fleury** the French cardinal who pursued, with Walpole, a policy
of peace. 84 **P—xed** infected with syphilis. 88 **Pug** a common name
for a pet dog. 97–8 **Whether . . . write** describing types of confine-
ment, notably in Bedlam for insanity. 99 **the Mint** a sanctuary for
debtors. 100 **Lee or Budgell** both for a time insane. 103 **Plums**
sums of £100,000. 103 **Shylock** an adaptation of the name of the
Earl of Selkirk. 104 **club their testers** pool their wealth. 106 **front**
brow.

Bare the mean heart that lurks beneath a Star;°
Can there be wanting, to defend her cause,
Lights of the Church, or guardians of the laws?   *110*
Could pensioned Boileau lash in honest strain
Flatterers and bigots even in Louis' reign?°
Could laureate Dryden pimp and friar° engage,
Yet neither Charles nor James° be in a rage?
And I not strip the gilding off a knave,   *115*
Unplaced, unpensioned, no man's heir, or slave?
I will, or perish in the generous cause:
Hear this, and tremble! you who 'scape the laws.
Yes, while I live, no rich or noble knave
Shall walk the world, in credit, to his grave.   *120*
To VIRTUE ONLY AND HER FRIENDS A FRIEND,
The world beside may murmur, or commend.
Know, all the distant din that world can keep,
Rolls o'er my grotto,° and but soothes my sleep.
There, my retreat the best companions grace,   *125*
Chiefs out of war, and statesmen out of place.
There ST. JOHN° mingles with my friendly bowl
The feast of reason and the flow of soul:
And he, whose lightning pierced the Iberian lines,°
Now forms my quincunx,° and now ranks my vines,   *130*
Or tames the genius of the stubborn plain,
Almost as quickly as he conquered Spain.
  Envy must own, I live among the Great,
No pimp of pleasure, and no spy of state,
With eyes that pry not, tongue that ne'er repeats,   *135*
Fond to spread friendships, but to cover heats;
To help who want, to forward who excel;
This, all who know me, know; who love me, tell;

---

108 **Star** the decoration for Knight of the Garter. 112 **even . . .
reign** in the absolute monarchy of Louis XIV. 113 **pimp and friar**
combined in Friar Dominick of Dryden's comedy, *The Spanish Friar.*
114 **neither Charles nor James** In fact, James II banned the play for
its satire on the Catholic clergy. 124 **grotto** an artificial cave on
Pope's estate. 127 **St. John** Bolingbroke, formerly with Harley at
the head of Queen Anne's government. 129 **he . . . Iberian lines**
the Earl of Peterborough, who captured Barcelona and Valencia in
1705–6. 130 **quincunx** a planting of five trees, one at the center of
the square formed by the rest.

And who unknown defame me, let them be
140 Scribblers or Peers, alike are *Mob* to me.
This is my plea, on this I rest my cause—
What saith my counsel, learnèd in the laws?
     F.   Your plea is good; but still I say, beware!
Laws are explained by men—so have a care.
145 It stands on record, that in Richard's times
A man was hanged for very honest rhymes.
Consult the Statute: *quart.* I think, it is,
Edwardi sext. or *prim. et quint. Eliz.*
See *Libels, Satires*—here you have it—read.
150   P.   *Libels* and *satires!* lawless things indeed!
But grave *Epistles,* bringing Vice to light,
Such as a King might read, a Bishop write,
Such as Sir ROBERT° would approve—
     F.   Indeed?
The case is altered—you may then proceed;
155 In such a cause the plaintiff will be hissed,
My Lords the Judges laugh, and you're dismissed.

153 **Sir Robert** Walpole.

THE SECOND SATIRE OF THE SECOND BOOK OF HORACE

TO MR. BETHEL°

(1734)

WHAT, and how great, the virtue and the art
To live on little with a cheerful heart;
(A doctrine sage, but truly none of mine)
Let's talk, my friends, but talk before we dine.
Not when a gilt buffet's reflected pride   5
Turns you from sound philosophy aside;
Not when from plate to plate your eyeballs roll,
And the brain dances to the mantling° bowl.
    Hear Bethel's sermon, one not versed in schools,
But strong in sense, and wise without the rules.   10
    Go work, hunt, exercise! (he thus began)
Then scorn a homely dinner, if you can.
Your wine locked up, your butler strolled abroad,
Or fish denied (the river yet unthawed),
If then plain bread and milk will do the feat,   15
The pleasure lies in you, and not the meat.°
    Preach as I please, I doubt our curious men
Will choose a pheasant still before a hen;
Yet hens of Guinea full as good I hold,
Except you eat the feathers green and gold.   20
Of carps and mullets why prefer the great,

To Mr. Bethel Hugh Bethel was an old and esteemed friend with
whom Pope maintained "constant, easy, and open commerce."
8 **mantling** sparkling.   16 **meat** food in general.

(Though cut in pieces ere my Lord can eat)
Yet for small turbots such esteem profess?
Because God made these large, the other less.

25   Oldfield° with more than harpy throat endued,
Cries "Send me, Gods! a whole hog barbecued!"
Oh blast it, south winds! till a stench exhale
Rank as the ripeness of a rabbit's tail.
By what criterion do ye eat, d' ye think,

30 If this is prized for sweetness, that for stink?
When the tired glutton labors through a treat,
He finds no relish in the sweetest meat,
He calls for something bitter, something sour,
And the rich feast concludes extremely poor:

35 Cheap eggs, and herbs, and olives still we see;
Thus much is left of old simplicity!
The robin redbreast till of late had rest,
And children sacred held a martin's° nest,
Till *beccaficos*° sold so devilish dear

40 To one that was, or would have been a Peer.
Let me extol a cat on oysters fed,
I'll have a party at the Bedford Head;°
Or even to crack live crawfish recommend,
I'd never doubt at court to make a friend.

45   'Tis yet in vain, I own, to keep a pother
About one vice, and fall into the other:
Between excess and famine lies a mean;
Plain, but not sordid; though not splendid, clean.
     Avidien, or his wife (no matter which,

50 For him you'll call a dog, and her a bitch)
Sell their presented° partridges, and fruits,
And humbly live on rabbits and on roots:
One half-pint bottle serves them both to dine,
And is at once their vinegar and wine.

55 But on some lucky day (as when they found
A lost bank-bill, or heard their son was drowned)

25 **Oldfield** a famous glutton. 38 **martin** European swallow. 39 **beccaficos** Italian name for small migratory birds esteemed as dainties in the autumn, when they have fattened on figs and grapes; here, fashionable diet for the socially ambitious. 42 **Bedford Head** a famous eating-house near Covent Garden. 51 **presented** those given to them.

At such a feast, old vinegar to spare,
Is what two souls so generous cannot bear:
Oil, though it stink, they drop by drop impart,
But souse the cabbage with a bounteous heart.   60

  He knows to live, who keeps the middle state,
And neither leans on this side, nor on that;
Nor stops, for one bad cork, his butler's pay,
Swears, like Albutius, a good cook away;
Nor lets, like Naevius, every error pass,   65
The musty wine, foul cloth, or greasy glass.

  Now hear what blessings temperance can bring:
(Thus said our friend, and what he said I sing)
First health: the stomach (crammed from every dish,
A tomb of boiled and roast, and flesh and fish,   70
Where bile, and wind, and phlegm, and acid jar,
And all the man is one intestine war)°
Remembers oft the schoolboy's simple fare,
The temperate sleeps, and spirits light as air.

  How pale, each Worshipful and Reverend guest   75
Rise from a clergy, or a City feast!°
What life in all that ample body, say?
What heavenly particle inspires the clay?
The soul subsides, and wickedly inclines
To seem but mortal, even in sound° divines.   80

  On morning wings how active springs the mind
That leaves the load of yesterday behind!
How easy every labor it pursues!
How coming to the poet every Muse!
Not but we may exceed, some holy time,°   85
Or tired in search of truth, or search of rhyme;
Ill health some just indulgence may engage,
And more the sickness of long life, old age;
For fainting age what cordial drop remains,
If our intemperate youth the vessel drains?   90

  Our fathers praised rank venison. You suppose,
Perhaps, young men! our fathers had no nose.

---

72 **intestine war** punning on civil war as well as digestive disturbance. 76 **City feast** of guild officers, addressed as "Worshipful."
80 **sound** (1) in body (2) in doctrine. 85 **holy time** holiday.

Not so: a buck was then a week's repast,
And 'twas their point, I ween, to make it last;
95 More pleased to keep it till their friends could come,
Than eat the sweetest by themselves at home.
Why had I not in those good times my birth,
Ere coxcomb-pies or coxcombs were on earth?
    Unworthy he, the voice of Fame to hear,
100 That sweetest music to an honest ear;
(For 'faith, Lord Fanny! you are in the wrong,
The world's good word is better than a song)
Who has not learned, fresh sturgeon and ham pie
Are no rewards for want, and infamy!
105 When Luxury has licked up all thy pelf,
Cursed by thy neighbors, thy trustees, thyself,
To friends, to fortune, to mankind a shame,
Think how posterity will treat thy name;
And buy a rope, that future times may tell
110 Thou hast at least bestowed one penny well.
    "Right," cries his Lordship, "for a rogue in need
To have a Taste is insolence indeed:
In me 'tis noble, suits my birth and state,
My wealth unwieldy, and my heap too great."
115 Then, like the sun, let Bounty spread her ray,
And shine that superfluity away.
Oh impudence of wealth! with all thy store,
How dar'st thou let one worthy man be poor?
Shall half the new-built churches° round thee fall?
120 Make quays, build bridges, or repair Whitehall:°
Or to thy country let that heap be lent,
As M * * o's was,° but not at five per cent.
    Who thinks that Fortune cannot change her mind,
Prepares a dreadful jest for all mankind.
125 And who stands safest? tell me, is it he
That spreads and swells in puffed prosperity,

---

119 **the new-built churches** Many of the new churches built under Queen Anne and George I suffered damage from the settling of the buildings into marshy ground; the cost of repairs was a constant concern. 120 **Whitehall** Most of the royal palace was destroyed by fire in 1698. 122 **As M * * o's was** the Duchess of Marlborough's; the Duke had been notoriously acquisitive and was reported to have profited greatly from military supplies.

Or blest with little, whose preventing care
In peace provides fit arms against a war?
    Thus BETHEL spoke, who always speaks his thought,
And always thinks the very thing he ought: *130*
His equal° mind I copy what I can,
And, as I love, would imitate the man.
In South Sea days° not happier, when surmised
The lord of thousands, than if now excised;°
In forest planted by a father's hand,   *135*
Than in five acres° now of rented land.
Content with little, I can piddle° here
On broccoli and mutton, round the year;
But ancient friends (though poor, or out of play)°
That touch my bell, I cannot turn away.   *140*
'Tis true, no turbots dignify my boards,
But gudgeons, flounders, what my Thames affords:
To Hounslow Heath I point and Banstead Down,
Thence comes your mutton, and these chicks my own:
From yon old walnut tree a shower shall fall;   *145*
And grapes, long lingering on my only wall,
And figs from standard and espalier° join;
The devil is in you if you cannot dine:
Then cheerful healths (your mistress shall have place),
And, what's more rare, a poet shall say grace.   *150*
    Fortune not much of humbling me can boast;
Though double taxed,° how little have I lost?
My life's amusements have been just the same,
Before, and after, standing armies° came.
My lands are sold, my father's house is gone;   *155*
I'll hire another's; is not that my own,

---

131 **equal** steady.   133 **South Sea days** at the time (1720) when the South Sea Bubble broke with the plummeting of the company's stocks; Pope lost heavily.   134 **excised** Walpole introduced what was taken to be a general excise in 1733 but withdrew it.   136 **five acres** the extent of Pope's leased property at Twickenham.   137 **piddle** trifle, toy with one's food.   139 **out of play** no longer in the game, i.e., in office.   147 **standard and espalier** trees growing naturally and fastened to a wall or lattice.   152 **double taxed** An extra tax was put upon Catholics' property after the Jacobite Rebellion of 1715.   154 **standing armies** strongly opposed by Tories as an expense and threat to the state.

And yours, my friends? through whose free-opening
    gate
None comes too early, none departs too late;
(For I, who hold sage Homer's rule the best,
160   Welcome the coming, speed the going guest.)
"Pray heaven it last!" (cries SWIFT) "as you go on;
I wish to God this house had been your own:
Pity! to build, without a son or wife:
Why, you'll enjoy it only all your life."
165   Well, if the use be mine, can it concern one,
Whether the name belong to Pope or Vernon?°
What's *Property?* dear Swift! you see it alter
Fro n you to me, from me to Peter Walter;°
Or, in a mortgage, prove a lawyer's share;
170   Or, in a jointure,° vanish from the heir;
Or in pure equity (the case not clear)
The Chancery° takes your rents for twenty year:
At best, it falls to some ungracious son,
Who cries, "My father's damned, and all's my own."
175   Shades, that to Bacon° could retreat afford,
Become the portion of a booby Lord;
And Hemsley, once proud Buckingham's delight,
Slides to a scrivener or a City knight.°
Let lands and houses have what lords they will,
180   Let us be fixed, and our own masters still.

---

166 **Vernon** the owner of Pope's land. 168 **Peter Walter** who was
buying up estates at the time; see note to *Satire* I, i, 3 170 **jointure**
settlement of an estate on a widow for her lifetime. 172 **Chancery**
the high court of equity, notoriously slow in settling cases. 175
Bacon Francis Bacon, whose estate near St. Albans finally passed
in Pope's day to a peer much ridiculed as a playwright. 178 **scriv-
ener . . . City knight** the estate that once belonged to the Duke of
Buckingham was sold to a London banker (City knight), Sir Charles
Duncombe for £90,000, "the greatest purchase ever made by any
subject of England."

THE FIRST EPISTLE OF THE FIRST BOOK OF HORACE

TO LORD BOLINGBROKE°

(1738)

ST. JOHN, whose love indulged my labors past,
Matures my present, and shall bound my last!
Why will you break the sabbath of my days?
Now sick alike of envy and of praise,
Public too long, ah let me hide my age!   *5*
See, modest Cibber° now has left the Stage:
Our generals now, retired to their estates,
Hang their old trophies o'er the garden gates,
In life's cool evening satiate of applause,
Nor fond of bleeding, even in BRUNSWICK's cause.°   *10*
   A Voice there is, that whispers in my ear,
('Tis Reason's voice, which sometimes one can hear)
"Friend Pope! be prudent, let your Muse take breath,
And never gallop Pegasus to death;
Lest stiff, and stately, void of fire or force,   *15*
You limp, like Blackmore on a Lord Mayor's horse."°

To Lord Bolingbroke Pope's friend, the brilliant Tory leader now
retired from politics, takes the place of Horace's Maecenas. Horace
was explaining why he had given up the writing of lyric poetry; he
was too old for it and had another, deeper interest. 6 **modest
Cibber** For his immodesty, see *Dunciad*, I. 10 **Brunswick's cause**
See note to *Satire*, 1, i, 24. 16 **Blackmore . . . horse** Blackmore's
poetry was highly regarded in the City of London if not elsewhere,
and his Pegasus is made the slow-paced horse that carries the Lord
Mayor.

Farewell then verse, and love, and every toy,
The rhymes and rattles of the man or boy;
What right, what true, what fit we justly call.
20 Let this be all my care—for this is all:
To lay this harvest up, and hoard with haste
What every day will want, and most, the last.
    But ask not to what doctors° I apply?
Sworn to no master, of no sect am I:
25 As drives the storm, at any door I knock:
And house with Montaigne now, or now with Locke.°
Sometimes a Patriot,° active in debate,
Mix with the world, and battle for the state,
Free as young Lyttleton,° her cause pursue,
30 Still true to virtue, and as warm as true:
Sometimes with Aristippus,° or St. Paul,°
Indulge my candor, and grow all to all;
Back to my native moderation slide,
And win my way by yielding to the tide.
35   Long, as to him who works for debt, the day;
Long as the night to her whose love's away
Long as the year's dull circle seems to run,
When the brisk minor pants for twenty-one:
So slow the unprofitable moments roll,
40 That lock up all the functions of my soul;
That keep me from myself; and still delay
Life's instant business to a future day:
That task, which as we follow, or despise,
The eldest is a fool, the youngest wise;
45 Which done, the poorest can no wants endure;°
And which not done, the richest must be poor.
    Late as it is, I put myself to school,
And feel some comfort, not to be a fool.

---

23 **doctors** teachers, especially dogmatic ones.   26 **Montaigne . . .
Locke** Opposed as extremes of informal and of systematic or regular
thought.   27 **Patriot** in general sense, but more pointedly a member
of the Opposition to Walpole.   29 **Lyttleton** a Whig in the Opposi-
tion, who tried to gain Pope's public support.   31 **Aristippus** the
Cyrenaic philosopher who held pleasures of the moment the chief
good.   31 **St. Paul** Cf. I Corinthians 9:22, "I am made all things to
all men," and Philemon 4:5, "Let your moderation be known unto
all men."   45 **can . . . endure** can want nothing.

Weak though I am of limb, and short of sight,
Far from a lynx, and not a giant quite;°   *50*
I'll do what Mead and Cheselden° advise,
To keep these limbs, and to preserve these eyes.
Not to go back, is somewhat to advance,
And men must walk at least before they dance.
    Say, does thy blood rebel, thy bosom move   *55*
With wretched avarice, or as wretched love?
Know, there are words, and spells, which can control
Between the fits this fever of the soul:
Know, there are rhymes, which fresh and fresh applied
Will cure the arrantest puppy of his pride.   *60*
Be furious, envious, slothful, mad, or drunk,
Slave to a wife, or vassal to a punk,°
A Swiss, a High Dutch, or a Low Dutch bear;
All that we ask is but a patient ear.
    'Tis the first virtue, vices to abhor;   *65*
And the first wisdom, to be fool no more.
But to the world no bugbear is so great,
As want of figure, and a small estate.
To either India see the merchant fly,
Scared at the spectre of pale Poverty!   *70*
See him, with pains of body, pangs of soul,
Burn through the Tropic, freeze beneath the Pole!
Wilt thou do nothing for a nobler end,
Nothing, to make Philosophy thy friend?
To stop thy foolish views, thy long desires,   *75*
And ease thy heart of all that it admires?
    Here, Wisdom calls: "Seek virtue first, be bold!
As gold to silver, virtue is to gold."
There, London's voice: "Get money, money still!
And then let virtue follow, if she will."   *80*
This, this the saving doctrine, preached to all,
From low St. James's up to high St. Paul;°
From him whose quills° stand quivered at his ear,

---

50 **Far . . . quite** Pope was becoming nearsighted, and he was under
five feet tall. 51 **Mead and Cheselden** physician and surgeon,
respectively, who attended Pope. 62 **punk** whore. 82 **From low
. . . St. Paul** by both low and high church preachers, also Whigs
and Tories. 83 **him . . . quills** the city clerk or scrivener.

To him who notches sticks° at Westminster.
85   Barnard° in spirit, sense, and truth abounds;
"Pray then, what wants° he?" Fourscore thousand
      pounds,
A pension, or such harness for a slave
As Bug now has, and Dorimant would have.
Barnard, thou art a Cit,° with all thy worth;
90   But wretched Bug, his Honor, and so forth.
    Yet every child another song will sing,
"Virtue, brave boys! 'tis virtue makes a King."
True, conscious honor is to feel no sin,
He's armed without that's innocent within;
95   Be this thy screen, and this thy wall of brass;
Compared to this, a Minister's an ass.
    And say, to which shall our applause belong,
This new court jargon, or the good old song?
The modern language of corrupted Peers,
100   Or what was spoke at CRESSY and POITIERS?°
Who counsels best? who whispers, "Be but great,
With praise or infamy, leave that to fate;
Get place and wealth, if possible, with grace;°
If not, by any means get wealth and place."
105   For what? to have a box where eunuchs sing,°
And foremost in the circle eye a King.
Or he, who bids thee face with steady view
Proud fortune, and look shallow greatness through:
And, while he bids thee, sets the example too?
110   If such a doctrine, in St. James's air,
Should chance to make the well-dressed rabble° stare;
If honest S*z° take scandal at a spark,
That less admires the palace than the park:

---

84 **who . . . sticks** the keeper of tallies of debt at the Royal Exchequer. 85 **Barnard** M.P. for the City of London, a leader of the Opposition to Walpole, a man of the highest reputation. 86 **wants** lacks. 89 **Cit** a City man, often used disparagingly. 100 **Cressy and Poitiers** the great 14th-century English victories in France. 103 **grace** with the frequent double reference to manners and to religious salvation. 105 **where . . . sing** at the opera, where *castrati* from Italy performed; George II often attended. 111 **rabble** Cf. "mob" in *Satire* II, i, line 140. 112 **honest S*z** keeper of the Privy Purse to George II.

Faith I shall give the answer Reynard° gave:
"I cannot like, dread Sir, your royal cave: *115*
Because I see, by all the tracks about,
Full many a beast goes in, but none come out."
Adieu to virtue, if you're once a slave:
Send her to court, you send her to her grave.
    Well, if a king's a lion, at the least   *120*
The people are a many-headed beast:°
Can they direct what measures to pursue,
Who know themselves so little what to do?
Alike in nothing but one lust of gold,
Just half the land would buy, and half be sold: *125*
Their country's wealth our mightier misers drain,
Or cross, to plunder provinces, the main;
The rest, some farm the poor-box, some the pews;°
Some keep assemblies,° and would keep the stews;°
Some with fat bucks° on childless dotards fawn;   *130*
Some win rich widows by their chine and brawn;
While with the silent growth of ten per cent,
In dirt and darkness hundreds stink content.
    Of all these ways, if each pursues his own,
Satire be kind, and let the wretch alone: *135*
But show me one who has it in his power
To act consistent with himself an hour.
Sir Job sailed forth, the evening bright and still,
"No place on earth (he cried) like Greenwich hill!"
Up starts a palace; lo, the obedient base   *140*
Slopes at its foot, the woods its sides embrace,
The silver Thames reflects its marble face.
Now let some whimsy, or that devil within
Which guides all those who know not what they mean,
But give the Knight (or give his Lady) spleen;°   *145*
"Away, away! take all your scaffolds down,

114 **Reynard** the fox of the fable in reply to the royal lion.   121
many-headed beast a term applied by Socrates in Plato's *Republic*.
128 **some farm . . . pews** Revenues were farmed out to collectors
for a percentage of the yield. Pews were commonly rented at the
time. The line may also allude to embezzlements by officers of the
Charitable Corporation, set up to relieve the poor.   129 **assemblies**
public ballrooms.   129 **stews** brothels.   130 **fat bucks** handsome
lovers.   145 **spleen** impulse, caprice.

"For snug's the word: My dear! we'll live in town."
   At amorous Flavio is the stocking thrown?
That very night he longs to lie alone.
150 The fool, whose wife elopes some thrice a quarter,
For matrimonial solace dies a martyr.
Did ever Proteus,° Merlin,° any witch,
Transform themselves so strangely as the rich?
Well, but the poor—The poor have the same itch;
155 They change their weekly barber, weekly news,°
Prefer a new japanner° to their shoes,
Discharge their garrets, move their beds, and run
(They know not whither) in a chaise and one;°
They hire their sculler,° and when once aboard,
160 Grow sick, and damn the climate—like a Lord.
   You laugh, half beau, half sloven if I stand,
My wig all powder, and all snuff my band;°
You laugh, if coat and breeches strangely vary,
White gloves, and linen worthy Lady Mary!°
165 But when no Prelate's lawn° with hairshirt lined,
Is half so incoherent as my mind,
When (each opinion with the next at strife,
One ebb and flow of follies all my life)
I plant, root up; I build, and then confound;°
170 Turn round to square, and square again to round;
You never change one muscle of your face,
You think this madness but a common case,
Nor once to Chancery, nor to Hales° apply;
Yet hang your lip, to see a seam awry!
175 Careless how ill I with myself agree,
Kind to my dress, my figure, not to me.
Is this my guide, philosopher, and friend?°
This, he who loves me, and who ought to mend?
Who ought to make me (what he can, or none,)

---

152 **Proteus** See note to *Dunciad,* I, 37.   152 **Merlin** the enchanter
of King Arthur's court.   155 **news** newspaper.   156 **japanner** boot-
black.   158 **chaise and one** light carriage drawn by one horse.   159
sculler oarsman.   162 **band** neckband.   164 **Lady Mary** Lady Mary
Wortley Montagu was notoriously slovenly.   165 **lawn** fine fabric
used in a bishop's attire.   169 **confound** destroy.   173 **Hales** physi-
cian at Bedlam.   177 **my guide . . . friend** Cf. *Essay on Man,* IV,
390.

That man divine whom wisdom calls her own;   *180*
Great without title, without fortune blessed;
Rich even when plundered, honored while oppressed;
Loved without youth, and followed without power;°
At home, though exiled, free, though in the Tower;°
In short, that reasoning, high, immortal thing,   *185*
Just less than Jove, and much above a King,
Nay, half in heaven—except (what's mighty odd)
A fit of vapors° clouds this demigod.

181–3 **Great . . . power** Bolingbroke's name was erased from the roll of peers and his estates forfeited in 1715. He returned from his exile abroad with a pardon in 1723 but was forbidden to resume his seat in the House of Lords; he became, nevertheless, a leader of the Opposition to Walpole for the next decade. He remained a close and much respected friend of Pope, Swift, and Gay.   184 **Tower** the Tower of London, which Bolingbroke escaped by flight from England. It should be observed that this portrait is a general one of the "man divine" Bolingbroke alone can teach one to become.   188 **vapors** spleen; hypochondria or melancholy.

THE SIXTH EPISTLE OF THE
FIRST BOOK OF HORACE

TO MR. MURRAY°

(1738)

"Not to admire,° is all the Art I know,
To make men happy, and to keep them so."
(Plain truth, dear Murray, needs no flowers of speech,
So take it in the very words of Creech.)°
5   This vault of air, this congregated ball,°
Self-centered sun, and stars that rise and fall,
There are, my friend! whose philosophic eyes
Look through, and trust the Ruler with his skies,
To him commit the hour, the day, the year,
10 And view this dreadful All without a fear.
    Admire we then what earth's low entrails hold,
Arabian shores, or Indian seas infold;°
All the mad trade of fools and slaves for gold?
Or popularity? or stars and strings?°
15 The mob's applauses, or the gifts of kings?
Say with what eyes we ought at courts to gaze,

To Mr. Murray William Murray, later Earl of Mansfield and Lord
Chief Justice, an eloquent orator in Commons, and pleader at the
bar of the House of Lords (line 49). 1 Not to admire Pope's ver-
sion of Horace's "nil admirari," i.e., be dazzled by nothing. 4
Creech Thomas Creech, the pedestrian translator of Horace, whom
Pope adapts in lines 1–2. 5 congregated ball peopled earth. 12
infold conceal. 14 stars and strings medals and ribbons of the
knightly orders.

And pay the great our homage of amaze?
   If weak the pleasures that from these can spring,
The fear to want them is as weak a thing:
Whether we dread, or whether we desire,   *20*
In either case, believe me, we admire;
Whether we joy or grieve, the same the curse,
Surprised at better, or surprised at worse.
Thus good or bad, to one extreme betray
The unbalanced mind, and snatch the man away;   *25*
For virtue's self may too much zeal be had;
The worst of madmen is a saint run mad.
   Go then, and if you can, admire the state
Of beaming diamonds, and reflected plate;
Procure a TASTE to double the surprise,   *30*
And gaze on Parian° charms with learned eyes:
Be struck with bright brocade, or Tyrian dye,°
Our birthday nobles' splendid livery.°
If not so pleased, at Council board rejoice,
To see their judgments hang upon thy voice;   *35*
From morn to night, at Senate, Rolls, and Hall,°
Plead much, read more, dine late, or not at all.
But wherefore all this labor, all this strife?
For fame, for riches, for a noble wife?°
Shall one whom nature, learning, birth, conspired *40*
To form, not to admire but be admired,
Sigh, while his Chloe blind to wit and worth
Weds the rich dulness of some son of earth?
Yet time ennobles, or degrades each line;
It brightened CRAGGS'S,° and may darken thine:° *45*
And what is fame? the meanest have their day,
The greatest can but blaze, and pass away.
Graced as thou art, with all the power of words,
So known, so honored, at the House of Lords:
Conspicuous scene! another yet is nigh,   *50*

31 **Parian** the white marble of which many classical statues were
made.   32 **Tyrian dye** Tyre was famous in antiquity for its dyes.
33 **birthday . . . livery** See notes to *Rape of the Lock*, I, 23, and
Dunciad, IV, 537.   36 **Senate . . . Hall** Parliament, Chancery, and
the High Court of Justice.   39 **noble wife** Cf. *Epistle to Dr. Ar-
buthnot*, line 393.   45 **Craggs** a prominent statesman of humble
birth.   45 **darken thine** Murray was of noble birth.

(More silent far) where kings and poets lie;°
Where MURRAY (long enough his country's pride)
Shall be no more than TULLY, or than HYDE!°
Racked with sciatics, martyred with the stone,
55 Will any mortal let himself alone?
See Ward by battered beaux invited over,
And desperate misery lays hold on Dover.°
The case is easier in the mind's disease;
There all men may be cured, whene'er they please.
60 Would ye be blest? despise low joys, low gains;
Disdain whatever CORNBURY° disdains;
Be virtuous, and be happy for your pains.
But art thou one, whom new opinions sway,
One who believes as Tindal° leads the way,
65 Who virtue and a Church alike disowns,
Thinks that but words, and this but brick and stones?
Fly then, on all the wings of wild desire,
Admire whate'er the maddest can admire.
Is wealth thy passion? Hence! from Pole to Pole,
70 Where winds can carry, or where waves can roll,
For Indian spices, for Peruvian gold,
Prevent° the greedy, and outbid the bold:
Advance thy golden mountain to the skies;°
On the broad base of fifty thousand rise,
75 Add one round hundred, and (if that's not fair)
Add fifty more, and bring it to a square.
For, mark the advantage; just so many score
Will gain a wife with half as many more,
Procure her beauty, make that beauty chaste,
80 And then such friends—as cannot fail to last.
A man of wealth is dubbed a man of worth,
Venus shall give him form, and Anstis° birth.

51 where . . . lie Westminster Abbey.   53 Tully . . . Hyde Cicero
and the first Earl of Clarendon, men of eloquence of different ages.
56–7 Ward . . . Dover two eminent quack doctors.   61 Cornbury
Henry Hyde, Viscount Cornbury, a friend of Pope, upon being of-
fered a pension, replied, "How could you tell, my Lord, that I was
to be sold? or, at least, how could you know my price so exactly?"
64 Tindal the anticlerical deist.   72 Prevent arrive before.   73 Ad-
vance . . . skies Cf. Essay on Man, IV, 73–6.   82 Anstis King at
Arms.

(Believe me, many a German prince is worse,
Who proud of pedigree, is poor of purse.)
His wealth brave Timon gloriously confounds;°   *85*
Asked for a groat, he gives a hundred pounds;
Or if three ladies like a luckless play,
Takes the whole house upon the poet's day.°
Now, in such exigencies not to need,
Upon my word, you must be rich indeed;   *90*
A noble superfluity it craves,
Not for yourself, but for your fools and knaves;
Something, which for your honor they may cheat,
And which it much becomes you to forget.
If Wealth alone then make and keep us blest,   *95*
Still, still be getting, never, never rest.

    But if to power and place your passion lie,
If in the pomp of life consist the joy;
Then hire a slave, or (if you will) a Lord
To do the honors, and to give the word;   *100*
Tell at your levee,° as the crowds approach,
To whom to nod, whom take into your coach,
Whom honor with your hand: to make remarks,
Who rules in Cornwall,° or who rules in Berks:
"This may be troublesome, is near the Chair;   *105*
That make three Members,° this can choose a Mayor."
Instructed thus, you bow, embrace, protest,
Adopt him son, or cousin at the least,
Then turn about, and laugh at your own jest.

    Or if your life be one continued treat,   *110*
If to live well means nothing but to eat;
Up, up! cries Gluttony, 'tis break of day,
Go drive the deer, and drag the finny prey;
With hounds and horns go hunt an appetite—
So Russel did, but could not eat at night,   *115*
Called happy dog the beggar at his door,
And envied thirst and hunger to the poor.
    Or shall we every decency confound,

---

85 **confounds** consumes. 88 **poet's day** the performance for the
author's benefit. 101 **levee** morning reception. 104 **Who . . . Corn-
wall** full of pocket boroughs and of votes easily controlled for a
price. 106 **makes . . . Members** controls three pocket boroughs.

Through taverns, stews, and bagnios° take our round,
120 Go dine with Chartres,° in each vice outdo
K—l's lewd cargo, or Ty—y's crew,°
From Latian sirens, French Circean feasts,
Return well travelled, and transformed to beasts,°
Or for a titled punk, or foreign flame,°
125 Renounce our country, and degrade our name?
  If, after all, we must with Wilmot° own,
The cordial drop of life is love alone,
And SWIFT cry wisely, "Vive la bagatelle!"°
The man that loves and laughs, must sure do well.
130 Adieu—if this advice appear the worst,
E'en take the counsel which I gave you first:
Or better precepts if you can impart,
Why do, I'll follow them with all my heart.

---

119 **bagnios** brothels. 120 **Chartres** Francis Chartres, gambler, debauchee, supporter of Walpole, "a man infamous for all manner of vices" (Pope). 121 **K—l's . . . crew** The Earl of Kinnoull and the Baron Tyrawley were notoriously immoral; both ambassadors, in Turkey and Portugal. Tyrawley, Horace Walpole reported, returned from Portugal with "three wives and fourteen children." 123 **transformed to beasts** like Odysseus' crew on the island of Circe, where they forgot their homes and were turned into swine. 124 **flame** (1) mistress (2) venereal disease. 126 **Wilmot** the Earl of Rochester, wrote of love as "That cordial drop Heaven in our cup has thrown,/To make the nauseous draught of life go down." 128 **bagatelle** trifle, joke.

EPILOGUE TO THE SATIRES

IN TWO DIALOGUES

(1738)

DIALOGUE I

Fr[iend]. NOT twice a twelvemonth you appear in print,
And when it comes, the court see nothing in't.
You grow correct, that once with rapture writ,
And are, besides, too *moral* for a wit.
Decay of parts, alas! we all must feel—   *5*
Why now, this moment, don't I see you steal?
'Tis all from Horace; Horace long before ye
Said, "Tories called him Whig, and Whigs a Tory;"°
And taught his Romans, in much better meter,
"To laugh at fools who put their trust in Peter."°   *10*
   But Horace, sir, was delicate, was nice;
Bubo° observes, he lashed no sort of *vice:*
Horace would say, Sir Billy° *served the crown,*
Blunt° could *do business,* H—ggins° *knew the town;*

8 Cf. *Satire* II, i, 68.   10 Cf. *Satire* II, i, 40.   12 **Bubo** "Some guilty
person very fond of making such an observation" (Pope).   13 **Sir
Billy** Sir William Yonge, a prominent Whig politician, of whom
Lord Hervey wrote, "His name was proverbially used to express
everything pitiful, corrupt, and contemptible."   14 **Blunt** Sir John,
director of the South Sea Company; upon its collapse he was
compelled to render his estate of almost £200,000.   14 **H—ggins**
John Huggins, warden of Fleet Prison; found guilty of extortion
and cruelty and tried for the murder of a prisoner, he was acquitted
because of the large number of prominent gentlemen who testified
on behalf of his character.

15 In Sappho° touch the *failings of the sex,*
In reverend bishops note some *small neglects,*
And own, the Spaniard° did a *waggish thing,*
Who cropped our ears, and sent them to the king.
His sly, polite, insinuating style
20 Could please at court, and make Augustus smile:
An artful manager, that crept between
His friend and shame, and was a kind of *screen.*°
But 'faith your very friends will soon be sore;
Patriots° there are, who wish you'd jest no more—
25 And where's the glory? 'twill be only thought
The Great Man° never offered you a groat.
Go see Sir Robert——

　　　P.　　　　　　　See Sir Robert!—hum—
And never laugh—for all my life to come?
Seen him I have, but in his happier hour
30 Of social pleasure, ill-exchanged for power;
Seen him, uncumbered with the venal tribe,
Smile without art, and win without a bribe.
Would he oblige me? let me only find,
He does not think me what he thinks mankind.°
35 Come, come, at all I laugh he laughs, no doubt;
The only difference is, I dare laugh out.

　　　F.　Why yes: with *Scripture* still you may be free;
A horselaugh, if you please, at *honesty;*
A joke on Jekyl,° or some odd *Old Whig*
40 Who never changed his principles, or wig:°
A patriot is a fool in every age,

15 **Sappho** Cf. *Satire* II, i, 83.   17 **Spaniard** The captain of a Spanish ship cut off the ear of Jenkins, an English ship captain, and told him to carry it to his master, the King. This helped to bring on war with Spain.   22 **screen** "A metaphor peculiarly appropriated to a certain person in power" (Pope); i.e., Sir Robert Walpole, who opposed all inquiries of Parliament into public frauds and was accused of being a "corrupt and all-screening minister."   24 **Patriots** a term applied to those in opposition to Walpole and the court "though some of them . . . had views too mean and interested to deserve that name" (Pope).   26 **Great Man** a common phrase for Walpole as first minister.   34 **what he . . . mankind** alluding to Walpole's reputed maxim, "All men have their price."   39 **Jekyl** "a true Whig in his principles, and a man of the utmost probity" (Pope).   40 **wig** The full-bottomed wig, which Jekyl still wore, had fallen out of fashion among the younger generation.

Whom all Lord Chamberlains° allow the stage:
These nothing hurts; they keep their fashion still,
And wear their strange old virtue, as they will.
    If any ask you, "Who's the man, so near   *45*
His prince, that writes in verse, and has his ear?"
Why, answer, Lyttleton,° and I'll engage
The worthy youth shall ne'er be in a rage:
But were his verses vile, his whisper base,
You'd quickly find him in Lord Fanny's° case.   *50*
Sejanus, Wolsey,° hurt not honest FLEURY,°
But well may put some statesmen in a fury.
    Laugh then at any, but at fools or foes;
These you but anger, and you mend not those.
Laugh at your friends, and, if your friends are sore,   *55*
So much the better, you may laugh the more;
To vice and folly to confine the jest,
Sets half the world, God knows, against the rest;
Did not the sneer of more impartial men
At sense and virtue, balance all again.   *60*
Judicious wits spread wide the ridicule,
And charitably comfort knave and fool.
    P.   Dear sir, forgive the prejudice of youth:
Adieu distinction, satire, warmth, and truth!
Come, harmless characters that no one hit;   *65*
Come, Henley's oratory,° Osborn's wit!°
The honey dropping from Favonio's° tongue,

---

42 **Lord Chamberlains** given power by the Licensing Act (1737) to
forbid performances of politically dangerous plays.   47 **Lyttleton**
"Sir George Lyttleton, Secretary of the Prince of Wales, distin-
guished both for his writings and speeches in the spirit of liberty"
(Pope), a strong opponent of Walpole and friend of Pope.   50 **Lord
Fanny** Hervey, who appears as Sporus in the *Epistle to Dr. Ar-
buthnot*, lines 305–33.   51 **Sejanus, Wolsey** "The one the wicked
minister of Tiberius; the other, of Henry VIII. The writers against
the court usually bestowed these and other odious names on the
minister" (Pope).   51 **Fleury** cardinal and minister to Louis XV of
France, whom the Patriots cited for wisdom and honesty.   66 **Hen-
ley's oratory** John Henley, an eccentric and popular preacher who
schooled gentlemen in elocution; cf. *Dunciad* III, 199.   66 **Osborn's
wit** James Pitt, a political journalist and party hireling, wrote in
defense of Walpole under many names, including Socrates and
Francis Osborne.   67 **Favonio's** from Favonius, the gentle west
wind.

The flowers of Bubo, and the flow of Y—ng!°
The gracious dew of pulpit eloquence,°
70   And all the well-whipped cream of courtly sense,
That first was H—vy's, F—'s next, and then
The S—te's, and then H—vy's once again.
O come, that easy Ciceronian style,
So Latin, yet so English all the while,
75   As, though the pride of Middleton and Bland,°
All boys may read, and girls may understand!
Then might I sing without the least offense,
And all I sung should be the *Nation's Sense;*°
Or teach the melancholy Muse to mourn,
80   Hang the sad verse on Carolina's urn,
And hail her passage to the realms of rest,
All parts performed, and *all* her children blest!°
So—satire is no more—I feel it die—
No *gazetteer*° more innocent than I—
85   And let, a-God's name, every fool and knave
Be graced through life, and flattered in his grave.
     F.   Why so? If satire knows its time and place,
You still may lash the greatest—in disgrace:
For merit will by turns forsake them all.

68 **Bubo . . . Y—ng** Bubb Dodington and Sir William Yonge, so
coupled in *Epistle to Dr. Arbuthnot,* line 280. Dodington was both
pretentious and dishonest; Yonge was described by Lord Hervey as
"talking eloquently without a meaning and expatiating agreeably
upon nothing beyond any man . . . that ever had the gift of speech."
69 In this line and following Pope refers to some florid flattery
which he believed Lord Hervey had composed. It was delivered
by Henry Fox as a parliamentary address of condolence on Queen
Caroline's death and became "The Senate's" (line 72) when Com-
mons accepted and sent it to the King. It reappeared in the form of
Hervey's Latin epitaph for the Queen.   75 **Middleton and Bland**
Conyers Middleton, Cambridge theologian and librarian, was at
work on a *Life of Cicero,* to be dedicated to Hervey in 1741. He
helped to correct the Latin of Hervey's epitaph, which Pope de-
scribed as "between Latin and English." Henry Bland, Provost of
Eton, translated the last act of Addison's *Cato* into Latin and had
it published through the friendship of Walpole. He may have been
consulted on Hervey's epitaph as well. Both would represent men
of learning used to give pretentious form to empty court flattery.
78 **Nation's Sense** court phrase for "consensus" or "official line."
82 Queen Caroline was reported to die without taking the last sac-
rament and without being reconciled to her son, the Prince of
Wales.   84 **gazetteer** a journalist paid by the government to present
its case.

Would you know when? exactly when they fall.   *90*
But let all satire in all changes spare
Immortal S——k,° and grave De——re.°
Silent and soft, as saints remove to Heaven,
All ties dissolved, and every sin forgiven,
These may some gentle ministerial wing   *95*
Receive, and place forever near a king!
There, where no Passion, pride, or shame transport,
Lulled with the sweet nepenthe° of a court;
There, where no father's, brother's, friend's disgrace
Once break their rest, or stir them from their place:°   *100*
But past the sense of human miseries,
All tears are wiped for ever from all eyes;°
No cheek is known to blush, no heart to throb,
Save when they lose a question,° or a job.°
    P.   Good Heaven forbid, that I should blast their   *105*
       glory,
Who know how like Whig ministers to Tory,
And when three sovereigns died, could scarce be vext,
Considering what a *gracious Prince* was next.
Have I, in silent wonder, seen such things
As pride in slaves, and avarice in kings;   *110*
And at a peer or peeress shall I fret,
Who starves a sister, or forswears a debt?
Virtue, I grant you, is an empty boast;
But shall the dignity of *vice* be lost?
Ye Gods! shall Cibber's son° without rebuke,   *115*
Swear like a lord, or Rich° outwhore a duke?

92 **Immortal S——k** "A title given to [Selkirk] by King James II.
He was of the Bedchamber to King William; he was so to King
George I; he was so to King George II" (Pope).   92 **grave De——re**
John West, first Earl De La Warr, an indefatigable supporter of
Walpole, "very skillful in all the forms of the House, in which he
discharged himself with great gravity" (Pope).   98 **nepenthe** a po-
tion that brings forgetfulness of grief or suffering.   100 **place** with
a pun upon political appointment.   102 Cf. Isaiah 25:8, "and the
Lord God will wipe away tears from off all faces." Here, as in
preceding lines, the moral obliviousness of the courtier is ironically
celebrated as a state of beatitude.   104 **question** parliamentary
motion.   104 **job** opportunity for personal profit or bribery.   115
Cibber's son Colley Cibber's son Theophilus, the actor; cf. *Dunciad*
III, 142.   116 **Rich** John Rich, theater manager; cf. *Dunciad* III,
261 ff.

A favorite's porter with his master vie,
Be bribed as often, and as often lie?
Shall Ward° draw contracts with a statesman's skill?
120 Or Japhet° pocket, like his Grace,° a Will?
Is it for Bond,° or Peter,° (paltry things)
To pay their debts, or keep their faith, like kings?
If Blount° dispatched himself, he played the man,
And so mayst thou, illustrious Passeran!°
125 But shall a printer,° weary of his life,
Learn from their books, to hang himself and wife?
This, this, my friend, I cannot, must not bear;
Vice thus abused, demands a nation's care:
This calls the Church to deprecate our Sin,
130 And hurls the thunder of the laws on *gin.*°
  Let modest Foster,° if he will, excel
Ten metropolitans° in preaching well;
A simple Quaker, or a Quaker's wife,
Outdo Landaffe° in doctrine,—yea in life:
135 Let humble Allen,° with an awkward shame,
Do good by stealth, and blush to find it fame.
Virtue may choose the high or low degree,
'Tis just alike to Virtue, and to me;
Dwell in a monk, or light upon a king,
140 She's still the same, beloved, contented thing.
Vice is undone, if she forgets her birth,

---

119 **Ward** a forger expelled from Parliament; cf. *Dunciad* III, 34.
120 **Japhet** Japhet Crook, convicted of forgery and fraud, condemned to stand in the pillory, have his ears cut off and his nose slit, forfeit his goods, and to be imprisoned for life. 120 **his Grace** Archbishop Wake handed the will of George I to his son, who suppressed it. 121 **Bond** Denis Bond, who embezzled the funds of the Charitable Corporation. 121 **Peter** Peter Walter, the moneylender, controlled many peers and died leaving £300,000. 123 **Blount** a deist author and suicide. 124 **Passeran** Alberto Radicati, Count of Passerano, a Piedmontese freethinker who fled to England, where he wrote a notorious defense of suicide, for which the translator and bookseller were also taken into custody. 125 **printer** as in fact happened in 1732. 130 **gin** whose exorbitant use was unsuccessfully restrained by an Act of 1736. 131 **Foster** Anabaptist minister and brilliant preacher whom Pope, it was reported, frequently went to hear. 132 **metropolitans** bishops. 134 **Landaffe** "A poor bishopric in Wales, as poorly supplied" (Pope). 135 **Allen** Ralph Allen, friend of Pope and Fielding, reformer of postal services, famous for his philanthropy.

And stoops from angels to the dregs of earth:
But 'tis the *fall* degrades her to a whore;
Let *greatness* own her, and she's mean no more:
Her birth, her beauty, crowds and courts confess,   *145*
Chaste matrons praise her, and grave bishops bless;°
In golden chains the willing world she draws,
And hers the gospel is, and hers the laws,
Mounts the tribunal, lifts her scarlet head,
And sees pale Virtue carted° in her stead.   *150*
Lo! at the wheels of her triumphal car,°
Old England's Genius, rough with many a scar,
Dragged in the dust! his arms hang idly round,
His flag inverted° trails along the ground!
Our youth, all liveried o'er with foreign gold,   *155*
Before her dance: behind her, crawl the old!
See thronging millions to the pagod° run,
And offer country, parent, wife, or son!
Hear her black trumpet through the land proclaim,
That "Not to be corrupted is the shame."   *160*
In soldier, churchman, patriot, man in power,
'Tis avarice all, ambition is no more!
See, all our nobles begging to be slaves!
See, all our fools aspiring to be knaves!
The wit of cheats, the courage of a whore,   *165*
Are what ten thousand envy and adore.
All, all look up, with reverential awe,
On crimes that scape, or triumph o'er the law:
While truth, worth, wisdom, daily they decry—
"Nothing is sacred now but villainy."   *170*
    Yet may this verse (if such a verse remain)
Show there was one who held it in disdain.

145–6 Alluding to Justinian's elevation of the prostitute **Theodora**
as his empress, and perhaps also to Sir Robert Walpole's scandalous
marriage in 1738 to Molly Skerrett, his mistress of many years and
the mother of two of his children. By the following lines (149) the
allusion expands to the Scarlet Whore of Revelations 17.   150
carted Prostitutes were punished by being exhibited from a cart.
151 **triumphal car** the conqueror's chariot.   154 **flag inverted** a ref-
erence to Walpole's foreign policy of peace at any price.   157
pagod (1) pagoda or shrine (2) idol (3) the name of a gold coin
used in India.

DIALOGUE II

Fr[iend], 'Tis all a libel—Paxton° (sir) will say.
P.   Not yet, my friend! tomorrow faith it may;
And for that very cause I print today.
How should I fret to mangle every line,
5   In reverence to the sins of *Thirty-nine!*
Vice with such giant strides comes on amain,
Invention strives to be before in vain;
Feign what I will, and paint it e'er so strong,
Some rising genius sins up to my song.
10   F.   Yet none but you by name the guilty lash;
Even Guthry° saves half Newgate by a dash.
Spare then the person, and expose the vice.
P.   How, sir! not damn the sharper, but the dice?
Come on then, satire! general, unconfined,
15   Spread thy broad wing, and souse° on all the kind.
Ye statesmen, priests, of one religion all!
Ye tradesmen, vile, in army, court, or hall!°
Ye reverend atheists.   F.   Scandal! name them, who?
     P.   Why that's the thing you bid me not to do.
20   Who starved a sister, who forswore a debt,
I never named; the town's inquiring yet.
The poisoning dame—   F.   You mean—
          P.   I don't.—   F.   You do.
P.   See, now I keep the secret, and not you!
The bribing statesman—   F.   Hold! too high you go.
25   P.   The bribed elector—   F.   There you stoop too
        low.

1 **Paxton** an official appointed to scan new publications for libel on the government.   11 **Guthry** The chaplain of Newgate Prison, who published the memoirs or confessions of criminals, often used no more than the initials of their names.   15 **souse** swooping like a hawk on its prey.   17 **hall** Westminster Hall, the chief law court of England.

P.   I fain would please you, if I knew with what: *26*
Tell me, which knave is lawful game, which not?
Must great offenders, once escaped the crown,
Like royal harts, be never more run down?
Admit your law to spare the knight requires,   *30*
As beasts of nature may we hunt the squires?
Suppose I censure—you know what I mean—
To save a bishop, may I name a dean?°
   F.   A dean, sir? no: his fortune is not made,
You hurt a man that's rising in the trade.   *35*
   P.   If not the tradesman who set up today,
Much less the prentice who tomorrow may.
Down, down, proud satire! though a realm be spoiled,°
Arraign no mightier thief than wretched Wild;°
Or, if a court or country's made a job,°   *40*
Go drench° a pickpocket, and join the mob.
   But, sir, I beg you (for the love of vice!)
The matter's weighty, pray consider twice;
Have you less pity for the needy cheat,
The poor and friendless villain, than the great?   *45*
Alas! the small discredit of a bribe
Scarce hurts the lawyer, but undoes the scribe.°
Then better sure it charity becomes
To tax directors, who (thank God) have plums;°
Still better, ministers; or, if the thing   *50*
May pinch even there—why, lay it on a king.
   F.   Stop! stop!
   P.   Must satire, then, nor rise nor fall?
Speak out, and bid me blame no rogues at all.
   F.   Yes, strike that Wild, I'll justify the blow.
   P.   Strike? why, the man was hanged ten years ago: *55*
Who now that obsolete example fears?
Even Peter° trembles only for his ears.

33 **dean** chief officer of a cathedral chapter, of lower rank than a
bishop.   38 **spoiled** despoiled.   39 **Wild** Jonathan Wild, thief, fence,
and informer; hanged in 1725 (cf. line 55).   40 **made a job** used
for personal profit.   41 **drench** a common punishment, either by
ducking or putting under a pump.   47 **scribe** scrivener or law clerk.
49 **plums** large round sums, usually £100,000.   57 **Peter** Peter
Walter (cf. *Dialogue* I, lines 10, 121), who just escaped the pillory
the year before.

   F.   What, always Peter? Peter thinks you mad,
You make men desperate, if they once are bad:
60 Else might he take to virtue some years hence—
   P.   As S———k, if he lives, will love the Prince.°
   F.   Strange spleen to S———k!
   P.   Do I wrong the man?
God knows, I praise a courtier where I can.
When I confess, there is who feels for fame,
65 And melts to goodness, need I Scarborough° name?
Pleased let me own, in Esher's peaceful Grove°
(Where Kent° and Nature vie for Pelham's love)
The scene, the master, opening to my view,
I sit and dream I see my Craggs° anew!
70   Even in a bishop I can spy desert;
Secker° is decent, Rundle° has a heart,
Manners with candor are to Benson° given,
To Berkeley,° every virtue under heaven.
    But does the court a worthy man remove?
75 That instant, I declare, he has my love:
I shun his zenith, court his mild decline;
Thus Somers° once, and Halifax,° were mine.
Oft, in the clear, still mirror or retreat,

61 **As . . . Prince** Cf. *Dialogue* I, line 92 ff. Because of the enmity
between the King and his son, Selkirk must now hate the Prince of
Wales, but as a true courtier will love him when he becomes king.
65 **Scarborough** a steady adherent of the royal interest but esteemed
by all parties for his honor and virtue.   66 **Esher's . . . grove** the
estate in Surrey of Henry Pelham, a loyal ministerial Whig.   67
Kent William Kent improved both the house and gardens at Esher.
Kent, a friend of Pope, did much to promote the "natural" garden,
and Esher was one of his finest works.   69 **Craggs** until his death
in 1721 a neighbor and friend of Pope, who wrote, "There never
lived a more worthy nature, a more disinterested mind, a more
open and friendly temper."   71 **Secker** Thomas Secker, Bishop of
Oxford, later Archbishop of Canterbury, famous for moderation,
tolerance, and discretion.   71 **Rundle** Thomas Rundle, Bishop of
Derry, of whom Pope wrote, "I never saw a man so seldom whom
I like so much."   72 **Benson** Martin Benson, Bishop of Gloucester.
73 **Berkeley** George Berkeley, Bishop of Cloyne, philosopher, and
friend of Swift and Pope.   77 **Somers** John Lord Somers, Lord
Keeper under William III. Pope knew him after his retirement and
found him both "a consummate statesman" and "a man of learning
and politeness."   77 **Halifax** Charles Montagu, first Earl of Hali-
fax; statesman, poet, and patron, a supporter of Pope's translation
of the *Iliad*.

I studied Shrewsbury,° the wise and great:
Carleton's° calm sense, and Stanhope's° noble flame,   *80*
Compared, and knew their generous end the same:
How pleasing Atterbury's° softer hour!
How shined the soul, unconquered in the Tower!
How can I Pulteney;° Chesterfield° forget,
While Roman spirit charms, and Attic wit: *85*
Argyle,° the state's whole thunder born to wield,
And shake alike the senate and the field:
Or Wyndham,° just to freedom and the throne,
The master of our passions, and his own.
Names, which I long have loved, nor loved in vain,   *90*
Ranked with their friends, not numbered with their train;
And if yet higher° the proud list should end,
Still let me say! No follower, but a friend.
    Yet think not, friendship only prompts may lays;
I follow *virtue*; where she shines, I praise: *95*
Point she to priest or elder, whig or tory,
Or round a Quaker's beaver, cast a glory.
I never (to my sorrow I declare)
Dined with the Man of Ross,° or my Lord Mayor.°
Some, in their choice of friends (nay, look not grave)   *100*
Have still a secret bias to a knave:
To find an honest man I beat about,
And love him, court him, praise him, in or out.

79 **Shrewsbury** Charles Talbot, Duke of Shrewsbury, minister in three reigns, ambassador to France, and Lord Lieutenant of Ireland.   80 **Carleton** Henry Boyle, Baron Carleton, held many public offices, including President of the Council under George I.   80 **Stanhope** commander of the British forces in Spain, 1708, and active in foreign policy later.   82 **Atterbury** Francis Atterbury, Bishop of Rochester, was imprisoned for correspondence with the Pretender in 1722. Pope testified in his behalf, but Atterbury was banished.   84 **Pulteney** William Pulteney was a leading opponent of Walpole and a brilliant speaker in Commons.   84 **Chesterfield** another opponent of Walpole and friend of Pope; later author of the famous *Letters to his Son.*   86 **Argyle** earlier a general, later an influential convert to the opposition against Walpole.   88 **Wyndham** a leader of the Tory opposition, a man of "the utmost judgment and temper" (Pope).   92 **yet higher** an allusion to Pope's friendship with the Prince of Wales.   99 **Man of Ross** John Kyrle, celebrated by Pope in the *Epistle to Bathhurst* (*Moral Essay* III) for the great public benefits he performed on an income of £500 a year.   99 **my Lord Mayor** Sir John Barnard, a religious and modest man, a great example of both private and public virtue.

F.   Then why so few commended?
P.   Not so fierce;
105 Find you the virtue, and I'll find the verse.
But random praise—the task can ne'er be done;
Each mother asks it for her booby son,
Each widow asks it for *the best of men*,
For him she weeps, and him she weds again.
110 Praise cannot stoop, like satire, to the ground;
The number may be hanged, but not be crowned.
Enough for half the greatest of these days,
To scape my censure, not expect my praise.
Are they not rich? what more can they pretend?
115 Dare they to hope a poet for their friend?
What Richelieu° wanted, Louis scarce could gain,
And what young Ammon° wished, but wished in vain.
No power the muse's friendship can command;
No power, when virtue claims it, can withstand:
120 To Cato, Virgil paid one honest line;°
O let my country's friends illumine mine!
—What are you thinking?   F.   Faith, the thought's
            no sin,
I think your friends are out, and would be in.
P.   If merely to come in, sir, they go out,
125 The way they take is strangely round about.
F.   They too may be corrupted, you'll allow?
P.   I only call those knaves who are so now.
Is that too little? Come then, I'll comply—
Spirit of Arnall!° aid me while I lie.
130 Cobham's° a coward, Polwarth° is a slave,
And Lyttleton° a dark, designing knave,

116 **Richelieu** (1585–1642) French cardinal, statesman, author; prin-
cipal minister of Louis XIII.   117 **Ammon** Alexander the Great
envied Achilles the fame that Homer had given him.   120 **line**
Aeneid VIII, 670: "And far apart, the good, and Cato giving them
laws." This is probably Cato Uticensis, who upheld republican
ideals against the first triumvirate.   129 **Arnall** Cf. *Dunciad* II, 315.
130 **Cobham** a distinguished general discharged for protesting Wal-
pole's actions, thereafter a leading opposition Whig; a friend of
Pope, to whom *Moral Essay* I is addressed.   130 **Polwarth** a disin-
terested and respected statesman, opposed to but admired by Wal-
pole.   131 **Lyttleton** an open leader of the opposition, a patron of
writers, to whom Fielding dedicated *Tom Jones* in 1749.

St. John° has ever been a wealthy fool—
But let me add, Sir Robert's° mighty dull,
Has never made a friend in private life,
And was, besides, a tyrant to his wife.   135
    But, pray, when others praise him, do I blame?
Call Verres, Wolsey,° any odius name?
Why rail they then, if but a wreath of mine,
Oh all-accomplished° St. John! deck thy shrine?
    What! shall each spur-galled hackney° of the day,   140
When Paxton° gives him double pots° and pay,
Or each new-pensioned sycophant, pretend
To break my windows if I treat a friend?°
Then wisely plead, to me they meant no hurt,
But 'twas my guest at whom they threw the dirt?   145
Sure, if I spare the minister, no rules
Of honor bind me, not to maul his tools;
Sure, if they cannot cut, it may be said
His saws are toothless, and his hatchet's lead.
    It angered Turenne,° once upon a day,   150
To see a footman kicked that took his pay:
But when he heard the affront the fellow gave,
Knew one a man of honor, one a knave;
The prudent general turned it to a jest,
And begged, he'd take the pains to kick the rest.   155
Which not at present having time to do—
    F.   Hold, sir! for God's sake, where's the affront to
        you?
Against your worship when had S———k writ?

---

132 **St. John** Henry, Viscount Bolingbroke, friend of Pope and
Swift, leader of the Tory government under Queen Anne, and of
the opposition to Walpole later; a man of learning and a brilliant
orator, to whom Pope addressed the *Essay on Man.*   133 **Sir Robert**
Walpole, here ironically dispraised in the "spirit" of the previous
lines; Walpole was personally attractive and totally indifferent to
his first wife's infidelities.   137 **Verres, Wolsey** Roman and English
models of men who used their office to gain great personal wealth.
139 **all-accomplished** "Lord Bolingbroke is something superior to
any thing I have seen in human nature" (Pope).   140 **hackney** hack
writer.   141 **Paxton** not only a censor (line 1) but director of Wal-
pole's journalistic campaigns.   141 **pots** of ale.   143 **treat a friend**
as was done at Twickenham when Pope was entertaining Boling-
broke and Bathurst.   150 **Turenne** (1611–75) Marshal of France.

Or P——ge° poured forth the torrent of his wit?
160 Or grant the bard whose distich all commend
[*In Power a servant, out of Power a friend*]°
To W——le guilty of some venial sin,
What's that to you who ne'er was out nor in?
     The Priest whose flattery bedropped the crown,
165 How hurt he you? he only stained the gown.
     And how did, pray, the florid youth offend,
Whose speech you took, and gave it to a friend?°
P.   Faith, it imports not much from whom it came;
Whoever borrowed, could not be to blame,
170 Since the whole House did afterwards the same.
Let courtly wits to wits afford supply,
As hog to hog in huts of Westphaly;
If one, through nature's bounty or his lord's,
Has what the frugal, dirty soil affords,
175 From him the next receives it, thick or thin,°
As pure a mess almost as it came in;
The blessed benefit, not there confined,
Drops to the third, who nuzzles close behind;
From tail to mouth, they feed and they carouse:
180 The last full fairly gives it to the *House*.
     F.   This filthy simile, this beastly line,
Quite turns my stomach——
     P.   So does flattery mine;
And all your courtly civet cats can vent,
Perfume° to you, to me is excrement.
185 But hear me further——Japhet,° 'tis agreed,
Writ not, and Chartres° scarce could write or read,
In all the courts of Pindus° guiltless quite;
But pens can forge, my friend, that cannot write.
And must no egg in Japhet's face be thrown,

---

159 **P——ge** Judge Page; cf. *Satire* II, i, 82.   161 A line from Bubb
Dodington's *Epistle to . . . Walpole*, published anonymously in
1726.   166–7 Cf. *Dialogue* I, 71–2.   175–80 An earlier couplet of
1715 reads "Now wits gain praise by copying other wits/As one
hog lives on what another sh——."   184 **Perfume** made from a sub-
stance extracted from a pouch near the sexual organs of the civet
cat.   185 **Japhet** Crook the forger; cf. *Dialogue* I, 120 and *Epistle
to Dr. Arbuthnot*, line 363.   186 **Chartres,** Francis; debauchee,
gambler, usurer; cf. *Epistle* I, vi, 120.   187 **Pindus** mountain in
Thessaly, a seat of the Muses.

Because the deed he forged was not my own?   190
Must never patriot then declaim at gin,
Unless, good man! he has been fairly in?
No zealous pastor blame a failing spouse,
Without a staring reason° on his brows?
And each blasphemer quite escape the rod,   195
Because the insult's not on man, but God?
      Ask you what provocation I have had?
The strong antipathy of good to bad.
When truth or virtue an affront endures,
The affront is mine, my friend, and should be yours.   200
Mine, as a foe professed to false pretense,
Who think a coxcomb's honor like his sense;
Mine, as a friend to every worthy mind;
And mine as man, who feel for all mankind.°
      F.   You're strangely proud.   205
      P.   So proud, I am no slave:
So impudent, I own myself no knave:
So odd, my country's ruin makes me grave.
Yes, ¹ am proud; I must be proud to see
Men not afraid of God, afraid of me:
Safe from the bar, the pulpit, and the throne,   210
Yet touched and shamed by ridicule alone.
      O sacred weapon! left for truth's defense,
Sole dread of folly, vice, and insolence!
To all but heaven-directed hands denied,
The muse may give thee, but the gods must guide.   215
Reverent I touch thee! but with honest zeal;
To rouse the watchmen of the public weal,
To virtue's work provoke the tardy Hall,°
And goad the prelate slumbering in his stall.
Ye tinsel insects! whom a court maintains,   220
That counts your beauties only by your stains,
Spin all your cobwebs o'er the eye of day!
The muse's wing shall brush you all away:
All his Grace preaches, all his lordship sings,

194 **staring reason** cuckold's horns. 204 From Terence's famous
line: "I am a man, and I think nothing human indifferent to me."
218 **Hall** Westminster Hall, as the seat of justice.

225 All that makes saints of queens, and gods of kings,
All, all but truth, drops deadborn from the press,
Like the last gazette, or the last address.°
    When black ambition stains a public cause,
A monarch's sword when mad vainglory draws,
230 Not Waller's wreath° can hide the nation's scar,
Nor Boileau turn the feather to a star.°
Not so, when diademed with rays divine,
Touched with the flame that breaks from virtue's shrine,
Her priestess Muse forbids the good to die,
235 And opes the Temple of Eternity.
There, other trophies deck the truly brave,
Than such as Anstis° casts into the grave;
Far other stars° than * and * * wear,
And may descend to Mordington from Stair:°
240 (Such as on Hough's unsullied miter shine,
Or beam, good Digby, from a heart like thine).°
Let Envy howl, while Heaven's whole chorus sings,
And bark at honor not conferred by kings;
Let Flattery sickening see the incense rise,
245 Sweet to the world, and grateful to the skies:
Truth guards the poet, sanctifies the line,
And makes immortal, verse as mean as mine.
    Yes, the last pen for freedom let me draw,
When truth stands trembling on the edge of law;
250 Here, last of Britons! let your names be read;

227 **address** the formal reply of Parliament to the King's opening speech.   230 **Waller's wreath** Edmund Waller's panegyrics to Oliver Cromwell.   231 **feather . . . star** Boileau, in his celebration of Louis XIV's conquest of the Lowlands, imitated Pindar's boldness by making the white feather in Louis's hat into a star or comet fatal to his enemies. Here the contrast is between this rhetorical "star" and the "rays divine" of line 232.   237 **Anstis** the chief herald at arms, who devised symbols of honor that were often cast into the grave of great peers.   238 **stars** symbols of the Order of the Garter; supply the names of the King and Prince of Wales, George and Frederick.   239 **to . . . Stair** The Earl of Stair was a distinguished soldier and envoy. Lord Mordington or his wife kept a gambling house.   240–1 "The one [Bishop Hough] an assertor of the Church of England in opposition to the false measures of King James II; the other [Lord Digby] as firmly attached to the cause of that king; both acting out of principle, and equally men of honor and virtue" (Pope).

Are none, none living? let me praise the dead,
And for that cause which made your fathers shine,
Fall by the votes of their degenerate line.
    F.   Alas! alas! pray end what you began,
And write next winter more *Essays on Man*.   255

THE DUNCIAD

TO DR. JONATHAN SWIFT

(1727–1743)

BOOK THE FIRST

THE Mighty Mother,° and her Son,° who brings
The Smithfield Muses° to the ear of kings,°
I sing. Say you, her instruments the great!°
Called to this work by Dulness, Jove, and Fate;
5   You by whose care, in vain decried and curst,
Still Dunce the Second° reigns like Dunce the First;
Say, how the goddess bade Britannia sleep,
And poured her spirit o'er the land and deep.
    In eldest time, ere mortals writ or read,
10 Ere Pallas° issued from the Thunderer's head,

---

1 **Mighty Mother** the goddess Dulness, with suggestions of the
Magna Mater, known as Cybele in Asia and associated with the
Greek Rhea; a goddess of the powers of nature, especially wild na-
ture, she was worshiped in erotic and often ecstatic rites inducing
prophetic rapture and insensibility to pain.   1 **Son** originally Lewis
Theobald, altered to the shamelessly incompetent poet laureate,
Colley Cibber, in the final version.   2 **Smithfield Muses** Smithfield
was the scene of the popular carnival of Bartholomew Fair. The
poem shows "the taste of the rabble" brought west (as Troy's cul-
ture was borne by Aeneas to Italy) to rule the arts at the court of
George I and II.   3 **great** aristocrats, men of influence, particularly
the Whigs who helped bring the Hanoverians to the throne.   6
Dunce the Second George II succeeded his father in 1727.   10 **Pal-
las** Athene sprang full-grown from the head of Zeus.

Dulness o'er all possessed her ancient right,°
Daughter of Chaos and eternal Night:°
Fate in their dotage this fair idiot gave,
Gross as her sire, and as her mother grave,
Laborious, heavy, busy, bold, and blind,   *15*
She ruled, in native anarchy, the mind.°
    Still her old empire to restore she tries,
For, born a goddess, Dulness never dies.
    O thou! whatever title please thine ear,
Dean, Drapier, Bickerstaff, or Gulliver!°   *20*
Whether thou choose Cervantes' serious air,°
Or laugh and shake in Rabelais' easy chair,°
Or praise the court, or magnify° mankind,
Or thy grieved country's copper chains° unbind;
From thy Boeotia° though her power retires,   *25*
Mourn not, my SWIFT, at aught our realm acquires,
Here pleased behold her mighty wings outspread
To hatch a new Saturnian° age of lead.
    Close to those walls° where Folly holds her throne,
And laughs to think Monroe° would take her down,   *30*
Where o'er the gates, by his famed father's hand,
Great Cibber's brazen, brainless brothers° stand;
One cell there is, concealed from vulgar eye,

11 her ancient right as one of the Titans who ruled before the sky-god, Zeus, gained power and imposed his order upon the universe. **12 Chaos . . . Night** Chaos was, according to Hesiod, the progenitor of all the gods. In *Paradise Lost*, II, Chaos and Night rule that portion of the universe that God has not ordered. **16 the mind** Dulness is both an external power and an internal, the ruler of the mind before it is ordered by reason. **20 Dean . . . Gulliver** The last three are the guises in which Swift wrote ironically; he became dean of St. Patrick's Cathedral, Dublin, in 1713. **21 Cervantes' . . . air** The ironic style of Don Quixote. **22 Rabelais' . . . chair** The comic fantasies of Gargantua and Pantagruel. **23 praise . . . magnify** with ironic reference to Swift's often scathing satire. **24 copper chains** Swift wrote *The Drapier's Letters* in 1720 to free Ireland of a debased and possibly inflationary copper coinage imposed by Sir Robert Walpole, the Prime Minister of England. **25 Boeotia** for the Greeks a land without culture, although the home of a few great men; here Ireland. **28 Saturnian** traditionally the Golden Age; but Saturn was also a symbol of lead; see line IV, 16. **29 those walls** Bedlam Hospital, the lunatic asylum. **30 Monroe** a physician there. **32 brothers** statues designed by Colley Cibber's father, a sculptor (actually of stone, not bronze).

The Cave of Poverty and Poetry.
35 Keen, hollow winds howl through the bleak recess,
Emblem of music° caused by emptiness.
Hence bards, like Proteus° long in vain tied down,
Escape in monsters, and amaze the town.
Hence Miscellanies spring, the weekly boast
40 Of Curll's° chaste press, and Lintot's rubric post.°
Hence hymning Tyburn's° elegiac lines,
Hence Journals,° Medleys, Mercuries, Magazines:
Sepulchral lies,° our holy walls to grace,
And New Year Odes,° and all the Grubstreet° race.
45   In clouded majesty here Dulness shone;
Four guardian virtues, round, support her throne:
Fierce champion Fortitude, that knows no fears
Of hisses, blows, or want, or loss of ears:°
Calm Temperance, whose blessings those partake
50 Who hunger and who thirst for scribbling sake:
Prudence, whose glass° presents the approaching jail:
Poetic Justice, with her lifted scale,
Where, in nice° balance, truth with gold she weighs,
And solid pudding against empty praise.
55   Here she beholds the chaos dark and deep,
Where nameless somethings° in their causes sleep,
Till genial Jacob,° or a warm third day,°
Call forth each mass, a poem, or a play:
How hints, like spawn, scarce quick° in embryo lie,
60 How newborn nonsense first is taught to cry,

36 **music** explained by an editor as "bowel music."   37 **Proteus** The
old man of the sea, who knew all things, could assume any shape
he wished to elude men's grasp and questioning.   40 **Curll's** Ed-
mund Curll, fined for publishing obscene books.   40 **Lintot's . . .
post** another bookseller, who posted title pages printed in red let-
ters.   41 **Tyburn** the scene of the gallows, where the condemned
criminals might sing psalms; elegies, often satirical, were published
at their death.   42 **Journals,** etc. names of popular periodicals.   43
lies flattering epitaphs inscribed on walls of churches.   44 **New
Year Odes** composed by the poet laureate.   44 **Grubstreet** center of
hack writing.   48 **loss of ears** an old penalty for seditious writing;
see I, 103n.   51 **glass** telescope.   53 **nice** precise.   56 **somethings**
unformed things not yet fully realized.   57 **Jacob** Jacob Tonson, the
publisher.   57 **warm . . . day** The proceeds of the third perform-
ance went to the playwright. A "warm" third day was a profitable
one; but "warm" also refers to the incubation process.   59 **quick**
alive.

Maggots° half-formed in rhyme exactly meet,
And learn to crawl upon poetic feet.°
Here one poor word an hundred clenches° makes,
And ductile° Dulness new meanders takes;
There motley° images her fancy strike,   65
Figures ill paired, and similes unlike.
She sees a mob of metaphors advance,
Pleased with the madness of the mazy dance:
How tragedy and comedy embrace;
How farce and epic get a jumbled race;   70
How Time himself stands still at her command,
Realms shift their place, and ocean turns to land.
Here gay description Egypt° glads with showers,
Or gives to Zembla° fruits, to Barca° flowers;
Glittering with ice here hoary hills are seen,   75
There painted° valleys of eternal green,
In cold December fragrant chaplets° blow,°
And heavy harvests nod beneath the snow.
    All these, and more, the cloud-compelling° queen
Beholds through fogs, that magnify the scene.   80
She, tinselled o'er in robes of varying hues,
With self-applause her wild creation views;
Sees momentary monsters rise and fall,
And with her own fool's colors gilds them all.
    'Twas on the day when * * rich and grave,°   85
Like Cimon,° triumphed both on land and wave:
(Pomps without guilt, of bloodless swords and maces,
Glad chains,° warm furs, broad banners, and broad faces)
Now night descending, the proud scene was o'er,
But lived, in Settle's° numbers, one day more.   90

61 **maggots** (1) grubs (2) foolish whimsies.   62 **feet** also referring
to versification.   63 **clenches** puns.   64 **ductile** fluid.   65 **motley** vari-
colored, like a fool's costume.   73 **Egypt** Egypt has almost no rain-
fall but depends on the Nile.   74 **Zembla** Nova Zembla near the
Arctic circle.   74 **Barca** Libyan desert.   76 **painted** bright-colored.
77 **chaplets** garlands.   77 **blow** blossom.   79 **cloud-compelling**
Homer's term for Zeus.   85 Supply Thorold, the Lord Mayor of
London, whose annual procession to Westminster by land and
water has just taken place.   86 **Cimon** Athenian victor at Salamis.
88 **chains** i.e., of office, therefore likely to make one "glad."   90
Settle Elkanah Settle, Poet to the City of London (a small-scale
counterpart of the court poet laureate) composed celebrations of
the Lord Mayor.

Now mayors and shrieves° all hushed and satiate lay,
Yet ate, in dreams, the custard of the day;
While pensive poets painful vigils keep,
Sleepless themselves, to give their readers sleep.
95 Much to the mindful queen the feast recalls
What city swans° once sung within the walls;
Much she revolves their arts, their ancient praise,
And sure succession down from Heywood's° days.
She saw, with joy, the line immortal run,
100 Each sire impressed and glaring in his son:
So watchful Bruin forms, with plastic° care,
Each growing lump, and brings it to a bear.
She saw old Prynne in restless Daniel° shine,
And Eusden eke out Blackmore's° endless line;
105 She saw slow Philips creep like Tate's° poor page,
And all the mighty mad in Dennis° rage.
   In each she marks her image full exprest,
But chief in Bays's° monster-breeding breast;
Bays, formed by nature stage and town to bless,
110 And act, and be, a coxcomb with success.
Dulness with transport eyes the lively dunce,
Remembering she herself was Pertness once.
Now (shame to Fortune!) an ill run at play°
Blanked his bold visage, and a thin third day:
115 Swearing and supperless the hero sate,
Blasphemed his gods, the dice, and damned his fate;
Then gnawed his pen, then dashed it on the ground,
Sinking from thought to thought, a vast profound!
Plunged for his sense, but found no bottom there,
120 Yet wrote and floundered on, in mere despair.°

91 **shrieves** sheriffs. 96 **swans** poets. 98 **Heywood's** John Heywood
in the reign of Henry VIII. 101 **plastic** shaping. 103 **Prynne** . . .
Daniel William Prynne (in 1633) and Daniel Defoe (in 1703) were
both pilloried for seditious writing. Prynne lost his ears. 104 **Eus-
den** . . . **Blackmore** Laurence Eusden, Cibber's predecessor as poet
laureate and a reputed alcoholic. Blackmore was court physician to
William III and a very copious poet. 105 **Philips** . . . **Tate** Two
weak poets, Ambrose Philips and Nahum Tate, once poet laureate.
106 **Dennis** Not only a furious critic, John Dennis admired the sub-
lime and the poet's "divine madness." 108 **Bays's** so called for the
bays or laurel crown. 113 **play** gambling. 119–20 Reminiscent of
Satan's flight through Chaos in *Paradise Lost*, II.

Round him much embryo, much abortion lay,
Much future ode, and abdicated play;
Nonsense precipitate,° like running lead,
That slipped through cracks and zigzags of the head;
All that on folly frenzy could beget,   125
Fruits of dull heat, and sooterkins° of wit.
Next, o'er his books his eyes began to roll,
In pleasing memory of all he stole,
How here he sipped, how there he plundered snug°
And sucked all o'er, like an industrious bug.   130
Here lay poor Fletcher's° half-eat scenes, and here
The frippery° of crucified Molière;
There hapless Shakespeare, yet of Tibbald° sore,
Wished he had blotted° for himself before.
The rest on outside merit° but presume,   135
Or serve (like other fools) to fill a room;
Such with their shelves as due proportion hold,
Or their fond parents dressed in red and gold;
Or where the pictures for the page atone,
And Quarles° is saved by beauties not his own.   140
Here swells the shelf with Ogilby° the great,
There, stamped with arms, Newcastle° shines complete:
Here all his suffering brotherhood retire,
And 'scape the martyrdom of jakes° and fire:
A Gothic library! of Greece and Rome   145
Well purged, and worthy Settle, Banks, and Broome.°
　　But, high above, more solid learning shone,
The classics of an age that heard of none;

123 **precipitate** in hurried motion. 126 **sooterkins** little animals supposedly bred in ladies by the small stoves placed under their petticoats in winter. 129 **snug** safely. 131 **Fletcher** Sir John Fletcher, the contemporary of Shakespeare. 132 **frippery** cast-off clothes or finery. 133 **Tibbald** Lewis Theobald edited Shakespeare and emended the text heavily. 134 **blotted** The tradition was that Shakespeare "never blotted a line." 135 **outside merit** not for use but display, because they fit the shelves (line 137), are lavishly bound (line 138) or illustrated (line 139). 140 **Quarles** Francis Quarles designed emblems, others' pictures with his poetic interpretations. Cf. *Rape of the Lock*, I, 148. 141 **Ogilby** voluminous translator of Homer and Virgil. 142 **Newcastle** The Duchess of Newcastle produced twelve large volumes. 144 **jakes** the privy, where old paper found its last use. 146 **Settle . . . Broome** poetic counterparts of Cibber.

There Caxton slept, with Wynkyn° at his side,
150   One clasped in wood, and one in strong cowhide;
There, saved by spice, like mummies, many a year,
Dry bodies of divinity appear:
De Lyra° there a dreadful front extends,
And here the groaning shelves Philemon° bends.
155   Of these, twelve volumes, twelve of amplest size,
Redeemed from tapers and defrauded pies,°
Inspired he seizes: these an altar raise:
An hecatomb° of pure unsullied lays
That altar crowns: a folio commonplace°
160   Founds the whole pile, of all his works the base:
Quartos, octavos, shape the lessening° pyre;
A twisted Birthday Ode completes the spire.
        Then he: "Great Tamer of all human art!
First in my care, and ever at my heart;
165   Dulness! whose good old cause I yet defend,
With whom my Muse began, with whom shall end;
E'er since Sir Fopling's periwig° was praise,
To the last honors of the butt° and bays:
O thou! of business the directing soul!
170   To this our head like bias to the bowl,°
Which, as more ponderous, made its aim more true,
Obliquely waddling to the mark in view:
O! ever gracious to perplexed mankind,
Still spread a healing mist before the mind;
175   And lest we err by wit's wild dancing light,°
Secure us kindly in our native night.
Or, if to wit a coxcomb make pretense,
Guard the sure barrier between that and sense;

149 **Caxton . . . Wynkyn** William Caxton and Wynkyn de Worde
were printers before the full revival of learning in Tudor England.
153 **De Lyra** His front (an epic term for brow) extends to five vol-
umes of commentaries.   154 **Philemon** Philemon Holland, volumi-
nous Elizabethan translator.   156 **tapers . . . pies** Old paper was
used to line candlesticks and bakers' tins.   158 **hecatomb** sacrifice
of a hundred oxen.   159 **commonplace** book in which one collected
notes and quotations from reading.   161 **lessening** pyramidal,
topped by the laureate's birthday ode to the King (line 162).   167
periwig the full wig worn by Cibber as actor in his first play.   168
butt the laureate was paid annually with a butt of wine.   170 **bowl**
bowling ball.   175 **wild . . . light** The will-o'-the-wisp often led men
to destruction.

Or quite unravel all the reasoning thread,
And hang some curious cobweb in its stead!   *180*
As, forced from wind-guns,° lead itself can fly,
And ponderous slugs cut swiftly through the sky;
As clocks to weight their nimble motion owe,
The wheels above urged° by the load below:
Me emptiness and Dulness could inspire,   *185*
And were my elasticity° and fire.
Some demon stole my pen (forgive the offense)
And once betrayed me into common sense:
Else all my prose and verse were much the same,
This, prose on stilts, that, poetry fallen lame.   *190*
Did on the stage my fops appear confined?°
My life gave ampler lessons to mankind.
Did the dead letter unsuccessful prove?
The brisk example never failed to move.
Yet sure had Heaven decreed to save the state,   *195*
Heaven had decreed these works a longer date.
Could Troy° be saved by any single hand,
This gray-goose weapon° must have made her stand.
What can I now? my Fletcher cast aside,
Take up the Bible,° once my better guide?   *200*
Or tread the path by venturous heroes trod,
This box° my thunder, this right hand my God?
Or chaired at White's° amidst the doctors° sit,
Teach oaths to gamesters, and to nobles wit?
Or bidst thou rather party to embrace?   *205*
(A friend to party thou, and all her race;
'Tis the same rope at different ends they twist;
To Dulness Ridpath is as dear as Mist.)°
Shall I, like Curtius,° desperate in my zeal,
O'er head and ears plunge for the commonweal?   *210*

---

181 **wind-guns** air rifles.   184 **urged** driven.   186 **elasticity** propelling force.   191 **confined** restrained.   197 **Troy** another echo (see note to I, 2) of the parallel of Cibber and Aeneas.   198 **weapon** his quill pen.   200 **Bible** Cibber's father meant him for the clergy. 202 **box** dice box.   203 **White's** a club for gambling.   203 **doctors** a term for loaded dice, with suggestions of Jesus in the temple. 208 **Ridpath . . . Mist** one a Whig, the other a Tory journalist.   209 **Curtius** the legendary hero who leaped into a chasm to save Rome.

Or rob Rome's ancient geese° of all their glories,
And cackling save the monarchy of Tories?
Hold—to the Minister° I more incline;
To serve his cause, O Queen! is serving thine.
215 And see! thy very gazetteers° give o'er,
Even Ralph repents, and Henley° writes no more.
What then remains? Ourself. Still, still remain
Cibberian° forehead, and Cibberian brain.
This brazen brightness, to the squire so dear;
220 This polished hardness, that reflects the peer;
This arch absurd, that wit and fool delights;
This mess, tossed up of Hockley Hole° and White's;
Where dukes and butchers join to wreathe my crown,
At once the bear and fiddle° of the town.
225   "O born in sin, and forth in folly brought!
Works damned, or to be damned! (your father's fault)
Go, purified by flames ascend the sky,
My better and more Christian progeny!°
Unstained, untouched, and yet in maiden sheets;
230 While all your smutty sisters° walk the streets.
Ye shall not beg, like gratis-given Bland,°
Sent with a pass, and vagrant through the land;
Not sail, with Ward,° to ape-and-monkey climes,
Where vile Mundungus° trucks° for viler rhymes:
235 Not sulphur-tipped emblaze an alehouse fire;
Not wrap up oranges, to pelt your sire!°
O! pass more innocent, in infant state,

211 **geese** They warned the Romans in the Capitol of the approach of the Gauls. 213 **Minister** Sir Robert Walpole, the Whig Prime Minister. 215 **gazetteers** hireling political journalists. 216 **Ralph . . . Henley** both writers in the pay of Walpole, against whom James Ralph had turned. 218 **Cibberian** with echoes of Milton's "Cimmerian darkness"; see note to III, 4. 222 **Hockley Hole** scene of bear-baiting, often preceded by playing on the fiddle (line 224). 224 **fiddle** also a jester. 228 **more . . . progeny** Cibber wrote: "My muse and my spouse were equally prolific." His son Theophilus and daughter Charlotte were both notorious. 230 **smutty sisters** copies of his works bound and offered for sale. 231 **Bland** His pamphlets for Walpole were sent post-free to all towns in England. 233 **Ward** Ned Ward's popular works were widely sold in the colonies. 234 **Mundungus** cheap tobacco. 234 **trucks** is bartered. 236 **pelt your sire** Oranges were sold in theatres and often thrown at actors.

To the mild limbo of our father Tate:
Or peaceably forgot, at once be blessed
In Shadwell's° bosom with eternal rest!   *240*
Soon to that mass of nonsense to return,
Where things destroyed are swept to things unborn."
   With that, a tear (portentous sign of grace!)
Stole from the master of the sevenfold° face:
And thrice he lifted high the birthday brand,   *245*
And thrice he dropped it from his quivering hand;
Then lights the structure, with averted eyes:
The rolling smoke involves° the sacrifice.
The opening clouds disclose each work by turns,
Now flames the Cid, and now Perolla burns;   *250*
Great Caesar roars, and hisses in the fires;
King John in silence modestly expires:
No merit now the dear Nonjuror claims,
Molière's old stubble in a moment flames.°
Tears gushed again, as from pale Priam's eyes   *255*
When the last blaze sent Ilion to the skies.
   Roused by the light, old Dulness heaved the head,
Then snatched a sheet of Thulè° from her bed;
Sudden she flies, and whelms it o'er the pyre;
Down sink the flames, and with a hiss expire.   *260*
   Her ample presence fills up all the place;
A veil of fogs dilates° her awful face:
Great in her charms! as when on shrieves and mayors
She looks, and breathes herself into their airs.
She bids him wait her to her sacred dome:°   *265*
Well pleased he entered, and confessed his home.
So spirits ending their terrestrial race.
Ascend, and recognize their native place.
This the Great Mother° dearer held than all

240 **Shadwell's** Thomas Shadwell, like Tate, was once poet laureate.
Cf. Luke 16:22. 244 **sevenfold** because of (1) actor's changes (2)
shamelessness. 248 **involves** enfolds. 250–4 **Now flames . . .
flames** a series of references to Cibber's plays, many of them adapta-
tions. 258 **Thulè** a poem by Ambrose Philips whose title designates
the northernmost region of earth; Pope is alluding to the "coldness
and heaviness" of Philips' writing as well as to the wet sheets of a
newly printed book. 262 **dilates** magnifies, as in I, 80. 265 **dome**
the Cave of Poverty and Poetry (I, 34). 269 **Great Mother** See
note to I, 1.

270 The clubs of quidnuncs,° or her own Guildhall:°
     Here stood her opium, here she nursed her owls,°
     And here she planned the imperial seat of fools.
         Here to her chosen all her works she shows;
     Prose swelled to verse, verse loitering into prose:
275 How random thoughts now meaning chance to find,
     Now leave all memory of sense behind:
     How prologues into prefaces° decay,
     And these to notes are frittered quite away:
     How index learning turns no student pale,
280 Yet holds the eel of science by the tail:°
     How, with less reading° than makes felons 'scape,
     Less human genius than God gives an ape,
     Small thanks to France, and none to Rome or Greece,
     A past, vamped,° future, old, revived, new piece,
285 'Twixt Plautus, Fletcher, Shakespeare, and Corneille,
     Can make a Cibber, Tibbald, or Ozell.°
         The goddess then, o'er his anointed head,
     With mystic words, the sacred opium shed.
     And lo! her bird (a monster of a fowl,
290 Something betwixt a Heidegger° and owl)
     Perched on his crown. "All hail! and hail again,
     My son! the promised land expects thy reign.
     Know, Eusden° thirsts no more for sack or praise;
     He sleeps among the dull of ancient days;

---

270 **quidnuncs** gossips, newsmongers; based on *quid nunc*, what news?   270 **her own Guildhall** any meeting place of a guild; here with reference to the famous one in the City of London.   271 **owls** the bird of Pallas Athene and a symbol of wisdom; but here, in its other traditional sense, as a bird of the night, unclean and stupidly solemn.   277 **prologues into prefaces** from verse prologues, often witty, into prose prefaces, notoriously verbose.   279–80 **index learning . . . tail** "The most accomplished way of using books at present is . . . to get a thorough insight into the index, by which the whole book is governed and turned, like fishes by the tail" (Swift, *A Tale of a Tub*, 1704).   281 **less reading** "Benefit of clergy" freed those clergymen who could prove their ability to read from trial in secular courts for felonies; this privilege was extended to laymen for many offenses.   284 **vamped** revamped.   286 **Cibber . . . Ozell** all three minor playwrights given to free but feeble use of others' works.   290 **Heidegger** a Swiss, famous for his ugliness, who was Master of the Revels under George II and manager of a London opera house. The not-quiteness of this creature recalls I, 284.   293 **Eusden** See note to I, 104.

Safe, where no critics damn, no duns° molest,   295
Where wretched Withers, Ward, and Gildon° rest,
And highborn Howard,° more majestic sire,
With fool of quality° completes the quire.°
Thou, Cibber! thou, his Laurel shalt support,°
Folly, my son, has still a friend at court.   300
Lift up° your gates, ye princes, see him come!
Sound, sound, ye viols; be the catcall dumb!
Bring, bring the madding bay, the drunken vine;
The creeping, dirty, courtly ivy° join.
And thou! his aide-de-camp, lead on my sons,   305
Light-armed with points,° antitheses, and puns.
Let Bawdry, Billingsgate, my daughters dear,
Support his front, and oaths bring up the rear:
And under his, and under Archer's° wing,
Gaming and Grubstreet skulk behind the King.   310
    "O! when shall rise a monarch all our own,
And I, a nursing mother, rock the throne;
'Twixt prince and people close the curtain draw,
Shade him from light, and cover him from law;
Fatten the courtier, starve the learnèd band,   315
And suckle armies,° and dry-nurse the land:
Till senates nod to lullabies divine,
And all be sleep, as at an ode of thine."
    She ceased. Then swells the Chapel Royal° throat:
"God save King Cibber!" mounts in every note.   320
Familiar White's, "God save King Colley!" cries;
"God save King Colley!" Drury Lane° replies:

295 **duns** bill collectors.   296 **Withers . . . Gildon** minor poets now
dead.   297 **Howard** known as "foolish Ned," author of six plays
and a much ridiculed epic poem.   298 **quality** aristocratic rank;
either Howard or John Lord Hervey, recently dead (for whom see
notes to *Epistle to Dr. Arbuthnot*, line 305).   298 **quire** choir; but
also the collection of pages, since all bad poets are so much paper.
299 **his Laurel . . . support** shall inherit Eusden's laureateship.   301
lift up Cf. Psalms 24:7 "Lift up your heads, O ye gates; and be ye
lift up, ye everlasting doors; and the King of glory shall come in."
304 **ivy** "emblematic of the . . . virtues of a court poet in particular"
(Pope).   306 **points** witty turns.   309 **Archer** Thomas Archer, as
Groom-Porter, presided over gambling at court; he died a very rich
man.   316 **armies** George II was criticized for supporting foreign
mercenary soldiers.   319 **Chapel Royal** where the laureate's odes
were performed to music.   322 **Drury Lane** resort of prostitutes.

To Needham's quick the voice triumphal rode,
But pious Needham dropped the name of God;°
325 Back to the Devil° the last echoes roll,
And "Coll!" each butcher roars at Hockley Hole.
   So when Jove's block descended from on high
(As sings thy great forefather Ogilby)°
Loud thunder to its bottom shook the bog,
330 And the hoarse nation croaked, "God save King Log!"

BOOK THE SECOND

High on a gorgeous seat, that far outshone
Henley's gilt tub,° or Flecknoe's Irish throne,°
Or that where on her Curlls the public pours,
All-bounteous, fragrant grains and golden showers,°
5 Great Cibber sat:° the proud Parnassian° sneer,
The conscious simper, and the jealous leer,

323–4 **Needham's . . . God** Mother Needham, who kept a well-known house of prostitution, protested her hope that she might "get enough by her profession to leave it off in time and make her peace with God." She died as a result of abuse in the pillory.   325 **Devil** The Devil Tavern, where laureate odes were rehearsed.   328 **Ogilby** as translator of Aesop's *Fables*. When the frogs begged Zeus for a king, he gave them a log. Later, dissatisfied, they chose a stork, who devoured them.   2 **Henley's . . . tub** Orator Henley was a very popular preacher. The dissenter's pulpit was often called a "tub" (cf. Swift's *A Tale of a Tub*); but Henley's was richly adorned. Cf. *Dunciad*, III, 199.   2 **Flecknoe's . . . throne** in Dryden's *MacFlecknoe* the former Irish priest crowns his successor to the throne of Dulness, Thomas Shadwell, the poet laureate.   3–4 **Curlls . . . showers** Edmund Curll, bookseller and publisher, stood on a platform in the pillory, where (Pope suggests) he was pelted with refuse, malt grains, rotten eggs, or the contents of chamber pots.   1–5 **High . . . sat** Cf. *Paradise Lost*, II, 1–5: "High on a Throne of Royal State, which far/Outshone the wealth of Ormus and of Ind,/Or where the gorgeous East with richest hand/Show'rs on her Kings Barbaric Pearl and Gold,/Satan exalted sat. . . ."   5 **Parnassian** as an exalted resident of Parnassus, the mountain of Apollo and the Muses.

Mix on his look: all eyes direct their rays
On him, and crowds turn coxcombs as they gaze.
His peers shine round him with reflected grace,
New edge their dulness, and new bronze their face.　　*10*
So from the sun's broad beam, in shallow urns
Heaven's twinkling sparks draw light, and point their
　　　horns.°
　　Not with more glee, by hands Pontific crowned,
With scarlet hats° wide-waving circled round,
Rome in her capitol saw Querno° sit,　　*15*
Throned on seven hills, the Antichrist° of wit.
　　And now the queen, to glad her sons, proclaims
By herald hawkers,° high heroic games.
They summon all her race: an endless band
Pours forth, and leaves unpeopled half the land.　　*20*
A motley mixture! in long wigs, in bags,°
In silks, in crapes,° in garters,° and in rags,
From drawing rooms, from colleges, from garrets,
On horse, on foot, in hacks, and gilded chariots:
All who true dunces in her cause appeared,　　*25*
And all who knew° those dunces to reward.
　　Amid that area wide they took their stand,
Where the tall maypole° once o'erlooked the Strand,
But now (so Anne and piety ordain)
A church collects the saints° of Drury Lane.　　*30*
　　With authors, stationers° obeyed the call,
(The field of glory is a field for all).
Glory, and gain, the industrious tribe provoke;
And gentle Dulness ever loves a joke.
A poet's form she placed before their eyes,　　*35*

---

12 **horns** of the crescent moon; by analogy, of Venus, the morning
star, which also has phases.　14 **scarlet hats** of cardinals.　15
Querno A poet made court jester by Pope Leo X and crowned with
laurel.　16 **Antichrist** associated in Revelations with the power of
Rome and the apocalyptic scarlet beast, whose seven heads can be
taken as the seven hills of Rome.　18 **hawkers** Dulness' heralds are
newspaper vendors.　21 **bags** wigs worn in bags, a youthful fashion.
22 **crapes** possibly clerical dress.　22 **garters** Order of the Garter,
England's highest decoration, newly revived by Walpole.　26 **knew**
knew how.　28 **maypole** removed in 1718, replaced by the new
church St. Mary le Strand.　30 **saints** the pious; here applied to the
prostitutes of Drury Lane.　31 **stationers** booksellers.

And bade the nimblest racer seize the prize;
No meagre, muse-rid mope, adust° and thin,
In a dun nightgown of his own loose skin;
But such a bulk as no twelve bards could raise,
40 Twelve starveling bards of these degenerate days.
All as a partridge plump, full-fed, and fair,
She formed this image of well-bodied air;
With pert flat eyes she windowed well its head;
A brain of feathers, and a heart of lead;
45 And empty words she gave, and sounding° strain,
But senseless, lifeless! idol void and vain!
Never was dashed out, at one lucky hit,
A fool so just a copy of a wit;
So like, that critics said, and courtiers swore,
50 A wit it was, and called the phantom Moore.°
    All gaze with ardor: some a poet's name,
Others a sword-knot° and laced° suit inflame.
But lofty Lintot in the circle rose:
"This prize is mine; who tempt° it are my foes;
55 With me began this genius, and shall end."
He spoke: and who with Lintot shall contend?
    Fear held them mute. Alone, untaught to fear,
Stood dauntless Curll; "Behold that rival here!
The race by vigor, not by vaunts is won;
60 So take the hindmost, Hell," he said, and run.
Swift as a bard° the bailiff leaves behind,
He left huge Lintot, and outstripped the wind.
As when a dabchick° waddles through the copse
On feet and wings, and flies, and wades, and hops;
65 So laboring on, with shoulders, hands, and head,
Wide as a windmill all his figure spread,
With arms expanded Bernard rows his state,

37 **adust** sallow.   45 **sounding** resonant, sonorous.   50 **Moore** James
Moore Smythe, a young man eager to be recognized as a wit, who
read unpublished works of Arbuthnot and Pope as his own and
tried by any means to fill the theater for his play.   52 **sword-knot**
ribbon tied to the hilt.   52 **laced** decorated with lace.   54 **tempt** try
for. This competition between rival publishers begins Pope's parody
of the epic games of Homer (*Iliad*, XXIII) and Virgil (*Aeneid*,
V).   61 **bard** i.e., a poet fleeing arrest for debt.   63 **dabchick** grebe,
an aquatic bird.

And left-legged Jacob° seems to emulate.
Full in the middle way there stood a lake,
Which Curll's Corinna° chanced that morn to make: 70
(Such was her wont, at early dawn to drop
Her evening cates° before his neighbor's shop,)
Here fortuned Curll to slide; loud shout the band,
And "Bernard! Bernard!" rings through all the Strand.
Obscene with filth the miscreant lies bewrayed,°   75
Fallen in the plash his wickedness had laid:
Then first (if poets aught of truth declare)
The caitiff vaticide° conceived a prayer.
    "Hear, Jove! whose name my bards and I adore,
As much at least as any God's, or more;   80
And him and his, if more devotion warms,
Down with the Bible,° up with the Pope's Arms."°
    A place there is, betwixt earth, air, and seas,
Where, from ambrosia, Jove retires for ease.
There in his seat two spacious vents appear,   85
On this he sits, to that he leans his ear,
And hears the various vows of fond mankind;
Some beg an eastern, some a western wind:
All vain petitions, mounting to the sky,
With reams abundant this abode supply;   90
Amused he reads, and then returns the bills
Signed with that ichor which from Gods distils.
    In office here fair Cloacina° stands,
And ministers to Jove with purest hands.
Forth from the heap she picked her votary's prayer,   95
And placed it next him, a distinction rare!
Oft had the goddess heard her servant's call,
From her black grottos° near the Temple Wall,
Listening delighted to the jest unclean
Of linkboys° vile, and watermen° obscene;   100
Where as he fished her nether realms for wit,

68 **left-legged Jacob** Dryden wrote of Jacob Tonson's "two left
legs." 70 **Corinna** Mrs. Thomas, who sold some of Pope's letters
to Curll for unauthorized publication. She had an extensive amor-
ous career. 72 **cates** delicacies. 75 **bewrayed** revealed. 78 **vati-
cide** murderer of poets. 82 **Bible** Curll's bookseller's sign. 82
Pope's Arms Lintot's sign (cross keys). 93 **Cloacina** goddess of the
sewers, or here, the privy. 98 **black grottos** coal wharves on the
Thames. 100 **linkboys** torch-carriers. 100 **watermen** ferrymen.

She oft had favored him, and favors yet.
Renewed by ordure's sympathetic force,
As oiled with magic juices° for the course,
105 Vigorous he rises; from the effluvia strong
Imbibes new life, and scours and stinks along;
Repasses Lintot, vindicates° the race,
Nor heeds the brown dishonors of his face.
    And now the victor stretched his eager hand
110 Where the tall Nothing° stood, or seemed to stand;
A shapeless shade, it melted from his sight,
Like forms in clouds, or visions of the night.
To seize his papers, Curll, was next thy care;
His papers light fly diverse, tossed in air;
115 Songs, sonnets, epigrams the winds uplift,
And whisk 'em back to Evans, Young, and Swift.°
The embroidered suit at least he deemed his prey;
That suit an unpaid tailor snatched away.
No rag, no scrap, of all the beau, or wit,
120 That once so fluttered, and that once so writ.
    Heavens rings with laughter: of the laughter vain,
Dulness, good queen, repeats the jest again.
Three wicked imps, of her own Grubstreet choir,
She decked like Congreve, Addison, and Prior;°
125 Mears, Warner, Wilkins° run: delusive thought!
Breval, Bond, Besaleel° the varlets caught.
Curll stretches after Gay, but Gay is gone,
He grasps an empty Joseph for a John:°
So Proteus,° hunted in a nobler shape,
130 Became, when seized, a puppy, or an ape.
    To him the goddess: "Son! thy grief lay down,
And turn this whole illusion on the town:

104 **oiled . . . juices** as witches use magic ointments to enable them
to fly.   107 **vindicates** wins.   110 **Nothing** the "poet's form" of II,
35.   116 **Evans . . . Swift** the original authors.   124 **Congreve . . .**
Prior three admirable writers, the playwright William Congreve, the
essayist and critic Joseph Addison, the poet Matthew Prior.   125
Mears . . . Wilkins "booksellers and printers cf much anonymous
stuff" (Pope).   126 **Breval . . . Besaleel** minor authors who had at-
tacked Pope.   128 **Joseph . . . John** Curll published several pam-
phlets as by Joseph Gay, hoping that they would be mistaken for the
works of the fine satiric poet John Gay.   129 **Proteus** See note to
I, 37.

As the sage dame, experienced in her trade,
By names of toasts retails each battered jade°
(Whence hapless Monsieur much complains at Paris   *135*
Of wrongs from Duchesses and Lady Marys);°
Be thine, my stationer! this magic gift;
Cook shall be Prior, and Concanen, Swift:°
So shall each hostile name° become our own,
And we too boast our Garth and Addison."   *140*
     With that she gave him (piteous of his case,
Yet smiling at his rueful length of face)
A shaggy tapestry, worthy to be spread
On Codrus'° old, or Dunton's° modern bed;
Instructive work! whose wry-mouthed portraiture   *145*
Displayed the fates her confessors° endure.
Earless° on high, stood unabashed Defoe,
And Tutchin° flagrant° from the scourge below.
There Ridpath, Roper,° cudgelled might ye view,
The very worsted still looked black and blue.   *150*
Himself among the storied chiefs° he spies,
As, from the blanket,° high in air he flies,
And "Oh!" (he cried) "what street, what lane but knows
Our purgings,° pumpings, blanketings, and blows?
In every loom our labors shall be seen,   *155*
And the fresh vomit run for ever green!"
     See in the circle next, Eliza° placed,

124 **jade** prostitute.   136 **Duchesses . . . Marys** titles assumed by (in
this case diseased) prostitutes; with a glance at Pope's enemy, Lady
Mary Wortley Montagu.   138 **Cook . . . Swift** Dulness substitutes
a feebly scurrilous writer for an excellent one in each case.   139
name Dulness is conquering the true wits by providing cheap sub-
stitutes under the same name.   144 **Codrus** an impoverished
Roman poet in Juvenal's third satire.   144 **Dunton** an abusive sati-
rist and poor bookseller.   146 **confessors** (pronounced with stress
on the first syllable) the adherents of Dulness.   147 **Earless** Defoe
never lost his ears; these are prophetic visions, not historical facts.
148 **Tutchin** sentenced to be whipped through several towns for
libel.   148 **flagrant** flaming.   149 **Ridpath, Roper** authors of scan-
dalous political journals on opposed sides.   151 **among . . . chiefs**
Curll sees his story as Aeneas finds tapestries in Dido's palace rep-
resenting the fate of the Trojan heroes, including his own.   152
blanket Curll was tossed in a blanket by the boys of Westminster
School for plagiarism.   154 **purgings** Pope, upon provocation, se-
cretly administered an emetic to Curll and later wrote an account
of the episode.   157 **Eliza** Eliza Haywood was the author of two
scandalous books.

Two babes of love close clinging to her waist;
Fair as before her works she stands confessed,
160 In flowers and pearls by bounteous Kirkall° dressed.
The goddess then: "Who best can send on high
The salient spout,° far-streaming to the sky;
His be yon Juno of majestic size,
With cow-like udders, and with ox-like eyes.°
165 This china jordan° let the chief o'ercome
Replenish, not ingloriously, at home."
    Osborne° and Curll accept the glorious strife,
(Though this his son dissuades, and that his wife).
One on his manly confidence relies,
170 One on his vigor and superior size.
First Osborne leaned against his lettered° post;
It rose, and labored to a curve at most.
So Jove's bright bow displays its watery round,
(Sure sign° that no spectator shall be drowned).
175 A second effort brought but new disgrace:
The wild Meander° washed the artist's face:
Thus the small jet, which hasty hands unlock,
Spurts in the gardener's eyes who turns the cock.
Not so from shameless Curll; impetuous spread
180 The stream, and smoking flourished o'er his head.
So (famed like thee for turbulence and horns)°
Eridanus° his humble fountain scorns;
Through half the heavens he pours the exalted urn;
His rapid waters in their passage burn.°
185   Swift as it mounts, all follow with their eyes:
Still happy impudence obtains the prize.
Thou triumphst, victor of the high-wrought day,

160 **Kirkall** He engraved her portrait for her published works. 162 **salient spout** upward jet (of urine). 164 **cow-like . . . eyes** Pope extends Homer's "ox-eyed (i.e., bright-eyed) Hera" to include other bovine attributes. 165 **jordan** chamber pot (as second prize). 167 **Osborne** bookseller who misrepresented his copies of Pope's works; "a man entirely destitute of shame," according to Dr. Johnson. 171 **lettered** covered with advertisements. 174 **sign** Jove's rainbow is a sign to man, as is God's after the deluge in Genesis 8:12–16. 176 **Meander** the winding river of Asia Minor. 181 **horns** River-gods were represented as horned figures with gushing urns. The horns also suggest Curll's cuckoldry. 182 **Eridanus** the river that flowed through the heavens. 184 **burn** with the suggestion of venereal disease.

And the pleased dame, soft-smiling, leadst away.
Osborne, through perfect modesty o'ercome,
Crowned with the jordan, walks contented home.   190
 But now for authors nobler palms remain;
Room for my lord! three jockeys in his train;
Six huntsmen with a shout precede his chair:
He grins, and looks broad nonsense with a stare.
His Honor's meaning Dulness thus exprest,   195
"He wins this patron, who can tickle° best."
 He chinks his purse, and takes his seat of state:
With ready quills the dedicators wait;
Now at his head the dextrous task commence,
And, instant, fancy feels the imputed sense;°   200
Now gentle touches wanton o'er his face,
He struts Adonis,° and affects grimace:
Rolli° the feather to his ear conveys,
Then his nice taste directs our operas:
Bentley° his mouth with classic flattery opes,   205
And the puffed orator bursts out in tropes.
But Welsted° most the poet's healing balm
Strives to extract from his soft, giving palm;
Unlucky Welsted! thy unfeeling master,
The more thou ticklest, gripes his fist the faster.   210
 While thus each hand promotes the pleasing pain,
And quick sensations skip from vein to vein;
A youth unknown to Phoebus,° in despair,
Puts his last refuge all in heaven and prayer.
What force have pious vows! The Queen of Love   215
His sister sends, her votaress, from above.
As, taught by Venus, Paris° learnt the art
To touch Achilles' only tender part;
Secure, through her, the noble prize to carry,
He marches off, his Grace's secretary.   220

196 **tickle** tickling with a feather was a well-known symbol of flattery.   200 **imputed sense** implied praise.   202 **Adonis** the beautiful youth loved by Venus.   203 **Rolli** a poet who taught Italian to gentlemen interested in opera.   205 **Bentley** either Richard Bentley, the great classical scholar, or (Pope asserts) his nephew Thomas, also an editor of Horace and a flattering dedicator.   207 **Welsted** the poet and critic.   213 **Phoebus** Apollo, god of poetry.   217 **Paris** With Venus' aid, his arrow found Achilles' one vulnerable part, his heel.

"Now turn to different sports" (the goddess cries)
"And learn, my sons, the wondrous power of noise.
To move, to raise, to ravish every heart,
With Shakespeare's nature, or with Jonson's art,
225 Let others aim: 'tis yours to shake the soul
With thunder° rumbling from the mustard bowl,
With horns and trumpets now to madness swell,
Now sink in sorrows with a tolling bell;
Such happy arts attention can command,
230 When fancy flags, and sense is at a stand.
Improve we these. Three catcalls be the bribe°
Of him, whose chattering shames the monkey tribe:
And his this drum, whose hoarse heroic bass
Drowns the loud clarion of the braying ass."
235   Now thousand tongues are heard in one loud din:
The monkey-mimics rush discordant in.
'Twas chattering, grinning, mouthing, jabbering all,
And noise and Norton, brangling and Breval,
Dennis and dissonance,° and captious° art,
240 And snip-snap short, and interruption smart,
And demonstration thin, and theses thick,
And major, minor,° and conclusion quick.
"Hold!" (cried the Queen) "a catcall each shall win;
Equal your merits! equal is your din!
245 But that this well-disputed game may end,
Sound forth, my brayers, and the welkin rend."
    As, when the long-eared milky mothers° wait
At some sick miser's triple-bolted gate,
For their defrauded, absent foals they make
250 A moan so loud, that all the guild° awake;
Sore sighs Sir Gilbert, starting at the bray,
From dreams of millions, and three groats to pay.
So swells each windpipe; ass intones to ass,
Harmonic twang! of leather, horn, and brass;

---

226 **thunder** Stage thunder was produced (like mustard) by beating
in a bowl. The dunces forsake literary art for spectacular stage
effects.   231 **bribe** prize.   238–9 **noise . . . dissonance** As W. K.
Wimsatt has observed, these proper names and types of noise be-
come equivalent and interchangeable.   239 **captious** confusing.
242 **major, minor** premises in a syllogism.   247 **milky mothers** Asses'
milk was considered medicinal.   250 **guild** neighborhood of the city.

Such as from laboring lungs the enthusiast° blows,   255
High sound, attempered to the vocal nose;
Or such as bellow from the deep divine;
There Webster! pealed thy voice, and Whitfield!° thine.
But far o'er all, sonorous Blackmore's° strain;
Walls, steeples, skies, bray back to him again.   260
In Tottenham fields, the brethren, with amaze,
Prick all their ears up, and forget to graze;
Long Chancery Lane retentive° rolls the sound,
And courts to courts return it round and round;
Thames wafts it thence to Rufus' roaring hall,°   265
And Hungerford° re-echoes bawl for bawl.
All hail him victor in both gifts of song,
Who sings so loudly, and who sings so long.
      This labor past, by Bridewell° all descend,
(As morning prayer and flagellation end)   270
To where Fleet-ditch° with disemboguing streams
Rolls the large tribute of dead dogs to Thames,
The king of dykes!° than whom no sluice of mud
With deeper sable blots the silver flood.
"Here strip, my children! here at once leap in,   275
Here prove who best can dash through thick and thin,
And who the most in love of dirt excel,
Or dark dexterity of groping well.
Who flings most filth, and wide pollutes around
The stream, be his the Weekly Journals° bound,   280
A pig° of lead to him who dives the best;
A peck of coals apiece shall glad the rest."
      In naked majesty Oldmixon° stands,

255 **enthusiast** fanatical preacher; they were famous for loudness
and nasal tones.   258 **Webster . . . Whitfield** opposed enthusiasts;
William Webster was a bitter anti-Methodist writer, George Whit-
field the celebrated field-preacher and (for a time) companion of
John Wesley.   259 **Blackmore's** mentioned here for his biblical
poetry rather than his six epics.   263 **retentive** Chancery cases were
slow in being settled, as a century later in Dickens' *Bleak House*.
265 **Rufus' . . . hall** Westminster Hall, built by William Rufus; a
scene of legal disputes.   266 **Hungerford** the public market.   269
Bridewell the house of correction for women.   271 **Fleet-ditch** then
an open sewer.   273 **dykes** canals.   280 **Journals** given to scandal
and party politics.   281 **pig** ingot.   283 **Oldmixon** an elderly critic
and partisan historian.

And Milo-like° surveys his arms and hands;
285 Then, sighing, thus, "And am I now threescore?
Ah why, ye Gods! should two and two make four?"
He said, and climbed a stranded lighter's height,
Shot to the black abyss, and plunged downright.
The senior's judgment all the crowd admire,
290 Who but to sink the deeper, rose the higher.
     Next Smedley° dived; slow circles dimpled o'er
The quaking mud, that closed, and oped no more.
All look, all sigh, and call on Smedley lost;
"Smedley" in vain resounds through all the coast.
295   Then ** essayed;° scarce vanished out of sight,
He buoys up instant, and returns to light:
He bears no token of the sabler streams,
And mounts far off among the swans of Thames.
     True to the bottom, see Concanen° creep,
300 A cold, long-winded native of the deep:
If perseverance gain the diver's prize,
Not everlasting Blackmore this denies:
No noise, no stir, no motion canst thou make,
The unconscious stream sleeps o'er thee like a lake.
305   Next plunged a feeble but a desperate pack,
With each a sickly brother at his back:°
Sons of a day! just buoyant on the flood,
Then numbered with the puppies in the mud.
Ask ye their names? I could as soon disclose
310 The names of these blind puppies as of those.
Fast by, like Niobe° (her children gone)
Sits Mother Osborne,° stupefied to stone!
And monumental brass° this record bears,
"These are,—ah no! these were, the Gazetteers!"

---

284 **Milo-like** a famous athlete of antiquity.   291 **Smedley** an Irish
clergyman, dean of Clogher, who savagely abused Swift and Pope.
295 **Then . . . essayed** Pope removed the name of Aaron Hill, a
"writer of genius and spirit."   299 **Concanen** an Irish journalist.
306 **at his back** some daily papers printed special issues on their
back pages.   311 **Niobe** When she boasted of her seven sons and
seven daughters before Leto, who had two, those two (Artemis and
Apollo) slew all of Niobe's children. Niobe wept until she was
turned into a column of stone.   312 **Mother Osborne** a term ap-
plied to this eldest of journalists.   313 **monumental brass** as in
church memorial plaques.

Not so bold Arnall;° with a weight of skull,   315
Furious he dives, precipitately dull.
Whirlpools and storms his circling arm invest,
With all the might of gravitation blest.
No crab more active in the dirty dance,
Downward to climb, and backward to advance.   320
He brings up half the bottom on his head,
And loudly claims the journals and the lead.
    The plunging prelate, and his ponderous Grace,°
With holy envy gave one layman place.
When lo! a burst of thunder shook the flood: 325
Slow rose a form,° in majesty of mud;
Shaking the horrors of his sable brows,
And each ferocious feature grim with ooze.
Greater he looks, and more than mortal stares:
Then thus the wonders of the deep declares.   330
    First he relates, how sinking to the chin,
Smit with his mien, the mud-nymphs sucked him in:
How young Lutetia,° softer than the down,
Nigrina black, and Merdamante° brown,
Vied for his love in jetty bowers below,   335
As Hylas° fair was ravished long ago.
Then sung, how shown him by the nut-brown maids
A branch of Styx here rises from the shades,
That tinctured as it runs with Lethe's streams,
And wafting vapors from the land of dreams,   340
(As under seas Alpheus'° secret sluice
Bears Pisa's offerings to his Arethuse)
Pours into Thames: and hence the mingled wave
Intoxicates the pert, and lulls the grave:
Here brisker vapors o'er the TEMPLE° creep,   345

---

315 **Arnall** author of "furious party-papers," he "writ for hire and
valued himself upon it" (Pope). 323 **prelate . . . Grace** possibly
Thomas Sherlock, Bishop of London, consistent supporter of Wal-
pole, and John Potter, Archbishop of Canterbury. 326 **a form** the
return of Smedley, lost in II, 293–4. 333 **Lutetia** classical name for
Paris, perhaps derived from *lutum* (mud). 334 **Merdamante** "filth-
loving." 336 **Hylas** "ravished by the water-nymphs and drawn into
the river," in Virgil, *Eclogue* VI (Pope). 341 **Alpheus** the river
runs under the sea at Pisa to mix with the fountain of Arethuse in
Sicily. 345 **Temple** the inns of court beside the Thames.

There, all from Paul's to Aldgate° drink and sleep.
 Thence to the banks where reverend bards repose,
They led him soft; each reverend bard arose;
And Milbourn° chief, deputed by the rest,
350 Gave him the cassock, surcingle,° and vest.
"Receive" (he said) "these robes which once were mine,
Dulness is sacred in a sound divine."
 He ceased, and spread the robe; the crowd confess
The reverend flamen in his lengthened dress.
355 Around him wide a sable army stand,
A lowborn, cell-bred, selfish, servile band,°
Prompt or to guard or stab, to saint or damn,
Heaven's Swiss,° who fight for any god, or man.
 Through Lud's famed gates,° along the well-known
  Fleet;
360 Rolls the black troop, and overshades the street,
Till showers of sermons, characters,° essays,
In circling fleeces whiten all the ways:
So clouds replenished from some bog below,
Mount in dark volumes, and descend in snow.
365 Here stopped the goddess; and in pomp proclaims
A gentler exercise to close the games.
 "Ye critics! in whose heads, as equal scales,
I weigh what author's heaviness prevails;
Which most conduce to soothe the soul in slumbers,
370 My H—ley's periods, or my Blackmore's numbers;°
Attend the trial we propose to make:
If there be man, who o'er such works can wake,
Sleep's all-subduing charms who dares defy,
And boasts Ulysses' ear° with Argus' eye;°
375 To him we grant our amplest powers to sit

346 **Paul's to Aldgate** from St. Paul's Cathedral east through the city to Aldgate. 349 **Milbourn** clergyman and critic who attacked Dryden. 350 **surcingle** girdle or belt for cassock. 356 **band** "such only of the clergy who . . . dedicate themselves for venal and corrupt ends to that of ministers and factions" (Warburton). 358 **Swiss** mercenary soldiers. 359 **Lud's . . . gate,** gate between Fleet Street and the western limit of the city, built by King Lud. 361 **characters** The "character" was a distinctive literary form deriving originally from Theophrastus. 370 **periods . . . numbers** prose and verse forms. 374 **Ulysses' ear** as he resisted the song of the Sirens. 374 **Argus' eye** He had a hundred eyes, some always open.

Judge of all present, past, and future wit;
To cavil, censure, dictate, right or wrong,
Full and eternal privilege of tongue."
   Three college sophs, and three pert templars° came,
The same their talents, and their tastes the same;   *380*
Each prompt to query, answer, and debate,
And smit with love of poesy and prate.
The ponderous books two gentle readers bring;
The heroes sit, the vulgar form a ring.
The clamorous crowd is hushed with mugs of mum,°   *385*
Till all, tuned equal, send a general hum.
Then mount the clerks, and in one lazy tone,
Through the long, heavy, painful page drawl on;
Soft, creeping, words on words, the sense compose,
At every line they stretch, they yawn, they doze.   *390*
As to soft gales top-heavy pines bow low
Their heads, and lift them as they cease to blow:
Thus oft they rear, and oft the head decline,
As breathe, or pause, by fits, the airs divine.
And now to this side, now to that they nod,   *395*
As verse, or prose, infuse the drowsy god.
Thrice Budgell° aimed to speak, but thrice suppressed
By potent Arthur,° knocked his chin and breast.
Toland and Tindal,° prompt at priests to jeer,
Yet silent bowed to Christ's No Kingdom Here.°   *400*
Who sat the nearest, by the words o'ercome,
Slept first; the distant nodded to the hum.
Then down are rolled the books; stretched o'er 'em lies
Each gentle clerk, and muttering seals his eyes.
As what a Dutchman plumps into the lakes,   *405*
One circle first, and then a second makes;
What Dulness dropped among her sons impressed
Like motion from one circle to the rest;
So from the midmost the nutation° spreads
Round and more round, o'er all the sea of heads.   *410*

379 **Templars** law students.   385 **mum** beer.   397 **Budgell** a gifted writer, unsettled by losses in the South Sea investment scheme, of which he spoke continually.   398 **Arthur** Blackmore's hero in two vast epics, now being read aloud.   399 **Toland and Tindal** deistic writers.   400 **Christ's . . . Here** the title of a long sermon or speech.
409 **nutation** nodding.

At last Centlivre° felt her voice to fail,
Motteux° himself unfinished left his tale,
Boyer° the state, and Law° the stage gave o'er,
Morgan° and Mandeville° could prate no more;
415 Norton,° from Daniel and Ostroea° sprung,
Blessed with his father's front, and mother's tongue,
Hung silent down his never-blushing head;
And all was hushed, as Folly's self lay dead.
    Thus the soft gifts of sleep conclude the day,
420 And stretched on bulks,° as usual, poets lay.
Why should I sing what bards the nightly Muse
Did slumbering visit, and convey to stews;°
Who prouder marched, with magistrates in state,
To some famed roundhouse,° ever open gate!
425 How Henley lay inspired beside a sink,
And to mere mortals seemed a priest in drink:
While others, timely, to the neighboring Fleet°
(Haunt of the Muses) made their safe retreat.

BOOK THE THIRD

BUT in her temple's last recess inclosed,
On Dulness' lap the anointed head reposed.
Him close she curtains round with vapors blue,

411 **Centlivre** Susanne Centlivre, a comic dramatist and ardent
Whig, friend of Cibber. Prolific writing or talk is the common ele-
ment in the next few lines.   412 **Motteux** a loquacious man, trans-
lator of Rabelais and Cervantes.   413 **Boyer** compiler of annals.
413 **Law** religious writer, attacker of the theatre. Each man relin-
quishes his absorbing subject as sleep overtakes him.   414 **Morgan**
deistic, self-styled "moral philosopher."   414 **Mandeville** Bernard
Mandeville's *The Fable of the Bees* was one of the greatest and
most widely criticized books of the age.   415 **Norton** Benjamin
Norton Defoe, son of Daniel by **Ostroea,** an oyster-wench.   420
bulks stalls, shop fronts.   422 **stews** brothels.   424 **roundhouse**
place of detention, lock-up.   427 **Fleet** debtors' prison.

And soft besprinkles with Cimmerian° dew.
Then raptures high the seat of sense o'erflow,   5
Which only heads refined from° reason know.
Hence, from the straw where Bedlam's prophet nods,
He hears loud oracles, and talks with gods:
Hence the fool's paradise, the statesman's scheme,
The air-built castle, and the golden dream,   10
The maid's romantic wish, the chemist's° flame,
And poet's vision of eternal fame.
   And now, on Fancy's easy wing conveyed,
The King descending views the Elysian shade.°
A slipshod Sibyl° led his steps along,   15
In lofty madness meditating song;
Her tresses staring from poetic dreams,
And never washed, but in Castalia's streams.°
Taylor,° their better Charon, lends an oar,
(One swan of Thames, though now he sings no more.)   20
Benlowes,° propitious still to blockheads, bows;
And Shadwell° nods the poppy on his brows.
Here, in a dusky vale where Lethe rolls,
Old Bavius° sits, to dip poetic souls,
And blunt the sense, and fit it for a skull   25
Of solid proof, impenetrably dull:
Instant, when dipped, away they wing their flight,
Where Brown and Mears° unbar the gates of light,
Demand new bodies, and in calf's array,°
Rush to the world, impatient for the day.   30
Millions and millions on these banks he views,

4 **Cimmerian** as in Homer's mythical land of constant mists and darkness. 6 **refined from** purged of. 11 **chemist's** alchemist's. 14 **Elysian shade** Cibber's fantasies include the epic descent to the underworld. 15 **Sibyl** The Cumaean Sibyl was consulted for her prophetic wisdom by Aeneas before his descent to the lower world. 18 **Castalia's streams** the fountain on Mt. Parnassus. 19 **Taylor** John Taylor, the water poet, was a voluminous writer as well as boatman. He died in 1654. 21 **Benlowes** a bad poet and patron of other bad poets. 22 **Shadwell** An addict, he died of an overdose of opium. 24 **Bavius** a bad Roman poet, Virgil's Cibber. 28 **Brown and Mears** "printers . . . for anybody" (Pope). 29 **calf's array** (1) fool's garb (2) calfskin binding.

Thick as the stars of night, or morning dews,
As thick as bees o'er vernal blossoms fly,
As thick as eggs at Ward° in Pillory.
35   Wondering he gazed: when lo! a sage appears,
By his broad shoulders known, and length of ears,
Known by the band and suit which Settle° wore
(His only suit) for twice three years before:
All as the vest, appeared the wearer's frame,
40 Old in new state, another yet the same.
Bland and familiar as in life, begun
Thus the great father° to the greater son.
    "Oh born to see what none can see awake!
Behold the wonders of the oblivious lake.
45 Thou, yet unborn, hast touched this sacred shore;
The hand of Bavius drenched thee o'er and o'er.
But blind to former as to future fate,
What mortal knows his pre-existent state?
Who knows how long thy transmigrating soul
50 Might from Boeotian° to Boeotian roll?
How many Dutchmen° she vouchsafed to thrid?°
How many stages through old-monks she rid?
And all who since, in mild benighted days,
Mixed the owl's ivy° with the poet's bays?
55 As man's meanders° to the vital spring
Roll all their tides, then back their circles bring;
Or whirligigs,° twirled round by skilful swain,
Suck the thread in, then yield it out again:
All nonsense thus, of old or modern date,
60 Shall in thee center, from thee circulate.
For this our Queen unfolds to vision true
Thy mental eye, for thou hast much to view:
Old scenes of glory, times long cast behind
Shall, first recalled, rush forward to thy mind:

34 **Ward** John Ward, expelled from Parliament for forgery. **37 Settle** See note to I, 90. **42 father** as Anchises in his prophecy to Aeneas. **50 Boeotian** See note to I, 25. **51 Dutchmen** believed to be heavy and unimaginative. **51 thrid** thread. **54 owl's ivy** the owl as pedant; cf. *Essay on Criticism,* line 706 and note. **55 meanders** See note to II, 176. **57 whirligigs** tops.

Then stretch thy sight o'er all her rising reign, 65
And let the past and future fire thy brain.
"Ascend this hill, whose cloudy point commands
Her boundless empire over seas and lands.
See, round the poles where keener spangles shine,
Where spices smoke beneath the burning Line,° 70
(Earth's wide extremes) her sable flag displayed,
And all the nations covered in her shade!
"Far eastward cast thine eye, from whence the sun
And orient° science their bright course begun:
One godlike monarch° all that pride confounds, 75
He, whose long wall the wandering Tartar bounds;
Heavens! what a pile! whole ages perish there,
And one bright blaze turns learning into air.
"Thence to the south extend thy gladdened eyes;
There rival flames with equal glory rise, 80
From shelves to shelves see greedy Vulcan° roll,
And lick up all their physic of the soul.
"How little, mark! that portion of the ball,
Where, faint at best, the beams of science fall:
Soon as they dawn, from hyperborean° skies 85
Embodied dark, what clouds of Vandals rise!
Lo! where Maeotis° sleeps, and hardly flows
The freezing Tanais° through a waste of snows,
The North by myriads pours her mighty sons,
Great nurse of Goths, of Alans,° and of Huns! 90
See Alaric's° stern port! the martial frame
Of Genseric!° and Attila's° dread name!
See the bold Ostrogoths on Latium fall;
See the fierce Visigoths on Spain and Gaul!
See, where the morning gilds the palmy shore 95

70 **Line** equator. 74 **orient** rising. 75 **One . . . monarch** The Em-
peror of China who built the Great Wall destroyed all books and
scholars so that learning would date from his reign. 81 **greedy
Vulcan** the burning of the great Ptolomean Library in Egypt (whose
inscription was *Medicina Animae,* or the "physic of the Soul");
ordered by the Caliph Omar I. 85 **hyperborean** of the extreme
north. 87 **Maeotis** the present Sea of Azor. 88 **Tanais** the river
Don. 90 **Alans** a Scythian people from the Caucasus. 91 **Alaric**
leader of the Visigoth sack of Rome, A.D. 410. 92 **Genseric** King of
the Vandals. 92 **Attila** King of the Huns, the so-called Scourge of
God.

(The soil° that arts and infant letters bore)
His conquering tribes the Arabian prophet draws,
And saving ignorance enthrones by laws.
See Christians, Jews, one heavy sabbath keep,
100   And all the western world believe and sleep.
      "Lo! Rome herself, proud mistress now no more
Of arts, but thundering against heathen lore;
Her gray-haired Synods damning books unread,
And Bacon° trembling for his brazen head.
105   Padua, with sighs, beholds her Livy° burn,
And even the Antipodes° Virgilius mourn.
See, the Cirque° falls, the unpillared temple nods,
Streets paved with heroes, Tiber choked with gods:
Till Peter's keys some christened Jove adorn,
110   And Pan to Moses lends his pagan horn;
See graceless° Venus to a Virgin turned,°
Or Phidias broken, and Apelles° burned.
      "Behold yon isle, by palmers, pilgrims trod,
Men bearded, bald, cowled, uncowled, shod, unshod,
115   Peeled,° patched, and piebald,° linsey-wolsey° brothers,
Grave mummers!° sleeveless some, and shirtless others.
That once was Britain—happy! had she seen
No fiercer sons, had Easter° never been.
In peace, great Goddess, ever be adored;

96 **Soil** The Near East, where the alphabet was invented, was the
scene of Mohammed's (the Arabian prophet's) first conquests.
104 **Bacon** Roger Bacon, the medieval philosopher, was said to have
made a brazen head that could speak; he seems to fear persecution
for his learning. 105 **Livy** The Roman historian was burned be-
cause of his full treatment of pagan rites. 106 **Antipodes** Virgilius,
8th-century bishop, was censured for believing in the existence of
the Antipodes. 107 **Cirque** circus, possibly the Colosseum, whose
stone was quarried for new buildings. 111 **graceless** (1) without
the accompanying three Graces (2) unchristian (3) amorous. 109–11
Till Peter's Keys . . . Virgin turned The Popes "spared some of the
temples by converting them to churches, and some of the statues by
modifying them into images of saints" (Pope). 112 **Phidias . . .
Apelles** Marble statues of these Greek sculptors or Roman copies
were burned to produce lime. 115 **Peeled** threadbare. 115 **piebald**
spotted. 115 **linsey-wolsey** a mixture of flax and wool; hence
"neither one thing nor the other." 116 **Mummers** mimes, actors.
118 **Easter** The proper date was the subject of wars.

How keen the war, if Dulness draw the sword!   *120*
Thus visit not thy own! on this blest age
Oh spread thy influence, but restrain thy rage!
  "And see, my son! the hour is on its way,
That lifts our goddess to imperial sway;
This favorite isle, long severed from her reign,   *125*
Dove-like,° she gathers to her wings again.
Now look through fate! behold the scene she draws!
What aids, what armies to assert her cause!
See all her progeny, illustrious sight!
Behold, and count them, as they rise to light.   *130*
As Berecynthia,° while her offspring vie
In homage to the mother of the sky,
Surveys around her, in the blest abode,
An hundred sons, and every son a god:
Not with less glory mighty Dulness crowned,   *135*
Shall take through Grubstreet her triumphant round;
And her Parnassus glancing o'er at once,
Behold an hundred sons, and each a dunce.
  "Mark first that youth° who takes the foremost place,
And thrusts his person full into your face.   *140*
With all thy father's virtues blessed, be born!
And a new Cibber shall the stage adorn.
  "A second see, by meeker manners known,
And modest as the maid that sips alone;
From the strong fate of drams° if thou get free,   *145*
Another Durfey,° Ward! shall sing in thee.
Thee shall each alehouse, thee each gill-house° mourn,
And answering gin-shops sourer sighs return.
  "Jacob,° the scourge of grammar, mark with awe,
Nor less revere him, blunderbuss of law.   *150*

---

126 **Dove-like** Cf. Psalms 91:4 "He shall cover thee with his feathers, and under his wings shalt thou trust." "This is fulfilled in the fourth book" (Pope).   131 **Berecynthia** Cybele, the Mighty Mother of the Gods (i.e., "of the sky," line 132).   139 **that youth** Theophilus Cibber, son of Colley and in most respects his successor as actor and writer.   145 **fate of drams** Ned Ward was not only a popular writer but also a tavern keeper; see note to I, 233.   146 **Durfey** popular song-writer and object of ridicule from Dryden's day. 147 **gill-house** Gill was a malt liquor treated with ground-ivy.   149 **Jacob** Giles Jacob, poet and biographer of poets, trained in the law.

Lo P—p—le's brow, tremendous to the town,
Horneck's fierce eye, and Roome's funereal frown.
Lo sneering Goode, half malice and half whim,
A fiend in glee, ridiculously grim.°
155 Each cygnet sweet of Bath and Tunbridge race,°
Whose tuneful whistling makes the waters pass:
Each songster, riddler, every nameless name,
All crowd, who foremost shall be damned to fame.
Some strain in rhyme; the Muses, on their racks,
160 Scream like the winding of ten thousand jacks:°
Some free from rhyme or reason, rule or check,
Break Priscian's° head, and Pegasus's° neck;
Down, down they larum,° with impetuous whirl,
The Pindars and the Miltons of a Curll.
165   "Silence, ye wolves! while Ralph to Cynthia° howls,
And makes night hideous—answer him, ye owls!
    "Sense, speech, and measure, living tongues and dead,
Let all give way—and Morris° may be read.
    "Flow, Welsted, flow! like thine inspirer, beer;
170 Though stale, not ripe; though thin, yet never clear;
So sweetly mawkish, and so smoothly dull;
Heady, not strong; o'erflowing, though not full.°
    "Ah Dennis! Gildon° ah! what ill-starred rage
Divides a friendship long confirmed by age?
175 Blockheads with reason wicked wits abhor,
But fool with fool is barbarous civil war.
Embrace, embrace, my sons! be foes no more!
Nor glad vile poets with true critics' gore.
    "Behold yon pair, in strict embraces joined;

151–4 **Lo P—p—le's . . . grim** All of these minor writers (the first is
William Popple) had attacked Pope; they are reduced here to facial
expressions.   155 **Bath . . . race** local poets at popular spas, whose
waters provide one of the senses of line 156.   160 **jacks** devices for
turning roasting spits.   162 **Priscian** standard Latin grammarian.
162 **Pegasus** the steed of poetry.   163 **larum** rush with cries.   165
Ralph to Cynthia James Ralph wrote a bad poem called "Night,"
thus to Cynthia, the moon.   168 **Morris** Bezaliel Morris, an inex-
haustible poet.   170–2 **Though stale . . . full** a parody of Sir John
Denham's famous lines on the Thames in *Cooper's Hill:* "Though
deep, yet clear, though gentle yet not dull,/Strong without rage,
without o'erflowing full."   173 **Dennis . . . Gildon** two acrimonious
critics, worthy of each other's respect.

How like in manners, and how like in mind! 180
Equal in wit, and equally polite,
Shall this a Pasquin, that a Grumbler° write;
Like are their merits, like rewards they share,
That shines a consul, this commissioner.
  "But who is he,° in closet close y-pent, 185
Of sober face, with learnèd dust besprent?
Right well mine eyes arede the myster wight,°
On parchment scraps y-fed, and Wormius hight.
To future ages may thy dulness last,
As thou preservest the dulness of the past! 190
  "There, dim in clouds, the poring scholiasts° mark,
Wits, who, like owls, see only in the dark,
A lumberhouse of books in every head,
For ever reading, never to be read!
  "But, where each science lifts its modern type,° 195
History her pot,° divinity his pipe,
While proud philosophy repines to show,
Dishonest sight! his breeches rent below;
Embrowned with native bronze, lo! Henley° stands,
Turning his voice, and balancing his hands. 200
How fluent nonsense trickles from his tongue!
How sweet the periods, neither said, nor sung!
Still break the benches,° Henley! with thy strain,
While Sherlock, Hare, and Gibson preach in vain.
Oh great restorer of the good old stage, 205
Preacher at once, and zany° of thy age!
Oh worthy thou of Egypt's wise abodes,
A decent° priest, where monkeys were the gods!
But fate with butchers° placed thy priestly stall,

182 **Pasquin . . . Grumbler** two weekly journals. 185 **he** the antiquarian Thomas Hearne, whose bookworm nature is rendered in archaic diction, like Spenser's. 187 **myster wight** "uncouth mortal" (Pope). 191 **scholiasts** commentators, annotators. 195 **type** emblem. 196 **pot** of ale. 199 **Henley** Orator Henley preached religion on Sundays, other matters on Wednesdays, reportedly calling himself the "restorer of ancient eloquence" and charging a shilling for admission (see line 205). 203 **benches** referring in part to the bishops (three of them are cited in line 204) who occupied benches in the House of Lords. Henley attacked church institutions. 206 **zany** clown. 208 **decent** fitting. 209 **butchers** Henley's oratory was in Newport Market, Butcher Row.

210 Meek modern faith to murder, hack, and maul;
And bade thee live, to crown Britannia's praise,
In Toland's, Tindal's, and in Woolston's days.°
    "Yet oh, my sons! a father's words attend:
(So may the fates preserve the ears you lend)
215 'Tis yours, a Bacon or a Locke to blame,°
A Newton's genius, or a Milton's flame:
But oh! with One, immortal One dispense,
The source of Newton's light, of Bacon's sense!
Content, each emanation of his fires
220 That beams on earth, each virtue he inspires,
Each art he prompts, each charm he can create,
Whate'er he gives, are given for you to hate.
Persist, by all divine in Man unawed,
But, learn, ye Dunces! not to scorn your God."°
225   Thus he, for then a ray of reason stole
Half through the solid darkness of his soul;
But soon the cloud returned—and thus the sire:
"See now, what Dulness and her sons admire!
See what the charms, that smite the simple heart
230 Not touched by nature, and not reached by art."
    His never-blushing head he turned aside,
(Not half so pleased when Goodman° prophesied)
And looked, and saw a sable sorcerer° rise,
Swift to whose hand a wingèd volume flies:
235 All sudden, gorgons hiss, and dragons glare,
And ten-horned fiends and giants rush to war.
Hell rises, Heaven descends, and dance on Earth:
Gods, imps, and monsters, music, rage, and mirth,
A fire, a jig, a battle, and a ball,
240 Till one wide conflagration swallows all.
    Thence a new world to nature's laws unknown,
Breaks out refulgent, with a heaven its own:

212 **In . . . days** citing three deists; like Henley, anticlerical. 215
blame attack, as enemies of Dulness. 224 **But, learn . . . God** i.e.,
not openly, lest you be charged with blasphemy. 232 **Goodman**
who, seeing Cibber in rehearsal, said, "If he does not make a good
actor, I'll be damned." Cibber reports his exultation at hearing this.
233 **sorcerer** Dr. Faustus, the hero of a series of popular farces
with elaborate stage effects (as in the next seven lines).

Another Cynthia her new journey runs,
And other planets circle other suns.
The forests dance, the rivers upward rise,   245
Whales sport in woods, and dolphins in the skies;
And last, to give the whole creation grace,
Lo! one vast egg° produces human race.
   Joy fills his soul, joy innocent of thought;
"What power," he cries, "what power these wonders   250
      wrought?"
"Son, what thou seekest is in thee! Look, and find
Each monster meets his likeness in thy mind.
Yet wouldst thou more? In yonder cloud behold,
Whose sarcenet° skirts are edged with flamy gold,
A matchless youth! his nod these worlds controls,   255
Wings the red lightning, and the thunder rolls.
Angel of Dulness, sent to scatter round
Her magic charms o'er all unclassic ground:
Yon stars, yon suns, he rears at pleasure higher,
Illumes their light, and sets their flames on fire.   260
Immortal Rich!° how calm he sits at ease
Mid snows of paper, and fierce hail of pease;
And proud his mistress' orders to perform,
Rides in the whirlwind, and directs the storm.°
   "But lo! to dark encounter in mid air   265
New wizards rise; I see my Cibber there!
Booth° in his cloudy tabernacle shrined,
On grinning dragons thou shalt mount the wind.
Dire is the conflict, dismal is the din,
Here shouts all Drury, there all Lincoln's Inn;   270
Contending theatres our empire raise,
Alike their labors, and alike their praise.
   "And are these wonders, Son, to thee unknown?
Unknown to thee? These wonders are thy own.

248 **one vast egg** These theatrical extravagances are a parody of cosmology, here of the myth of the cosmic egg from which the universe was hatched.   254 **sarcenet** thin silk.   261 **Rich** theatrical manager in Lincoln's-Inn-Field, deviser of pantomimes.   264 **whirlwind . . . storm** Cf. Nahum 1:3 "The Lord hath his way in the whirlwind and in the storm, and the clouds are the dust of his feet." 267 **Booth** joint-manager with Cibber of the Theatre in Drury Lane, in competition with Rich.

275 These Fates reserved to grace thy reign divine,
     Foreseen by me, but ah! withheld from mine.
     In Lud's old walls though long I ruled, renowned
     Far as loud Bow's stupendous bells resound;
     Though my own aldermen conferred the bays,
280 To me committing their eternal praise,
     Their full-fed heroes, their pacific mayors,
     Their annual trophies,° and their monthly wars:°
     Though long my party built on me their hopes,
     For writing pamphlets, and for roasting popes;°
285 Yet lo! in me what authors have to brag on!
     Reduced at last to hiss in my own dragon.°
     Avert it, Heaven! that thou, my Cibber, e'er
     Shouldst wag a serpent tail in Smithfield fair!
     Like the vile straw that's blown about the streets,
290 The needy poet sticks to all he meets,
     Coached, carted, trod upon, now loose, now fast,
     And carried off in some dog's tail at last.
     Happier thy fortunes! like a rolling stone,
     Thy giddy dulness still shall lumber on,
295 Safe in its heaviness, shall never stray,
     But lick up every blockhead in the way.
     Thee shall the patriot, thee the courtier taste,
     And every year be duller than the last.
     Till raised from booths, to theatre, to court,
300 Her seat imperial Dulness shall transport.
     Already opera prepares the way,
     The sure forerunner of her gentle sway:
     Let her thy heart, next drabs° and dice, engage,
     The third mad passion of thy doting age.
305 Teach thou the warbling Polypheme° to roar,
     And scream thyself° as none e'er screamed before!

---

282 **annual trophies** on Lord Mayor's Day.   282 **monthly wars** military exercises of the City Trainbands.   284 **roasting popes** Settle was employed to write anti-Catholic tracts.   286 **my own dragon** in a booth at Smithfield. To another actor's St. George, Settle played the dragon in a costume of green leather that he had devised.   303 **drabs** whores.   305 **Polypheme** Cibber translated the Italian opera *Polifemo*.   306 **scream thyself** Cibber's voice was shrill and often cracked when he raised it.

To aid our cause, if Heaven thou canst not bend,
Hell thou shalt move; for Faustus° is our friend:
Pluto with Cato thou for this shalt join,
And link the Mourning Bride to Proserpine.°   310
Grubstreet! thy fall should men and gods conspire,
Thy stage shall stand, ensure it but from fire.°
Another Aeschylus appears! prepare
For new abortions,° all ye pregnant fair!
In flames, like Semele's,° be brought to bed,   315
While opening Hell spouts wildfire at your head.
    "Now, Bavius,° take the poppy from thy brow,
And place it here! here all ye heroes bow!
This, this is he, foretold by ancient rhymes:
The Augustus born to bring Saturnian° times.   320
Signs following signs lead on the mighty year!°
See! the dull stars roll round and reappear.
See, see, our own true Phoebus wears the bays!
Our Midas° sits Lord Chancellor of plays!
On poets' tombs see Benson's° titles writ!   325
Lo! Ambrose Philips° is preferred for wit!
See under Ripley° rise a new Whitehall,°

308 **Faustus** The pantomime hero, like Marlowe's, trafficked with the Devil.   309–10 **Pluto with Cato . . . Proserpine** alluding to the custom of coupling a tragedy and a farce in one evening, here Addison's *Cato* and Congreve's *Mourning Bride* coupled with the *Lover of Pluto and Proserpine*.   312 **fire** a favorite if dangerous effect in pantomime, especially the hellfire of Faustus.   314 **new abortions** Aeschylus' tragedy of the Furies threw children into fits and induced miscarriages; here abortions of art are also implied.   315 **Semele** When Semele prayed that Zeus might come to her in all his power, she was consumed in flames by his lightning; Dionysus was born of her ashes.   317 **Bavius** like Maevius, a bad poet of Virgil's day. 320 **Saturnian** See note to I, 28.   321 **Mighty year** the great cycle of time in which prophecy will be fulfilled.   324 **Midas** who, judging between the performances of Apollo and Pan, gave the prize to Pan; he was rewarded by Apollo with asses' ears.   325 **Benson** William Benson for political reasons displaced Sir Christopher Wren as royal architect; he built a lavish monument to Milton in Westminster Abbey and commissioned a Latin translation of *Paradise Lost*; see IV, 109–12 where he appears as "bold Benson."   326 **Ambrose Philips** a poet of ability but uncertain taste; his verses for children won him the nickname of Namby Pamby.   327 **Ripley** see note to *Epistle to Burlington*, line 18.   327 **new Whitehall** perhaps the new Admiralty building, but plans for a new royal palace at Whitehall had long been considered.

While Jones' and Boyle's united labors° fall:
While Wren° with sorrow to the grave descends,
330 Gay° dies unpensioned with a hundred friends,
Hibernian politics,° O Swift! thy fate;
And Pope's, ten years° to comment and translate.
     "Proceed, great days! till learning fly the shore,
Till birch° shall blush with noble blood no more,
335 Till Thames see Eton's sons for ever play,
Till Westminster's whole year be holiday,
Till Isis' elders reel, their pupils' sport,
And Alma Mater lie dissolved in Port!"
     "Enough! enough!" the raptured monarch cries;
340 And through the ivory gate° the vision flies.

BOOK THE FOURTH

YET, yet a moment, one dim ray of light
Indulge, dread Chaos, and eternal Night!°
Of darkness visible° so much be lent,

328 **Jones' . . . united labors** The works of Inigo Jones in London
had fallen into serious disrepair. Richard Boyle, Earl of Burlington,
had restored his Covent Garden church and sponsored the publica-
tion of his architectural designs. 329 **Wren** Sir Christopher and
Inigo Jones were England's greatest architects up to Pope's day;
Wren had built great city churches as well as St. Paul's, but he was
dismissed after fifty years' service. 330 **Gay** John Gay, in spite of
his friend's efforts, never won a suitable court appointment. 331
Hibernian politics Swift resented his failure to win a church office
in England and regarded his career in Ireland as exile, although he
was deeply involved in Irish politics at times. 332 **ten years** Pope's
work in translating Homer and editing Shakespeare lasted from
1713 to 1725. 334 **birch** used for caning schoolboys. Pope moves
up through the public schools (Eton and Westminster) to the uni-
versities (Isis or Oxford), where the pleasures of the wine cellar
replace those of the library. 340 **ivory gate** through which false
dreams pass; the horn gate releases the true. 2 **Chaos . . . Night**
See note to line I, 12. The "restoration of this empire is the action
of the poem" (Pope and/or Warburton, hereafter P-W; and War-
burton alone, W). 3 **darkness visible** used of Hell in *Paradise Lost*
I, 63.

As half to show, half veil, the deep intent.
Ye Powers! whose mysteries restored I sing,   *5*
To whom Time bears me on his rapid wing,
Suspend a while your force inertly strong,
Then take at once the poet and the song.

    Now flamed the Dog-star's° unpropitious ray,
Smote every brain, and withered every bay;   *10*
Sick was the sun, the owl forsook his bower,
The moon-struck prophet felt the madding hour:
Then rose the seed of Chaos, and of Night,
To blot out order, and extinguish light,
Of dull and venal a new world to mold,   *15*
And bring Saturnian days of lead and gold.°

    She mounts the throne: her head a cloud concealed,
In broad effulgence all below revealed;°
('Tis thus aspiring Dulness ever shines)
Soft on her lap her laureate son reclines.   *20*

    Beneath her footstool, *Science* groans in chains,
And *Wit* dreads exile, penalties, and pains.
There foamed rebellious *Logic,* gagged and bound,
There, stripped, fair *Rhetoric* languished on the ground;
His blunted arms by *Sophistry*° are borne,   *25*
And shameless *Billingsgate* her robes adorn.
Morality, by her false guardians drawn,
Chicane in furs, and *Casuistry* in lawn,°
Gasps, as they straiten° at each end the cord,
And dies, when Dulness gives her Page° the word.   *30*
Mad *Máthesis*° alone was unconfined,
Too mad for mere material chains to bind,
Now to pure space lifts her ecstatic stare,
Now running round the circle, finds it square.
But held in tenfold bonds the *Muses* lie,   *35*

---

9 **Dog-star's** of Sirius, visible in the late, hot summer. 16 **lead and gold** See note to I, 28; here parallel with "dull and venal." 18 **all below revealed** P-W cite the old adage: "The higher you climb, the more you show your arse." 25 **sophistry** Dulness "admits something *like* each science, or casuistry, sophistry, etc." (P-W) 28 **furs . . . lawn** law (ermine robes of the judge) and church (the fine linen sleeves of a bishop). 29 **straiten** tighten. 30 **Page** punning on Sir Francis Page, a famous "hanging judge." 31 **Máthesis** pure mathematics, unlimited by application.

Watched both by Envy's and by Flattery's eye:
There to her heart sad Tragedy addrest
The dagger wont to pierce the tyrant's breast;
But sober History restrained her rage,
40 And promised vengeance on a barbarous age.
There sunk Thalia,° nerveless, cold, and dead,
Had not her sister Satire held her head:
Nor couldst thou, Chesterfield!° a tear refuse,
Thou weptst, and with thee wept each gentle° Muse.
45   When lo! a harlot form° soft sliding by,
With mincing step, small voice, and languid eye;
Foreign her air, her robe's discordant pride
In patchwork fluttering, and her head aside.
By singing peers upheld on either hand,
50 She tripped and laughed, too pretty much to stand;
Cast on the prostrate Nine° a scornful look,
Then thus in quaint recitativo spoke.
    "O *Cara! Cara!* silence all that train:
Joy to great Chaos! let Division° reign:
55 Chromatic tortures° soon shall drive them hence,
Break all their nerves, and fritter all their sense:
One trill shall harmonize joy, grief, and rage,
Wake the dull Church, and lull the ranting stage;
To the same notes thy sons shall hum, or snore,
60 And all thy yawning daughters cry, *encore.*
Another Phoebus, thy own Phoebus,° reigns,
Joys in my jigs, and dances in my chains.
But soon, ah soon, rebellion will commence,
If music meanly borrows aid from sense:

41 **Thalia** the Muse of comedy, enervated by the censorship of the Licensing Act, 1737.   43 **Chesterfield** who spoke eloquently against the Act.   44 **gentle** as opposed to the low-born substitutes.   45 **harlot form** Opera, tremendously popular with the importation of Italian singers, was resented for its tendency to destroy the fusion of sound and sense in the native English song tradition.   51 **Nine** the Muses.   54 **Division** i.e., breaking up each of a succession of long notes into a number of short ones, and so dwelling on a single syllable of the word being sung.   55 **Chromatic tortures** elaborate variations introducing notes which do not belong to the diatonic scale.   61 **thy own Phoebus** referring to the French term *phebus*: "an appearance of light glimmering over the obscurity, a semblance of meaning without any real sense" (Bouhours, cited by P-W).

Strong in new arms, lo! giant Handel° stands,   *65*
Like bold Briareus,° with a hundred hands;
To stir, to rouse, to shake the soul he comes,
And Jove's own thunders follow Mars's drums.
Arrest him, Empress; or you sleep no more—"
She heard, and drove him to the Hibernian shore.   *70*
    And now had Fame's posterior trumpet° blown,
And all the nations summoned to the throne.
The young, the old, who feel her inward sway,
One instinct seizes, and transports away.
None need a guide, by sure attraction led,   *75*
And strong impulsive gravity° of head:
None want° a place, for all their center found,
Hung to the goddess, and cohered around.
Not closer, orb in orb,° conglobed are seen
The buzzing bees about their dusky queen.   *80*
    The gathering number, as it moves along,
Involves a vast involuntary throng,
Who gently drawn, and struggling less and less,
Roll in her vortex,° and her power confess.
Not those alone who passive own her laws,   *85*
But who, weak rebels, more advance her cause:
Whate'er of dunce in college or in town
Sneers at another, in toupee or gown;°
Whate'er of mongrel no one class admits,
A wit with dunces, and a dunce with wits.   *90*
    Nor absent they, no members of her state,

---

65 **Handel** whose increase of "hands" in chorus and orchestra (suggested in the next line) "proved so much too manly for the fine gentlemen of his age, that he was obliged to remove his music into Ireland" (P-W). The *Messiah* was first performed in Dublin in 1741. The power of Handel's music, as opposed to precious, feminine Opera, is made clear in line 67 below. 66 **Briareus** The giant of a hundred hands fought for the Olympians against the Titans. 71 **posterior trumpet** "her second or more certain report" (P-W), but cf. also IV, 18. 76 **gravity** (1) solemnity (2) gravitational attraction, as in lines 81–4. 77 **want** lack. 79 **orb in orb** Cf. Milton's account of the angels in *Paradise Lost* V, 594–6: "Thus when in Orbs/ Of circuit inexpressible they stood,/Orb within Orb." 84 **Rolls . . . vortex** eddy around her. 88 **toupee or gown** in curled periwig (as a man of fashion) or in academic gown.

Who pay her homage in her sons, the Great;°
Who, false to Phoebus, bow the knee to Baal;°
Or, impious, preach his word without a call.
95 Patrons, who sneak from living worth to dead,
Withhold the pension, and set up the head;°
Or vest dull Flattery in the sacred gown;
Or give from fool to fool the laurel crown.
And (last and worst) with all the cant of wit,
100 Without the soul, the Muse's hyprocrite.°
    There marched the bard and blockhead, side by side,
Who rhymed for hire, and patronized for pride.
Narcissus,° praised with all a parson's power,
Looked a white lily sunk beneath a shower.
105 There moved Montalto° with superior air;
His stretched-out arm displayed a volume fair;
Courtiers and patriots in two ranks divide,
Through both he passed, and bowed from side to side:
But as in graceful act, with awful eye
110 Composed he stood, bold Benson° thrust him by:
On two unequal crutches propped he came,
Milton's on this, on that one Johnston's name.
The decent knight retired with sober rage,
Withdrew his hand, and closed the pompous page.
115 But (happy for him as the times went then)
Appeared Apollo's mayor and aldermen,°
On whom three hundred gold-capped youths° await,
To lug the ponderous volume off in state.
    When Dulness, smiling—"Thus revive the wits!
120 But murder first, and mince them all to bits;

92 **Great** nobles, men in power.   93 **Baal** any false god, presumably
power or wealth.   96 **withhold . . . head** i.e., fail to support when
alive and parasitically honor after death.   100 **the Muse's hyprocrite**
"who thinks the only end of poetry is to amuse" (W).   103 **Narcissus**
Lord Hervey, an epileptic, had a very white face; he was heavily
flattered in the dedication of Dr. Middleton's *Life of Cicero*.   105
Montalto Sir Thomas Hanmer, pompous and portly, published a
lavish edition of Shakespeare at his own expense.   110 **Benson** See
note to III, 325; he published several editions of Arthur Johnston's
Latin version of the Psalms.   116 **Apollo's . . . aldermen** dignitaries
of Oxford, whose press published Hanmer's Shakespeare.   117 **gold-
capped youths** with the gold tassel of the Gentleman-Commoner.

As erst Medea° (cruel, so to save!)
A new edition of old Aeson gave;
Let standard authors, thus, like trophies born,
Appear more glorious as more hacked and torn,
And you, my critics! in the chequered shade,   125
Admire new light through holes yourselves have made.
        "Leave not a foot of verse, a foot of stone,
A page, a grave, that they can call their own;
But spread, my sons, your glory thin or thick,
On passive paper, or on solid brick.   130
So by each bard an alderman° shall sit,
A heavy lord shall hang at every wit,
And while on Fame's triumphal car they ride,
Some slave of mine° be pinioned to their side."
        Now crowds on crowds around the goddess press,   135
Each eager to present their first address.
Dunce scorning dunce beholds the next advance,
But fop shows fop superior complaisance.°
When lo! a specter° rose, whose index hand
Held forth the virtue of the dreadful wand;   140
His beavered brow a birchen garland wears,
Dropping with infant's blood, and mother's tears.
O'er every vein a shuddering horror runs;
Eton and Winton° shake through all their sons.
All flesh is humbled, Westminster's bold race   145
Shrink, and confess the genius° of the place:
The pale boy Senator yet tingling stands,
And holds his breeches close with both his hands.
        Then thus. "Since man from beast by words is known,
Words are man's province, words we teach alone.°   150

121 **Medea** who had Aeson's daughters cut him up and boil him in
order to restore him to youth; this worked for Aeson but not Pelias,
whom Medea wished to destroy.   131 **Alderman** such as Alderman
Barber, the printer, who proudly placed his own name on the monu-
ment he erected to Samuel Butler.   134 **slave of mine** as in Rome,
where a slave was chained beside a triumphant general as he rode
through the city.   138 **complaisance** tolerance.   139 **specter** Dr.
Busby, the famous headmaster of Westminster School, carrying his
birch cane ("dreadful wand") for discipline.   144 **Eton and Winton**
where Busby's students are now enrolled.   146 **genius** presiding
spirit or deity.   149–50 **Since man . . . teach alone** The humanist
view that eloquence is wisdom expressed is here reduced to a con-
cern for words to the neglect of thought.

When reason doubtful, like the Samian letter,°
Points him two ways, the narrower is the better.
Placed at the door of learning, youth to guide,
We never suffer it to stand too wide.
155 To ask, to guess, to know, as they commence,
As fancy opens the quick spring of sense,
We ply the memory, we load the brain,
Bind rebel wit, and double chain on chain,
Confine the thought, to exercise the breath;
160 And keep them in the pale of words till death.
Whate'er the talents, or howe'er designed,
We hang one jingling padlock° on the mind:
A poet the first day he dips his quill;
And what the last? a very poet still.
165 Pity! the charm works only in our wall,
Lost, lost too soon in yonder house or hall.°
There truant Wyndham every Muse gave o'er,
There Talbot° sunk, and was a wit no more!
How sweet an Ovid, Murray° was our boast!
170 How many martials were in Pulteney° lost!
Else sure some bard, to our eternal praise,
In twice ten thousand rhyming nights and days,
Had reached the work, the all that mortal can;
And South° beheld that masterpiece of man."
175   "Oh" (cried the goddess) "for some pedant reign!
Some gentle James,° to bless the land again;
To stick the doctor's° chair into the throne,
Give law to words, or war with words alone,

151 **Samian letter** the letter Y, emblem of the crossroads of choice.
162 **jingling padlock** exercises in composing Greek and Latin verses.
166 **house or hall** Westminster Hall or the House of Commons.
167–8 **Wyndham . . . Talbot** two brilliant members of Parliament.
169 **Murray** a student of Busby ("our boast"). Awarded a prize
for a Latin poem at Oxford, he became a distinguished statesman
rather than a poet.   170 **Pulteney** Gifted in epigram like Martial, he
used his skill as political writer and orator in opposition to Walpole.
174 **South** "Dr. South declared a perfect epigram as difficult a per-
formance as an epic poem, and the critics say, 'an epic poem is the
greatest work human nature is capable of' " (P-W). The epigram
becomes the culmination of Busby's and Dulness' verbalism.   176
James James I was a famous pedant and the first English monarch
to espouse the divine right of kings.   177 **doctor's** teacher's.

Senates and courts with Greek and Latin rule,
And turn the Council to a grammar school!   *180*
For sure, if Dulness sees a grateful day,
'Tis in the shade of arbitrary sway.°
O! if my sons may learn one earthly thing,
Teach but that one, sufficient for a king:
That which my priests, and mine alone, maintain,   *185*
Which as it dies, or lives, we fall, or reign:
May you, may Cam and Isis,° preach it long!
The RIGHT DIVINE of kings to govern wrong."
    Prompt at the call, around the goddess roll
Broad hats, and hoods, and caps, a sable shoal: *190*
Thick and more thick the black blockade extends,
A hundred head of Aristotle's friends.
Nor wert thou, Isis! wanting to the day,
Though Christ Church° long kept prudishly away.
Each staunch polemic, stubborn as a rock,   *195*
Each fierce logician, still expelling Locke,°
Came whip and spur, and dashed through thin and thick
On German Crousaz, and Dutch Burgersdyck.°
As many quit the streams that murmuring fall
To lull the sons of Margaret and Clare Hall,°   *200*
Where Bentley° late tempestuous wont to sport
In troubled waters, but now sleeps in port.
Before them marched that awful Aristarch;°
Ploughed was his front with many a deep remark:
His hat, which never vailed° to human pride,   *205*
Walker° with reverence took, and laid aside.
Low bowed the rest: he, kingly, did but nod;

181–2 **For sure . . . sway** "no branch of learning thrives well under arbitrary government but verbal" (W). 187 **Cam and Isis** the universities of Cambridge and Oxford. 194 **Christ Church** the college at Oxford whose dons resisted Dulness most successfully. 196 **Locke** actually censured in 1703 by the heads of Oxford, where Aristotelian philosophy was still strong. 198 **Crousaz . . . Burgersdyck** two logicians. 200 **Margaret and Clare Hall** St. John's and Clare College in Cambridge. 201 **Bentley** As master of Trinity College, Cambridge, Richard Bentley had been at odds with his Fellows but was now at rest; but see III, 338. 203 **Aristarch** Bentley, here named for Aristarchus, Homeric commentator and corrector. 205 **vailed** yielded. 206 **Walker** the vice-master of Trinity.

So upright° Quakers please both man and God.
"Mistress! dismiss that rabble from your throne:
210 Avaunt——is Aristarchus yet unknown?
Thy mighty scholiast, whose unwearied pains
Made Horace dull, and humbled Milton's strains.°
Turn what they will to verse, their toil is vain,
Critics like me shall make it prose again.
215 Roman and Greek grammarians! know your better:
Author of something yet more great than letter;°
While towering o'er your alphabet, like Saul,°
Stands our Digamma,° and o'ertops them all.
'Tis true, on words is still our whole debate,
220 Disputes of *Me* or *Te,* of *aut* or *at,*
To sound° or sink in *cano,* O or A,
Or give up Cicero° to C or K.
Let Freind affect to speak as Terence spoke,
And Alsop° never but like Horace joke:
225 For me, what Virgil, Pliny may deny,
Manilius or Solinus shall supply:°
For Attic phrase in Plato let them seek,
I poach in Suidas° for unlicensed Greek.
In ancient sense if any needs will deal,
230 Be sure I give them fragments, not a meal:
What Gellius or Stobaeus° hashed before,
Or chewed by blind old scholiasts o'er and o'er.
The critic eye, that microscope of wit,
Sees hairs and pores, examines bit by bit;
235 How parts relate to parts, or they to whole,

208 **upright** (1) honest (2) not bowing in prayer, as Aristarchus will not bow before Dulness. 212 **Milton's strains** which Bentley, as editor, arrogantly corrected on the pretext that Milton's blindness allowed numerous errors to appear. 216 **letter** the invention of a single letter by other grammarians. 217 **Saul** taller than any of his people. 218 **Digamma** a letter restored by Bentley in his projected edition of Homer; taller than ordinary letters. 221 **sound** stress. 222 **Cicero** the pronunciation of whose name was disputed. 223-4 **Freind . . . Alsop** two scholars who catch the spirit of the ancients. 226 **Manilius . . . supply** As a philologist, Bentley is not interested in literature but in words; for his purposes minor authors are as useful as major. 228 **Suidas** a dictionary writer and collector of strange words. 231 **Gellius or Stobaeus** who collected fragments of ancient writers in their works.

The body's harmony, the beaming soul,°
Are things which Kuster, Burman, Wasse° shall see,
When man's whole frame is obvious to a *flea*.
  "Ah, think not, Mistress! more true Dulness lies
In folly's cap, than wisdom's grave disguise.   240
Like buoys, that never sink into the flood,
On learning's surface we but lie and nod.
Thine is the genuine head of many a house,
And much divinity without a Noῦs.°
Nor could a Barrow work on every block,   245
Nor has one Atterbury° spoiled the flock.
See! still thy own, the heavy canon° roll,
And metaphysic smokes involve the pole.
For thee we dim the eyes, and stuff the head
With all such reading as was never read: 250
For thee explain a thing till all men doubt it,
And write about it, Goddess, and about it:
So spins the silkworm small its slender store,
And labors till it clouds itself all o'er.
  "What though we let some better sort of fool   255
Thrid° every science, run through every school?
Never by tumbler through the hoops was shown
Such skill in passing all, and touching none.
He may indeed (if sober all this time)
Plague with dispute, or persecute with rhyme.   260
We only furnish what he cannot use,
Or wed to what he must divorce, a Muse:
Full in the midst of Euclid dip at once,
And petrify a genius to a dunce:
Or set on metaphysic ground to prance,   265
Show all his paces, not a step advance.
With the same cement, ever sure to bind,
We bring to one dead level every mind.

236 **beaming soul** the soul irradiating the body with form. 237
Kuster . . . Wasse editors and philologists. 244 **without a** Noῦs
"Noῦs was the Platonic word for mind, or the first cause, and that
system of divinity is here hinted at which terminates in blind nature
without a νοῦς" (P-W). 245-6 **Barrow . . . Atterbury** both eloquent
preachers, Isaac Barrow a fine mathematician, Francis Atterbury
a classical scholar. 247 **canon** (1) churchman (2) artillery (cannon).
256 **thrid** thread.

Then take him to develop, if you can,
270 And hew the block off, and get out the man.°
But wherefore waste I words? I see advance
Whore, pupil, and laced governor° from France.
Walker! our hat"———nor more he deigned to say,
But, stern as Ajax' specter,° strode away.
275   In flowed at once a gay embroidered race,
And tittering pushed the pedants off the place:
Some would have spoken, but the voice was drowned
By the French horn, or by the opening° hound.
The first came forwards, with as easy mien,
280 As if he saw St. James's° and the Queen.
When thus the attendant orator° begun:
"Receive, great Empress! thy accomplished son,
Thine from the birth, and sacred° from the rod,
A dauntless infant! never scared with God.
285 The sire saw, one by one, his virtues wake:
The mother begged the blessing of a rake.
Thou gav'st that ripeness, which so soon began,
And ceased so soon, he ne'er was boy, nor man.
Through school and college, thy kind cloud o'ercast,
290 Safe and unseen° the young Aeneas past:
Thence bursting glorious, all at once let down,°
Stunned with his giddy larum° half the town.
Intrepid then, o'er seas and lands he flew:°
Europe he saw, and Europe saw him too.
295 There all thy gifts and graces we display,
Thou, only thou, directing all our way!
To where the Seine, obsequious as she runs,
Pours at great Bourbon's feet her silken sons;°
Or Tiber, now no longer Roman, rolls,
300 Vain of Italian arts, Italian° souls:

270 **And hew . . . man** the traditional notion that in every block of
stone there is a statue waiting to be freed. 272 **governor** tutor.
274 **Ajax' specter** which turns sullenly from Ulysses, *Odyssey*, XI.
278 **opening** giving tongue. 280 **St. James's** the royal palace. 281
Orator the "governor" of line 271. 283 **sacred** exempt. 290 **un-
seen** as Aeneas enters Carthage veiled in cloud by his mother, Venus.
291 **let down** revealed, freed. 292 **larum** alarm, commotion. 293 **he
flew** on the Grand Tour. 298 **Bourbon's feet . . . sons** France is
seen as an absolute monarchy encouraging courtly luxury or ef-
feminacy. 300 **Italian** i.e., in place of Roman .

To happy convents, bosomed deep in vines,
Where slumber abbots, purple as their wines:
To isles of fragrance, lily-silvered vales,
Diffusing languor in the panting gales:
To lands of singing, or of dancing slaves,   *305*
Love-whispering woods, and lute-resounding waves.
But chief her shrine where naked Venus keeps,
And Cupids ride the Lion of the Deeps;°
Where, eased of fleets, the Adriatic main
Wafts the smooth eunuch and enamored swain.   *310*
Led by my hand, he sauntered Europe round,
And gathered every vice on Christian ground;
Saw every court, heard every king declare
His royal sense, of operas or the fair;°
The stews° and palace equally explored,   *315*
Intrigued with glory, and with spirit whored;
Tried all *hors d'oeuvres,* all *liqueurs* defined,
Judicious drank, and greatly daring dined;
Dropped the dull lumber of the Latin store,°
Spoiled his own language, and acquired no more;   *320*
All classic learning lost on classic ground;
And last turned *air,* the echo of a sound!
See now, half-cured,° and perfectly well-bred,
With nothing but a solo° in his head;
As much estate, and principle, and wit,   *325*
As Jansen, Fleetwood, Cibber° shall think fit;
Stolen° from a duel, followed by a nun,
And, if a borough choose him,° not undone;
See, to my country happy I restore
This glorious youth, and add one Venus more.   *330*
Her too receive (for her my soul adores)°

308 **the Lion of the Deeps** the winged lion, emblem of Venice, no
longer a great naval and mercantile power, famous instead as the
brothel of Europe.   314 **of operas or the fair** The royal conversa-
tions recall the interests of George II.   315 **stews** brothels.   319
Dropped . . . store forgot his Latin.   323 **half-cured** of a venereal
disease.   324 **solo** like "air" (line 322), the reduction of substance
to sound; see IV, 159–60.   326 **Jansen . . . Cibber** all gamblers, the
last two theatre-managers, hence tutors to youth.   327 **Stolen** es-
caped.   328 **borough choose him** Members of Parliament could not
be arrested for debt.   331 **my soul adores** Both tutor and pupil
seem attached to the former nun.

So may the sons of sons of sons of whores,
Prop thine, O Empress! like each neighbor throne,
And make a long posterity thy own."
335   Pleased, she accepts the hero, and the dame,
Wraps in her veil, and frees from sense of shame.
       Then looked, and saw a lazy, lolling sort,
Unseen at church, at senate, or at court,
Of ever-listless loiterers, that attend
340   No cause, no trust, no duty, and no friend.
Thee too, my Paridel!° she marked thee there,
Stretched on the rack of a too easy chair,
And heard thy everlasting yawn confess
The pains and penalties of idleness.
345   She pitied! but her pity only shed
Benigner influence on thy nodding head.
       But Annius,° crafty seer, with ebon wand,
And well-dissembled emerald on his hand,
False as his gems, and cankered° as his coins,
350   Came, crammed with capon, from where Pollio° dines.
Soft, as the wily fox is seen to creep,
Where bask on sunny banks the simple sheep,
Walk round and round, now prying here, now there;
So he; but pious, whispered first his prayer.
355   "Grant, gracious Goddess! grant me still to cheat,
O may thy cloud still cover the deceit!
Thy choicer mists on this assembly shed,
But pour them thickest on the noble head.
So shall each youth, assisted by our eyes,
360   See other Caesars, other Homers° rise;
Through twilight ages hunt the Athenian fowl,°
Which Chalcis gods, and mortals call an owl,
Now see an Attys, now a Cecrops° clear,

341 **Paridel** Spenser's name for a wandering courtly squire. 347 **Annius** named for an early collector, monk of Viterbo, and a famous forger of antiquities. 349 **cankered** corrupt. 350 **Pollio** named for the Roman patron. 360 **other Caesars . . . Homers** possibly forged manuscripts; more tellingly, substitute models, i.e., the heroics of collecting and the supreme value of rarity. 361 **Athenian fowl** Athenian coins were stamped with an owl. 363 **Attys . . . Cecrops** forged coins professedly issued by the ancient king of Lydia or the mythical founder of Athens.

Nay, Mahomet!° the pigeon at thine ear;
Be rich in ancient brass, though not in gold, 365
And keep his Lares,° though his house be sold;
To headless Phoebe° his fair bride postpone,
Honor a Syrian prince° above his own;
Lord of an Otho,° if I vouch it true;
Blest in one Niger,° till he knows of two." 370
    Mummius° o'erheard him; Mummius, fool-renowned,°
Who like his Cheops stinks above the ground,
Fierce as a startled adder, swelled, and said,
Rattling an ancient sistrum° at his head.
    "Speakst thou of Syrian princes? Traitor base! 375
Mine, Goddess! mine is all the hornèd race.°
True, he had wit, to make their value rise;
From foolish Greeks to steal them, was as wise;
More glorious yet, from barbarous hands to keep,
When Sallee rovers° chased him on the deep. 380
Then taught by Hermes,° and divinely bold,
Down his own throat he risked the Grecian gold;
Received each demigod,° with pious care,
Deep in his entrails—I revered them there,
I bought them, shrouded in that living shrine, 385
And, at their second birth, they issue mine."
    "Witness, great Ammon!° by whose horns I swore,"
(Replied soft Annius) "this our paunch before
Still bears them, faithful; and that thus I eat,

364 **Mahomet** Mohammed, who forbade all images, here represented on a coin or medal with the white pigeon he claimed (according to legend) was the angel Gabriel. 366 **Lares** statues of household gods. 367 **headless Phoebe** a mutilated statue of Diana, which preempts the place of a living bride. 368 **Syrian prince** presumably as represented on a rare medal. 369 **Otho** coin of a Roman Emperor who ruled very briefly. 370 **Niger** another Emperor of short reign, whose coins would be very rare. 371 **Mummius** dealer in Egyptian antiquities. 371 **fool-renowned** "a compound epithet in the Greek manner, *renowned by fools*, or *renowned for making fools*" (Pope). 374 **sistrum** Egyptian musical instrument. 376 **horned race** the successors of Alexander, supposedly born of the gods, represented with horns on their medals. 380 **Sallee rovers** pirate ships from Morocco. 381 **Hermes** god of commerce but also the patron of thieves. 383 **demigod** coins of emperors who claimed that status; with suggestions of the eucharist, sustained by "pious care" and culminating in the Second Coming of line 386. 387 **Ammon** Jupiter Ammon, from whom Alexander and his heirs claimed descent; cf. line 376.

390   Is to refund the medals with the meat.
      To prove me, Goddess! clear of all design,
      Bid me with Pollio sup, as well as dine:
      There all the learned shall at the labor stand,
      And Douglas° lend his soft, obstetric hand."
395   The goddess smiling seemed to give consent;
      So back to Pollio, hand in hand, they went.
           Then thick as locusts blackening all the ground,
      A tribe, with weeds and shells fantastic crowned,
      Each with some wondrous gift approached the Power,
400   A nest, a toad, a fungus, or a flower.
      But far the foremost, two, with earnest zeal,
      And aspect ardent to the throne appeal.
           The first thus opened: "Hear thy suppliant's call,
      Great Queen, and common Mother of us all!
405   Fair from its humble bed I reared this flower,°
      Suckled and cheered, with air, and sun, and shower,
      Soft on the paper ruff its leaves° I spread,
      Bright with the gilded button tipped its head,
      Then throned in glass, and named it Caroline:°
410   Each maid cried, charming! and each youth, divine!
      Did nature's pencil° ever blend such rays,
      Such varied light in one promiscuous blaze?
      Now prostrate! dead! behold that Caroline:
      No maid cries, charming! and no youth, divine!
415   And lo the wretch! whose vile, whose insect lust
      Laid this gay daughter of the spring in dust.
      Oh punish him, or to the Elysian shades
      Dismiss my soul, where no carnation fades!"
           He ceased, and wept. With innocence of mien,
420   The accused stood forth, and thus addressed the queen.
           "Of all the enamelled race,° whose silvery wing
      Waves to the tepid zephyrs of the spring,
      Or swims along the fluid atmosphere,

---

394 **Douglas** a famous obstetrician and collector of editions of
Horace.   405 **flower** a reference to the efforts in the age to produce
a perfect carnation.   407 **leaves** petals.   409 **Caroline** for the Queen,
an ardent gardener; P-W pursue the theme of idolatry of lines
359–86 by citing a gardener who advertised his favorite flower as
"*my* Queen Caroline."   411 **pencil** paintbrush.   421 **enamelled race**
colorful butterflies.

Once brightest shined this child of heat and air.
I saw, and started from its vernal bower   *425*
The rising game,° and chased from flower to flower.
It fled, I followed; now in hope, now pain;
It stopped, I stopped; it moved, I moved again.°
At last it fixed, 'twas on what plant it pleased,
And where it fixed, the beauteous bird° I seized: *430*
Rose or carnation was below my care;
I meddle, Goddess! only in my sphere.
I tell the naked fact without disguise,
And, to excuse it, need but show the prize;
Whose spoils this paper° offers to your eye,   *435*
Fair even in death! this peerless *butterfly.*"
   "My sons!" (she answered) "both have done your
      parts:
Live happy both, and long promote our arts!
But hear a mother, when she recommends
To your fraternal care, our sleeping friends.°   *440*
The common soul, of Heaven's more frugal make,
Serves but to keep fools pert, and knaves awake:
A drowsy watchman, that just gives a knock,
And breaks our rest, to tell us what's a-clock.
Yet by some object every brain is stirred;   *445*
The dull may waken to a hummingbird;
The most recluse, discreetly opened find
Congenial matter in the cockle kind;°
The mind, in metaphysics at a loss,
May wander in a wilderness of moss;°   *450*
The head that turns at superlunar things,
Poised with a tail, may steer on Wilkins' wings.°
   "O! would the sons of men once think their eyes

425–6 **started . . . game** the idiom of the huntsman.   427–8 Cf.
Eve's words (*Paradise Lost,* IV, 462–3) on first seeing her reflection
in water and, without recognizing what it is, adoring it: "I started
back,/It started back; but pleased I soon returned,/Pleased it re-
turned as soon."   430 **bird** any winged creature; here the butterfly.
435 **this paper** on which the butterfly is mounted.   440 **sleeping
friends** Cf. line IV, 345.   448 **cockle kind** collections of scallop
shells.   450 **moss** of which 300 species had been identified.   452
Wilkins' wings John Wilkins in the 17th century proposed flights to
the moon.

And reason given them but to study *flies!*
455 See nature in some partial narrow shape,
And let the author of the whole escape:
Learn but to trifle; or, who most observe,
To wonder at their maker, not to serve!"°
"Be that my task" (replies a gloomy clerk,
460 Sworn foe to mystery,° yet divinely dark;
Whose pious hope aspires to see the day
When moral evidence° shall quite decay,
And damns implicit faith,° and holy lies,
Prompt to impose,° and fond to dogmatize:)
465 "Let others creep by timid steps, and slow,
On plain experience lay foundations low,
By common sense to common knowledge bred,
And last, to Nature's Cause through Nature led.°
All-seeing in thy mists, we want no guide,
470 Mother of arrogance, and source of pride!
We nobly take the high priori road,°
And reason downward, till we doubt of God:
Make Nature still encroach° upon his plan;
And shove him off as far as e'er we can:
475 Thrust some mechanic cause into his place,
Or bind in matter, or diffuse in space.°

458 **wonder . . . serve** to lose themselves in natural wonder and neg-
lect divine laws of morality.   460 **mystery** religious mysteries.   462
moral evidence the probability of the historical facts of the Bible,
believed by some to decay as the events became more remote.   463
implicit faith belief upon authority, unquestioning adherence.   464
Prompt to impose the freethinker seen as dogmatically rejecting
dogma, self-deceiving while he attacks "holy lies."   468 **Nature's
Cause . . . led** For this empirical, inductive procedure cf. *Essay on
Man*, IV, 332.   471 **high priori road** the deductive or a priori
method, such as Descartes takes in his *Meditations*.   473 **Nature
. . . encroach** explain away Providence by natural ("mechanic")
causes, or create some metaphysical natural principle (such as Ralph
Cudworth's plastic nature) to displace or limit a theistic God.
475–6 **Thrust . . . space** "the first of these follies is that of Descartes;
the second of Hobbes; the third of some succeeding Philosophers"
(P-W). The last may include Henry More, the Cambridge Platonist,
who separated extension from materiality in order to attribute ex-
tension or pure space to spirit; space for More is "an obscure repre-
sentation of the essential presence of the divine being." More in
turn influenced Newton's conception of absolute space. (See E. L.
Burtt, *The Metaphysical Foundations of Modern Science*.)

Or, at one bound o'erleaping° all his laws,
Make God man's image, man the final cause,°
Find virtue local, all relation scorn,°
See all in *self*,° and but for self be born: *480*
Of naught so certain as our *reason* still,
Of naught so doubtful as of *soul* and *will*.°
Oh hide the God still more! and make us see
Such as Lucretius° drew, a God like Thee:
Wrapped up in self, a God without a thought,   *485*
Regardless of our merit or default.
Or that bright image to our fancy draw,
Which Theocles° in raptured vision saw,
While through poetic scenes the Genius roves,
Or wanders wild in academic groves;   *490*
That NATURE our society° adores,
Where Tindal° dictates, and Silenus° snores."
    Roused at his name, up rose the bousy sire,
And shook from out his pipe the seeds of fire;°
Then snapped his box,° and stroked his belly down: *495*
Rosy and reverend, though without a gown.°
Bland and familiar to the throne he came,
Led up the Youth, and called the goddess *Dame*.

477 **o'erleaping** like Satan overleaping the walls of Paradise (*Paradise Lost*, IV, 181).   478 **Make God . . . cause** as in the *Essay on Man*, see human happiness as the end of the universe and God as subservient to that end.   479 **Find virtue . . . scorn** make morality relative to local customs rather than absolute, universal, or dependent upon God's will.   480 **self** the final contraction of scale, in contrast to the opening movement of *Essay of Man*, IV, 361ff.   482 **soul and will** The metaphysical and moral principle of human nature are neglected by the dogmatic rationalism of the freethinkers.   484 **Lucretius** whose philosophical poem *De Rerum Natura* (following Epicurean thought) seeks to free man of his fears of anthropomorphic gods and presents nature as an impartial divine force free of the limitations and narrow human concerns (therefore, for the "gloomy clerk," like Dulness, sublimely indifferent to all distinctions of value).   488 **Theocles** the philosophical visionary in Shaftesbury's *The Moralists*, here taken as an enthusiastic worshiper of nature (his "Genius"), cultivating Platonic ecstasy in the natural landscape.   491 **our society** the association of freethinkers.   492 **Tindal** the deist; see II, 399; III, 212.   492 **Silenus** the fat, drunken, and debauched companion of Dionysius who appears in Virgil's Sixth Eclogue; here associated with Thomas Gordon, a political writer whom Walpole made Commissioner of the Wine Licenses. 494 **seeds of fire** parodying Epicurean language for atoms.   495 **box** snuffbox.   496 **without a gown** not a priest.

Then thus. "From priestcraft happily set free,
500 Lo! every finished son returns to thee:
First slave to words, then vassal to a name,°
Then dupe to party; child and man the same;
Bounded by nature, narrowed still by art,
A trifling head, and a contracted heart.
505 Thus bred, thus taught, how many have I seen,
Smiling on all, and smiled on by a queen.
Marked out for honors, honored for their birth,
To thee the most rebellious things on earth:
Now to thy gentle shadow all are shrunk,
510 All melted down, in pension, or in punk!°
So K——, so B——° sneaked into the grave,
A monarch's half, and half a harlot's slave.
Poor W——° nipped in folly's broadest bloom,
Who praises now? his chaplain on his tomb.
515 Then take them all, oh take them to thy breast!
Thy *Magus,*° Goddess! shall perform the rest."
    With that, a WIZARD OLD his *Cup* extends;
Which whoso tastes, forgets his former friends,
Sire, ancestors, himself. One casts his eyes
520 Up to a *star,*° and like Endymion° dies:
A *feather,*° shooting from another's head,
Extracts his brain; and principle is fled;
Lost is his God, his country, everything;
And nothing left but homage to a king!
525 The vulgar herd turn off to roll with hogs,°
To run with horses, or to hunt with dogs;
But, sad example! never to escape
Their infamy, still keep the human shape.

501 **name** reputation.   510 **punk** whore.   511 **So K——, so B——**
Kent, Berkeley; two noblemen, both holders of the highest royal
honor, Knight of the Garter; possibly indebted to one of George I's
mistresses ("harlot's slave").   513 **W——** Wharton or Warwick,
both of whom died young.   516 **Magus,** adept in occult arts, high
priest, the wizard of the next line; Sir Robert Walpole "is sug-
gested, whose use of bribery is embodied in the 'Cup of Self-love' "
(P-W).   520 **star** worn by Knights of the Garter or of the Bath.
520 **Endymion** Loved by the Moon, he was thrown into perpetual
sleep and visited by her each night.   521 **feather** worn in the cap
of Knights of the Garter.   525 **roll with hogs** with suggestion of
those transformed by Circe's enchantment.

But she, good goddess, sent to every child
Firm impudence, or stupefaction mild;   *530*
And straight succeeded, leaving shame no room,
Cibberian forehead, or Cimmerian° gloom.

    Kind self-conceit to some her glass applies,
Which no one looks in with another's eyes:
But as the flatterer or dependent paint,   *535*
Beholds himself a patriot, chief, or saint.

    On others Interest her gay livery° flings,
Interest that waves on party-colored° wings:
Turned to the sun, she casts a thousand dyes,
And, as she turns, the colors fall or rise.   *540*

    Others the Siren Sisters° warble round,
And empty heads console with empty sound.
No more, alas! the voice of fame they hear,
The balm of Dulness trickling in their ear.
Great C——, H——, P——, R——, K——,°   *545*
Why all your toils? your sons have learned to sing.
How quick ambition hastes to ridicule!
The sire is made a peer, the son a fool.

    On some, a priest succinct in amice white°
Attends; all flesh is nothing in his sight!   *550*
Beeves, at his touch, at once to jelly turn,
And the huge boar is shrunk into an urn:°
The board with specious° miracles he loads,
Turns hares to larks, and pigeons into toads.
Another (for in all what one can shine?)   *555*
Explains the *sève* and *verdeur*° of the vine.
What cannot copious sacrifice atone?°

<hr>

532 **Cimmerian** See note to III, 4.   537 **livery** costume worn by re-
tainers, whether courtiers or servants.   538 **party-colored** a pun on
"party" and "vari-colored."   541 **Siren Sisters** perhaps the muses of
opera, but see note to IV, 324.   545 **Great . . . K——** noblemen
ambitious for their families.   549 **priest . . . white** a chef dressed
in a white cap, counterpart of the priestly "amice" worn over head
and shoulders with white vestments.   551–2 **Beeves . . . urn** culi-
nary miracles, where beef is reduced (a form of transubstantiation)
to jelly, or boned meats are given decorative or amusing shapes as
in the ingenious transformations in line 554.   553 **specious** striking,
showy.   556 **sève . . . verdeur** fineness of flavor and briskness of
sparkling wines.   557 **sacrifice atone** The yield of luxuries by fa-
mous French districts (Perigord, Bayonne) seen as religious offer-
ings (libations accompanied by operatic music, as in line 559).

Thy truffles, Perigord! thy hams, Bayonne!
With French libation, and Italian strain,
560 Wash Bladen white, and expiate Hays's° stain.
Knight° lifts the head, for what are crowds undone
To three essential partridges in one?°
Gone every blush, and silent all reproach,
Contending princes mount them in their coach.
565   Next bidding all draw near on bended knees,
The Queen confers her *titles* and *degrees*.
Her children first of more distinguished sort,
Who study Shakespeare at the Inns of Court,°
Impale a glowworm, or virtú° profess,
570 Shine in the dignity of F.R.S.°
Some, deep Freemasons,° join the silent race
Worthy to fill Pythagoras's place:°
Some botanists, or florists at the least;
Or issue members of an annual feast.°
575 Nor passed the meanest unregarded; one
Rose a Gregorian, one a Gormogon.°
The last, not least in honor or applause,
Isis and Cam° made Doctors of her Laws.
    Then, blessing all, "Go, children of my care!
580 To practice now from theory repair.
All my commands are easy, short, and full:

560 **Bladen . . . Hays** two notorious gamblers who "lived with utmost magnificence at Paris and kept open tables frequented by persons of the first quality of England and even by princes of the blood of France" (P-W). The form of Bladen's name suggests the proverbial "wash blackamoors white."   561 **Knight** the cashier of the South Sea Company, who fled England at its collapse in 1720.   562 **three essential . . . one** two partridges dissolved with sauce for a third, with clear reference to the mystery of the Trinity (three persons in one essence).   568 **Shakespeare . . . Court** lawyers who neglect their proper tasks to dabble in Shakespeare criticism.   569 **virtú** amateur pursuit of arts or sciences (hence "virtuosity").   570 **F.R.S.** Fellow of the Royal Society, a title often granted at the time to untrained noblemen.   571 **Freemasons** "where taciturnity is the *only* essential qualification, as it was the *chief* of the disciples of Pythagoras" (P-W).   572 **Pythagoras's place** referring to the ascetic brotherhood of Pythagoras which pursued mathematical and religious mysteries at Croton in southern Italy, *ca.* 600–450 B.C. (see IV, 31).   574 **annual feast** held by various groups, such as the Freemasons and the Royal Society.   576 **Gregorian . . . Gormogon** members of societies founded in ridicule of the Freemasons.   578 **Isis and Cam** Oxford and Cambridge bestowed honorary degrees.

My sons! be proud, be selfish, and be dull.
Guard my prerogative,° assert my throne:
This nod confirms each privilege your own.
The cap and switch° be sacred to his Grace;   585
With staff and pumps° the Marquis lead the race;
From stage to stage° the licensed° Earl may run,
Paired with his fellow charioteer the sun;
The learnèd Baron butterflies design,°
Or draw to silk Arachne's subtile line,°   590
The Judge to dance his brother Sergeant° call;
The Senator at cricket urge the ball;
The Bishop stow (pontific luxury!)°
An hundred souls of turkeys in a pie;
The sturdy Squire to Gallic masters° stoop,   595
And drown his lands and manors in a soup.
Others import yet nobler arts from France,
Teach kings to fiddle, and make senates dance.°
Perhaps more high some daring son may soar,°
Proud to my list to add one monarch more;   600
And nobly conscious, princes are but things
Born for first ministers, as slaves for kings,
Tyrant supreme! shall three estates° command,
And MAKE ONE MIGHTY DUNCIAD OF THE LAND!"
  More she had spoke, but yawned—all nature nods: 605

583 **prerogative** royal powers unlimited by law or accountability,
sometimes used tyrannically.   585 **cap and switch** of a jockey; here
awarded to a lord devoted to horseracing.   586 **staff and pumps** the
equipment of grooms or footmen.   587 **stage to stage** driving a
stagecoach, as the Earl of Salisbury did.   587 **licensed** as coach-
owners were; also "privileged."   589 **design** study and draw.   590
draw . . . line try to obtain silken thread from spiders' webs (see
Swift, *Gulliver's Travels*, III, Ch. 5).   591 **Sergeant** barrister; the
"call of sergeants" involved ceremonies much like a dance.   593
pontific luxury such as was in fact enjoyed by the Bishop of Dur-
ham in Pope's day.   595 **Squire to Gallic masters** the cultivation of
fashionable foreign tastes (here a costly "soup") by traditionally
conservative country squires.   598 **dance** "either after their Prince"
or, banished, "to Siberia" (P-W). In *Gulliver's Travels*, I, Ch. 3,
courtiers are chosen for office in Lilliput for their agility in dancing
on a rope.   599 **more high . . . soar** Walpole, as First Minister, had
virtually ruled England from 1721 until his fall in 1742, shortly be-
fore this was published.   603 **three estates** Walpole controlled
through appointment, bribery, and appeal to interest the nobility,
the clergy, and the merchants.

What mortal can resist the yawn of gods?°
Churches and chapels° instantly it reached;
(St. James's first, for leaden G——° preached)
Then catched the schools;° the hall scarce kept awake;
610　The convocation gaped, but could not speak:
Lost was the nation's sense, nor could be found,
While the long solemn unison went round:
Wide, and more wide, it spread o'er all the realm;
Even Palinurus° nodded at the helm:
615　The vapor mild o'er each committee crept;
Unfinished treaties in each office slept;
And chiefless armies dozed out the campaign;
And navies yawned for orders on the main.
　　O Muse! relate (for you can tell alone,
620　Wits have short memories, and dunces none)
Relate, who first, who last resigned to rest;
Whose heads she partly, whose completely blessed;
What charms could faction, what ambition lull,
The venal quiet, and entrance the dull;
625　Till drowned was sense, and shame, and right, and
　　　　wrong—
O sing, and hush the nations with thy song!
　　*　　　*　　　*　　　*　　　*　　　*　　　*
　　In vain, in vain—the all-composing hour
Resistless falls: the Muse obeys the power.
She comes! she comes! the sable throne behold
630　Of *Night* primeval, and of *Chaos* old!
Before her, *Fancy's* gilded clouds decay,

---

606 **the yawn of gods** "the Great Mother composes all, in the same manner as Minerva at the period of the Odyssey" (P-W).　607 **chapels** place of dissenters' worship.　608 **leaden G——** Bishop Gilbert was eloquent; for the point of "leaden" see IV, 16.　609 **then catched the schools** "The progress of this yawn is judicious, natural, and worthy to be noted. First it seizeth the churches and chapels; then catcheth the schools, where, though the boys be unwilling to sleep, the masters are not; next Westminster Hall [the chief law courts], much more hard indeed to subdue, and not totally put to silence even by the Goddess; then the Convocation [of the clergy], which though extremely desirous to speak yet cannot; even the House of Commons, justly called the Sense of the Nation [see line 611] is *lost* (that is to say *suspended*) during the yawn" (P-W).　614 **Palinurus** the pilot of the ship of Aeneas; here Walpole, pilot of the ship of state.

And all its varying rainbows die away.
Wit shoots in vain its momentary fires,
The meteor drops, and in a flash expires.
As one by one, at dread Medea's strain,°   635
The sickening stars fade off the ethereal plain;
As Argus' eyes° by Hermes' wand opprest,
Closed one by one to everlasting rest;
Thus at her felt approach, and secret might,
Art after *Art* goes out, and all is night.   640
See skulking *Truth* to her old cavern° fled,
Mountains of casuistry heaped o'er her head!
Philosophy, that leaned on Heaven before,
Shrinks to her second cause,° and is no more.
Physic of *Metaphysic*° begs defense,   645
And *Metaphysic* calls for aid on *Sense!*°
See *Mystery* to *Mathematics*° fly!
In vain! they gaze, turn giddy, rave, and die.
Religion blushing veils her sacred fires,
And unawares *Morality* expires.   650
Nor public flame, nor private, dares to shine;
Nor human spark is left, nor glimpse divine!
Lo! thy dread empire, CHAOS! is restored;
Light dies before thy uncreating word:°
Thy hand, great anarch! lets the curtain fall;   655
And universal darkness buries all.

635 **dread Medea's strain** In Seneca's *Medea,* the enchantress, seeking revenge for Jason's desertion, calls back to life all the monstrous serpents and sings an incantation that causes the sun to halt and the stars to fall.   637 **Argus' eyes** placed all over his body so that some might always remain open.   641 **Truth . . . cavern** "alludes to the saying of Democritus, that truth lay at the bottom of a deep well" (P-W).   643-4 **leaned on Heaven . . . second cause** as in IV, 471-82, explains away all divinity by natural causation.   645 **Physic of Metaphysic** natural science turning to traditional speculative metaphysics for its ground (Pope had originally written "the Stagirite's defense").   646 **Metaphysic . . . Sense** metaphysics in turn depending upon sense data, creating with line 645 a vicious circle.   647 **Mystery to Mathematics** religious mystery seeking deductive mathematical demonstration, perhaps infecting mathematics with an occult and mystical strain such as that of the Pythagoreans. 654 **uncreating word** referring to the terms (based on the Greek *logos*) "wisdom" and "word," applied to the Son, that is, to Christ as creator, and orderer.

🅜 MERIDIAN

LANGUAGE POWER!

☐ **HOW TO READ A POEM by Burton Raffel.** This book is not only a guide to understanding poetry, but a celebration of poetry as well. Raffel's discussion always focuses on specific poems. He includes more than 200 full-length poems, from Shakespeare to Marianne Moore, to help his readers appreciate what makes a poem memorable. (006821—$7.95)

☐ **THE STORY OF LANGUAGE by Mario Pei.** From the dawn of time to the mid-twentieth century . . . world-renowned linguist Mario Pei discusses the formation and development of language—the tool by which mankind has advanced from savagery to civilization. "A good book for both reading and reference."—*The New York Times* (006848—$9.95)

☐ **THE EVIL IMAGE: Two Centuries of Gothic Short Fiction and Poetry edited and introduced by Patricia L. Sharda and Nora Crow Jaffe.** The dark side of the literary imagination shadows these pages of terror with more than fifty selections from writers of every period and style including Daniel Defoe, Lord Byron, Thomas Hardy, and William Faulkner. (006368—$8.95)

☐ **THE CONTEMPORARY AMERICAN POETS edited by Mark Strand.** A comprehensive anthology of American poetry since 1940. The balanced selection of 92 leading poets includes Robert Lowell, John Berryman, Theodore Roethke, Elizabeth Bishop, Richard Wilbur, and Alan Dugan. Biographies. (005922—$6.95)

Prices slightly higher in Canada.

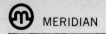 MERIDIAN

TIMELESS VERSE FOR YOUR LIBRARY

☐ **THE SELECTED POETRY AND PROSE OF SHELLEY edited and with an Introduction by Harold Bloom.** This collection recaptures Shelley's entire creative development from his earliest accomplishments through his final poetic achievements, with such selections as: *Prometheus Unbound,* "Ode to the West Wind," *On a Future State and A Defense of Poetry.* (006597—$7.95)

☐ **THE SELECTED POETRY AND PROSE OF WORDSWORTH edited and with an Introduction by F. Hartman.** This volume includes Wordsworth's immortal lyrics, ballads, sonnets, and autobiographical poems, as well as a generous selection of his prose—including his *Preface to Lyrical Ballads,* one of the landmark critical statements in our literature. (007410—$7.95)

☐ **THE COMPLETE POETRY AND SELECTED CRITICISM OF EDGAR ALLAN POE edited and with an Introduction by Allen Tate.** This volume contains some of Poe's finest critical essays as well as all of his immortal poems, among them such unforgettable works as "Tamberlane," "Al Aaraaf," "The Raven," "The Bells," and "Annabel Lee." (007054—$7.95)

☐ **THE SELECTED POETRY OF BROWNING selected and with an Introduction by George Ridenour.** Included among the 40 poems in this volume are "My Last Duchess," Soliloquy of the Spanish Cloister," "Fra Lippo Lippi," as well as excerpts from his magnum opus, "The Ring and the Book"; plus a chronology of Browning's life, footnotes keyed to the text, and an extensive bibliography. (007119—$7.95)

Prices slightly higher in Canada.

SELECTED POETRY FROM MERIDIAN

☐ **THE SELECTED POETRY OF WILLIAM BLAKE edited and with an Introduction by David V. Erdman.** Poems include the great lyrics, the longer political and religious poems, such famous works as *Songs of Innocence* and *Songs of Experience*, as well as the poet's Notebook and letters. With chronology, footnotes and bibliography.
(005698—$6.95)

☐ **THE SELECTED POETRY OF POPE edited and with an Introduction by Martin Price.** Presented here in their entirety are several of Pope's principal works, including *Windsor Forest, Essay on Man, Essay on Criticism* and his masterpiece, *The Duncaid.*
(006074—$5.95)

☐ **THE SELECTED POETRY OF DONNE. Edited and with Introduction by Marius Bewley.** Includes the complete *Songs and Sonnets; Elegies, Epithalamions* and *Satyres; The Second Anniversary; The Progress of the Soul;* and selections from *Letters to Several Personages* and the *Divine Poems;* and other works. Chronology, footnotes, bibliography included. (005175—$4.95)

☐ **THE SELECTED POETRY AND PROSE OF BYRON edited and with an Introduction by W. H. Auden.** Byron stands out among his contemporaries of the English Romantic period as the only poet of unquestioned brilliance whose genius was largely comic. Included in this edition are: "Beppo"; "Epistle to Augusta"; "The Vision of Judgment"; selections from *Don Juan, Childe Harold, English Bards and Scotch Reviewers, Hints from Horace;* numerous letters; and extracts from Byron's *Journal* of 1816 and his *Diary* of 1821.
(006589—$7.95)

All prices higher in Canada.

Buy them at your local bookstore or use this convenient coupon for ordering.

NEW AMERICAN LIBRARY, INC.
P.O. Box 999, Bergenfield, New Jersey 07621

Please send me the PLUME and MERIDIAN BOOKS I have checked above. I am enclosing $_____(please add $1.50 to this order to cover postage and handling.) Send check or money order—no cash or C.O.D.'s. Prices and numbers are subject to change without notice.

Name_____

Address_____

City_____State_____Zip Code_____

Allow 4-6 weeks for delivery.
This offer subject to withdrawal without notice.